Gay and Lesbian Literature Since World War II: History and Memory

Gay and Lesbian Literature Since World War II: History and Memory has been co-published simultaneously as *Journal of Homosexuality,* Volume 34, Numbers 3/4 1998.

Gay and Lesbian Literature Since World War II: History and Memory

Sonya L. Jones, PhD
Editor

Gay and Lesbian Literature Since World War II: History and Memory, edited by Sonya L. Jones, was simultaneously issued by The Haworth Press, Inc., under the same title, as a special issue of *Journal of Homosexuality,* Volume 34, Numbers 3/4, 1998, John P. DeCecco, Editor.

The Harrington Park Press
An Imprint of
The Haworth Press, Inc.
New York • London

ISBN 1-56023-102-5

Published by

The Harrington Park Press, 10 Alice Street, Binghamton, NY 13904-1580 USA

The Harrington Park Press is an Imprint of The Haworth Press, Inc., 10 Alice Street, Binghamton, NY 13904-1580 USA.

Gay and Lesbian Literature Since World War II: History and Memory has been co-published simultaneously as *Journal of Homosexuality,* Volume 34, Numbers 3/4 1998.

Cover design by Thomas J. Mayshock Jr.

Library of Congress Cataloging-in-Publication Data

Gay and lesbian literature since World War II : history and memory / Sonya L. Jones, editor
p. cm.
Published also as v. 34, nos. 3/4 1998 of the Journal of homosexuality.
Includes bibliographical references and index.
ISBN 0-7890-0349-X (alk. paper). – ISBN 1-56023-102-5 (alk. paper)
1. Gays' writings, American–History and criticism. 2. Homosexuality and literature–United States–History–20th century. 3. American literature–20th century–History and criticism. 4. Lesbians in literature. 5. Gay men in literature. I. Jones, Sonya L.
PS153.G38G39 1997
810.9'920664–dc21 97-48394
CIP

INDEXING & ABSTRACTING

Contributions to this publication are selectively indexed or abstracted in print, electronic, online, or CD-ROM version(s) of the reference tools and information services listed below. This list is current as of the copyright date of this publication. See the end of this section for additional notes.

- ***Abstracts in Anthropology***, Baywood Publishing Company, 26 Austin Avenue, P.O. Box 337, Amityville, NY 11701
- ***Abstracts of Research in Pastoral Care & Counseling***, Loyola College, 7135 Minstrel Way, Suite 101, Columbia, MD 21045
- ***Academic Abstracts/CD-ROM***, EBSCO Publishing Editorial Department, P.O. Box 590, Ipswich, MA 01938-0590
- ***Academic Search: database of 2,000 selected academic serials, updated monthly,*** EBSCO Publishing, 83 Pine Street, Peabody, MA 01960
- ***Alternative Press Index,*** Alternative Press Center, Inc., P.O. Box 33109, Baltimore, MD 21218-0401
- ***Applied Social Sciences Index & Abstracts (ASSIA) (Online: ASSI via Data-Star) (CD-Rom: ASSIA Plus)***, Bowker-Saur Limited, Maypole House, Maypole Road, East Grinstead, West Sussex RH19 1HH England
- ***Book Review Index,*** Gale Research, Inc., P.O. Box 2867, Detroit, MI 48231
- ***Cambridge Scientific Abstracts***, *Risk Abstracts*, 7200 Wisconsin Avenue #601, Bethesda, MD 20814
- ***CNPIEC Reference Guide: Chinese National Directory of Foreign Periodicals,*** P.O. Box 88, Beijing, People's Republic of China
- ***Criminal Justice Abstracts***, Willow Tree Press, 15 Washington Street, 4th Floor, Newark NJ 07102

(continued)

- *Criminology, Penology and Police Science Abstracts*, Kugler Publications, P.O. Box 11188, 1001 GD-Amsterdam, The Netherlands
- *Current Contents: Clinical Medicine/Life Sciences (CC: CM/LS) (weekly Table of Contents Service), and* **Social Science Citation Index.** *Articles also searchable through* **Social SciSearch,** *ISI's online database and in ISI's* **Research Alert** *current awareness service,* Institute for Scientific Information, 3501 Market Street, Philadelphia, PA 19104-3302
- *Digest of Neurology and Psychiatry*, The Institute of Living, 400 Washington Street, Hartford, CT 06106
- *Excerpta Medica/Secondary Publishing Division*, Elsevier Science, Inc., Secondary Publishing Division, 655 Avenue of the Americas, New York, NY 10010
- *Expanded Academic Index*, Information Acccss Company, 362 Lakeside Drive, Forest City, CA 94404
- *Family Studies Database (online and CD/ROM)*, National Information Services Corporation, 306 East Baltimore Pike, 2nd Floor, Media, PA 19063
- *Family Violence & Sexual Assault Bulletin*, Family Violence & Sexual Assault Institute, 1121 East South East Loop # 323, Suite 130, Tyler, TX 75701
- *Higher Education Abstracts,* Claremont Graduate University, 231 East Tenth Street, Claremont, CA 91711
- *HOMODOK/"Relevant" Bibliographic database, Documentation Centre for Gay & Lesbian Studies, University of Amsterdam (selective printed abstracts in "Homologie" and bibliographic computer databases covering cultural, historical, social and political aspects of gay & lesbian topics),* c/o HOMODOK-ILGA Archive, O.Z. Achterburgwal 185, NL-1012 DK Amsterdam, The Netherlands
- *IBZ International Bibliography of Periodical Literature*, Zeller Verlag GmbH & Co., P.O.B. 1949, d-49009 Osnabruck, Germany

(continued)

- ***Index Medicus***, National Library of Medicine, 8600 Rockville Pike, Bethesda, MD 20894
- ***Index to Periodical Articles Related to Law***, University of Texas, 727 East 26th Street, Austin, TX 78705
- ***INTERNET ACCESS (& additional networks) Bulletin Board for Libraries ("BUBL") coverage of information resources on INTERNET, JANET, and other networks.***
    - <URL:http://bubl.ac.uk/>
    - The new locations will be found under <URL:http://bubl.ac.uk/link/>.
    - Any existing BUBL users who have problems finding information on the new service should contact the BUBL help line by sending e-mail to <bubl@bubl.ac.uk>.

  The Andersonian Library, Curran Building, 101 St. James Road, Glasgow G4 0NS, Scotland
- ***Leeds Medical Information,*** University of Leeds, Leeds LS2 9JT, United Kingdom
- ***MasterFILE: updated database from EBSCO Publishing,*** 83 Pine Street, Peabody, MA 01960
- ***Mental Health Abstracts (online through DIALOG)***, IFI/Plenum Data Company, 3202 Kirkwood Highway, Wilmington, DE 19808
- ***MLA International Bibliography,*** Modern Language Association of America, 10 Astor Place, New York, NY 10003
- ***National Women's Health Resource Center,*** 5255 Loughboro Road, NW, Washington, DC 20016
- ***PASCAL,*** c/o Institute de L'Information Scientifique et Technique. Cross-disciplinary electronic database covering the fields of science, technology & medicine. Also available on CD-ROM, and can generate customized retrospective searches. INIST/CNRS-Service Gestion des Documents Primaires, 2, allée du Parc de Brabois, F-54514 Vandoeuvre-les-Nancy, Cedex, France [http//www.inist.fr]
- ***Periodical Abstracts, Research I*** (***general and basic reference indexing and abstracting data-base from University Micro-films International (UMI), 300 North Zeeb Road, P.O. Box 1346, Ann Arbor, MI 48106-1346***), UMI Data Courier, P.O. Box 32770, Louisville, KY 40232-2770

(continued)

- ***Periodical Abstracts, Research II (broad coverage indexing and abstracting data-base from University Microfilms International (UMI), 300 North Zeeb Road, P.O. Box 1346, Ann Arbor, MI 48106-1346)***, UMI Data Courier, P.O. Box 32770, Louisville, KY 40232-2770
- ***PsychNet***, PsychNet Inc., P.O. Box 369, Georgetown, CO 80444
- ***Public Affairs Information Bulletin (PAIS)***, Public Affairs Information Service, Inc., 521 West 43rd Street, New York, NY 10036-4396
- ***Religion Index One: Periodicals, the index to Book Reviews in Religion, Religion Indexes: RIO/RIT/IBRR 1975- on CD/ROM,*** American Theological Library Association, 820 Church Street, 3rd Floor, Evanston, IL 60201-5613
  - E-mail: atla@atla.com
  - WWW: http://atla.library.vanderbilt.edu/atla/home.html
- ***Sage Family Studies Abstracts (SFSA),*** Sage Publications, Inc., 2455 Teller Road, Newbury Park, CA 91320
- ***Social Planning/Policy & Development Abstracts (SOPODA)***, Sociological Abstracts, Inc., P.O. Box 22206, San Diego, CA 92192-0206
- ***Social Sciences Index (from Volume 1 & continuing)***, The H.W. Wilson Company, 950 University Avenue, Bronx, NY 10452
- ***Social Science Source: coverage of 400 journals in the social sciences area; updated monthly;*** EBSCO Publishing, P.O. Box 2250, Peabody, MA 01960-7250
- ***Social Work Abstracts***, National Association of Social Workers, 750 First Street NW, 8th Floor, Washington, DC 20002
- ***Sociological Abstracts (SA)***, Sociological Abstracts, Inc., P.O. Box 22206, San Diego, CA 92192-0206
- ***Studies on Women Abstracts***, Carfax Publishing Company, P.O. Box 25, Abingdon, Oxfordshire OXI4 3UE, United Kingdom
- ***Violence and Abuse Abstracts: A Review of Current Literature on Interpersonal Violence (VAA),*** Sage Publications, Inc., 2455 Teller Road, Newbury Park, CA 91320

Book reviews are selectively excerpted by the Guide to Professional Literature of the Journal of Academic Librarianship.

SPECIAL BIBLIOGRAPHIC NOTES

related to special journal issues (separates) and indexing/abstracting

- ☐ indexing/abstracting services in this list will also cover material in any "separate" that is co-published simultaneously with Haworth's special thematic journal issue or DocuSerial. Indexing/abstracting usually covers material at the article/chapter level.
- ☐ monographic co-editions are intended for either non-subscribers or libraries which intend to purchase a second copy for their circulating collections.
- ☐ monographic co-editions are reported to all jobbers/wholesalers/approval plans. The source journal is listed as the "series" to assist the prevention of duplicate purchasing in the same manner utilized for books-in-series.
- ☐ to facilitate user/access services all indexing/abstracting services are encouraged to utilize the co-indexing entry note indicated at the bottom of the first page of each article/chapter/contribution.
- ☐ this is intended to assist a library user of any reference tool (whether print, electronic, online, or CD-ROM) to locate the monographic version if the library has purchased this version but not a subscription to the source journal.
- ☐ individual articles/chapters in any Haworth publication are also available through the Haworth Document Delivery Service (HDDS).

ABOUT THE EDITOR

Sonya L. Jones, PhD, is Professor of English and interdisciplinary studies at Allegheny College where she has served as Chair of Faculty Council, Chair of the Gay and Lesbian Studies Minor, and on the Steering Committee of the Committee in Support of Gay, Lesbian, and Bisexual People. She has taught seminars in Twentieth Century Gay and Lesbian Literature and directed senior theses ranging from Oscar Wilde to Adrienne Rich. An early lesbian-feminist activist, Dr. Jones founded and managed the Atlanta-based Vanity Press (1975-80), and plans for re-issuing her 1976 novel, *The Legacy*, are underway. Under her direction, *Gay and Lesbian Literature Since World War II: History and Memory* became a conference by the same name held at Allegheny College in April 1997, and from that event, a new vision emerged. Jones is currently at work compiling an edition of the *Journal of Homosexuality* titled *A Sea of Stories: The Shaping Power of Narrative in Gay and Lesbian Cultures*, which will feature an expanded version of John De Cecco's "History and Memory" keynote address in which he explored his twenty years as Editor of the *Journal of Homosexuality*. Dr. Jones holds a doctorate from Emory University's Graduate Institute of the Liberal Arts, and her recent publications include a collection of poems, *Small Claims, Large Encounters* (Brito & Lair, 1995).

CONTENTS

Introduction 1
Sonya L. Jones

The Calamus Root: A Study of American Gay Poetry Since World War II 5
Walter Holland

The Purloined *Ladder*: Its Place in Lesbian History 27
Manuela Soares

"What Is Going on Here?": Baldwin's *Another Country* 51
Laura Quinn

Writing the Fairy *Huckleberry Finn*: William Goyen's and Truman Capote's Genderings of Male Homosexuality 67
Gary Richards

Inscribing a Lesbian Reader, Projecting a Lesbian Subject: A Jane Rule Diptych 87
Marilyn R. Schuster

Built Out of Books: Lesbian Energy and Feminist Ideology in Alternative Publishing 113
Kate Adams

Bertha Harris's *Lover*: Lesbian *and* Postmodern 143
Amanda C. Gable

Breaking the Silence, Dismantling Taboos: Latino Novels on AIDS 155
Alberto Sandoval Sánchez

Nietzsche, Autobiography, History: Mourning and *Martin and John* 177
John Champagne

Resources for Lesbian Ethnographic Research in the Lavender Archives 205
Alisa Klinger

The Will to Remember: The Lesbian Herstory Archives of New York 225
Joan Nestle

Index 237

ALL HARRINGTON PARK PRESS BOOKS
ARE PRINTED ON CERTIFIED
ACID-FREE PAPER

Introduction

Sonya L. Jones

Allegheny College

The summer of 1976 was hot, and the drive from Atlanta to Omaha was long. As our yellow Saab hummed along interconnecting freeways across the flatlands of Kansas through the cornfields of Iowa, my mind began to race with expectations.

Would June Arnold, cofounder of Daughters, Inc., be as nice as she sounded on the phone when she called to invite The Vanity Press to the first conference of Women in Print (WIP)? Or, was she using her good manners to disguise the intensely radical nature of the event? Would we as a group of publishers explore concrete ways to do business differently in a world of giant corporations that seemed more intent on devouring each other than in issuing good books? Or, would we draft a collective resolution to blow up the offices of Random House?

Each woman who heeded the call to a summer camp in Nebraska–discussions of which are now available in the work of scholars such as Kate Adams and Alisa Klinger–no doubt arrived with her own political agenda and ideas for positioning her press in the growing network of lesbian publishers. During the course of the week together, there were moments thick with tension, and there were moments of unforgettable solidarity.

Though I, a Southerner who had come out in a quiet, quasi way at

---

Sonya L. Jones has been a lesbian-feminist since the seventies when she founded the Atlanta-based Vanity Press. She is Associate Professor of English and interdisciplinary studies at Allegheny College. Correspondence may be addressed: Department of English, Allegheny College, Meadville, PA 16335. E-mail: sjones@alleg.edu

[Haworth co-indexing entry note]: "Introduction." Jones, Sonya L. Co-published simultaneously in *Journal of Homosexuality* (The Haworth Press, Inc.) Vol. 34, No. 3/4, 1998, pp. 1-4; and: *Gay and Lesbian Literature Since World War II: History and Memory* (ed: Sonya L. Jones) The Haworth Press, Inc., 1998, pp. 1-4; and: *Gay and Lesbian Literature Since World War II: History and Memory* (ed: Sonya L. Jones) Harrington Park Press, an imprint of The Haworth Press, Inc., 1998, pp. 1-4. Single or multiple copies of this article are available for a fee from The Haworth Document Delivery Service [1-800-342-9678, 9:00 a.m. - 5:00 p.m. (EST). E-mail address: getinfo@haworth.com].

another summer camp in the midsixties, dare not speak for women whose histories differ from mine, I daresay that no woman who went to Omaha in 1976 remained unchanged by a decade which Walter Holland in the opening essay of this volume calls the "golden age" of homosexual publishing. In gay and lesbian circles, the seventies were on fire. They were a time of massive awakening and, as such, were characterized by energies strong enough to make Prometheus look like a petty thief.

* * *

If Virginia Woolf was right in claiming that human nature changed about 1910–was she serious or was she camping?–we might also say that a gay and lesbian literary tradition began to emerge about 1948, the year thousands of baby boomers were born, yours truly included, the same year Truman Capote published his first novel, *Other Voices, Other Rooms*. I say, "began to emerge," give or take a few years, because homoerotic behavior, the defining characteristic of the "tradition," is by no means a postwar phenomenon. The natural scientists tell us it's as old as fish. Neither are texts which represent same-sex desires new to the years following Hitler's defeat. The forties were ripe with lesbian pulps, and many male writers made careers of encoding gay desire. As Alisa Klinger notes in her essay on "lavender archives," beginning in 1950, Barbara Grier, founder of the Naiad Press, and her partner, Donna McBride, began to amass 9,000 gay and lesbian titles ranging back through history. They have donated this collection to the Gay and Lesbian Center of the San Francisco New Main Public Library.

Gay and Lesbian Literature Since World War II: History and Memory is an attempt to chronicle the multifaceted explosion in gay and lesbian writing that has taken place in the second half of the twentieth century. According to Manuela Soares in her essay studded with quotes from key lesbian figures, Grier included, the pages of *The Ladder*, first published by the Daughters of Bilitis in October 1956, contained lesbian fiction and poetry, and the "purloined" magazine went on to publish writers like Rita Mae Brown. Its male counterpart, *One*, first appeared three years earlier in September 1953.

At least three important historical moments follow postwar soundings to signal cultural shifts which, in turn, shifted literary concerns and perspectives. They operate like echoes in this volume: the riots at the Stonewall Inn in 1969, the politicized activities of the lesbian "bookwomen" of the seventies, and the onset of AIDS.

In selecting essays for this volume, I have looked for range in subject matter as well as balance of gay and lesbian concerns; I have included work by established scholars and work by young theoreticians and archivists who have initiated new areas of investigation in their doctoral dissertations. While Walter Holland's essay on gay poetry provides an overview of the time period, Gary Richards focuses on two gay writers from the Southern Renaissance–Truman Capote and William Goyen. Despite Allen Tate's claim in "A Southern Mode of the Imagination" that there never was a Southern Renaissance because there was nothing to be reborn, Richards makes a good case for a truly fugitive kind of renaissance. To complement the wealth of information presented in these essays, I have chosen two single-author pieces for the in-depth insights they afford: Marilyn Schuster's feminist mapping of Jane Rule's short fiction "Dulce" and "Home Movie" and John Champagne's reading of Dale Peck's *Martin and John* alongside Friedrich Nietzsche on history and Sigmund Freud on mourning.

Theorizing about lesbian texts began in the seventies when lesbianism intersected with various forms of feminism, American and French. Proliferation of scholarly interest in and theorizing about gay texts came a bit later in the early eighties. Publication of the 1978 English translation of Michel Foucault's *The History of Sexuality* was a catalyst, and as the Reagan decade wore on, a flurry of gay work was fueled by the devastating onslaught of AIDS.

George C. Wolfe, who directed the first Broadway production of Tony Kushner's *Angels in America*, has suggested that there is no Other any more. We are now performing in each other's story–each other's Other. The gay liberation movement has been accused of being too white, but the culture itself is assuredly made up of all colors and cultures. Its "melting pot" tendencies may, in fact, be a way in which gay culture continues to threaten the straight world: gay sex is hard enough to tolerate; sex and race in bed together is just too much. Laura Quinn's essay on teaching James Baldwin's *Another Country* at a small college in Middle America and Alberto Sandoval Sánchez's analysis of four Latino novels dealing with AIDS reveal faces of a tradition that is anything but pale. Both essays challenge us to think about the formal elements of gay texts–who sleeps where when, who gets the boy in the end–in responsible and complicated ways.

An important function of volumes like *Gay and Lesbian Literature Since World War II* is to correct errors of scholarly neglect. Invariably, given the market-driven forces of history, some writers become household words while others are relegated to being so-called "writers' writers." In my view, what this volume did not need was another essay on Adrienne Rich. No disrespect intended; Rich's work is as foundational to lesbian literature as the "rockshelf forming underneath everything that grows" in her poem titled "Transcendental Etude" (*The Dream of a Common Language* 1977). What this volume needed and sadly did not find was an essay on Audre Lorde. What this volume needed badly and found at the eleventh hour in the work of Amanda Gable, a young Southerner at Georgia Institute of Technology in Atlanta, of all places, was an intelligent discussion of Bertha Harris's *Lover*. Woolfian in its scope and wit, *Lover* may well be the aesthetic achievement of lesbian fiction to date. Certainly it is a metacultural product of the lesbian feminist seventies worthy of being read, time and again, for its "deliriously hypnotic" prose, to cop Wayne Kostenbaum's description from the *Voice Literary Supplement* (October 1993, 8). *Lover*, undeniably, is a trouble-making "pleasure dome," a gorgeous touchstone of a novel.

* * *

The summer of 1996 was too long in coming to northwestern Pennsylvania. Huddled in sweaters, we sat around a seminar table sipping coffee. Our third faculty workshop in gay and lesbian studies sponsored by the Fund for the Improvement of Post Secondary Education was ready to start at Allegheny College, the institution which granted John De Cecco, editor of the *Journal of Homosexuality*, a B.S. in biology fifty years ago, and I was feeling a Proustian wave of nostalgia.

Twenty years had passed. June Arnold was no longer with us on the planet; the raucous disagreements between cultural lesbians who frequented Ms. Garbo's in pearls and separatists who hung out at the Tower Lounge in flannel shirts had gone the way of all flesh; even ALFA (the Atlanta Lesbian Feminist Alliance) had closed its house and donated its books to Emory University, its manifestos on vegetarian nonmonogamy to Duke University.

No serious thinker at our table would have advocated "closet nostalgia" for long or exchanged the relative openness of the midnineties for a return to secrecy and shame. Nor would anyone there have wished to promote an anxiety of otherness as the best avenue to literary inspiration. At the same time, no one was naive enough to deny that it takes a certain amount of anguish to make a creative explosion. We were hip to the dangers of neocolonialism embedded in the academic enterprise; we were willing to take seriously Joan Nestle's caution: "If we ask decorous questions of history, we will get a genteel history."

As I sipped coffee and listened to us trying to make sense of a tradition that ranges from Plato to Minnie Bruce Pratt, I wondered where we might be headed now as the new millennium closes in. Will we look back on the century that gave us identity(ies) as a time of mixed blessings–a bursting forth curbed by years of plague? Will we come to think of the half-century from 1948 to 1998 as the Queer Renaissance? We have a richly textured literary history to help point our way, and we have, in Nestle's words, "a new generation of rememberers who we hope will keep the door open to the multiplicities" of lesbian and gay culture.

History and memory are, after all, slippery issues. It will serve us well to remember that Saab used to be a dyke car, and "queer" used to be a word that dared not speak its name.

The Calamus Root: A Study of American Gay Poetry Since World War II

Walter Holland

City University of New York

SUMMARY. This paper traces the development of gay poetry in America after World War II. A taxonomy and publishing history is outlined for various poetic movements. An overview is given of the aesthetic and thematic characteristics of the tradition and its connection to homosexual writing in the nineteenth century. *[Article copies available for a fee from The Haworth Document Delivery Service: 1-800-342-9678. E-mail address: getinfo@haworth.com]*

Walter Holland holds a BA in Literature from Bard College and an MA in Creative Writing from City College. He is currently a doctoral student in English Literature at the City University of New York. His dissertation covers the same topic as this article and bears the same title. A book of poetry, *A Journal of the Plague Years*, appeared in 1992 from Magic City Press. His novel, *The March*, was published by Masquerade Books in October 1996. His poems have appeared in various journals and anthologies, notably *Poets for Life* and *Jugular Defenses*. He would like to thank Alfred Corn, Howard Frey, Sonya Jones, Steven Kruger, Carl Morse, Felice Picano, Richard Wandel, Joseph Wittreich, and Ian Young for their assistance in making this article possible. This essay is dedicated to the memory of David Craig Austin, Nick Bamforth, Joe Bartlett, David Frechette, Essex Hemphill, Craig Reynolds, and Assotto Saint. Correspondence may be addressed: c/o Howard Frey, Magic City Press, P.O. Box 236, Planetarium Station, New York, NY 10024-0236.

[Haworth co-indexing entry note]: "The Calamus Root: A Study of American Gay Poetry Since World War II." Holland, Walter. Co-published simultaneously in *Journal of Homosexuality* (The Haworth Press, Inc.) Vol. 34, No. 3/4, 1998, pp. 5-25; and: *Gay and Lesbian Literature Since World War II: History and Memory* (ed: Sonya L. Jones) The Haworth Press, Inc., 1998, pp. 5-25; and: *Gay and Lesbian Literature Since World War II: History and Memory* (ed: Sonya L. Jones) Harrington Park Press, an imprint of The Haworth Press, Inc., 1998, pp. 5-25. Single or multiple copies of this article are available for a fee from The Haworth Document Delivery Service [1-800-342-9678, 9:00 a.m. - 5:00 p.m. (EST). E-mail address: getinfo@haworth.com].

To date, few studies have ventured to trace a gay poetic tradition from the broad historical perspective of its many-faceted locales, cultural sites, interests, styles, and voicings. Just as the Harlem Renaissance was an explosive period for African-American writing, the renaissance that took place in gay poetry after World War II was equally formative. Following the Stonewall Riots in 1969, the seventies, eighties, and nineties were rich periods for gay poetry across North America, particularly in New York City and San Francisco. As a cultural phenomenon, gay literature has blended with a growing diversification of the American tradition into the multicultural canon, its literary transmission paralleling social and historical changes in American society. This essay aims to provide an overview of gay poetry from World War II to the present.

The theoretical and historical work of the last two decades from Faderman to Foucault, Duberman to Katz, Sedgwick to Sinfield, has given us vocabularies and theoretical constructs to speak about the culture and experience of gay people. It is now possible to formulate and reappropriate a "canon" of American gay poetry and to identify emerging poetical concerns which have made this poetry both unique and timely. It is also possible to study the development of gay culture and aesthetics in relation to this literature and to recontextualize the writings of former authors whose work was never appreciated nor read with attention to a shared gay sensibility. The literature of gay poets may now be more fully studied in regard to the social milieu, community, and publishing industry which informed and supported it.

The postmodernist concerns of multiculturalism and diversity, and the early modernist constructions (especially of a Black-African-American literary tradition during the Harlem Renaissance), have helped reshape our view of the "other" and given us clear evidence of how the place of the "other" has been a powerful catalyst for new experiments in language and form. It has helped us posit a theory of how such an "other" is constructed in the dominant culture and how textuality reflects this construction.

World War II and the war effort at home changed the social fabric of America. Large numbers of young men were mobilized far from home for the first time creating larger social freedoms. Greater numbers of single men and the easy availability of work made a single life outside the constraints of marriage and family possible. Urban and suburban areas became steadily more populous. The exodus from Europe of many intellectuals and artists also gave America a new cultural heritage and sophistication. Americans enjoyed a prolonged postwar boom which afforded them economic mobility, freedom, and leisure time. New York became the cultural capitol of the world in the face of a devastated Europe.

In the fifties, a growing homophile movement in America led to the foundation of both the Mattachine Society and the Daughters of Bilitis, with their respective magazines *ONE* and *The Ladder.* The Beat poetry movement and the writers of Black Mountain College exerted their influence. Olson, Creeley, and the gay poet Robert Duncan were practitioners of "open," "organic" form or "projective verse." Ginsberg's "Howl" (1956) made a striking impression on a whole generation of younger gay writers. Auden and his lover Chester Kallman were living in New York and friendly with the psychotherapist and poet, Paul Goodman. Harold Norse, the West Coast poet, was Auden's secretary in New York City before leaving for Europe. Jack Spicer and Robert Duncan were on the West Coast, as were Paul Mariah and Thom Gunn. Abstract Expressionism was making a powerful new statement in the art scene. Aesthetes such as James Merrill would drive into the City from Stonington and have lunches with literary friends. Howard Moss showed up at fashionable gay parties and newcomers such as Richard Howard were being introduced to Ginsberg, Baldwin, and Edward Albee. Edward Field was struggling as an actor and attending parties at May Swenson's along with Ralph Pomeroy. O'Hara, Ashbery, and Schuyler had formed their close friendships and were night after night out on the town as part of the "New York School."

This postwar period saw an unprecedented number of poets who were conscious of their homosexuality and of a gay culture and sensibility, although the terms "gay culture" and "gay sensibility" had not been fully coined. These writers sought one another out. They read and reflected upon the homoerotic verse of previous generations: Cavafy in Egypt; Whitman, Hartley, Hughes, and Crane in America; Wilde and the Uranian poets of England; Stefan George of Germany; Rimbaud and Verlaine in France; Strato of Ancient Greece and Catullus, Martial, and Juvenal of Ancient Rome. They also knew of such forties gay writers as George Barker, Robert Friend, and Dunstan Thompson and were titillated by previous homosexual anthologies of poetry such as Edward Carpenter's *Ioläus* (1926). There were other gay writers as well who were exerting their influence, everyone from Henry James to Jean Genet to James Baldwin. The postwar gay poets had numerous friendships. They moved in a gay social and cultural sphere, cognizant of other gay happenings in the worlds of art, photography, history, theater, and music. Their work anticipated the explosive gay liberation movement of the late sixties and early seventies.

The Stonewall Riots of 1969 in New York City acted as a catalyst for social change and for the formation of a national gay political front. The creation of gay "ghettos" in places such as New York's West Village and

Fire Island, Provincetown in Massachusetts, the Castro district in San Francisco, and Key West in Florida could be compared to locales such as Paris at the turn of the century or in the twenties, and Berlin in the twenties and early thirties, all acting as sites of gay cultural and literary production.

Many influential gay literary magazines and newspapers took their start during the seventies and eighties: *Come Out!* (1969); *Gay Liberator, Manroot, Sebastian Quill, Gay Sunshine, Gay Post, Ain't It Da Truth* (1970s); *RFD* (1974); *Mouth of the Dragon* (1974); *Fag Rag* (1976); *Christopher Street* (1976); *Blacklight, Habari-Daftari, Yemonja* (later *Blackheart*, which lasted for three issues), *Moja: Black and Gay* (all of the early 1980s); *The James White Review* (1983); and *Other Countries Journal* (1988). A growing small-press movement included: Jonathan Williams's Jargon Society (founded in 1951), John and Elaine Gill's Crossing Press (1960s and 1970s), Ian Young's Catalyst (1970), Good Gay Poets (c. 1980), Alyson Publications (c. 1980), Bhakti Books (c. 1987), Black Star Press (c. 1987), Amelia (c. 1985), Little Caesar Press, Seahorse Press (1977), Galiens Press (1989), Amethyst Books (c. 1990), Hanging Loose Press (c. 1990), and Alice James Books (c. 1992). All helped to foster a renaissance in gay poetry. I say renaissance because, indeed, a strong tradition had already begun at the end of the last century in America and Europe.

The need to reevaluate the American poetic canon from the perspective of a gay poetic history and taxonomy, and to rethink the work of both prominent and lesser-known American authors comes from the way in which the relevance of a gay sensibility and a gay poetic voice have been so easily dismissed by the mainstream heterosexual press. A review of various mainstream anthologies and histories that have already covered modern and postmodern American poetry–for instance those of Donald Allen and George F. Butterick, A. Poulin, Jr., Marjorie Perloff, David Perkins, Helen Vendler, and Donald Hall–reinforces such a need for reevaluation.

If I look at a book such as David Perkins's *A History of Modern Poetry: Modernism and After* or A. Poulin, Jr.'s essay "Contemporary American Poetry: The Radical Tradition," I am struck by the possibilities if not the necessity for reassessing American poetry from a gay and lesbian perspective. Poulin writes:

> Until recently the sexual preferences of some of this century's great poets were among the best-kept secrets in literary history–in large part because they were rightfully considered irrelevant to the poetry. Consequently, Allen Ginsberg's and Robert Duncan's poems about aspects of their homosexuality, as well as Adrienne Rich's open and moving explorations of her own sexual preference in some of her

more recent poems, may be somewhat startling to some readers. (Poulin 688)

Poulin sees it as "rightfully irrelevant" that several of the major American poets of the twentieth century (Ginsberg, Duncan, Rich) happened to be gay or lesbian, failing to understand, from Gertrude Stein to the present, how the displacements of gay identity and the creation of its "otherness" forced new and exciting experimentations in form, a more inventive language for expressing gender, race, and desire; and situated such poets at the crucial center of the movement toward what Poulin himself calls "the personalization of American poetry since 1945" (688).

Perkins writes of O'Hara, Ashbery, Schuyler, and the "New York School" that "their work was light, witty, sophisticated, and ebullient, and beneath their bright surfaces were serious implications" (Perkins 528). Perkins also notes that "these poets were friends, referred to one another in their poems, lived in New York City, and described or alluded in their verses to its sophisticated pleasures" (Perkins 529). He mentions in the same paragraph these poets' affinities to the paintings of Fairfield Porter and the music of John Cage. What Perkins fails to see is how some of these artists were uniquely connected by their gay lifestyles, gay friendships, or gay proclivities. The gay poets of the "New York School" were influenced by gay or bisexual artists such as Rauschenberg, Johns, and Rivers, as well as abstract expressionists such as Kline, de Kooning, and Pollock. The sophistication, as well as the wittiness of their work, was inherited from both the lyrics of Noel Coward and the flippancy of Oscar Wilde. Gay camp humor and sociability invigorated their writing or at least touched its surface along with the erudition of Proust, Cavafy, and Auden. John Cage was homosexual (the lover of the dancer Merce Cunningham), and among the "serious implications" beneath the surface of O'Hara's, Schuyler's, and Ashbery's work was their homosexuality or homosexual Eros.

While one cannot segregate "gay and lesbian poets" from the broader influences of the American heterosexual tradition they lived in, nor deny their participation in its development, I am convinced that a separate tradition is there to be uncovered by careful and sensitive reading. Many writers have undertaken such a reading.

In December 1976 Barry Laine in *Chistopher Street* magazine wrote an article entitled "Gay Poetry Reaches Adolescence." Laine discusses the nineteenth century and how the "first poetic closets" began "to inch open," albeit with much ambiguity, with the work of Emily Dickinson, Walt Whitman, and Hart Crane. He mentions Wilde and the homosexual themes which emerge in the French and Mediterranean poetry of Verlaine,

Cavafy, Cocteau, and Lorca. He extolls Ginsberg's "Howl" (1956) as presenting a "sexually explicit homosexual poetry," but one which was lost within the larger "import of the Beat movement." Laine summarizes:

> Ultimately, what neither Ginsberg, nor Frank O'Hara or Jack Spicer, nor somewhat earlier writers like Stein or Auden, ever possessed was an at-large cultural identity that integrated their poetry and their homosexuality. In that sense, the first gay poem was born when the first beer bottle smashed through the glass at the Stonewall Inn in 1969. (Laine 34)

Laine, however, leaves unexplored in his piece, the concept of a gay poetic tradition and the thematic, stylistic, and theoretical influences and developments that occurred over time.

The mythic view of Stonewall as the moment when a deep wall of silence and invisibility was magically lifted and gay identity and culture were instantly constituted has been deconstructed by the work of George Chauncey whose *Gay New York* (1994) shows the existence of a rich and diverse "gay" past even at the start of the century. It has also been explored recently by the broad and far-reaching discussion of Ian Young in *The Stonewall Experiment: A Gay Psychohistory* (1995) which looks at the gradual development and psychic origins, if you will, from Wilde and Carpenter onward, of many of gay life's myths and fantasies.

Robert K. Martin's *The Homosexual Tradition in American Poetry* (1979), Gregory Woods's *Articulate Flesh: Male Homo-Eroticism and Modern Poetry* (1987), Thomas Yingling's *Hart Crane and the Homosexual Text* (1990), Claude Summers's *Gay Fictions: Wilde to Stonewall* (1990), David Bergman's *Gaiety Transfigured* (1991), Michael Moon's *Disseminating Whitman* (1991), Byrne S. Fone's *Masculine Landscapes* (1992) and *A Road to Stonewall* (1995), and Claude Summers's recent *The Gay and Lesbian Literary Heritage* (1995), have done much toward laying a framework for a gay critical inquiry in gay poetry. Their essays have given a context and language with which texts may be closely read for their homosexual influences.

There is a wide body of literature which presently can be employed in the study of gay poetry as well: anthologies such as Ian Young's *The Male Muse* (1973), Felice Picano's *A True Likeness: Lesbian & Gay Writing Today* (1980), Winston Leyland's *Angels of the Lyre* (1975) and *Orgasms of Light* (1977), Stephen Coote's *Penguin Book of Homosexual Verse* (1983), Ian Young's *The Son of the Male Muse* (1983), Joseph Beam's *In the Life* (1986), Carl Morse and Joan Larkin's *Gay and Lesbian Poetry in Our Time* (1988), Michael Klein's *Poets for Life* (1989), Essex Hemphill's

Brother to Brother (1991), Assotto Saint's *The Road Before Us* (1991), *Here to Dare* (1992), *Milking Black Bull* (1995), Rudy Kikel's *Gents, Bad Boys, and Barbarians* (1994), *The Badboy Book of Erotic Poetry* (1995) edited by David Laurents, Michael Lassell's *The Name of Love: Classic Gay Love Poems* (1995) and *Eros in Boystown: Contemporary Gay Poems About Sex* (1996). These books have proved invaluable at identifying gay poets of the post-World War II period. The fine introductions to their anthologies by Essex Hemphill, Winston Leyland, Carl Morse, and Ian Young have proved helpful as well in piecing together a gay poetic history.

* * *

The thematic concerns, tropes, topoi, and traditions that emerged in the earliest works by poets who were homosexual (especially of the last century) found their way into gay American verse after World War II. One concern was the cult of Platonism which established homosexual Eros in the context of classical myth, comradeship, manly virtue, and chivalry, and which tended to mimic classical religious and highly literary poetic forms. This concern drew on classic examples of homosexual love: Zeus and Ganymede, Poseidon and Pelops, Phoebus Apollo and Hyacinthus, Heracles and Hylas, Achilles and Patroclus, Hadrian and Antinous, and Jonathan and David (Summers 508-513; 594-600). Another concern dealt with the Christ-image of suffering and martyrdom and the death of the comrade, often employing the elegiac verse form. This poetry tended to follow Christian iconography to evidence male to male love as a virtuous expression. Tennyson, Symonds, William Johnson, Oscar Wilde, Lord Alfred Douglas, Bayard Taylor, Edwin Bradford, Edward Lefroy, and other Uranian poets all reflected many of these concerns.

Other gay poets followed the pagan writings of Catullus, as well as the French symbolists and decadents who pursued a frank and unadulterated eroticism. The decadents invited open forms or simple ballads which used raw vernacular language and slang and were quite erotic. More contemporary gay poets such as Dennis Cooper, Allen Ginsberg, Harold Norse, and Charles Shively all share affinities with the French decadents. Rimbaud, Verlaine, and later Genet especially created a model of the homosexual rebel and the homosexual demimonde. Within this arena, gay poets took their "criminality" in the mind of society and their "carnality" very seriously—embracing pleasure so that their work seems to proclaim itself and discredit the bourgeois values that censored it.

In summary, by the forties, a gay sensibility or aesthetic in poetry had arrived which had been influenced by nineteenth-century concerns of classicism and ancient mythology; and utopian and pastoral homoerotic views of ancient Greece (Cavafy), rural England (the Uranians), and democratic America (Walt Whitman); by powerfully pagan and rebellious erotic Mediterranean verse (Genet, Rimbaud, Verlaine); by a very effete gay urbanity based on high aestheticism, stylization, and camp (Wilde, Auden, Isherwood, and Merrill); by an abstract and encoded modern gay urban verse (Crane); by a dramatic exploration of racial identity and mythography (Baldwin, Hughes); and a growing sense of mysticism, ritual, and counter-cultural dissent (Duncan, Ginsberg, Spicer). Gay poetry was influenced as well by other cultures. It had absorbed the blues culture of Harlem African-American life and had been fed by the sensuous romanticism of Spanish gay verse (Lorca).

* * *

The forties in America saw the advent of what I will term 'The Gay Beat Period.' During and after World War II a generation of single gay men heard the call to travel and sought the urban culture of New York, San Francisco, Los Angeles, and Boston as well as cities abroad. These early gay poets drew on a new freedom in "open form," predominantly perfected by Charles Olson, Robert Duncan, the Black Mountain experience, and the emotionalism and mysticism of the countercultural protest of the 'San Francisco Renaissance.' They were also influenced by the surrealism of Breton, Cocteau, and Lautreamont. These writers took up Whitman's legacy of frankness, direct speech, an everyday vernacular, and an unabashed celebration of the homoerotic. Unlike Crane, they felt free to speak their desire in simple, less opaque terms. They enthusiastically looked to the past to rediscover homoerotic verse forms. They drew on the American experience of William Carlos Williams and his delight in the American vernacular.

They shared the new social mobility and disruption prompted by World War II and the vast mobilization of single young men. They reveled in travel: Norse lived in Europe for many years and visited Algeria; Ginsberg made his well-documented forays to India, Mexico, and Morocco. They moved through the Bohemian enclaves of New York City, San Francisco, and Paris (the famous 'Beat' Hotel). Like Whitman they felt a comradeship with the open road, the democratics of desire, and the working-class experience. They shared an iconoclastic streak or, in the case of Spicer, courted a new wave of mysticism. They drew from the Dadaists, the surrealists, and the abstract expressionists to invigorate new poetic forms–"found" poetry, the "cut-up" of Byron Geysin, Burroughs, etc.

Their stance as liberationists was seen in both their raw, masculine unconventionality and their fascination with the extremes of decadence and romanticism of earlier eras–Blake, Whitman, Rimbaud, Verlaine, and Lorca–as well as their affinity to Buddhism and Eastern philosophy. Harold Norse, Allen Ginsberg, Steve Jonas, John Giorno, John Wieners, Jack Spicer, Robert Duncan, Charles Henri Ford, Edouard Roditi, and Maurice Kenny were some writers of this period. Paul Mariah, Ralph Pomeroy, and Richard Tagett are transitional poets from a Beat individualism and counter-cultural aesthetic toward a newer gay subcultural liberationist perspective. Rene Ricard, a more contemporary gay poet, has continued the surrealist work of Wieners.

'The Gay Intelligentsia or Poets of Gay Urbanity' were broadly speaking, though not all, urban dandies of the forties, fifties, sixties, and seventies who settled in New York City, were part of its small, gay, intellectual, and academic community, and, early in their careers, moved into positions as curators, museum administrators, editors, art critics, journalists, book reviewers, and academic teachers. Bonded by various interrelationships and associations, many were familiar with the older Auden and his circle. Auden, indeed, with Chester Kallman (Auden's lover) and Paul Goodman, as well as the poetry editor of *The New Yorker* Howard Moss, moved in this New York gay intellectual set, a savvy "academic" group that mentored younger writers and courted other intellectuals. Auden, Merrill, later O'Hara and the fiction writer Edmund White became centers for this constellation of intellectuals. O'Hara's group included Ashbery and Schuyler, Merrill's included the poetry critic David Kalstone and poets Alfred Corn and Sandy McClatchy. More recent gay writers such as David Craig Austin, David Bergman, Henri Cole, Mark Doty, Daniel Hall, Scott Hightower, Timothy Liu, Richard McCann, Paul Monette, Reginald Shepherd, Carl Phillips, Gregory Woods, and Wayne Koestenbaum continue to reflect characteristics of this academic style and tradition. Indeed they form a newer generation of Academic gay poets very much a part of the contemporary queer scene.

Highly educated, well versed in European and American traditions, erudite, as well as interested in a new gay aestheticism, these poets shared a deep interest in culture, art, and fashion and in the traditions of Auden, Cavafy, Crane, Gide, James, Proust, Whitman, and Wilde. They aspired to a high cultural profile and ushered in a new sense of urbanity. Indeed, one might argue that twentieth-century Urbanity was a homosexual creation (as gays and lesbians–Oscar Wilde and Gertrude Stein, most importantly–were its supreme, often strategic practitioners).

These poets looked to the spectacle of the urban and the international as signifier for their gay sensibility. Gay verse became performative. Their interest in culture, both high culture and popular culture, was informed by a greater self-consciousness of forming a gay vanguard.

This gay urbanity ranged from the more formal academic gentility of Auden, Merrill, McClatchy, and Howard to the affable sociability of Goodman, Corn, and Schuyler; from the witty, rebellious 'Personism' of Frank O'Hara to the mandarin 'nostalgia of the infinite' (a term O'Hara describes in his Personism manifesto) of Ashbery.

The homosexuality of these poets was often less spoken than implied by their wit, erudition, high-art-low-art slummings, and their deep knowledge of the artful dissembling of discourse. Their verse explored their inner circles of gay friendship.

Auden, Merrill, Schuyler, Howard, Corn, and McClatchy in particular reflected a style sometimes similar to the Genteel poets of American Civil War times. By linking them to the privileged and homosexual Genteel poets of another century, I am not suggesting they were all affected or marked by prudery. Their writing is in no way pedantic, arch, or obscure. Auden, Schuyler, and Corn have a wonderful affinity to the social day-to-day and can be outrageously campy. Corn in particular has a love of Whitman, and his work shows at times an evocative spirituality. Corn, Schuyler, and Merrill all have a love of nature and have written in a myriad of poetic forms. These writers often chose English verse forms such as blank verse, sonnets, and terza rima for their poetry.

Frank O'Hara actually represents a fascinating transition poet where many gay thematic concerns and styles come together. He is the bridge from an underground marginalized 'Beat' other (that he was certainly part of in the fifties and early sixties) to a highly visible and self-conscious gay intellectual aesthetic. For the first time a 'gay voice' became widely heard. His life and death (in 1966) ushered in the gay high culture of the seventies and eighties.

O'Hara found in the cultural crossroads of New York City a nexus of cultural sensations. The appropriation of art and artifice, the mixing of styles both high and low, and the growing movement toward Op and Pop on the heels of Abstract Expressionism showed the inherent potential for the gay artist as not only "keeper of the code" and the "cultural flame" ('flame' in its more camp element) but its trickster as well. O'Hara created a very self-conscious and stylized gay poetic, one noted for its wit, sophistication, and attention to society and glamour. "Steps" and "Poem [Lana Turner has collapsed!]" are perfect examples of O'Hara at his most sophisticated and playful. Poems like "Hotel Transylvanie," "To You," and "Homosexuality" speak directly to O'Hara's gay self. Society and gossip, as with Proust, became a means for gay men to look out of the closet and participate in the dominant culture. Inevitably a 'gay society' or a gay aesthetic was built around a certain elitism. An urban identity based on culture and knowledge became formulated around O'Hara's numerous friends and immediate success. O'Hara's position at the Museum of Modern Art, his travels through the party scene of gallery openings, art world happenings, Fire Island, and the Hamptons, and his flirtations with high and low society had established a new sense of a "gay intelligentsia," dressed flamboyantly in the accoutrements of glamour and culture. Warhol solidified this gay popular aesthetic, and the cult of "gay aestheticism" or the gay urban dandy was truly entrenched.

Warhol and O'Hara influenced other gay poets who were still part of the surrealist gay Beat movement of Wieners, notably, Gerard Malanga.

The advent of Charles Ortleb's *Christopher Street* in 1976 (with the assistance of Michael Denneny, Bertha Harris, Blanche Boyd, and Richard Howard) with its high literary style and intellectualism was perhaps the high point of this gay New York urbanity.

In the midseventies a style of rebellious, erotic, gay liberation poetry took the scene. Many of the poets in this movement lived in Boston and were published in Charles Shively's *Fag Rag* magazine (1976). They also found a home in the rural gay periodical *RFD* (1975). These 'Poets of the Pagan' or '*Fag Rag* Poets' were the carnivorous saints, barbarians, bad boys, and sexual outlaws of their time. Many of them were members of what Rudy Kikel has called the "Boston School." Born of an aggressive radical activism, they celebrated the erotic, the revolutionary, the defiant, and alternatively the pastoral. An extension in many ways of the rebelliousness of the gay Beat writers and Ginsberg, Orlofsky, and Giorno's radical faggotry, these writers appropriated that which had been labeled pornographic and criminal. In later years they supported groups such as NAMBLA (The North American Man/Boy Love Association) and the "Radical Faeries."

The movement also embraced mysticism and the pagan celebration of the body. Just as feminism and the women's movement sought to reclaim the female body from patriarchal control, gay "pagan" poets attempted to reenvision the male body, celebrating its receptivity, sensuality, and spiritual essences. This erotic gay poetry balanced itself between the sacred and the profane. The West Coast poet James Broughton is a strong example of this spiritual celebration of the male body.

Magicians, fairies, "cocksuckers," "faggots," and "queens" of all persuasions became the mythical beasts of this gay urban and pastoral verse. Their raw style, evocative of Verlaine and Rimbaud's celebration of the male sexual anatomy and Genet's fascination with the underworld and the criminal, proclaimed a new sexual freedom. Less taxed by form, often uneven in language, this verse could be highly charged and provocative, or spiritual, pastoral, and tantric. Franklin Abbott, Steve Abbott, Antler, Tommi Avicolli, Walta Borawski, James Broughton, Kirby Congdon, Louie Crew, Gavin Dillard, Jim Eggling, Jim Everhard, Allen Ginsberg, Walter Griffin, Will Inman, Gabriel Lampert, Larry Mitchell, Edmund Miller, Carl Morse, Peter Orlovsky, Chuck Ortleb, Crazy Owl, Steve Pallagi, David Pini, Kenneth Pitchford, Jim Regan, Ron Schreiber, Charles Shively, Aaron Shurin, Randy Smallwood, David Sunseri, Bill Taorimino, and Roger Weaver all wrote at various times from this perspective.

Aaron Shurin's "A Waist" and "Pilgrimage" focus on the male body. "Conversions/Winter Solstice" is filled with sexual ritual and mysticism. Charles Shively's "Immediately" and Antler's "What Every Boy Knows" are sexually explicit poems of desire. Chuck Ortleb's "Militerotics" is an award-winning work (the 1976 Fels Award in poetry) which looks defiantly at repressed homosexuality and its role in male violence, war, and sadism, and rejects that drive for power via violence. Morse's "Dream of the Artfairy" is a classic mix of the political ode and an invocation to the new radicalism of gay identity. Walta Borawski's "Live Free or Die" and "Power of One" are powerful statements about the formulation and assertion of individual gay identity.

Gavin Dillard in his extended cycle of poems from *The Naked Poet* (1989) and *Pagan Love Songs* (1987) establishes himself in the vernacular of a gay folk balladeer. His works are evocative of the folk lyrics of Leonard Cohen from the sixties. There is a great innocence to Dillard's work.

'The Gilded Poets' is a title drawn from the work of Felice Picano to label the sensibility in the next broad group of extremely eclectic and gifted poets. These writers arrived on the heels of gay liberation in the late sixties and early seventies and continued their work in the eighties. Many were steeped in a gay subculture at a younger age and wrote from the particular vantage of its colorful, romantic acculturation. Like Edward Field, Thom Gunn, Maurice Kenny, Ralph Pomeroy, and Tennessee Williams, some had been writing since the forties and fifties.

Their work, indeed, was drawn to the locales and haunts of a masculine erotic subculture. Many came of age at a time in the seventies when lesbians and gay men had been polarized into separate communities and cultures. Their writing bears a certain lyrical, romantic, theatrical sheen or, as in Gunn, a raw economy of vision. Like Frank O'Hara, many were interested in American popular culture and its camp appeal, or, as in Williams (and even in Richard Howard), the vernacular of the gay "queen," worldly, complex, tragic, and bitchy. They were drawn to the drama of the gay bar and its rituals, to cruising and the urban haunts of gay men. Writers such as Darryl Hine and Robert Peters have enjoyed academic careers.

Homosexuality is "out" in the work of these 'Gilded Poets' and becomes their point of departure, rather than providing a gritty background. All of these writers shared in the hedonistic culture after Stonewall. They had experienced, as Gunn writes in his poem "Lament," "Those normal pleasures of the sun's kingdom/The hedonistic body basks within/ And takes for granted–summer on the skin." If they were poets of summer, pleasure, skin, and the body, they were also part of a golden age for American gay literary publishing. Many participated in starting the first gay poetry presses and their work celebrated and adorned gay newspapers, gay political leaflets, and gay journals. Poetry was everywhere.

Their works appeared primarily in gay magazines/journals/newspapers such as: *ManRoot* (1969), *Gay Sunshine* (1970), *Mouth of the Dragon* (1974), *RFD* (1975), *Fag Rag* (1976), *Come Out!* (1969); and anthologies such as Ian Young's *The Male Muse* (1973), Winston Leyland's *Angels of the Lyre* (1975) and *Orgasms of Light* (1977), Felice Picano's *A True Likeness* (1980), and Ian Young's *Son of the Male Muse* (1983). They also continue to be published in reviews such as *Christopher Street* (1976) and *The James White Review* (1983). Some wrote from the special political perspective of the postliberation seventies and eighties. Many exhibited a youthful Byronic vision of sexual liberation and a growing confidence in a gay poetic voice.

Some were poets who shared in the club-drug scene of New York and San Francisco, the ghetto culture, taking their imagery and stylistic from the music of the times, the movie and TV culture, and the glimmering surfaces and fast-track lives they experienced. Fire Island, Provincetown, the Castro were some of their haunts. Many were connected by literary and social friendships, and chose a poetry that was sophisticated, clever, and autobiographical, following in the footsteps of O'Hara and Schuyler. Their style varied from the formal simplicity of Gunn with his metered regularity and the sonnets of Rudy Kikel to the open forms of David Trinidad and Edward Field. They often looked at the coming-out experience and the rituals of gay culture: cruising, adolescence, American pop culture, relationships, love, sex, and obsession. Perry Brass has written poems of great lyrical grace which have been set to music by several gay composers of the eighties.

Dennis Cooper wrote from an aesthetic found in sex, drugs, sadomasochism, and a hypermasculine cult. His poems are loaded with anger and libidinous desire but strangely unable to connect. He writes sometimes from a particular nihilistic stance. He borrows his spirit from Rimbaud and Genet. Poems such as Cooper's "Hustlers," "Being Aware," "ABBA," "First Sex," and "The Blank Generation" establish his hostile use of language, its rawness of tone, and its alienation.

Gunn, the master of tight, simple forms, uses a terse masculine language in works such as "Lines for My 55th Birthday," "Looks," "To Isherwood Dying," and "The Stealer." He has been writing since the fifties and his work transcends many gay perspectives, connecting frequently with the darker social humanism of Auden and Isherwood. There is a solitariness to his vision, a hypermasculine eroticism, and a toughness of language and attack.

Field, like Schuyler, pursues a poetry of the personal that is sociable, self-examining, chatty, and democratic. His work swings from the gay domestic to the erotic to the international.

All these 'Gilded Poets' were part of a diverse golden age for gay poetry. They mirrored a highly charged gay cultural scene. They were influenced by the homoerotic photography of Bruce Weber, Herb Ritts, and Mapplethorpe, who were creating lasting images of masculine desire. These photos built upon the earlier work of the painter Thomas Eakins and the photography of F. Holland Day, Baron von Gloeden, and later George Platt Lynes. Some were sparse and clean and pedestrian as poets, writing from a new sense of the masculine. Many relied on a sense of theater, fashion, romanticism, and atmospherics. They lived in the time of a highly stylized Gay Arts Movement which included gay performers such as Charles Ludlum, Ethyl Eichenberg, and Jack Smith; gay musicians such as John Cage, Boy George, and Freddy Mercury; gay choreographers such as Alvin Ailey, Robert Joffery, Michael Bennett, Bill T. Jones, and Arnie Zane; and gay visual artists such as Haring, Mapplethorpe, and Warhol. They were also writers of differing talents, ages, political persuasions, and gifts. Felice Picano wrote essays, reviews, and screenplays and spent time in the movie industry. Tim Dlugos wrote novels, book reviews, and articles on gay culture. Carl Morse wrote plays, edited anthologies, and promoted new gay and lesbian writers with his Open Lines reading series in New York in 1981. These were poets who experimented in more than one form. Mark Ameen, Jack Anderson, Perry Brass, Joe Cady, Dennis Cooper, Daniel Diamond, Tim Dlugos, Edward Field, Robert Gluck, Thom Gunn, Darryl Hine, John Iozia, Maurice Kenny, Rudy Kikel, Michael Lassell, Sean Lawrence, Paul Mariah, Carl Morse, Robert Peters, Felice Picano, Ralph Pomeroy, Steven Riel, Simon Sheppard, David Trinidad, James White, Tennessee Williams, and Ian Young were some of the writers.

In the sixties Adrian Stanford was already exploring an alternative gay experience, a sensibility born of African-American myth and style, of the blues and jazz, of drag queens and street hustlers. Trying to find a separate voicing for a gay black man, these lyrical poems evoked the raunchy blues style of Bessie Smith and other blues and jazz figures of the Harlem Renaissance. Stanford's powerful influence culminated in the publication by Good Gay Poets Press in 1977 of his seminal book of poetry, *Black and Queer.*

The Harlem Renaissance in essence continued and never fully ended, and the issues of race, gender, and class that it began to articulate were picked up by a new generation of black gay writers. Marked with the political stances of the Black Arts Movement and the Black Civil Rights Movement of the sixties, poets such as Stanford had a fresh political and cultural take on empowerment and self-expression. Also, black gay writers could draw upon the work of black lesbian poets such as Audre Lorde and Pat Parker, and the prose writings of James Baldwin and Samuel R. Delany.

As the literature of the gay, black experience in the eighties broadened to include Caribbean and Atlantic Rim cultures as well as gay black internationalism, a rich renaissance in poetry with a startling mix of metaphors and imagery was born. This work adopted gay black slang in both traditional and nontraditional verse forms. The language of blues poems, reggae, and rap were appropriated–for instance–into haiku and tanka.

A powerful connection to the myths of an African tradition were manifested in poems which drew from the Yoruban legend of the adodi–homosexual shamans and healers who empowered their communities. Like the Berdache, the adodi held special powers by virtue of their transgendered knowledge.

The black, male poets of this generation had a sensitivity to myth and the rhetorical power which verse and language played in their communities. These poets shared with black women writers an interest in the exploration of race, class, and gender and the new conceptualization of community, sisterhood, and brotherhood. The work also reflected the powerful political concerns of black gay men who had experienced the upheaval of the Civil Rights era and the homophobia of the black church and black heterosexual community.

Many of these poets of this extended Harlem Renaissance found their start in Michael J. Smith's anthology *Black Men/White Men* (1983) and Joseph Beam's groundbreaking black gay anthology *In the Life* (1986).

Many were members of the influential New York black writers' collectives Blackheart and Other Countries (founded by Daniel Garrett). R. G. Dildy, Melvin Dixon, Salih Michael Fisher, David Frechette, D. Rubin Greene, Roy Gonsalves, Craig G. Harris, Essex Hemphill, Redvers Jeanmarie, Brad Johnson, Cary Alan Johnson, Steve Langley, C. R. Pouncy, Alden Reimonenq, Craig A. Reynolds, Colin Robinson, Phillip Robinson, Assotto Saint, Adrian Stanford, Arthur T. Wilson, Richard Witherspoon, and Donald W. Woods were all part of this first generation of gay 'poets-of-color' who tried to explore their separate identities outside the domain of the then dominant white gay culture. Gay, black fiction/non-fiction writers and playwrights also included in this group were Shawn Brown, M.E. Fuller, Daniel Garrett, Cary Alan Johnson, Phillip Richardson, Allan B. Williams, Allen Wright, and Ali Wadud. This first wave hit in the mid to late eighties and was centered primarily in New York although Hemphill lived in Philadelphia, Reynolds in Washington, and Robinson in Boston.

Many of these writers were self-published and attempted to revitalize a tradition founded in the heyday of the Harlem Renaissance when *Fire!* (1926) was collectively published with Richard Bruce Nugent's short story "Smoke, Lilies and Jade." Looking back to the work of Hughes and Cullen, they shared in the legacy of jazz and blues forms as well as a vivid imagistic diversity and lyricism which drew from the drama and rhetorical power of black literature and slave narratives. They explored the uses of ritual, theater, music, and performance to heighten their work. They also looked to other gay writers such as Walter Thurman and Alain Locke for their gay black legacies. As with Jean Toomer's anthology *Cane*, whose publication marked a high point for the Harlem Renaissance, gay black anthologies such as *In the Life* (1986), *Brother to Brother* (1991), and *Other Countries Journal* (1988) followed Toomer's format of mixing prose and poetry to portray the broadest possible spectrum of gay Afro-American life. By reprinting such Harlem Renaissance works as Nugent's "Smoke, Lilies and Jade" or making allusions to the novels of Wallace Thurman (Thurman's *The Infants of Spring* [1932] featured a gay character), Hemphill, Saint, Dixon, and others were further underscoring their link to the Harlem Renaissance period.

An early poem such as Stanford's "Sacrifice" printed in *ONE* magazine in the sixties shows his great talent for creating poetic imagery and weaving a powerful mythic language around African-American experience. "Remembrance of Rittenhouse Square" which first appeared in *ONE* in 1965 (and later in Essex Hemphill's *Brother to Brother* anthology) is a seminal poem for its invocation of the black drag queen as deity and its revival of the 'blues' poem in a new gay context. Stanford's richly imaginative language in this poem becomes an originary moment for the creation of a true gay black voice.

Essex Hemphill's "Family Jewels," "Cordon Negro," "Visiting Hours," and "American Wedding" establish Hemphill's acute understanding of the workings of racism and homophobia, and his adept ability at finding images both painful and powerful to link black gay male culture with broader racial issues in his community.

Melvin Dixon in "Change of Territory," "Hemispheres," and "King of Crossroads" explores the personal mythology (already begun by Audre Lorde) of being gay and Afro-American and having been richly educated in the traditions of western culture.

Poems such as "Processional," "Souvenir," and "Arc-En-Ciel" by the Haitian-born Assotto Saint, as well as his later poems "The Queen's Etiquette" and "Heart & Soul" draw upon an interesting language of voodoo, mysticism, theater, and defiance to make his personal statement. The work of Saint bears a relationship to the lyrical imagery of Redvers Jeanmarie who like other Caribbean poets finds a language rich in color and ritual. "Raga" and "The English Language" are two poems which relate directly to the Caribbean experience and issues of gayness, brotherhood, and allegiance.

A second wave of gay poets-of-color appeared in the late eighties and early nineties. The careers of these writers were shaped and influenced by the earlier pioneering works of James Baldwin, Samuel R. Delany, Essex Hemphill, Assotto Saint, Audre Lorde, and Pat Parker. They took as their mandate the task of further delineating their varied cultural experiences as gay African- or Caribbean-Americans.

This movement took its advent with three seminal anthologies of Assotto Saint, *The Road Before Us: 100 Gay Black Poets* (1991), *Here to Dare* (1992), and *Milking Black Bull* (1995). Some of the second wave of Afro-American and Caribbean poets who were part of this multicultural movement included Thom Bean, Carl Cook, Rodney Dildy, Thomas Glave, Thomas Grimes, Umar Hasan, B. Michael Hunter, G. Winston James, Bob McNeil, Reginald Patterson, Robert E. Penn, Reginald Shepherd, and Vega.

This gay poets-of-color movement also reached to cultures other than Afro-American and Caribbean-American. Francisco X. Alarcon on the West Coast, a poet of Hispanic descent, was at work at this time. Roy Gonsalves's *Perversion* (1990) spoke of the gritty urban experience of gays in the ghetto from both an African-American and Hispanic perspective. Indeed, Hispanic gay writing was discovered for its deep and varied roots in Lorca, Jaime Gil de Biedma, and Cernuda. Jaime Manrique, New York novelist and poet, and a native of Columbia, would publish in 1995 *My Night with Federico Garcia Lorca.* This seminal collection of poetry shows the creative link of Hispanic gay poets to the tradition of Lorca.

A poetry of AIDS emerged in the eighties especially with the advent of Michael Klein's 1989 anthology *Poets for Life*, the start of the magazine *Art & Understanding* by David Wagonner, and the 1993 anthology *Sojourner: Black Gay Voices in the Age of AIDS*. Poets such as David Craig Austin, Raul Martinez-Avila, Charles Barber, David Bergman, Glenn Besco, Steven Blaski, William Bory, Robert Boucheron, Rafael Campo, Dan Conner, Mark Doty, Kenny Fries, Tony J. Giordano, Brad Gooch, Walter Holland, Michael Klein, Michael Lassell, Michael Lynch, Paul Monette, Gustavo Motta, Michael Niemoeller, Michael Pelonero, Ron Schreiber, and James Turcotte are a few among the many who have dealt movingly with the subject of death and dying. They have also addressed the concerns of a generation of gay writers confronted by the issue of loss, absence, anger, and the search for inner resolve.

One form of elegy which gained acceptance was the very long narrative, reminiscent of Tennyson, and the prose poems of Cavafy and Ginsberg. These verses dealt with AIDS, loss, and memory, and are notable for their decorum and control, their lyrical beauty and evocative loss.

Another form of elegy was defiant and tightly restricted in ever-confined metrical units. This work was informed by the angry, rhetorical language of ACT-UP. Melvin Dixon, Roy Gonsalvez, and Assotto Saint were the more accomplished practitioners of these short lyric forms.

In dealing with AIDS, poets such as James Merrill, Sandy McClatchy, and Mark Doty chose elegant refined surfaces to their works where lyrical excess seemed to emphasize a certain emptiness underneath and a poignant sense of absence.

Love Alone (1988) by Paul Monette became exemplary of the new attention and elevated artistry of the elegy form. By his wonderful compression of anger, memory, rage, admiration, and sorrow into a language wholly contemporary and American, Monette established AIDS elegiac verse as a genre which would dominate gay poetry for years to come.

Michael Lynch's *These Waves of Dying Friends* (1989), Kenny Fries's *The Healing Notebooks* (1990), Michael Lassell's *Decade Dance* (1990), my own *A Journal of the Plague Years* (1992), William Bory's *Orpheus in His Underwear* (1993), Mark Doty's *My Alexandria* (1993), Walta Borawski's *Lingering in a Silk Shirt* (1994), David Bergman's *The Care and Treatment of Pain* (1994), Assotto Saint's *Wishing for Wings* (1994), and Michael Niemoeller's *Stone Made Flesh* (1995) have all helped establish a new breadth and sophistication for the "gay AIDS elegy."

The "queer" poets who arrived in the nineties after the death of so many of their predecessors represent a broader and more multicultural perspective. Some among them continue to explore their varied cultural heritages such as Reggie Cabico and Craig Hickman. Others such as Carl Phillips and Reginald Shepherd carry the legacy of African-American experience in a more postmodern, abstract style. Many of them bring fine skills honed in poetry workshops at universities across the country. Many were around in the seventies and eighties and continue to bring, like the 'Gilded Poets,' a romantization to the rituals of male bar culture and cruising. Others are part of 'Generation Q,' those young, twenty-something queer writers who were born at the time of the Stonewall Rebellion in 1969 or shortly thereafter.

Queer poets represent continued influences in the growth of performance poetry from the Nuyorican Poets Cafe in New York City and from the Boston and West Coast area slam culture. Anthologies such as *Premonitions: The Kaya Anthology of New Asian North American Poetry* (1995, Kaya Press) and *Aloud: Voices from the Nuyorican Poets Cafe* (1994), in which queer writers are associated and included with more multicultural and mainstream authors, reflect new alliances in publishing.

For the first time, they are a generation raised from adolescence by the gay community. They have read its theory, attended its massive marches, games, and celebrations, and enjoyed its growing visibility. Many have led open lives from early ages. They now share in the transitional culture from gay to queer. If gay was a libertarian, aggressive spirit and rebellion born of the sexual revolution and a cult of masculinity, as well as a defining need to retrieve that culture and history from a closeted and oppressive past, queer is a broader, less stable, cross-gendered, multicultural entity, one that questions the categories of race and gender and sex, distrusts discourse, and revels in the aporia.

At the end of the twentieth century, thirty years post-Stonewall, these writers evidence a new economy of language, a more skilled and confident poetic voice, and a greater variety of subject matter and range of feeling. No longer restrained to the Beat exigency for travel, rebellion, mysticism, decadence, and the democratic; no longer wholly committed to liberationist eroticism and political posturings, nor enamored of the surfaces of a highly refined and mandarin knowledge of cognoscenti culture, nor drawn to the originary separateness and urgencies of the black gay movement; these younger poets speak from diverse spectrums of queer life. The pressure to speak the male body is still present but now without the weighted hand of performative anxiety. A new queer domesticity has become prominent as young gays and lesbians integrate their lives into middle-class America and the American heartland. Love poetry anthologies are growing ever more popular. Queer culture is adapting to its newfound commercial consumerism and popularity. Slick magazines are on every newstand. Anthologies such as *Generation Q* (1996) are presenting new voices from those growing up in the age of information.

Many of these poets have been schooled and nurtured by numerous writing workshops and academic programs across the country. They have heard their peers read at open-mike gay and lesbian readings. They have been influenced by newer trends in contemporary American mainstream poetry from the Language Poetry of the West and East Coasts (Charles Bernstein, Michael Palmer, Lyn Hejinian, Barbara Guest, John Yau) to the style commonly presented in journals such as *Paris Review, Ploughshares*, and *The Iowa Review*. This "Best American Poetry" poetry appears to be characterized by quiet introspection, small and delicate fields of vision, a new domesticity, and a language of crisp prosaic exactitude. It also represents a darker American realism, one that senses the political in the personal. It grapples with issues of environment, twelve-step self-help programs, childhood sexual abuse, mothers and daughters, fathers and sons, alcoholism, gardening, domestic life, and a myriad of everyday experiences with measured reason and eloquence. Its practitioners include mainstream older and younger poets such as: John Ash, Hayden Carruth, Jorie Graham, Marilyn Hacker, Robert Hass, Lynda Hull, Stanley Kunitz, Phillip Levine, Carol Muske, Mary Oliver, Molly Peacock, Gerald Stern, and David Wojahn.

Still others are drawn to recent queer "zines" such as *Fruit* which look for the offbeat in gay and lesbian writing. A need to push toward ever more forbidden and marginalized material takes on issues of adolescence and gender formation, sadomasochism, incest, religion, colonialism, androgyny, transexualism, and multiculturalism.

Recent anthologies such as *Gents, Bad Boys, & Barbarians: New Gay Male Poetry* published in 1995 by Alyson Publications and edited by Rudy Kikel; Lynn Crosbie and Michael Holmes's *Plush* (1995); and David Laurents's *The Badboy Book of Erotic Poetry* (1995) identify many strong new gay/queer poets of this generation along with others who are beginning to make their mark. Ken Anderson, Jeffery Beam, Mark Bibbins, Regie Cabico, Rafael Campo, Tom Carey, Justin Chin, Jeffrey Conway, Steven Cordova, Mark Doty, Ron Drummond, S. K. Duff, Daniel Hall, Craig Hickman, Scott Hightower, Walter Holland, Matthew Howard, C.K. Jones, Nathan Kernan, Michael Klein, Dean Kostos, Michael Lassell,

Joseph Like, Timothy Liu, Richard McCann, John T. Medeiros, Rondo Mieczkowski, Thomas Paul Miller, M. S. Montgomery, Christopher Murray, Jon Nalley, Peter Pereira, Carl Phillips, George Piggford, William Reichard, Lawrence Schimmel, Reginald Shepherd, Winthrop Smith, Dan Stone, Jerl Surratt, G. R. Taylor, Fabian Thomas, Gary Paul Wright, and Gregory Woods are just a few of these writers.

The discontinuities of gender construction and cultural ethnicity find their way into the verse of these writers. The problems of discourse, family, and other diverse experiences such as bisexual and transgendered perspectives as well as those of writers with disabilities are making themselves known. Not wedded to the ivory tower closet or the aesthetic isolation of a previous generation, they are more accepted and published in both mainstream and alternative presses. The issue of gayness has now shifted from liberation sexual politics to organized community and social life.

Some of these poets are more balanced in their approach, more varied and contemplative than many of their predecessors. They have the advantage of a diverse and active gay/queer poetic tradition to draw upon. They have begun, in the wake of AIDS, the process of rebuilding a gay/queer poetry community. Some have chosen to return to the transformative power of the erotic as basis for a shared sense of community and knowledge. As recent anthologies of gay male poetry go more mainstream, as evidenced by the success of St. Martin's Press' *The Name of Love: Classic Gay Love Poems* (1995) and more recently *Eros in Boystown* (St. Martin's Press, 1996), gay/queer poetry moves beyond its adolescence. However, the transition toward "queerness" at the end of the century has turned gay, lesbian, and straight culture inside out. A new "individualism" and theory of "identity" outside the old formulas of gender, biological sex, race, and sexual orientation is beginning to develop. Queer poets will need to synthesize a new language outside of the aging vocabulary of a passing century to better capture the shifting paradigm.

WORKS CITED

Laine, Barry. "Gay Poetry Reaches Adolescence." *Christopher Street*. December, 1976. 34-42.

Perkins, David, ed. *A History of Modern Poetry: Modernism and After*. Cambridge, MA: Harvard University Press, 1987.

Poulin, A., Jr., ed. *Contemporary American Poetry*. Boston: Houghton Mifflin, 1985.

Summers, Claude J., ed. *The Gay and Lesbian Literary Heritage: A Reader's Companion to the Writers and Their Works, from Antiquity to the Present*. New York: Henry Holt, 1995.

The Purloined *Ladder*: Its Place in Lesbian History

Manuela Soares

New York, New York

SUMMARY. This essay traces *The Ladder* from its initial publication in October 1956 as the official vehicle of the lesbian rights group the Daughters of Bilitis to its final issue as a privately published magazine in August 1972. By excerpting quotes from key lesbian figures of the time, it seeks to trace *The Ladder*'s history from amateur newsletter to a more polished literary magazine–a reflection of the shift in the culture's perspective of itself from "variant" to "lesbian." *[Article copies available for a fee from The Haworth Document Delivery Service: 1-800-342-9678. E-mail address: getinfo@haworth.com]*

In 1967, the *New York Times* joined the trend for multimedia ownership and set up a book publishing division known as The New York Times Book Co., which included Quadrangle Publishing and The Arno Press.

Manuela Soares is Managing Editor of hardcover books for a major New York publisher. An independent scholar who lives in New York City, she recently published *Butch/Femme* (Crown, 1995), a series of photographic images representing these roles in lesbian culture. Under the auspices of the Lesbian Herstory Archives, she has been collaborating for several years with Sara Yager, Kelly Anderson, and Trista Sordillo on a video project documenting the history of the Daughters of Bilitis. Clips from the video had their most recent public preview at an Allegheny College symposium, April 25, 1995.

[Haworth co-indexing entry note]: "The Purloined *Ladder*: Its Place in Lesbian History." Soares, Manuela. Co-published simultaneously in *Journal of Homosexuality* (The Haworth Press, Inc.) Vol. 34, No. 3/4, 1998, pp. 27-49; and: *Gay and Lesbian Literature Since World War II: History and Memory* (ed: Sonya L. Jones) The Haworth Press, Inc., 1998, pp. 27-49; and: *Gay and Lesbian Literature Since World War II: History and Memory* (ed: Sonya L. Jones) Harrington Park Press, an imprint of The Haworth Press, Inc., 1998, pp. 27-49. Single or multiple copies of this article are available for a fee from The Haworth Document Delivery Service [1-800-342-9678, 9:00 a.m. - 5:00 p.m. (EST). E-mail address: getinfo@haworth.com].

Founded as a reprinter of historical and scholarly collections aimed at the library market, Arno published books in many different areas, including medieval literature.

In 1975, Arno introduced a new series on homosexuality–"Lesbians and Gay Men in Society, History, and Literature." The Arno Series on Homosexuality reprinted books as well as entire collections of major periodicals with gay themes. Among the reprinted magazines was a complete nine-volume set of *The Ladder* (Parr, 1975), the official publication of the first lesbian rights group in America, the Daughters of Bilitis, founded in San Francisco in October 1955.

In reprinting many of these classic works, the Arno Press gave a new generation of scholars access to important gay and lesbian literature and history, as well as the complete collection of one of the most important lesbian/feminist publications in the United States, *The Ladder*.

From the magazine's first publication in October 1956 until the final issue in August 1972, *The Ladder* included discussions on the major issues in the homosexual movement–politics, the law, religion–and examinations of social phenomena such as butch/femme and coming out, as well as fiction and poetry. As a result, the pages of *The Ladder* provide a history of the lesbian rights movement in the United States as it existed in the latter half of the twentieth century.

The orange library-bound books in the Homosexual series include over fifty titles, both fiction and nonfiction–classics of lesbian and gay literature as well as many little-known gems. Among the titles in the series were: Mercedes de Acosta's memoirs, *Here Lies the Heart* (1960), about her relationships with Greta Garbo and Marlene Dietrich; Ann Bannon's *Odd Girl Out* (1957), *I Am a Woman* (1959), *Women in the Shadows* (1959), and *Journey to a Woman* (1960); Jane Rule's *Desert of the Heart* (1964); as well as even earlier works: Gale Wilhelm's *We Too Are Drifting* (1935), Natalie Barney's *Aventures de l'esprit* (1929), *The Life of Radclyffe Hall* (1961) by Una Troubridge, and *Poèmes de Renée Vivienne* (1923-24). The only other periodical Arno reissued in the series was a six-volume reprint of the *Mattachine Review* (volumes 1-13, 1955-1966), the official publication of the Mattachine Society, a gay men's group founded in Los Angeles in 1951 by Harry Hay. Named for a secret fraternity of unmarried French townsmen in the Middle Ages, the Society's statement of purpose reflected its interest in self-education and community organizing as well as its Communist organizational model.

Using copies of *The Ladder* from the collection of Barbara Grier, the last editor of *The Ladder,* Arno reprinted every issue, from volume 1, number 1 (October 1956), to volume 16, numbers 11 and 12 (August/September 1972). Oddly, they never included the first cover of the magazine, though the same graphic was used for the first twelve issues of the journal–October 1956 through September 1957–printed in varying colors of ink and paper.

Grier wrote a brief introduction to the reprint series, but there was no other commentary about *The Ladder* or The Daughters of Bilitis.[1] This essay will attempt to review the history of *The Ladder* and some of the ways in which it impacted the lesbian community.

Although *The Ladder* was actually the second lesbian publication in America, "that we know of," adds Lesbian Herstory Archives founder Joan Nestle (Nestle, 1987), it was the most widely read publication of its kind, with a rich 16-year history.[2] Subscribers to *The Ladder* were limited initially to a handful of chapter members and their friends, mostly in San Francisco, becoming a few hundred nationwide within a few years, and finally several thousand by the time it ceased publication. What made *The Ladder* unique was its dedicated following and the fact that it was passed from reader to reader and reached a far larger audience than their subscription list would initially indicate. Because there was no access to the mainstream media, the first three gay periodicals, *ONE* magazine, *The Mattachine Review*, and *The Ladder* built up their initial circulation almost entirely by being passed from hand to hand.[3] Circulation remained small because so many readers did not subscribe.

The experience that lesbian activist Judith Schwarz describes in a 1988 interview reflects what many women felt about *The Ladder*. Schwarz, who worked at a photo processing lab, relates:

> I would buy it at the newsstand and you had to prove you were twenty-one to buy it. . . . And it said "For adults only" even then [1964] . . . I think I picked up a copy of *The Ladder* before I went to DOB and joined it. Anyway *The Ladder* was really important and I would take it to work. After I finished reading it, I would put it in a darkroom bag and put it in the darkroom and I would let other women know where it was or we would pass it to other women, like we were passing film back and forth because that's the environment we were working in . . . over 30 women, and sometimes up to 50 in the summertime when we hired lots of extra people, were reading that one copy. (Schwarz, 1987)

Few publications have had the impact on their readership as did *The Ladder*. As the official publication of the first lesbian rights organization in the United States, *The Ladder* was meant to connect its membership and keep it apprised of DOB events. Founded in 1955 by eight women, DOB as a national organization collapsed in 1970 as the women's movement began to gain momentum. Most notable among the founding members were Del Martin and Phyllis Lyon, who guided the organization through the first ten years of its life. Over the course of its fifteen-year history, DOB developed into a national organization with chapters in major American cities–first in San Francisco and later on in New York, Boston, Chicago, Dallas, Los Angeles, and other cities across the United States–and even included a chapter in Australia. Even today, a chapter still exists in Boston, Massachusetts.

Though the Daughters was originally viewed as a social club and an alternative to the bars, it soon began to provide vital services to lesbian women throughout the San Francisco Bay area.

DOB's primary goals were outlined in the organization's statement of purpose:

1. Education of the variant, with particular emphasis on the psychological, physiological, and sociological aspects, to enable her to understand herself and make her adjustment to society in all its social, civic and economic implications–this to be accomplished by establishing and maintaining as complete a library as possible of both fiction and non-fiction literature on the sex deviant theme; by sponsoring public discussions on pertinent subjects to be conducted by leading members of the legal, psychiatric, religious and other professions; by advocating a mode of behavior and dress acceptable to society.
2. Education of the public at large through acceptance first of the individual, leading to an eventual breakdown of erroneous taboos and prejudices; through public discussion meetings aforementioned; through dissemination of educational literature on the homosexual theme.
3. Participation in research projects by duly authorized and responsible psychologists, sociologists and other such experts directed towards further knowledge of the homosexual.
4. Investigation of the penal code as it pertains to the homosexual, proposal of changes to provide an equitable handling of cases involving this minority group, and promotion of these changes through due process of law in the state legislatures.

DOB's four goals were printed in virtually every issue until April/May 1970, when *The Ladder*, as the property of the Daughters of Bilitis, ceased to exist.

In San Francisco, as in other major U.S. cities, homosexual bars were raided on a regular basis and harassment of homosexuals was a common practice. Gay men and women were often unaware of their rights. Billye Talmadge, an early member of DOB San Francisco, recalls the time,

> we were not that far away from the Senator McCarthy witchhunts. . . . And so there was tremendous fear, and people had no idea of their rights as just human beings. They didn't know that it was not against the law to *be* a homosexual, what one *did* was what was against the law if you got caught. And so what we were after, actually, was kind of twofold. One, to keep our people out of the bars because they were hotspots of arrest and harassment. And two, to educate them to their rights as people and that's really what we started . . . just very small right here in San Francisco, and then . . . the second part of that was to educate the public to the best of our ability. (Talmadge, 1987)

Del Martin recalls the early days of DOB:

> After about a year we had 12 members, and decided to try to go all out to get some other members. And we started what we called public discussion groups and we also started *The Ladder*, the publication.
>
> The public discussion groups were held downtown in a small auditorium and the audience, of course, the lesbian and gays who came, were the public. This gave them the freedom, then, to come to hear about the organization or to learn about their rights without giving themselves away–they were part of the public. And occasionally we'd pick up a member or two. But at least we were giving them information that they didn't have. At times we've been questioned about how come we got all these professional people to come to these meetings and talk about us. At that time we had psychiatrists, psychologists, marriage counselors, attorneys, professional people who came and spoke because we needed validation. Everybody was scared. They were afraid. They could be arrested, they could lose their jobs, they could be picked up by their families and if they were still underage, parents would, if they found out about them, send them to a shrink immediately or institutionalize them. And there was a lot to be afraid of–it wasn't just paranoia. It was just after the time of the McCarthy hearings and a purge of homosexuals from the State Department, and of course, there were all these purges of the Armed Services. It was a very scary time, and in some ways more scary because women always had more problems economically, so that if you worked your way up the academic ladder, for instance, you're not going to jeopardize that because you had to be so much better than men would have been. (Martin, 1987)

Although originally conceived as a calendar of events and house organ for the organization, the early issues of *The Ladder* included an amazing variety of information and revealed ambitious plans for the future.

The first issue (vol. 1, no. 1, October, 1956) reflects the organization's interests. In the pages of *The Ladder* members could read about upcoming business meetings, social gatherings (bowling, softball, picnics, brunch), and discussions (a panel, "What Are You Afraid Of?"; as well as a lecture, attorney Benjamin M. Davis on "The Lesbian and the Law").

The first issue also included an editorial, "The Positive Approach," written by Del Martin about self-esteem and living happily in a heterosexual society; editors offered an assurance of security about the mailing list titled "Your name Is Safe!" And in *Readers Respond . . .* , letters from members expressed eagerness for the new journal:

> "How about a poetry page in your publication? I might contribute some of mine for consideration . . . "
>
> M.R., San Francisco

> "We plan to tell all women writing to *ONE* of the Daughters and of *The Ladder*. I hope to have an editorial on it in the next issue. Best wishes for your success."
>
> Ann Carll Reid
> Editor, *ONE* magazine

The 5 1/2 × 8 1/2 booklet format DOB decided upon made *The Ladder* more of a periodical than a newsletter. Folding the 8 1/2 x 11 inch paper in half was considered an easier shape to mail than folding it into thirds or mailing it as a full letter-size sheet. The booklet form, with center staples and a cover, also lent itself more readily to fiction and poetry and longer nonfiction essays.

That the staff of *The Ladder* did not see themselves as an up-and-coming literary journal, however, is evident from the artwork on the cover, which never changed for the first 12 issues. Though *The Ladder* was often criticized as being amateurish because the level of writing was inconsistent, it provided vital information and connected gay women with each other for the first time on a national level. For many lesbian women in isolation throughout the country, *The Ladder* was a beacon of hope–it carried within its pages the message that there were many other gay women in the United States and that they were organizing, and perhaps most importantly, the overall tenor of *The Ladder* conveyed the message that being gay was sane and acceptable.[4]

The publication used the word "variant" until 1967, when it was changed to "lesbian." Use of the word "variant" reflected one of DOB's main purposes–integration of the variant into society. In 1955, "lesbian" was considered too highly charged a word.

Initially, *The Ladder* was "integrationist," a stance which became anathema to radical lesbian feminists of the late 1960s and early 1970s, but according to Joan Nestle, "under that flag of assimilation," lesbians began to discover "self-respect. On its pages," says Nestle:

> could be found all aspects of our culture, including the very things that in some sense, [it] took a public stance of disownership on, like butch/femme women, sexuality in a more blatant sense. So it was a very complicated cultural product and it played a very complex role. And if you see it for instance with the bar women culture existing at the same time, and then the DOB culture, and then the unaffiliated women, it forms a very complex network. (Nestle, 1987)

Phyllis Lyon was *The Ladder's* first editor, but she chose to use a pseudonym, Ann Ferguson. Using a pseudonym was standard practice in a homophobic heterosexist society where being discovered could mean the loss of a job, housing, or custody of a child. Both Martin and Lyon felt the need to be open about their activities, however, especially since they were the group's leaders. And since Lyon never learned to answer to her "pseud," she shortly decided to give it up ("Ann Ferguson is Dead!" vol. 1, no. 4).

According to Martin, soon after the first issue, the Daughters began receiving letters from women across the country. One of the women who responded wholeheartedly to the new publication was only known by her pseudonym–Gene Damon–for many years. In fact, Barbara Grier never used her real name officially in the pages of *The Ladder*, though she wrote under many pseudonyms, including Vern Niven, Lennox Strong, Marilyn Barrow, Dorothy Lyle, Irene Fisk, among others (Grier, 1987). According to Grier, the reason she used several pen names was that she contributed so much material to the pages of *The Ladder* she felt she *had* to use other names, but it is interesting to note that unlike Martin, Lyon, and Gittings, among others in those early days, Grier never allowed her real name to be used.

As Gene Damon, she began a regular column in the March 1957 issue (vol. 1, no. 6) that ran in every issue until the magazine's demise. *Lesbiana* was a bibliography of lesbian literature (fiction, nonfiction, drama, poetry), which Grier published as a book a few years later. The first four entries were *The Collected Works of Pierre Louys*, *The Well of Loneliness* by

Radclyffe Hall, *Wind Woman* by Carol Hales, and *Claudine at School* by Colette.

In its sixteen years of publishing, *The Ladder* had only five editors. Each left a distinct mark on the publication. Phyllis Lyon was the first editor and remained so until 1960, when Del Martin gave up her duties as DOB president to take over the publication. Martin remained editor until Barbara Gittings took over in 1963.

Working with a small group of dedicated women, Del Martin and Phyllis Lyon built The Daughters of Bilitis into a national organization, in part through publishing *The Ladder.* At first they pooled the names of friends and acquaintances, guaranteeing anonymity and a closely guarded mailing list. For this reason, there was usually only one copy of the mailing list. *The Ladder* was mailed in a plain brown wrapper, a fact later immortalized by Rita Mae Brown in her collection of essays (including three that appeared in *The Ladder*) *Plain Brown Wrapper.*

During the time that Martin and Lyon edited *The Ladder*, the publication's primary purpose was to announce events organized by DOB (and other homophile organizations) relevant to the Daughters' agenda, to discuss issues of interest to their readers–social, political, religious, and historical–and to provide a sense of connectedness to other lesbians around the country. It was also a powerful networking tool. DOB continued to challenge laws that ostracized and restricted gays in San Francisco and news of their efforts had an effect on women around the country. By the end of 1958, another DOB chapter was founded by Barbara Gittings in New York City.

In addition to their political work, DOB provided a haven for many women and, through the pages of *The Ladder*, mitigated the sense of isolation felt by lesbians and gay men across the country.

The Ladder also investigated and documented the lives of lesbian women through their fiction and poetry, as well as historical pieces on Radclyffe Hall and Queen Christina of Sweden. The quality of writing was uneven, and the early artwork amateurish and cartoon-like. That, and the fact that DOB was named after the title character (one of Sappho's many lovers) in a collection of erotic poetry by Pierre Louys, turned some women away from *The Ladder.*[5] Noted science fiction and fantasy author Marion Zimmer Bradley also contributed to its pages in the very early days of the publication. However, even though "It did get me in contact with a few people. . . . Eventually, I didn't want to be associated with something so amateurish. . . . The "Songs of Bilitis" were disgusting . . . written by one of those drooling voyeurs" (Bradley, 1988). But for most of the women who read it, *The Ladder* provided positive perspectives on lesbian life and ways of connecting with like-minded others.

From being mailed discreetly to a few hundred women around the country, and then passed from hand to hand among friends, *The Ladder* began being distributed nationally on newsstands in major cities. But anonymity and privacy were major issues in the 1950s and 1960s. In an early issue, Phyllis Lyon wrote a short piece about the DOB mailing list ("Where did we get your name?" vol. 1, no. 5, February, 1957). *ONE* magazine had been accused of violating their promise and giving their mailing list to DOB.[6] In the piece, Lyon denies using *ONE*'s list and states that they had acquired names by badgering and bullying everyone they knew into giving their names and the names of friends who might be interested in the Daughters and *The Ladder*. The editorial ends with a plea for new members–"If your name is on our mailing list then a friend of yours sent it along. How about sending the names of your friends?" However, Martin and Lyon did in fact begin *The Ladder* mailing list by not only sending it to everyone they and all their friends could think of, but to every woman attorney listed in the San Francisco phone book!

Though it was aimed at a lesbian audience, *The Ladder* also carried a substantial amount of information for men, including regular coverage of Mattachine and *ONE* events, as well as a regular column, during Del Martin's tenure as editor, titled "The Masculine Viewpoint." When *The Ladder* (vol. 5, no. 4, January 1960) ran Dr. Frank Caprio's study "The Sexually Adequate Female," it also included his study of men, "The Sexually Adequate Male."

There were several recurrent, and popular, themes in the pages of *The Ladder*. Reflecting DOB's third primary goal, research was high on the list. It frequently examined why women and men were gay and supported the general feeling that if homosexuality could be explained, then perhaps it would be better understood by heterosexual society.

Prior to DOB's involvement with research, most studies of lesbians had been done on criminal and psychiatric populations when they were done at all. To make sure that the research was legitimate, DOB formed a research committee and appointed Florence Conrad as research director. Conrad was a DOB member who had an academic background and taught economics at a junior college in California (Marcus, 1992). In addition to finding and reviewing proposed studies using DOB members, Conrad reviewed relevant books, reported on talks about homosexuality by members of the psychiatric community, and was generally supportive of DOB members' participation in research.

In June 1958, DOB sent out questionnaires to subscribers to *The Lad-*

der, but it wasn't until the September 1959 issue (vol. 3, no. 12) that DOB devoted an entire issue of *The Ladder* to the results of the questionnaire.

More than 500 questionnaires had been sent out to *The Ladder* subscribers, and over the course of one year, 160 had been returned. Of these, only 157 were deemed usable (some men had replied and these questionnaires were eliminated from the study). DOB's purpose in sending out the questionnaire was, briefly: to gather general data on lesbians who would not otherwise come to the attention of researchers; to get an idea of the response to such a questionnaire; to gain experience in writing and analyzing such questionnaires; and to stimulate interest and encourage further research by publishing their findings.

They found that the respondents were almost entirely Caucasian, "largely of U.S. citizenship, born or reared in varying (40) states of the Union or (10) foreign countries. The bulk–almost three-quarters of the group–come from urban rather than rural backgrounds. Ages vary from 19 to 62, with a median age of 32 years."

The income level and education of the group also appeared to be higher than the national average, as was the percentage of professionals. It was noted that the respondents appeared to be "living a relatively stable, responsible mode of life by certain conventional, if superficial, standards" (p. 9).

The respondents' own evaluations of themselves showed that "64% had not found it difficult to adjust to their homosexuality. A still larger proportion (83%) considered themselves to be well-adjusted now; and 92% reported that they 'get along well with people in general' " (p. 25).

In fact, these subscribers to *The Ladder* were so well adjusted that "less than 30% of the group (45 persons) reported having had psychotherapy. Something less than three-quarters of the remainder felt they had no need for it. Less than 10% indicated they would like to have therapy" (pp. 25-26).

Regarding sex roles, in answer to the question–"In your homosexual relationship(s) do you consider yourself predominantly feminine, masculine, or neither?"–those who answered "masculine" and "neither" accounted for about one third each of the replies. About 21% answered "feminine" and only 5% did not reply to the question (p. 24).

Another interesting finding showed that for the majority of the respondents, their fellow workers were not aware of their sexual orientation (p. 26), even though most of the respondents also reported having an equal number of homosexual as well as heterosexual friends (p. 26).

In conclusion, the report showed "a group with a high homosexual component, both on self-rating and on the basis of actual experience, but with more heterosexual experience than might have been guessed" (p. 26).

The view of research and participation by members of the homophile movement would change in the early 1960s. By the time Barbara Gittings began her tenure as editor of *The Ladder* with the March 1963 issue, the research debate had started to grow. Gittings, the founder of the New York chapter of DOB in 1958, and her lover, Kay Tobin, took on the responsibility of putting together each issue and then sending the material to California, where DOB members would type, print, and mail it.

The December 1963 (vol. 8, no. 3) issue of *The Ladder* (p. 8) carried a report on the 1963 convention of the East Coast Homophile Organizations (ECHO), of which DOB was a founding member, in Philadelphia. Among the speakers were Dr. Albert Ellis, a psychologist with a national reputation. Ellis's address to a packed auditorium, "The Right of Man to be Wrong," had a powerful impact on the audience. As *The Ladder* reported, "It is a tribute to the entire audience that they sat in well-mannered silence through what might have been described as an hour of castigation. To Dr. Ellis's statement that he had decided that the exclusive homosexual is a psychopath, the following retort by one of the guests: 'Any homosexual who would come to you for treatment, Dr. Ellis, would *have* to be a psychopath.' The applause which supported this remark might indicate the feelings of the most of the group."

Just a few years earlier, groups like DOB had been happy to have even speakers with homophobic views address them. As Del Martin points out in reference to one or two unsympathetic Church leaders, DOB asked to speak to their members. "We'd already been called every name under the sun, the point is, we have finally made contact with the Church and can begin a dialogue."[7]

One of the speakers at the ECHO Conference who followed Ellis's presentation was Dr. Frank Kameny, who spoke about "The Homosexual and the United States Government." Formerly employed as an astronomer for the U.S. Army Map Service, Kameny had been dismissed in 1957 for being a homosexual. Rather than suffer in silence, Kameny fought his dismissal through every means then available. In 1961, he helped to organize and found the vocal Washington, D.C., Mattachine Society. He was to have a profound effect on the homosexual community's thinking about the issue of research.

By 1963, Conrad had persuaded DOB to cooperate with Dr. Ralph Gundlach, a New York-based psychologist, in another full-scale research study on lesbians, and once again, DOB sent out questionnaires to members. In the July 1963 issue, she asked that each DOB member and subscriber to *The Ladder* participate by responding to the questionnaire, because "such a study can advance the cause of genuine understanding of the lesbian" (vol. 7, no. 9, June 1963, p. 4). Anonymity, of course, was guaranteed.

The August 1964 issue (vol. 8, no. 11, p. 11) reports that Dr. Gundlach presented his initial findings at DOB's third national convention in New York City the previous June. Gundlach, associate director of research at the Postgraduate Center for Mental Health, was conducting a study titled "The Early Family Life and Sexual Patterns of Adult Women." Gundlach's initial report was titled "More Lesbians than Non-Lesbians Report Rape–Why?" and his basic premise was that "early experiences determine in a major way whether a person becomes heterosexual or bisexual or asexual." Citing evidence that showed the "overwhelming importance of social training," Gundlach said he was stunned when 32.4% of the 200 women who filled out questionnaires responded yes to the question, "Have you ever been the subject of a rape or attempted rape?" Of these women, 37% said they were 11 years old and under at the time.

For many DOB members, Gundlach's findings about rape and his sudden focus on them worried members, who thought that it reinforced the view of lesbians as women who got that way because of bad experiences with men.

According to Barbara Gittings, "Some members of DOB began to see what was coming and that we were not necessarily going to be helped by participating in this research" (Gittings, 1988).

Another factor in the growing debate over research was Frank Kameny, who was outspoken in his belief that research was not going to benefit the homosexual community. As *The Ladder* editor, Gittings was profoundly influenced by Kameny's views.

> My thinking didn't change until Frank Kameny came along and he said plainly and firmly and unequivocally that homosexuality is no kind of sickness or disease or disorder or malfunction, it is fully on par with heterosexuality and it is fully the equal of heterosexuality. Whew, that knocked me for a loop. I'd never heard anybody come right out and say things that boldly before. He said, "The hell with their research, the hell with their causation theories, why are we bothering to spend all this time and effort trying to find out how we got to be this way. Our problem is we need our rights, let them do the research if they are so concerned about it. We shouldn't be helping them with it. We have to go out and get our rights." And it was a revelation. This was a whole new philosophy. . . . And suddenly I found that I was looking at things that had happened in the past in a

> very different light and I was taking a position that was increasingly diverging from DOB's positions. So I became, in a way, a kind of radical, which is rather amusing now, but I was against DOB's policies in some areas as a result of my thinking changing on the sickness issue in part. (Gittings, 1988)

A few years younger than her San Francisco counterparts, Gittings embraced Kameny's argument against cooperating with research and further fueled the debate by including essays by Florence Conrad, who still strongly believed in it ("Research Is Here to Stay," vol. 9, nos. 10 & 11, July/August), and Kameny, who rejected it ("Emphasis on Research Has Had Its Day," vol. 10, no. 1, October).

As *The Ladder* editor, Gittings introduced fresh perspectives to the magazine. Her editorship reflected a change from the repression of the McCarthy era of the midfifties to the polite picketing of the early 1960s. The overall quality of the publication was better, and there were several innovations, among them, adding "A Lesbian Review" to the cover of the journal and using photographs of attractive women on the cover.[8]

"The photo covers were a major breakthrough," Gittings says, "because this was our image to the world, including other lesbians who were not part of the movement. And this is the message, 'we are whole and happy and healthy and this is what we look like and never mind what the world says' " (Gittings, 1988).

Gittings also wanted to "discuss the issues of the day" and was not interested in having the magazine merely reflect past events. Although past events were reported, Gittings was much more interested in exploring the "controversies of the day." Accordingly, "Kay and I engineered a series of debates in the pages of the magazine that I think were very productive, at least they were for those of us who were involved in them, I don't know that we got a great response from the readership, which was pretty apathetic, but I think that getting letters from readers, which we did publish, was an interesting part for me. It's always interesting to know what people think" (Gittings, 1988).

One of the major functions of *The Ladder* as far as the national organization was concerned was informing members of the DOB conventions. In fact, it was only through the pages of *The Ladder* that the organization The Daughters of Bilitis communicated with its members on a national level. Each chapter had a newsletter or sent flyers out locally, but the organization could only address the collective membership–as well as many other nonmembers all over the country–through *The Ladder*. So, when Gittings was particularly late delivering copy for the issue announcing the next convention, which was to include representatives of local government, members of the clergy, and others, and was titled "Putting San Francisco on the Spot," it proved to be the proverbial "straw." The leadership in San Francisco demanded she resign.[9]

And the search was on once again for someone to take over as editor. Martin and Lyon persuaded their longtime friend Helen Sandoz, who lived in Los Angeles, to take over. "Sandy," who used the pseudonym Helen Sanders, had been one of the founding members of the Los Angeles chapter in November 1958. Sandoz's tenure as editor was less political than Gittings and more aligned with the earlier conception of *The Ladder* as the official publication of The Daughters. Sandoz liked the "sweet stories" that were always included in *The Ladder* and which she felt were balanced by the political reportage of local events by her partner, Sten Russell, who was a regular reporter for *ONE*.

According to Sandoz:

> I just gave up on the idea of trying to have a really serious type magazine. There was just that little element of being serious up to a point and beyond that it was better not to. Now I had Stella to report conventions and things like that and if arguments came up we reported it. Sometimes half of the magazine would be that way, but rarely. We tried to balance it out with a couple of short stories, maybe a poem or two, with letters, news about other chapters, just an assortment of things–like a house organ in a sense. (Sandoz, 1987)

Her vision of *The Ladder* was a magazine that like-minded women would enjoy reading and she felt she had reader support:

> I just figured that what these people wanted was a little romance in their life, a little poetry, a nice little story, a little success, and I think I was successful with it because for the most part people kept paying their money, re-upping on it and I had a lot of letters [that] thanked me for it. These would come from people that somebody had loaned it to them and they'd read it. Maybe they'd say, well, they couldn't have it come to their home, but they did read it and they enjoyed it. (Sandoz, 1987)

Though the pages of *The Ladder* during Sandoz's tenure reflected a more lighthearted approach in some ways (with editorials written by Ben the Cat), there was also serious coverage of movement activities and articles about issues of continuing interest to members, such as religion and research. The research argument had continued to evolve and in the January 1968 issue of *The Ladder*, Dr. Mark Freedman published an article titled "Homosexuality Among Women and Psychological Adjustment." Dr. Freedman's study compared women in DOB with a women's volunteer division of a national service organization.

Freedman's study showed no differences between the two groups in a "global measure of psychological adjustment." Freedman argued that the psychological functioning of those who engaged in homosexual activity was as good as those who engaged in heterosexual activity. He argued further that the prevailing view which associated homosexuality with disturbance in personality functioning was a consequence of most psychiatrists dealing with homosexuals in clinical settings only. It is important to note here that it would be five more years before the American Psychiatric Association removed homosexuality from its "disease" classification in December 1973.

In 1968, Barbara Grier, living in the midwest, was still working on *The Ladder*, writing the *Lesbiana* column as Gene Damon, as well as the American Women series (as Lennox Strong), and other articles as Vern Niven. She was also Poetry Editor. Actively seeking a greater role in shaping *The Ladder* and its content, Grier wrote daily from Kansas City to Sandoz until she finally stepped down as editor at the DOB convention in Denver in the spring of 1968.[10] At the DOB convention, Grier was named editor of *The Ladder* and Rita LaPorte became national president.

Barbara Grier's first issue as editor was September 1968 (vol. 12, nos. 11 & 12), in which she announced that the next issue would be 48 pages long. She promised "to take a more active look at the current world. Beginning with this issue, we will make every effort to present a more balanced magazine, with the emphasis on better quality writing in every area."

Grier's ideas about running *The Ladder* were often at odds with the Daughters' own policies. And while Grier was the editor, she still had to deal long distance with DOB's governing board who had their own ideas about the organization and the publication. *The Ladder* had always carried a statement regarding the opinions voiced in its pages–"The Ladder is regarded as a sounding board for various points of view on the homophile and related subjects, and does not necessarily reflect the opinion of the organization except such opinions as are specifically acknowledged by the organization." However, the Daughters still paid the bills and the publication was mailed from San Francisco, so they retained control over it. The National Officers and Chapter Presidents, who were also part of the Board, had their own interests and issues, but their main concern was the organization, not the publication. And their primary interest was the political aspects of the movement at the time; they were much less concerned about the literature.

It is important to note that 1970 was a time of terrific unrest and upheaval in American life–in addition to the civil rights movement, the women's movement began to emerge, the homophile movement of the 1950s and early 1960s had been radicalized by the Stonewall uprising in 1969 and was now called "gay liberation," and the Vietnam War was adding to the general chaos.

Many gay women felt ostracized and rejected by their heterosexual sisters and wanted no part of the women's movement, while others wanted to focus on lesbian liberation–and wanted nothing to do with any men, gay included, while others felt that gay men and women had to continue to work together. Suddenly there were greater divisions and political rifts than ever before.

In the middle of the birth of identity politics, another storm was brewing. Increasingly at odds with the national leadership, and afraid that her supporter at DOB San Francisco–national president Rita LaPorte–might lose the election at the next DOB Convention in August of 1970, and that her position as editor of *The Ladder* might be threatened, Grier and LaPorte decided to take matters into their own hands. Just a few months prior to the convention, Barbara Grier and Rita LaPorte kidnapped *The Ladder*. Taken from interviews conducted with the key players, the following excerpts tell the story in their own words:

Barbara Grier begins:

> I haven't the remotest idea when we first discussed it. . . . Rita and I both felt, really, that we were spending an awful lot of time fooling around and not a whole lot of time working on *The Ladder* and that she was tired of dealing with the people in San Francisco and it wasn't going to get any better and why didn't we just walk into the sunset. Now I didn't have to go anywhere. I was always totally removed, I was in Kansas City and I was out of touch in a sense and Rita and I . . . I didn't know how it could be logistically worked out. I remember that we did talk about that and she said it was nothing, it was a matter of saying DOB is in this cage and we will be in this and taking nothing but *The Ladder* mailing list and a few back issues . . . and some current stuff that was on file, but see, I was the editor of *The Ladder* so I had all the manuscript crap. (Grier, 1987)

Phyllis Lyon was the first to discover what had happened:

> Rita was here in San Francisco as National President and she just went down to the addressograph company and said, you know, 'I'm Rita LaPorte and I'm president of DOB' . . . the woman at the place

knew her, and [when] she said she wanted all the plates . . . she got them . . . .

And we didn't find out until it was a *fait accompli*. The woman at the addressograph company called me but by the time she thought to call me and mention it, it had already happened. So . . . then we tried to figure out what to do. Oh my goodness, *The Ladder* is gone. . . . The Purloined Ladder . . . Mostly people wanted to file suit, everybody was pretty annoyed, if not furious. And we consulted with attorneys and because the things had been taken across a state line, it became a federal case, and after a while I guess saner minds prevailed. (Lyon, 1987)

For security reasons, there were only two copies of *The Ladder* mailing list: the copy at the addressograph company and one copy at the DOB San Francisco office. Having only two copies was a precaution DOB took in order to protect the names on the list and to make sure that these names were not easily accessible. LaPorte not only took the addressograph plates, she took the only remaining copy of the mailing list from the DOB San Francisco office. DOB member Judith Schwarz remembers arriving at the San Francisco office after the mailing list had been taken:

I remember coming in and finding the whole place in disarray, the membership list missing, and all the stuff about *The Ladder* missing. So everybody thought it was the cops or the FBI. I mean, it was just so clear it had to be them. What lesbian would come and do a thing like this, you know, who would dare? And it turned out to be one faction of women who wanted to take *The Ladder* away from the San Francisco group whom they felt, and maybe rightly so some of it, that the mail wasn't getting answered, that things weren't being done the way that they wanted to see them done, it wasn't a professional magazine yet, they wanted slicker covers, they wanted a more professional feel to it, they wanted it to be fuller and they wanted, you know, professionalism brought into it. (Schwarz, 1987)

Grier had her own reasons for taking *The Ladder*:

The Ladder was the last thing to be considered in everything and in my head I probably realized if there were no *Ladder*–if you don't have *The Ladder*–you don't have an organization. But I did not take *The Ladder* away to prove that their organization would fall apart at their feet. It had nothing to do with that. Because that was not my intention. My intention was to wrest *The Ladder* away from people who were not paying enough attention to it. (Grier, 1987)

Barbara Gittings comments:

> There was one more DOB conference and that was 1970 in New York City and it really was the last hurrah for DOB as a national organization. Because that was the point just after *The Ladder* as the property of DOB had been stolen and it was–it occupied the attention of DOB for most of that conference. They weren't able to do very much about thinking or expanding or continuing the organization because in effect, the props had been knocked out from under them with the theft of *The Ladder* and I think it was just the last touch and DOB as a national organization really never recovered and was not a national organization after that. (Gittings, 1988)

Grier continues:

> I am sure that Rita's and my taking *The Ladder* away from DOB killed it and you have to understand that none of these things were done with malice aforethought or with intention to damage. I mean I was just as much a light-eyed maniac then as I am now in terms of the mission. The mission is that the lesbians shall inherit the earth, you see. (Grier, 1987)

The June/July issue, the first issue of *The Ladder* published by Grier and Rita LaPorte from the Reno, Nevada, address, still maintained the facade of being the official publication of the Daughters of Bilitis. The contents page included the same masthead "Published bi-monthly by the Daughters of Bilitis, Inc., a non-profit organization" but with a few key alterations–the address was the Reno P.O. box Rita LaPorte had rented and inside the front cover, the Daughters statement of purpose was gone, replaced with a Gene Damon editorial titled "Once More With Feeling." The editorial, a plea for more reader contributions as writers, cartoonists, and photographers, included a request for the names of women who might be interested in *The Ladder*:

> If you have shy friends who might be interested in DOB but who are, for real or imagined reasons, afraid to join us–write to me. I will send you a sample copy of THE LADDER, a copy of "WHAT IS DOB?", and a copy of the article, "Your Name Is Safe," which shows why NO ONE at any time in any way is ever jeopardized by belonging to DOB or by subscribing to THE LADDER.

By the following issue, all pretense to being a part of the Daughters of Bilitis was dropped and the inside front cover had a new statement of purpose:

> THE LADDER, published by Lesbians and directed to ALL women seeking full human dignity, had its beginning in 1956. It was then the only Lesbian publication in the U.S. It is now the only women's magazine openly supporting Lesbians, a forceful minority within the women's liberation movement.
>
> Initially, THE LADDER'S goal was limited to achieving the rights accorded heterosexual women, that is, full second-class citizenship. In the 1950s women as a whole were as yet unaware of their oppression. The Lesbian knew. And she wondered silently when her sisters would realize that they too share many of the Lesbian's handicaps, those that pertained to being a woman.
>
> THE LADDER'S purpose today is to raise all women to full human status, with all of the rights and responsibilities this entails; to include ALL women, whether Lesbian or heterosexual.
>
> OCCUPATIONS have no sex and must be opened to all qualified persons for the benefit of all.
>
> LIFE STYLES must be as numerous as human beings require for their personal happiness and fulfillment.
>
> ABILITY, AMBITION, TALENT–
> THESE ARE HUMAN QUALITIES

In the August/September 1970 issue (vol. 14, nos. 11 & 12), both Grier and LaPorte wrote editorials about the new direction of the magazine. In her editorial "The Undefeatable Force," LaPorte outlined *The Ladder*'s commitment to women: "With this issue, *The Ladder*, now in its 14th year, is no longer a minority publication. It stands squarely with all women, that majority of human beings that has known oppression longer than anyone." She goes on to say that tolerance is not enough, but that we must "replace our fear of those who differ from us with a joy that so many differences exist."

Grier's editorial in the same issue, "Women's Liberation Catches Up to The Ladder," calls for "true human civil rights for all" and states "until women are free it isn't likely any group [blacks or homosexuals] will make it." Grier ends with, "We either work together or doom a few more hundreds of generations of women yet unborn to the spheres available to them today," which she identifies as "caring for children, church, and kitchen."

Grier continued to work with many of the women who had helped her in the past; she expanded the publication by adding more pages and using smaller type. Rita LaPorte was given the title Director of Promotion and wrote editorials from time to time. Grier was also completely dedicated to improving the quality and reputation of the journal. Though art had been a focus in the pages of *The Ladder* from time to time, under Grier it took on new importance. An Art Editor was added and work by noted artists such as Audrey Flack, Romaine Brooks, and Georgia O'Keeffe began appearing on the cover more frequently. When Sarah Whitworth took over as Art Editor, she contributed a regular column about art from a feminist perspective, including articles on lesbian and feminist images in Greek art and mythology, political art, and the feminist movement. Such notable lesbian writers as Jill Johnston, Jane Rule, Jane Chambers, Martha Shelley, and Rita Mae Brown contributed to Grier's vision of lesbian literature and culture. It is important to note that in keeping with their commitment to women, not just lesbians, both gay and straight women contributed to *The Ladder.*

Anita Cornwell wrote about her experiences as a black woman. Her thinking changed from her earliest article, where she is clear about her allegiance to women's rights ("Open Letter to a Black Sister," vol. 16, nos. 1 & 2, October/November 1971) and lesbian rights ("Letter to a friend," vol. 16, nos. 3 & 4, December/January 1971/1972) to her last article ("From a Soul Sister's Notebook," vol. 16, nos. 9 &10, June/July 1972), where she is equally clear about her commitment to blacks and her identification and allegiance first by color, then by gender, and thirdly, by sexual orientation.

Rita Mae Brown regularly contributed articles and poetry to *The Ladder* through the end of 1970 and throughout 1971 and 1972. In addition to her poetry, in the pages of *The Ladder* Brown also related her experiences with women's (both straight and gay) vivid and often vicious homophobia in "Take A Lesbian to Lunch" (April/May 1972), and took a candid look at the prevailing sexist culture in "Viewing Sexism" (April/May 1971) that still resonates today ("Sex is used to sell everything in our country. If you packaged shit, called it 'Fabulous Feces' and utilized a woman in the advertising campaign, it would sell").

Grier's "light-eyed" fanaticism produced a rich and important contribution to lesbian literature, culture, and politics. Her dedication has had a far-reaching impact as she went on to found Naiad Press in Tallahassee, Florida. As Grier notes, *The Ladder* went on to become incredibly successful, but

> it grew too big, we didn't have advertising income and we actually got so big, so fast, we did what they call plateau out, which is grow beyond your cash flow income and reach the point where you cannot go on. And that strictly was a matter of I didn't know as much then about the publishing business as I do today. (Grier, 1987)

In the April/May 1971 issue, *The Ladder* announced it would no longer be available on the newsstands, because the magazine was having a difficult time supporting itself and it made more money on individual subscribers than it did on newsstand sales (vol. 15, nos. 7 & 8).

The last issue appeared in August 1972 and featured an editorial "Catholicism and the Lesbian" by Rita LaPorte, an interview with Barbara Love and Sidney Abbott and a review of their recently published book *Sappho Was a Right-On Woman*, an article titled "The Challenge of Teaching Women's Liberation in Jr. High School," by Judy Fowler, Sarah Whitworth's column "Journeys in Art," and quite a bit of poetry and fiction.

While *The Ladder*'s growth paralleled the emergence of an identity, a culture, and a movement, its demise signaled an important cultural shift. From a hidden, marginalized group, gay women transformed themselves into a proud and vocal part of both the gay and women's liberation movements. The variant had to die so that the lesbian might live.

NOTES

1. Barbara Grier writes in her introduction to the series that the first issue of *The Ladder* was published in the fall of 1957. In fact, the first issue was published in the fall of 1956.

2. Lisa Ben's publication *Vice Versa* was the first lesbian publication in America. First published in Los Angeles in 1947, only nine issues were ever produced and distributed very locally in California.

3. In fact, even as late as the 1960s in New York, "when gays things were opening up in a lot of ways, the wonderful, liberal *Village Voice* would not accept a classified ad for gay publications." Barbara Gittings interview, Philadelphia, PA, 1988.

4. It is useful to note here that homosexuality as a clinical category for mental illness was not changed until 1973, when the American Psychiatric Association deleted homosexuality from their "disease" classification.

5. In the "privately printed" edition for William Godwin, Inc. (New York) in 1933, Louys' dedication to *The Songs of Bilitis* reads: "This little book of antique love is respectfully dedicated to the young daughters of future society."

6. *ONE*, like the Mattachine Society, referred women to DOB, even though they also had women members in their own organizations.

7. This dialogue led to the formation by DOB and Mattachine of The Council on Religion and the Homosexual. With CRH, ministers could meet with the gay community. On New Year's Day 1965, CRH–members of DOB and SIR and Mattachine, along with members of the clergy and their wives–held a ball that the local police raided, arresting several people. This clearly demonstrated to the members of the clergy the kind of persecution and police harassment that gays in their communities suffered on a regular basis.

8. The first and only photograph on the cover of *The Ladder* had appeared in 1958, but photos were not used again until Gittings became editor and then they became a regular feature.

9. As Gittings puts it: "when the tensions that had built up between me and the national board, over a whole variety of things, were just too much and over a reasonable matter that turned unreasonable, they asked me to leave, so I did." Barbara Gittings, Philadelphia, PA, 1988.

10. "We went to Denver and I said to myself, 'Self, you are going to put this damn thing in this suitcase and you are going to give it to this broad that's been sending you a letter and a half for the last five years' and I did. I had simply had it up to here. I just . . . I couldn't stand her anymore, I couldn't stand the whole idea of it anymore." Helen Sandoz, Costa Mesa, California, 1987.

REFERENCES

Bannon, Ann. (1975). *I am a woman*. Homosexuality: Lesbians and gay men in society, history, and literature. Leslie Parr (Ed.). New York: Arno Press.

Bannon, Ann. (1975). *Journey to a woman*. Homosexuality: Lesbians and gay men in society, history, and literature. Leslie Parr (Ed.). New York: Arno Press.

Bannon, Ann. (1975). *Odd girl out*. Homosexuality: Lesbians and gay men in society, history, and literature. Leslie Parr (Ed.). New York: Arno Press.

Bannon, Ann. (1975). *Woman in the shadows*. Homosexuality: Lesbians and gay men in society, history, and literature. Leslie Parr (Ed.). New York: Arno Press.

Barney, Natalie. (1975). *Aventures de l'esprit*. Homosexuality: Lesbians and gay men in society, history, and literature. Leslie Parr (Ed.). New York: Arno Press.

Bradley, Marion Zimmer. (1988). Interview with the author, Berkeley, California. DOB Video Project for the Lesbian Herstory Archives, New York.

de Acosta, Mercedes. (1975). *Here lies the heart*. Homosexuality: Lesbians and gay men in society, history, and literature. Leslie Parr (Ed.). New York: Arno Press.

Gittings, Barbara. (1988). Interview with the author, Philadelphia, Pennsylvania. DOB Video Project for the Lesbian Herstory Archives, New York.

Grier, Barbara. (1987). Interview with the author, Tallahassee, Florida. DOB Video Project for the Lesbian Herstory Archives, New York.

Louys, Pierre. (1933) *The songs of Bilitis*. New York: William Godwin, Inc.

Lyon, Phyllis. (1987). Interview with the author, San Francisco, California. DOB Video Project for the Lesbian Herstory Archives, New York.

Lyon, Phyllis. (1988). Interview with the author, San Francisco, California. DOB Video Project for the Lesbian Herstory Archives, New York.
Marcus, Eric. (1992). *Making history, The struggle for gay and lesbian equal rights, 1945-1990*. New York: HarperCollins.
Martin, Del. (1987). Interview with the author, San Francisco, California. DOB Video Project for the Lesbian Herstory Archives, New York.
Martin, Del. (1988). Interview with the author, San Francisco, California. DOB Video Project for the Lesbian Herstory Archives, New York.
Nestle, Joan. (1987). Interview with the author, New York City. DOB Video Project for the Lesbian Herstory Archives, New York.
Parr, Leslie. (Ed.). (1975). *The Ladder, Vols. I-XVI*. Homosexuality: Lesbians and gay men in society, history, and literature. New York: Arno Press.
Rule, Jane. (1975). *Desert of the heart*. Homosexuality: Lesbians and gay men in society, history, and literature. Leslie Parr (Ed.). New York: Arno Press.
Sandoz, Helen. (1987). Interview with the author, Costa Mesa, California. DOB Video Project for the Lesbian Herstory Archives, New York.
Schwarz, Judith. (1987). Interview with the author, New York City. DOB Video Project for the Lesbian Herstory Archives, New York.
Talmadge, Billye. (1987). Interview with the author, San Francisco, California. DOB Video Project for the Lesbian Herstory Archives, New York.
Troubridge, Una. (1975). *The Life of Radclyffe Hall*. Homosexuality: Lesbians and gay men in society, history, and literature. Leslie Parr (Ed.). New York: Arno Press.
Vivien, Renée. (1975). *Poèmes de Renée Vivien*. Homosexuality: Lesbians and gay men in society, history, and literature. Leslie Parr (Ed.). New York: Arno Press.
Wilhelm, Gale. (1975). *We too are drifting*. Homosexuality: Lesbians and gay men in society, history, and literature. Leslie Parr (Ed.). New York: Arno Press.

"What Is Going on Here?": Baldwin's *Another Country*

Laura Quinn

Allegheny College

SUMMARY. This paper uses two teaching experiences with Baldwin's 1962 novel *Another Country* to frame a discussion of the complicated critical history of this literary work and its relation to Baldwin's literary reputation. The contested relationship between the categories of race and sexuality in the novel is tracked and its political implications explored. *[Article copies available for a fee from The Haworth Document Delivery Service: 1-800-342-9678. E-mail address: getinfo@haworth.com]*

Eugenia W. Collier began an essay on *Another Country* in the seventies (1977) with this observation: "James Baldwin's novel *Another Country* has, as the cliche says, something for everyone–in this instance, something offensive for everyone" (38). Perhaps this is why I masochistically (and, as some of my students might claim, sadistically) chose to teach the novel in a new course called "Alternative Traditions in American Litera-

---

Laura Quinn completed a doctorate in literature at University of Minnesota in 1981 and is an associate professor at Allegheny College in Meadville, Pennsylvania, where she teaches African-American Literature and Women's Studies. Her research interests are in black writers of the forties and fifties and in the relation of politics to literature. Correspondence may be addressed: Department of English, Allegheny College, Meadville, PA 16335. E-mail: lquinn@alleg.edu

[Haworth co-indexing entry note]: "'What Is Going on Here?': Baldwin's *Another Country*." Quinn, Laura. Co-published simultaneously in *Journal of Homosexuality* (The Haworth Press, Inc.) Vol. 34, No. 3/4, 1998, pp. 51-65; and: *Gay and Lesbian Literature Since World War II: History and Memory* (ed: Sonya L. Jones) The Haworth Press, Inc., 1998, pp. 51-65; and: *Gay and Lesbian Literature Since World War II: History and Memory* (ed: Sonya L. Jones) Harrington Park Press, an imprint of The Haworth Press, Inc., 1998, pp. 51-65. Single or multiple copies of this article are available for a fee from The Haworth Document Delivery Service [1-800-342-9678, 9:00 a.m. - 5:00 p.m. (EST). E-mail address: getinfo@haworth.com].

ture" to forty undergraduates at a small liberal arts college in Middle America in 1990. My choice produced a teaching nightmare. For the two weeks we spent on the novel, most of the class made resolute eye contact with the floor, refusing to respond to even the most harmless questions about textual detail. My efforts to engage them metacritically by asking that we talk about why it was so hard to talk about the text only brought about deeper commitment to the floor, ball caps pulled further down over lowered eyes, hair that was wont to fall into faces solicited and left fallen. This had been, up to this point, a lively discussion class despite its size. We had read other potentially disturbing texts by African-American writers (the particular "alternative" tradition that we were exploring historically) including works in which gay/lesbian sexuality figured explicitly or implicitly. Richard Bruce Nugent's "Smoke, Lilies and Jade" (1926) and Nella Larsen's *Passing* (1929) had proved to be discussable, and students had felt free to express discomfort with gay/lesbian readings of these works while, nonetheless, engaged in the project of those readings collectively. *Another Country* was clearly another matter, though. The eyes were not about to leave the floor.

On the last day of our "discussion" of the novel, as I unilaterally discussed Book Three (entitled "Toward Bethlehem"), I gave up all hope of raising eyes or voices and read aloud the sex scene between Vivaldo and Eric, the most prolonged and graphically depicted sexual encounter in the novel, the one that critic Robert Bone (1965) disparaged as a "rectal revelation" for Vivaldo and for the novel, "heralding, presumably, a fresh start for all and a new era of sexual and racial freedom" (234). An intrepid African-American woman student raised her eyes and her hand to ask this question: "What is going on here?" I read–misread?–her question as being about the scene in the text, attempted to engage her and the rest of the class in shaping an answer to her query (to no avail), and, finally, provided my own teacherly answer: What was going on was the discovery of sexual desire and emotional need on the part of two men who had hitherto been nonsexual friends. One of these men identified himself as heterosexual and the other as gay, both were in love with others at the time of the encounter, and the sexual moment was treated lyrically and at length and lovingly because Baldwin wished to make a claim for its redemptive and liberating potential. As I developed what I believed to be an answer to my brave student's question–doing so with teacherly passion and conviction–I realized simultaneously that I was not addressing her question at all. Her "What is going on here?" was meant to ask why we were reading this text, why I, a white feminist teacher, had imposed this reading experience on them, why, in particular, I had taken the most angst-producing (for all kinds of constituencies) part of the novel and read it aloud in class. Her question was a good one. I write this essay as part of an ongoing (but also irresponsibly belated) attempt to respond to it.

Five years after my first shot at teaching *Another Country* I featured it again in a very different context, that of a junior seminar entitled "Native Sons and Fathers: Richard Wright, Ralph Ellison, and James Baldwin." To a group of thirteen relatively sophisticated English majors, I assigned *Native Son* (1940), *Invisible Man* (1951), and *Another Country*, along with collateral, contextualizing primary and secondary works. I hedged my bet that this would be a different kind of engagement with Baldwin's novel by describing to the thirteen seminarians my earlier experience with the teaching of this book, a confessional anecdote that they listened to gravely and with great appearance of interest. This was, of course, an utterly manipulative maneuver, designed crassly to protect myself from a recurrence of the earlier disaster and less crassly (I hoped) to enable them to begin their engagement with the novel as self-consciously "advanced" readers who, having been informed of their predecessors' paralyzed silence, wouldn't on a bet let that happen to them. This class engaged the novel with level-eyed volubility. My immediate anxiety was alleviated, and I felt I could safely claim that, given an appropriate context (in the form of a narrower historical focus and more secondary material), a smaller, more advanced class, and more time spent on close reading of the novel, *Another Country* could be productively taught. Of course, I would be telling the truth and lying at the same time. My seminar students evaded the novel and its cruces every bit as resolutely as the silent floor-gazers had. They used their advanced reading skills and my cautionary tale to discover all the ways in which the novel makes available its own avoidance. Exploring their well-intentioned stratagems as well as the earlier class's silent alarm has been, for me, instruction in reading *Another Country*.

There are three general issues I wish to explore in this essay in light of the contested critical response to this novel and my own students' complex responses: the first of these is the relationship between the categories of race and sexuality in the text; the second is the structure or form of the novel and the implications of its *elaboration* (by which I mean, largely, its early killing off of its protagonist and subsequent decentering of the novel's narrative and perspectival focus); the third is what we might call the "politics" of the novel, that is, the claim or argument that it might be making. The sources of meaning that I am interested in here are interstitial: it is the novel's tensions and contradictions that make it mean most richly; it is, further, the particular shape that much of the critical debate over the novel has taken that speaks more loudly than any one reading does; finally, it is in the space between what my students were able to do with the novel and what they were not that the novel is illuminated.

There are two basic–and contradictory–readings of the relation between race and sexuality that bear upon *Another Country*. One is most frequently and infamously represented (albeit, in exaggerated form) by Eldridge Cleaver's critique of Baldwin in *Soul on Ice* (1968). For Cleaver, the black homosexual is a race traitor:

> The white man has deprived him of his masculinity, castrated him in the center of his burning skull, and when he submits to the change and takes the white man for his lover as well as Big Daddy, he focuses on "whiteness" all the love in his pent up soul and turns the razor edge of hatred against "blackness"–upon himself, what he is, and all those who look like him, remind him of himself. (103)

This kind of racialized reading sees homosexuality as a phenomenon and mechanism of hegemonic whiteness. (It does not, of course, imagine black men as partners.) Black nationalist arguments about homosexuality as genocidal to black community, as a Western/European form of decadence, rely on this equation. More moderate critics of Baldwin see him as deauthorized as a black spokesman by virtue of his sexuality and his affirmative representations of gay sexuality in some of his fiction.[1] Oppositional gay readings, conversely, see race as displaced (that is, a kind of stand-in for) sexual difference and racial and sexual oppression as (sometimes) figuratively interchangeable. Particularly in the works of Harlem Renaissance writers such as Countee Cullen, Langston Hughes, Claude McKay, Nella Larsen have gay readings found fertile ground for their claims for sexual differences being encoded in the discourses of racial difference, knowability, and "passing" potential.[2]

For Baldwin, who was able (and willing) to write about gay sexuality in un-encoded ways in *Another Country*, race and sexuality get unravelled in some senses. The black male protagonist of the first part of the novel, Rufus Scott, suffers–unto death–from racial oppression and ensuing rage and hopelessness. Though he has engaged in both consensual sex with a desired male partner (Eric) and exigent "ass-peddling" in the depths of his fall from grace, homophobic oppression does not contribute to Rufus's particular hell. It is the prison of a *racial* history that both produces and constrains his destructive relationship with Southern white Leona; no agonizing over sexual identity gets factored into the torments of that affair, except perhaps for his paranoid triangular conviction that if Leona desires him, she must be balling other black men as well. The novel's other black character, Rufus's sister Ida–who survives and supplants him in the narrative–is unproblematically heterosexual (though her heterosexuality, as always in Baldwin's characters, is shot through with destructiveness) and mildly homophobic at that. Very importantly, then, one kind of difference does not stand in for another in the novel.

Moreover, racial oppression in the novel has a stature that homophobia does not have–witness Ida's rage and the kind of space that gets made for it by the narrative and the white characters. Eric's sexuality, on the other hand, is treated as a safer, because more concealable, difference.[3] The psychological and material danger that a gay man might experience would be a function of street sex, of promiscuity, of meaninglessness. The novel does not choose to examine the kind of systemic, institutionalized oppression that a stable gay couple might encounter.[4] Implicitly, thus, the categories of race and sexuality in the novel, in relation to their vulnerability to oppression, are disentangled. In this sense, homosexuality, in the form of gay male sexuality, as a long-term identification or a meaningful interval in the lives of otherwise heterosexually identified characters, is normalized in *Another Country*–by which I mean that it offers itself up as a relatively unproblematized possibility to anyone (at least to any male).

This, I believe, is a large part of what silenced my first larger class and led the seminar to chatter about love rather than sex in the novel, a shift that the text makes fully possible (though not inevitable). When homosexuality as a category is interchangeable with race, both being seen as targets of discrimination and injustice, a stance of liberal tolerance is easy (for some) to come to–certainly, easy to speak of in a classroom setting. What Baldwin does in *Another Country*–ironically out of the conservatism of his own commitment to sexual privacy (see note 3)–is to feature race as something *out there*, visible, calling for public attention. Same-sex (male) sexuality, on the other hand, might be behind any closed door, even our own, might sneak up on us as Vivaldo's desire for Eric sneaks up on him–"what is going on here?" What *Another Country* poses to readers, students and otherwise, goes well beyond the challenges that a novel like Puig's *Kiss of the Spider Woman* (1978 or the film version of 1985) or the movie *The Crying Game* (1992) present. In both of the latter representations of heterosexual men confronting same-sex exigencies, mitigating conditions–prison, cross-dressing, etc.–cushion the panic that many students/readers/viewers experience. Despite the emotional extremity of much of *Another Country*, the setting, even given its urbanity and low-level bohemianism, is insufficiently exotic to provide distance between readers and the desires that arrive when possibilities arise for characters whose lives we recognize.

A key scene in midnovel highlights the irony of Baldwin's conservatism and the paradoxical threat it poses to 1990s student readers, acculturated to particular discourses of diversity and tolerance. After hearing Ida sing at a night club, a group consisting of Vivaldo, Ida, Eric, and a sleazy talent agent named Ellis walk through a crowded Central Park. Eric–the gay man in the group–is being questioned about his acting career by Ellis:

> Coming toward them on the path, were two glittering, loud-talking fairies. He pulled in his belly, looking straight ahead. . . . The birds of paradise passed; their raucous cries faded.
>
> Ida said, "I always feel so *sorry* for people like that."
>
> Ellis grinned. "Why should you feel sorry for them? They've got each other."
>
> The four of them now came abreast, Ida putting her arm through Eric's.
>
> "A couple of the waiters on my job are like that. The way some people treat them–! They tell me about it, they tell me everything. I like them, I really do. They're very sweet. And, of course, they make wonderful escorts. You haven't got to worry about them." (262-3)

The students in my seminar landed on this passage with energy and indignation. They judiciously pointed out that, while Ida's and Ellis's attitudes may be under fire here, the narrative voice that characterizes these figures as "glittering, loud-talking fairies" and "birds of paradise" is harder–perhaps impossible–to read as self-critical. We talked about Baldwin's "generation," about closets and glass closets, about internalized homophobia, about the particular pressures faced by Baldwin as a leader in an African-American literati, about Eldridge Cleaver's attack on him and the fact that, by some accounts, Baldwin took that attack seriously.[5] Additionally, I gave them John Lash's 1964 article, "Baldwin Beside Himself: A Study in Modern Phallicism," which makes an argument for seeing sanctioned gay male sexuality in *Another Country* as being very particularly (and, I would claim, conservatively) "a modern cult of phallicism, the fear and admiration and worship of the male sex organ" (48). Thus the overt effeminacy of the "birds of paradise" falls outside the pale of acceptability within *Another Country*'s economy of redemptive sexuality. I think students came to terms, thereby, with the notion that gay male sexuality is neither monolithic nor historically fixed in its pressures and interests. What I think was more difficult to take in was the possibility that the "normalized," that is the phallic, privatized sexuality in the novel and the paradoxical flagrancy of its presentation, its claim on the reader, is far more potentially threatening than any identifiable glittering fairies would be. Like Ida, we can put our arms through Eric's and reintegrate him; but later in the novel Vivaldo will not tell Ida of his sexual interval with Eric, though she confesses her infidelity with Ellis. Eric is deniable within the world of the novel but not in the textual experience of the reader–Baldwin's extended and lavishly developed account of Vivaldo and Eric's sex makes the reader know and live with their privacy and their pleasure.

It is this forced knowing in the face of our not wanting to know (or needing to know, within the privatized sexual space that Baldwin wants to occupy) that is set against Ida's relentlessly paradoxical claim that whites can't know blacks, yet "you've got to know, you've got to know what's happening" (347). The black woman student's question–"What is going on here?"–was, I believe, as much about Baldwin's telling some of us more than we want to know about "private" matters as it was about my using my professorial authority to deliver this unwanted knowledge. That the private business of sexuality overtakes the novel's racial narrative and leaves it behind is a by-product of the structural elaboration of *Another Country* and another crux for the reader.

Another Country, over four hundred pages long, kills off its black male protagonist on page eighty-eight. Rufus Scott's tragic suicide/sacrifice has a healthy afterlife in the novel, of course, and his death brings the remaining characters together and gives them all something besides the miseries in their own lives to share, to grieve over, and to produce white guilt. After Rufus disappears as the center of consciousness, that capacity shifts around from Vivaldo to Cass to Eric, leaving the other key characters Ida, Richard, Yves, and the minor figures Ellis and Jane out of the attached narrative loop–while we spend time with them in the company of the others, we do not get access to their private thoughts. These shifts and selectivities in narrative perspective ask to be read more fully than they have been in the critical literature on the novel. Further, the novel is divided into three books, each with titles and epigraphs that also ask to be read, that insist on making meaning. There is not space enough in this essay to respond to all of the invitations that this text extends to the reader by means of its self-consciously elaborate structural apparatus. Yet, both professional critical response to the novel and my seminar students' preoccupation tend to focus on the *characters* as the formal device of consequence in the novel. There is logic in this focus; the characters are highly and skillfully developed, and the novel's as well as the novelist's ideological commitment to the priorities of identity and individualism enables such a concentration.[6] But such a focus also enables the evasions of some of the novel's implications, particularly those which readers of many stripes–liberal, homophobic, the sexually panic-stricken, puritanical–may be particularly avid about evading.

Let me illustrate. My students smartly identified *Another Country* as a novel of fully rounded realistic characters in comparison to the sociologically pressured characterizations of *Native Son* and the stylized figures in *Invisible Man*, the other "blockbuster" black novels we studied in detail in the seminar. They further noted that Baldwin is much more interested in relationships, in "romantic" and familial relationships than either of the other novelists seem to be. These truths about *Another Country*, are, of course, part of what makes the sexual fluidity in the novel as threatening as it is; as with Baldwin's conservative view of homosexuality as a privatized choice, the naturalized conventionalism of relationships and domesticity in the novel work to shape readerly expectations, and to insert loving gay male sex into those expectations is, in effect, to normalize it. What is also true, however, of all the relationships in the novel–of all relationships everywhere, no doubt–is that they are troubled; the business of the narrative is to trouble them. The troubles are various, but the tendency of a reading which naturalizes character is to conflate these troubles, to universalize them–everybody fights with his/her partner, everybody has crises of trust and self-confidence; everybody, above all, cheats sexually. Roger Rosenblatt's dismissive characterization of 1974 illustrates this critical strategy:

> *Another Country* is designed as a modern Inferno. Lovers throw themselves at each other in lust and violence. Rufus torments Leona, and Leona, merely by being white, torments him. Ida cheats on Vivaldo, and breaks his heart. Richard and Cass despise each other because of the falsity of their life, particularly of their artistic life. Ellis, the television executive who is going to launch Ida's career, treats Ida like a whore. Everyone betrays everyone else. Cass has an affair with Eric; Eric with Vivaldo; Vivaldo with Ida; Ida with Ellis. . . . Sexual gluttony is ubiquitous. (92)

There is no possibility, reading thus, of seeing any one relationship among these characters as more or less promising than any other. If characters, in their confusion and trouble, stumble into the bed of a partner of the same sex, what else can be expected of ubiquitous sexual gluttony?

Yet, the relationship which marks Part One: "Easy Rider"–that of Rufus and Leona–is light-years more destructive than any other in the novel, is old news, a devastating script, rote-read by the black blues man Rufus and the white trash version of Little Eva, as Leona is called by Rufus's friend (16-18). That the novel structurally knocks off this racialized heterosexual nightmare early on needs to be read against the final and triumphant positioning of Yves–the French boy-man lover of Eric–as he arrives in New York on an airplane in the last paragraph of the novel:

> He looked up. Eric leaned on the rail of the observation deck, grinning, wearing an open white shirt and khaki trousers. He looked very much at ease, at home, thinner than he had been, with his short hair spinning and flaming about this head. Yves looked up joyously, and waved, unable to say anything. *Eric.* And all his fear left him, he was certain, now, that everything would be all right. He whistled to himself as he followed the line which separated him from the Americans, into the examination hall. But he passed his examination with no trouble, and in a very short time; his passport was eventually stamped and handed back to him, with a grin and a small joke, the meaning, but not the good nature of which escaped him. Then he was in a vaster hall, waiting for his luggage, with Eric above him, smiling down on him through glass. Then even his luggage belonged to him again, and he strode through the barriers, more high-hearted than he had ever been as a child, into that city which the people from heaven had made their home. (435-6)

That there may be trouble ahead for this romance is the reading-beyond-the-ending that my students brought to bear upon the utopian strains of this finish. Eric has earlier expressed fears of losing Yves in the New World, and students and critics alike are all too eager to point out that Eric "cheated" on Yves with *both* Cass and Vivaldo just prior to this rhetorically rhapsodic reunion. All of the above are true. Is the ringing rhetoric ironic, then? Is the novel not thrilled with the possibility that Yves and Eric represent? At the level of character and relationship, we can't come to much in this ending; Eric and Yves are no less flawed and vulnerable than anyone else as characters, their relations no more stable. But that the novel believes in (and has meticulously recorded since the opening of Book Two) the small miracles of connection which have made up the larger miracle of this relationship is structurally clear. The tenuousness of the possibility of their "making it" is not evaded; Book Three is cautiously titled "Toward Bethlehem," and its epigraph from Shakespeare's Sonnet LXV is about fragility:

> How with this rage shall beauty hold a plea,
> Whose action is no stronger than a flower?

Even the ending paragraph quoted above hovers over the material details of disembarkation and customs, indulgently letting Yves's small victories seem magical and momentous. If there is delusion in all of this, if the novel has enabled a cynical take on this ending, it has also allowed itself a Gatsby-like power and affection for this ending and this beginning.

Much more could be said about elliptical formal strategies that can be and have been deployed in order to, in my view, *underread* the assertions and affirmations implicit in the novel's architecture. Most notably, the critical neglect of the French episodes in which Eric and Yves's relationship gets shaped is revealing. My seminar students, to their credit, were happy to talk about the Chartres setting of the couple's first lovemaking, with the looming phallic cathedral towers, their "dogmatic and pagan presence" pursuing and ironizing their union (218). Perhaps it is easier to talk about phallic symbols than about phalluses, and certainly Eric's careful, slow, tender approach to sex with the much younger Yves as well as the clear sexual identity markers that both bear throughout this episode make it accessible to liberal tolerance. But to read this episode as laying groundwork for the *claim* about the health and redemptive potential of this relationship in the world of the novel proves difficult. Yves is prophetic on the eve of Eric's departure for New York when he says to his lover, "People do not take the relations between boys seriously, you know that. We will never know many people who believe we love each other" (223).

On the other hand, critic Robert Bone, in his classic *The Negro Novel in America* (1958, revised 1965) aggressively overreads the first paragraph of Book Two: "Any Day Now," in the interest of not taking relations between boys very seriously. He describes the following as "highly charged, symbolic prose" with which Baldwin "tends to endow his diffuse sexuality with mythic significance" and to bring "into metaphorical relation the idea of homosexuality and the idea of Africa" (232):

> Eric sat naked in his rented garden. Flies buzzed and boomed in the brilliant heat, and a yellow bee circled his head. Eric remained very still, then reached for the cigarettes beside him and lit one, hoping the smoke would drive the bee away. Yves' tiny black-and-white kitten stalked the garden as though it were Africa, crouching beneath the mimosas like a panther and leaping into the air. (183)

Surely this is a domesticated and diminutive mythology. The garden is rented, after all, the insects are bothersome, and the kitten is tiny. Like the luggage and passport in the novel's final paragraph, inflationary moments in the life of Eric and Yves's relationship are always brought down, via detail, to the material constraints of their lives. It is the demythologizing gesture rather than the concomitant mythologizing one that bodes well for their future. Both overreading and underreading the depiction of this central relationship in *Another Country* are important strategies of resistance to the "politics" of the novel.

Many Baldwin critics converge (from various political positions) on the Albert Murray thesis, developed in 1970, that Baldwin "reneged on the artistic promise of 'Everybody's Protest Novel' and 'Many Thousands Gone'" in which he rejects the social protest novel as a literary form, renounces the literary paternity of Richard Wright, and projects himself and his own artistic practice as an antidote (qtd. in Porter, 157). According to the Murray thesis, Baldwin writes his own version of the social protest novel, substituting sexual claims for racial ones and subordinating artistic concerns to didactic ones. Not everyone has a problem with this move on Baldwin's part. Many critics think social protest is a worthy fictional undertaking but are critical of the politics that Baldwin evinces or fails to evince in his fiction. Others see novels such as *Giovanni's Room* (1956) and *Another Country* as brave, even radical pathbreaking texts. My seminar students, interestingly, resisted the notion that *Another Country* had a thesis of its own or made a claim or implied a politics. For them the novel was just about relationships and people and how hard life was for everybody. This is the underbelly of contemporary liberal politics–the blinkering of difference. But it is also a function of the decentering of the novel after Rufus's textual disappearing act. We are offered a figure like Vivaldo who serves as a red herring, leading us to think that he is "it" after Rufus's exit. Vivaldo, as "faux" center of the post-Rufus novel covers up and covers for the narrative usurpation that Eric undertakes–making it possible for the reader to "skip" Eric if the reader so wishes (and as my seminar tried hard to do). One might argue that Baldwin freed himself up to do what he wished with Eric, having deployed Vivaldo as a narrative decoy. If, however, we will not be decoyed as readers, if we take the relations between boys seriously, do we read the novel as a celebration of gay male love? What are we then to do with the infamously elongated sex scene between Vivaldo and Eric that prefaces Yves's tremulously triumphant arrival? What are we to do with Eric's affair with Cass?

Of course, there are "explanations"–psychological, characterological, therapy industry explanations–for all this sexual gluttony. Eric gives heterosexuality one last shot before cementing his commitment to Yves–thus Cass finds her way to his bed? Cass is drawn to Eric because he is an antidote to her conventional relations with macho husband Richard, who can't write real novels, only best-sellers? Vivaldo needs to ghost-fuck Eric as a surrogate Rufus, out of guilt for not having "loved" Rufus enough to save him from suicide? Or to confirm for himself that he really wants to be with a woman, with Ida? We can speculate endlessly about motivation and desire, and this is what students who have gotten beyond staring at the floor are eager to do. Again, such reading strategies and foci are arguably evasions of the larger questions raised by the novel. What does it all add up to, and how do we add it up? Where do we land? In what "country"?

Readings of the novel's political claims vary widely in both substance and degree of complexity. Among those who believe, either happily or unhappily, that the novel means to affirm a certain kind of sexuality as being of a higher order than others, there is confusion about whether the ideal is homosexual or bisexual. David Bergman (1991) points out that Baldwin is "careful to make all his characters bisexual" and that "despite Bone's and Cleaver's assertions that Baldwin elevated homosexuality, gay black men such as Samuel Delaney found his portraits far from affirming" (165). Donald Gibson (1977) says that the radicalism in Baldwin lies in the suggestion that "the bisexual male is . . . the apogee of human development" (12). German critic Fletcher Dubois (1991), on the other hand, celebrates *Another Country*'s mutually male sex scenes as "a lifeline in the very troubled waters of my adolescence" (89). While the novel's male characters may engage in bisexual behavior, they don't tend to identify themselves as such. The novel's sex scenes themselves don't tend to support the claim that bisexuality is a desideratum; with the exception of the vague and underdeveloped encounter between Cass and Eric, heterosexual love scenes (between Rufus and Leona, Vivaldo and Ida) are either actually violent or depicted violently, by means of military and colonial metaphor. It is hard to argue that the final airport reunion of Eric and Yves and all that it promises is a paean to bisexuality, which is, in fact, a threat to the commitment the two have made to each other. Bergman in his essay on gay black literature in *Gaiety Transfigured* (1991) provides insight into Baldwin's connection to bisexuality as expressed in his one and only nonfiction treatment of gay sexuality, the critique of André Gide in "The Male Prison," which appears in *Nobody Knows My Name* (1961):

> Although he does not mention bisexuality, one can see why it becomes so important to Baldwin: a homosexuality derived from a fear of the other sex, or a heterosexuality derived from a contempt of one's own are merely different forms of racism. Consequently, Baldwin sees Gide's prison as "not very different from the prison inhabited by, say, the heroes of Mickey Spillane" (105). Both the homosexual and the ultra-macho heterosexual are ruled by the need to control and contain their fears and contempt. (169-70)

Shelton Waldrep (1993) similarly cites Baldwin for "his courage and opposition to Cleaver's overwrought ideal of male sexuality," claiming that Cleaver attacks Baldwin "with a vicious combination of misogyny and homophobia" (170, 169). But Waldrep goes on to point out that a black feminist position like that of Audre Lorde might counter that "Baldwin ignores much complexity within gender debate by his positing of brotherly love as a panacea for society's ills. She would say that Baldwin is too brotherly and leaves the unique experiences of women out of the picture" (179). Or, as one of my seminar students did point out, there are no lesbian references in this novel, only Rufus calling Vivaldo's old girlfriend Jane a bull dagger (31). The women characters are afforded little opportunity for or provided with little interest in sisterly love, and misogynistic rhetoric is rife. If bisexuality is an ideal in the novel, it appears to be male.

James Levin (1991) encapsulates what we might term a liberal reading of *Another Country* as a political project or social protest novel: "By intertwining the themes of racial prejudice and homophobia, he hoped to stigmatize homophobia and make it as unacceptable as any other kind of bigotry" (188). He argues further that Baldwin used his position as a leading black writer in the early sixties to effect such attitudinal change. Such a claim may be true. Certainly, this is a political goal which, however, would not have been subversive or terrifying enough to keep my first set of students of the novel staring at that floor. Stigmatizing homophobia is a liberal gesture. Even going beyond that gesture to one of affirmation of gay identity is (or ought to be) liberally manageable. The novel makes all such readings possible. It also reconfigures its world and places a pair of men at the center. That's the part that's hard for many to read. Out of the tension between Baldwin's own conservative commitment to sexual privacy and his willingness to indulge fictionally in the committed representation of gay male sexuality and relationality, we get a book that puts at risk our disbelief in the love between boys and in the possibility of a world (*another country*?) in which such love would figure largely, even centrally and centripetally in relation to the desires and interests of others. In fact, the centripetal force of that love might be so strong that heterosexual men and women are drawn into its orbit? Is that what is going on here?

NOTES

1. See the treatment of Baldwin in classic African-American studies such as Robert A. Bone's *The Negro Novel in America* (1958, revised 1965) and Bernard Bell's *The Afro-American Novel and Its Tradition* (1987) as well as the work of white critic of the African-American novel Roger Rosenblatt in his 1974 study, *Black Fiction*.

2. See, for instance, the work of Gregory Woods, Eric Garber, and Deborah McDowell.

3. See the works cited by Shelton Waldrep and David Bergman for explication of Baldwin's commitment to a sexual ethic of privacy.

4. It's important to note–and my seminar students did–that same-sex sexuality is always male in the novel. The other country of *Another Country*, as one student remarked, "doesn't seem to know or care about lesbians."

5. See David Bergman, page 166 of *Gaiety Transfigured*, for a discussion of the adjustment in his public persona that Baldwin made after Cleaver's attack.

6. See Waldrep, page 176, and Klein, pages 17-18, for discussions of Baldwin's preoccupation with identity and his commitment to individualism.

WORKS CITED

Baldwin, James. *Another Country*. 1960. New York: Vintage, 1993.

______. *Nobody Knows My Name: More Notes of a Native Son*. New York: Dial, 1961.

Bell, Bernard W. *The Afro-American Novel and Its Tradition*. Amherst: U Mass P, 1987.

Bergman, David. *Gaiety Transfigured: Gay Self-Representation in American Literature*. U Wisconsin P, 1991.

Bone, Robert A. *The Negro Novel in America* . Rev. ed. New Haven: Yale UP, 1965.

Cleaver, Eldridge. *Soul on Ice*. New York: McGraw-Hill, 1968.

Collier, Eugenia W. "The Phrase Unbearably Repeated." *James Baldwin: A Critical Evaluation*. Ed. Therman B. O'Daniel. Washington, DC: Howard UP, 1977. 38-46.

DuBois, Fletcher. "With Only the Rain as Witness: James Baldwin and Britain's Section 28." *James Baldwin: His Place in American Literary History and His Reception in Europe*. Ed. Jakob Kollhofer. Frankfurt am Main: Peter Lang, 1991. 89-94.

Garber, Eric. "A Spectacle in Color: The Lesbian and Gay Subculture of Jazz Age Harlem." *Hidden from History: Reclaiming the Gay and Lesbian Past*. Ed. Martin Bauml Duberman, Martha Vicinus, and George Chauncey, Jr. Harmondsworth, Middlesex: Penguin, 1991. 318-333.

Gibson, Donald. "James Baldwin: The Political Anatomy of Space." *James Baldwin: A Critical Evaluation*. Ed. Therman B. O'Daniel. Washington, DC: Howard UP, 1977. 3-18.

Klein, Marcus. "A Question of Identity." *James Baldwin*. Ed. Harold Bloom. New York: Chelsea, 1986. 17-36.

Lash, John S. "Baldwin Beside Himself: A Study in Modern Phallicism." *James Baldwin: A Critical Evaluation*. Ed. Therman B. O'Daniel. Washington, DC: Howard UP, 1977. 47-55.

Levin, James. *The Gay Novel in America*. New York: Garland, 1991.

McDowell, Deborah. Introduction to Nella Larsen's *Quicksand* and *Passing*. New Jersey: Rutgers UP, 1986. ix-xxxv.

Porter, Horace. *Stealing the Fire: The Art and Protest of James Baldwin*. Middletown, CT: Wesleyan UP, 1989.

Rosenblatt, Roger. *Black Fiction*. Cambridge: Harvard UP, 1974.

______ . "Out of Control: *Go Tell It On the Mountain* and *Another Country*." *James Baldwin*. Ed. Harold Bloom. New York: Chelsea, 1986. 77-96.

Waldrep, Shelton. " 'Being Bridges': Cleaver/Baldwin/Lorde and African-American Sexism and Sexuality." *Critical Essays: Gay and Lesbian Writers of Color*. Ed. Emmanuel S. Nelson. New York: Harrington Park Press, 1993. 167-180.

Woods, Gregory. "Gay Re-Readings of the Harlem Renaissance Poets." *Critical Essays: Gay and Lesbian Writers of Color*. Ed. Emmanuel S. Nelson. New York: Harrington Park Press, 1993. 127-142.

Writing the Fairy *Huckleberry Finn*: William Goyen's and Truman Capote's Genderings of Male Homosexuality

Gary Richards

University of New Orleans

SUMMARY. After rehearsing persisting representations of same-sex desire in the Southern Renaissance's literary production, this essay charts how novels by Truman Capote and William Goyen reveal contradictory genderings of male homosexuality. Capote's *Other Voices, Other Rooms* collapses male gay identity with effeminacy, while Goyen's *The House of Breath* replicates this model but also contrasts it with a coexisting and competing one in which masculine men can physically act upon gay desire. Thus, contrary to the theorizations of Michel Foucault and David Halperin, these representations suggest the absence of a unified model of mid-twentieth-century male homosexuality. *[Article copies available for a fee from The Haworth Document Delivery Service: 1-800-342-9678. E-mail address: getinfo@haworth.com]*

In *Epistemology of the Closet* Eve Kosofsky Sedgwick sets herself the task of scrutinizing the relation of gay/lesbian studies to current debates

---

Gary Richards teaches in the Department of English, University of New Orleans. Correspondence may be addressed: Department of English, University of New Orleans, New Orleans, LA 70148-2315. E-mail: gnreg.uno.edu

[Haworth co-indexing entry note]: "Writing the Fairy *Huckleberry Finn*: William Goyen's and Truman Capote's Genderings of Male Homosexuality." Richards, Gary. Co-published simultaneously in *Journal of Homosexuality* (The Haworth Press, Inc.) Vol. 34, No. 3/4, 1998, pp. 67-86; and: *Gay and Lesbian Literature Since World War II: History and Memory* (ed: Sonya L. Jones) The Haworth Press, Inc., 1998, pp. 67-86; and: *Gay and Lesbian Literature Since World War II: History and Memory* (ed: Sonya L. Jones) Harrington Park Press, an imprint of The Haworth Press, Inc., 1998, pp. 67-86. Single or multiple copies of this article are available for a fee from The Haworth Document Delivery Service [1-800-342-9678, 9:00 a.m. - 5:00 p.m. (EST). E-mail address: getinfo@haworth.com].

about the literary canon, and, although she ultimately deems the relation tortuous, she argues for the absolute centrality of gay/lesbian inquiry. According to Sedgwick,

> We can't possibly know in advance about the Harlem Renaissance, any more than we can about the New England Renaissance or the English or Italian Renaissance, where the limits of a revelatory inquiry are to be set, once we begin to ask–as it is now beginning to be asked about each of these Renaissances–where and how the power in them of gay desires, people, discourses, prohibitions, and energies were manifest. We know enough already, however, to know with certainty that in each of these Renaissances they were central. (No doubt that's how we will learn to recognize a renaissance when we see one.) (58-59)

Sedgwick's argument is both attractive and persuasive, yet her catalogue of renaissances is incomplete. There remains at least one desperately in need of gay/lesbian inquiry: the so-called Southern Renaissance of the mid-twentieth century. Steeped in New Criticism and social conservativism, southern literary studies have resisted theories of gender and sexuality that have proliferated since the 1970s, and, as a result, the queerness of this region's literature has been minimized. The predominant grammar of these studies is often that which Sedgwick characterizes as prevailing in treatments of sexual otherness: "It didn't happen; it doesn't make any difference; it didn't mean anything; it doesn't have interpretive consequences" (53). Many studies do not even attempt to explain away queerness and instead simply let it go unnoted.

This silence in southern literary studies should not be taken to indicate a comparable one in actual southern literary production. In part because of its gothic spectacles of deviancy, the Southern Renaissance has a particularly lavender tint, especially the drama and fiction in the two decades during and after World War II. In plays such as *A Streetcar Named Desire* (1947), *Cat on a Hot Tin Roof* (1955), and *Suddenly Last Summer* (1958), Tennessee Williams foregrounds issues of gay desire from southern perspectives, just as Carson McCullers does in her fiction. *The Heart Is a Lonely Hunter* (1940), for example, presents a devoted domestic partnership between two men, while *Reflections in a Golden Eye* (1941) depicts an array of misdirected erotic–and specifically homoerotic–desires within the military's subculture. *The Ballad of the Sad Café* (1943) continues this focus on gay desire but also presents McCullers's recurring figure of the gender-transitive woman who, culturally assumed to be lesbian, is nevertheless heterosexual. Indeed, this figure–Mick Kelly in *The Heart Is a*

Lonely Hunter, Amelia Evans in *The Ballad of the Sad Café*, and Frankie Addams in *The Member of the Wedding* (1946)–is the one most persistently associated with McCullers. In the space cleared by this prewar and wartime fiction for such depictions, a number of novels arose in quick succession, each interrogating gayness from a specific vantage point of the homosocial matrix: Calder Willingham's *End as a Man* (1947), Hubert Creekmore's *The Welcome* (1948), and Thomas Hal Phillips's *The Bitterweed Path* (1950). A decade later Lillian Smith complicated these interrogations with *One Hour* (1959), a novel climaxing with the brutal murder of a gender-transitive man held to be gay by his homophobic community.

In contrast to these presentations of homosexuality, another set of contemporary southern novels explores same-sex desire in relation to race. Smith's *Strange Fruit* (1944), for instance, focuses on a miscegenistic heterosexual affair yet also depicts lesbianism and its stringent censorship. Harper Lee's *To Kill a Mockingbird* (1960) and McCullers's *Clock Without Hands* (1961) replicate this double-stranded structure. Lee's novel privileges racial tensions in its narration but also includes a wealth of sexual deviancy either encoded in characters' gender transitivity or symbolized within Boo Radley, victim of social intolerance. McCullers's novel centralizes broader racial tensions but also explores a young white boy's anxious gay desire for a black friend. This dual focus on race and homosexuality appears in the fiction of southern African-Americans as well. In *The Long Dream* (1958), for example, Richard Wright analyzes the ways compulsory heterosexuality disciplines black men's potentially homoerotic investments. These and similar texts concerned with same-sex desire culminated to form such a queer-themed subset of southern literary production that it threatens to characterize all of the region's literature, in both the broader currents of academic literary studies and the popular imagination. When, with polemical absolutes, Leslie Fiedler claims in a revised edition of *Love and Death in the American Novel* that post-World War II American fiction can be divided into "the Jewish-heterosexual wing . . . [and] the Southern-homosexual" (490), his understanding of the South's literature is thus not wholly without support.

Given the diversity of these writers in age, class, race, sex, and–perhaps most significantly–sexuality, it is not surprising that their work, rather than constituting a coherent, traceable gay literary tradition, offers contradictory representations of homosexuality and therefore disrupts whatever continuities have been imposed upon these texts. By juxtaposing two of the most prominent gay-themed southern novels of this era, this essay charts some of the more divergent representations of same-sex desire within this subset of southern literature, those revealing contradictory understandings of relationships of gender and same-sex desire. In *Other Voices, Other Rooms* (1948), Truman Capote's first novel, the effeminate adolescent Joel Knox awakens to desire for his gay uncle within the gothic surroundings of a forsaken Louisiana plantation. With amazing consistency, this narrative equates male homosexuality with gender transitivity, simplistically holding the two to be mutually and exclusively indicative of one another. In contrast, the lyric monologues imagined by Boy Ganchion, the narrator of William Goyen's *The House of Breath* (1950), posit that same-sex desire may be as pronounced in the masculine man as in the effeminate and that this is, in fact, the more culturally valued gendering of male homosexuality.

* * *

If Eve Sedgwick is correct, the flurry of scholarship dealing with same-sex desires and erotic interactions produced following the appearance of the introductory volume of Michel Foucault's *The History of Sexuality* has not been without cost. Sedgwick maintains that, in its "historical search for a Great Paradigm Shift" in understandings of same-sex relations, this scholarly work has tended to reify a knowable, stable contemporary homosexual identity, an identity she clearly holds as suspect. This scholarship, Sedgwick asserts, "has tended inadvertently to *re*familiarize, *re*naturalize, damagingly reify an entity that it could be doing much more to subject to analysis" and therefore is "still incomplete . . . in counterposing against the alterity of the past a relatively unified homosexuality that 'we' *do* 'know today'" (44-45). Despite the significant work in several disciplines that has been done to check this reification during the last half decade, there often still persists "the notion that 'homosexuality as we conceive of it today' itself comprises a coherent definitional field rather than a space of overlapping, contradictory, and conflictual definitional forces" (45).

To substantiate this claim, Sedgwick contrasts two divergent understandings of the relationships between gender and homosexuality. Returning to Foucault's "act of polemical bravado," his offering of 1870 as the "birth of modern homosexuality" (44), Sedgwick clarifies that Foucault seemingly understands contemporary "homosexuality in terms of gender inversion and gender transitivity" (45-46). He asserts in *The History of Sexuality* that, unlike the earlier sodomite, the person whose forbidden acts made him or her "a temporary aberration," the homosexual is "a personage, a past, a case history, and a childhood, in addition to being a type of life, a life form, and a morphology, with an indiscreet anatomy and possibly a mysterious physiology." Perhaps most crucially, homosexual identity is constituted "less by a type of sexual relations than by a certain quality of sexual sensibility, a certain way of inverting the masculine and the feminine in oneself" (43). That is, for Foucault as Sedgwick presents him, the modern homosexual is constituted by the absence of gender attributes that society deems appropriate for that sex and the simultaneous manifestation of gender attributes socially appropriate only for the other sex.

In contrast to Foucault, who posits a homosexuality that has been relatively consistent in its manifestations and knowability since 1870, David M. Halperin offers a more historically mutable sexuality, yet one that has followed a unidirectional, supervening progression. He accepts Foucault's privileging of the mid-nineteenth century as the moment of an epistemic shift in understandings of sexuality, the moment of "the formation of the great . . . experience of 'sexual inversion,' or sex-role reversal, in which some forms of sexual deviance are interpreted as, or conflated with, gender deviance" (9). Halperin asserts, however, that mid- and presumably late-twentieth-century homosexuality emerged "out of inversion" and has as its "highest expression . . . the 'straight-acting and -appearing gay male,' a man distinct from other men in absolutely no other respect besides that of his 'sexuality' " (9). Thus, for Halperin, gender intransitivity rather than transitivity defines 'modern homosexuality.'

Sedgwick concludes that what must be acknowledged is the simultaneous existence of both of these paradigms and the slippage between–and perhaps even outside of–these two. For her, "the most potent effects of modern homo/heterosexual definition tend to spring precisely from the inexplicitness or denial of the gaps *between* long-coexisting minoritizing and universalizing, or gender-transitive and gender-intransitive, understandings of same-sex relations." Indeed, the broadest project of *Epistemology of the Closet* is self-admittedly "to show how issues of modern homo/heterosexual definitions are structured, not by the supersession of one model and the consequent withering away of another, but instead by the relations enabled by the unrationalized coexistence of different models during the times they do coexist." In short, Sedgwick's "first aim is to denaturalize the present, rather than the past–in effect, to render less destructively presumable 'homosexuality as we know it today' " (47-48). To anatomize 'our' contemporary homosexuality, to question the ways in which it has already been defined through its fragmentations, to interrogate its performances within culturally and historically specific settings: this is the work called for but by no means completed in *Epistemology of the Closet.*

* * *

With these contrasting models of same-sex desire in mind, one easily detects in Capote's *Other Voices, Other Rooms* a Foucauldian understanding of gendered homosexuality. Like the Foucault of Sedgwick's consideration, Capote holds 'modern' homosexuality and gender transitivity to be mutually and exclusively indicative of one another. Gay men are effeminate; effeminate men are gay. Without exception, each man struggling to negotiate his desire for another man in the novel displays gendered performances deemed socially appropriate of women. Consider first Uncle Randolph, the novel's sole adult whose identity is centrally informed by same-sex desire. Remembering when he first sees his ostensible girlfriend Delores with Pepe Alvarez, Randolph recalls his tentative acknowledgment of gay desire: "I looked at Pepe: his Indian skin seemed to hold all the light left in the air, his flat animal-shrewd eyes, bright as though with tears, regarded Delores exclusively; and suddenly, with a mild shock, I realized it was not she of whom I was jealous, but him" (147). Much like Henry James's May Bartram, Dolores identifies and reassures Randolph of his gay identity: "Afterwards, and though at first I was careful not to show the quality of my feelings, Dolores understood intuitively what had happened: 'Strange how long it takes us to discover ourselves; I've known since first I saw you' " (147). For Capote, this identity is inescapable, and, years after Pepe violently rejects Randolph, he still sends out daily letters to random places in hopes of contacting Pepe: "[D]eep inside lay a thick stack of letters, sealed, as he [Joel] found, in watergreen envelopes. It was like the stationery his father had used when writing Ellen. And the spidery handwriting was identical: Mr Pepe Alvarez, c/o the postmaster, Monterrey, Mexico. Then Mr Pepe Alvarez, c/o the postmaster, Fukuoka, Japan. Again, again" (111).

Randolph's erotic investments are not, however, confined to Pepe Alvarez. Indeed, Joel's uncle has an ongoing penchant for hypermasculine, often nonwhite men. He paints and collects images of such men, and his curio cabinet features among its treasures "several plush-framed daintily painted miniatures of virile dandies with villainous mustaches" (87). Even more captivating for Randolph, however, are actual African-American men such as the servant Zoo's lover Keg. Randolph consistently casts Keg in homoerotic terms, as in the telling of his near-fatal attack on Zoo. "This happened more than a decade ago, and in a cold, very cold November," Randolph recounts to Joel. "There was working for me at the time a strapping young buck, splendidly proportioned, and with skin the color of swamp honey" (77). Despite Keg slitting Zoo's throat "from ear to ear" and thus, Randolph carps, ruining "a roseleaf quilt my great-great aunt in

Tennessee lost her eyesight stitching" (80), the black man's powerful body still tempts Randolph.

That Randolph's objects of desire are invariably hypermasculine bodies highlights the contrasting representations of him as anything but manly. Indeed, Capote establishes Randolph's effeminacy to excess:

> As he puckered his lips to blow a smoke ring, the pattern of his talcumed face was suddenly complete: it seemed composed now of nothing but circles: though not fat, it was round as a coin, smooth and hairless; two discs of rough pink colored his cheeks, and his nose had a broken look, as if once punched by a strong angry fist; curly, very blond, his fine hair fell in childish yellow ringlets across his forehead, and his wide-set, womanly eyes were like sky-blue marbles. (78-79)

Randolph's clothing does little to cover and therefore negate this unmasculine body. His wardrobe consists of breezy seersucker kimonos "with butterfly sleeves" and rather androgynous "tooled-leather sandals" (85). When such frills are removed or inadvertently opened, they reveal an insistently feminine body: "Randolph, clutching the bedpost, heaved to his feet: the kimono swung out, exposing pink substantial thighs, hairless legs" (121). Like his face, Randolph's torso has virtually no hair, stock element of virility, and readers are thus confronted with a body conspicuously lacking male secondary sexual characteristics.

As much as his bodily appearance and dress, Randolph's behavior reinforces his lack of conventional masculinity. His handwriting is the first hint of this effeminacy. When Joel shows Radclif the letter from Randolph "penned in ink the rusty color of dried blood" that formed "a maze of curlicues and dainty i's dotted with daintier o's," the trucker contemptuously asks himself, "What the hell kind of man would write like that?" (8). Readers soon learn that, much like this handwriting, Randolph is himself excessively delicate. He giggles "in the prim, suffocated manner of an old maid" (77) and forces the residents of Skully's Landing to defer to his delicate constitution. Moreover, Randolph is, as Amy refers to him, a "[s]ilver-tongued devil" (76) ready with a quip, an exaggerated hand motion, and a dash of French for every occasion–not unlike the gay Capote himself. This campiness culminates in Randolph's most blatantly gender-transitive performances, his cross-dressing as "the queer lady" with "white hair . . . like the wig of a character from history: a towering pale pompadour with fat dribbling curls" (67). Capote thus offers in the novel's sole gay man one so insistently gender-transitive as to attempt to eradicate, if only momentarily, all traces of masculinity.

Although Joel's performances of gender are less socially violating than his uncle's, they are nevertheless sufficiently transitive to anticipate Joel's ultimate gayness. Capote consistently scripts his autobiographical protagonist as effeminate, beginning in the novel's first pages. Radclif reflectively eyes the boy as the two travel to Skully's Landing. He "had his notions of what a 'real' boy should look like, and this kid somehow offended them." Joel "was too pretty, too delicate and fair-skinned; each of his features was shaped with a sensitive accuracy, and a girlish tenderness softened his eyes, which were brown and very large" (4). Joel's activities and mannerisms are no less effeminate, and he behaves as a stereotypical girl: carrying a change purse rather than a wallet, neatly organizing his possessions, whimpering, blushing violently, crying out of homesickness. As a result, other characters dismiss him as unmanly, as Idabel Thompkins's recurring orders to Joel reveal. "Out a the way, sissy-britches" (108), she shouts, later demanding, "Go on home and cut out paper dolls, sissy-britches" (109).

Given Capote's understanding that gayness and lack of masculinity mutually constitute one another, it is not surprising that the novel culminates in the effeminate Joel's acknowledgment of a gay identity. His comfort with and resemblance to Randolph foreshadow precisely this recognition. Joel feels "very much at ease with Randolph" (75) throughout the novel and at moments even literally mirrors his uncle: "So he questioned the round innocent eyes [of Randolph], and saw his own boy-face focused as in double camera lenses" (86). Even then "sometimes he [Joel] came near to speaking out his love for him" (211). The fateful trip to the Cloud Hotel with Randolph allows Joel to articulate this love, and the novel closes with his metaphorical acceptance of the gay identity he shares with his uncle. From Randolph's window the "queer lady" "beckoned to him, shining and silver, and he knew he must go: unafraid, not hesitating, he paused only at the garden's edge where, as though he'd forgotten something, he stopped and looked back at the bloomless, descending blue, at the boy he had left behind" (231).

What thus remains absent in *Other Voices, Other Rooms* is the physical actualization of gay desire. Capote may be deferring to readers' potential aversions to overt gay sexuality or to any sexual explicitness. But regardless of reasons for this absence, because contemporary readers and critics, like Capote, understood gender transitivity as a marker of same-sex desire, they immediately recognized homosexuality as the novel's central preoccupation despite a lack of sexual explicitness. In fact, the often homophobic reviews of *Other Voices, Other Rooms* frankly outed the novel. As Capote's biographer Gerald Clarke notes, *Time*, for instance, deemed the book "immature and its theme . . . calculated to make the flesh crawl. . . . The distasteful trappings of its homosexual theme overhang it like Spanish moss" (155). Within the private realm, this acknowledgment of the "homosexual theme" was even more candid. Clarke relates that when Capote pressured his onetime mentor George Davis, fiction editor of *Mademoiselle*, into an evaluation of the novel, a hesitant Davis finally asserted, "I suppose someone had to write the fairy *Huckleberry Finn*" (158).

* * *

In contrast to Capote, William Goyen does not signal gender transitivity as a consistent, culturally readable marker of homosexuality. In *The House of Breath*; his approximation of "the fairy *Huckleberry Finn*," Goyen posits same-sex desire and the physical interactions fueled by this desire to be as pronounced in aggressively masculine men as in effeminate ones. He conspicuously parallels the narrator's two uncles, the foppish and therefore aptly named Folner 'Follie' Ganchion and his older masculine brother Christy, as both desiring other men and engaging in homosexual activity despite their exaggerated differences in gender. However, in Boy's privileging of Christy's model of homosexuality over Folner's, Goyen ultimately depicts the masculine gay man as preferable to the feminine one. Goyen thus differs from Capote and his Foucauldian foreclosure of gay desire in the gender intransitive man and instead replicates Halperin's notions that the "highest expression" of male homosexuality is the "straight-acting and -appearing gay male."

Goyen does, nevertheless, acknowledge the existence of male homosexuality as represented in Capote's Uncle Randolph. Goyen offers in Folner a gay man who is gender transitive to the extreme of cross-dressing. It begins as a child in the town of Charity, he recalls, when his mother "dressed me like a girl when I was little and called me 'Follie'" (141). When given the freedom of an adult to dress himself, Folner continues to cross-dress despite Charity's strict demands for gender conformity. Granny Ganchion recalls her son's initial steps towards adult cross-dressing: "You know Folner's done strange things like goin away with a show and everyone says there was something wrong with him–the time he came home in patent leather shoes and had a permanent wave in his blonde hair proved it" (147). Such behavior apparently intensifies once Folner abandons Charity for San Antonio and ultimately New York. When he commits suicide and his body is returned to Charity for burial, it is accompanied by trunks stamped "GAYETY SHOWS AND COMPANY" (135-136) and packed with the paraphernalia that unequivocally outs him: "false faces, with tragic-gay bent down eyes, women's wigs, tubes of make-up grease, and spangles spilled over the clothes like dried fishscales" (136). Granny remembers "box after box of costumes with spangles and rhinestones and boafeathers" and, like the townspeople, wonders, "Can this be all that's left of Folner Ganchion to come back from San Antone: spangles and rhinestones and boafeathers?" (148).

With the exception of his mother and Boy, Folner's family despises him for this effeminacy. In an imagined confrontation Boy recalls to Folner that at the funeral "Aunty sat hating you, even dead. Even laid in a coffin she despised you like a snake," and Christy Ganchion "sat out in front of the church in the car, would not come in, sullen and wretched" (123). Even the minister uses the occasion to air his repugnance of Folner. "The sermon was a long and sad one," Boy remembers, one that emphasizes Folner's sinfulness: "It told about all the family, about your young life in Charity and your work in the Church. . . . You had been a bright boy. You had sinned. The Lord save your soul" (126). The acts of Folner's adult life negate the catalogue of youthful achievements, irrevocably damning him in Charity's eyes: "What does he say, Brother Ramsey, in his talking, in his sermon? He is condemning Follie to hellfire" (128).

Critic Robert Phillips has rightly argued that, despite Folner's familial and communal condemnation, there emerges a bond between him and Boy. This bond seemingly arises from Boy's resemblance to Folner, one of which the older man is acutely aware. Much like Randolph, who recognizes himself in Joel, Folner finds a youthful mirroring of himself in Boy. The nephew also senses these similarities. When Boy mentally inventories the loft of the Ganchions' homeplace, Boy imagines Folner speaking to him: " 'I give you this glass,' your voice whispers, 'in which to see a vision of yourself, for this is why you've come. My breath is on the glass and you must wipe away my breath to see your own image.' In the mirror I cannot see myself but only an image of dust. I brush it off–and then see my portrait there. For a moment I look like Folner!" (136-137). Boy's reflection of Folner's image and, by extension, his identity is so pronounced that he does indeed seem, as Phillips terms it, to function as "an alter-ego for the narrator" (39). Thus, as in the model for gay mentorship that Capote offers, the adolescent struggling with negotiations of sexual identity finds the effeminate gay man the most recognizable and accessible model.

Goyen goes on to suggest, however, that this model is nevertheless unsatisfactory. As with Uncle Randolph's, Folner's exemplary identity posits a direct and inescapable correlation between same-sex desire and gender transitivity. In a society committed to disciplining perceived deviancies, this model's requisite performances of gender secure the gay man's social alienation. Because Boy directly witnesses alienation in Charity's responses to Folner, his is an uneasy acceptance of the model of homosexuality that Folner offers. "It is hard to be in the world and bone of your bone" (132), Boy confesses to Folner. At no time does Boy realize this more strongly than as he sits listening to Brother Ramsey's homophobic sermon at Folner's funeral. Boy reflects that his homosexuality, that which supposedly must replicate Folner's, is an immense burden. "The Lord hath hung this millstone upon my neck," Boy thinks, "and I know what for and I have never told. It is a lavalier of wickedness. It is the enormous rotten core of Adam's Apple" (128).

Folner Ganchion is not, however, the only model of homosexuality with whom Goyen presents Boy in the novel. Unlike Capote, Goyen significantly complicates the circulations of erotic desire and their relationships to Boy's identity with the inclusion of his other uncle, the masculine Christy. "[B]lack-headed and swarthy among the other towheads" (129) of the family, he is the physical opposite of Folner: "Christy was big and had dark wrong blood and a glistening beard, the bones in his russet Indian cheek were thick and arched high and they curved round the deep eye-cavities where two great silver eyes shaped like bird's eggs were set in deep—half-closed eyes furred round by grilled lashes that laced together and locked over his eyes" (157-158). Goyen's imagery repeatedly animalizes Christy, yet no flitting exotic birds characterize him as they do Folner. Goyen instead conveys Christy's identity via great hulking beasts or those given to violence—oxen, dogs, falcons, horses—all animals typically associated with masculine realms. These links to animals are more than imagistic, however. The narrative repeatedly documents Christy's fascination with and incessant discussion of animals' genitals and their frequently violent sexual acts. A then-titillated Boy remembers that Christy "would say whispered things about animals: udders, the swinging sex of horses, the maneuvers of cocks, bulls' ballocks and fresh sheep—he was in some secret conspiracy with all animals" (161). Christy even admits to the voyeuristic, erection-forming pleasure he takes in watching animals mate: "(Lyin in the fields all afternoon one afternoon, watchin for the stallion to take the mare. . . . I waited and waited and just about dark Good Lord it happened. How the mare screamed and how the stallion leapt with's hooves in the air like a great flyin horse of statues. . . . As I laid in the fields, somewhere in me was fillin with blood, and suddenly somewhere I was full and throbbin with blood)" (177). A somewhat less than subtle Goyen reinforces this conspicuous focus on males and their genitals by making Christy a personified phallus. "He had a circumcision-like scar,"

Boy recalls, "pink and folded, on his brown neck over which he would gently rub his fingers and tell me how it was a knifecut because of love" (159).

Despite Christy's literal phallocentrism, his often terrifying violence, his withdrawn personality, and the rarity of his interactions with Boy, a significant bond forms between the two, especially when Christy facilitates–perhaps unwittingly and perhaps not–Boy's first orgasm and thus circuitously introduces him to masturbation. The anthropomorphized river of Boy's memory reminds him of his awakening to autoeroticism and Christy's role in that experience: "Once, when you were swimming, naked, it happened for the first time to you in me. Christy stood on the bank and told you and Berryben to jump and touch my bottom and see who could come up to the top first" (29-30). As with Capote's lyricism, Goyen's is obfuscatory, yet the diction and actions imply that Boy gets an erection and ultimately climaxes. The River continues: "and you were struggling to come up first, rising rising rising, faster, faster, when some marvelous thing that can happen to all of us happened to you, wound up and burst and hurt you, hurt you and you came up, changed, last to the top trembling and exhausted and sat down on my banks in a spell" (30). While the orgasm bewilders Boy, the older Christy fully understands what has occurred and even encourages Boy to attempt another climax. "Christy knew," the River reminds Boy, "and tried to make you jump into me again" (30).

Although Boy remains oblivious to his potential same-sex desire for some time, the novel's progression clarifies that Christy is the likely fuel of Boy's autoeroticism. And, just as Boy's same-sex desires crystalize for both him and readers as Goyen's narrative progresses, so too do Christy's own same-sex desires become more clearly identifiable. These desires are initially ambiguous in large part because Goyen adroitly manipulates the instability inherent in male homosociality or, in an even more complicating move, has Christy do so. As in the scene of Boy's first orgasm, Christy seemingly stands as the masculine man who thrives on and even orchestrates fraternal interactions. At least on Christy's part, however, these interactions do not necessarily work to discipline and/or exclude male homosexuality. Rather, he may gratify same-sex desires by exploiting the physical contact and displays of sexuality that male homosociality 'legitimately' allows between men. Consider, for instance, the fishing trip that Boy remembers from his childhood:

> I had lain listening all night to a conversation . . . about women and certain Charity women; and then one man had said (it was Christy, my uncle) while he thought I was asleep, that he wondered if I had

> any hairs down there yet and drank his homebrew and said let's wake him up to see, and chuckled. I had lain trembling and waiting for them to come, knowing they would find what they came to see, quite a few, and lovely golden down, and they had been my secret; but they never came, only made me feel a guilt for secrets. (23)

While this passage documents Boy's not fully conscious desire to have other men gaze at his pubescent body, it also establishes the ambiguity of Christy's desire to subject Boy to precisely this scrutiny. Simple curiosity may prompt Christy's urge to examine Boy's genitals, to see if his body has become 'manly enough' for his 'full participation' in the homosocial and ostensibly heterosexual realm of the hunt and its talk of women. On the other hand, Christy may be manipulating homosociality's allowances for these supposedly asexual interactions to gratify visually his desire for Boy's adolescent body.

Christy's vexed relationship with his brother Folner suggests that this gaze may indeed be prompted by homoerotic desire, that Christy ultimately sets up Boy as a sort of surrogate for Folner. As discussed, Christy rejects Folner, refusing even to attend his funeral since, like the rest of Charity, Christy despises Folner's violations of gender. "He hated Folner," Boy recalls of Christy, "said he had to squat to pee and didn't have enough sense to pour it out of a boot" (160). Goyen complicates this hatred, however, by preceding it with Christy's intense love of Folner as a child. This devotion is so fierce that Christy violates his otherwise consistent performances of masculinity with displays of affection that he–and presumably the rest of Charity–perceive to be feminine:

> I was Follie's mother all those years, makes me part woman and I know it and I'll never get over it. How I rocked him and how I slept warm with him at nights, rolled up against my stomach and how I never left him day nor night, bless his little soul, settin on the gallry with him on my knee while I watched the others comin and goin across the pasture to town and back from town, to Chatauquas and May Fetes. (160)

Christy is clearly anxious at having performed in this manner. It "makes me part woman and I know it," he asserts, adding that "I'll never get over it." However, the gratification that arises from this transgression of gender outweighs the anxiety, and Christy remembers his parenting of Folner with amazing tenderness.

The brothers' close relation falters when the transgression of gender is no longer momentary and does not end with Christy. Moreover, it fails to insure a gratification for him that compensates for the social disapproval engendered by the supposedly deviant performance. When Folner too begins to enact roles socially scripted as feminine, Christy's gender anxiety reaches such levels that he reassumes only strict masculine roles and rejects Folner almost altogether because he will not perform comparably. "What was it got hold of him?" the perplexed Christy asks himself of Folner. "Took to swingin in the gallry swing all day, by hisself, turned away from me, somethin wild got in his eye, and then Mama took him back. Began to wear Mama's kimona and highheeled shoes and play show, dancin out from behind a sheet for a curtain; and then I turned away from him" (160-161). At least in this case, a temporary sacrifice of masculinity leads not to a reinscription of stable masculinity but rather to even more exaggerated violations of gender norms. In his tending to Folner, Christy may be less than conventionally masculine, but he is far from cross-dressing. Moreover, as Christy's reflections suggest, Folner's rejection of his brother is equally anxiety-inducing in that the social approval that Christy sacrifices to mother Folner is not compensated by his reciprocal devotion. Quite the contrary, Folner flatly rejects his brother. Boy thus seems correct in his assessment of his uncles, that Christy "had raised him like a mother until Folner turned away from him and hated him, and then Christy said he was a sissy and a maphrodite" (161).

As Boy further recalls, the relationship between the two brothers does not end here, however. Despite their mutual rejections, "they joined again in the woods–where I joined them too; and now we all join in the world" (161). As usual, Goyen is extraordinarily vague; nevertheless, the narrative suggests that the nonsexual physical contact expressive of the brothers' original mutual devotion metamorphoses into sexual physical contact, perhaps so gratifying that it outweighs the reciprocal disgust. The unique combination of their antithetical performances of gender and latent homosexuality allows the brothers to become what seems compatible–albeit clandestine–sexual partners. That is, through an enactment of recurrent cultural elisions of gender and sexual preferences–ones in which activity and in particular sexual activity such as penetration mark masculinity, and passivity and in particular sexual passivity such as being penetrated orally and/or anally mark femininity–the brothers find themselves able to enact a 'classic' butch-femme homosexual relationship, here within a specifically incestuous context.

Goyen's narrative never clarifies exactly what goes on between the two brothers in the woods or if these interactions haunt Christy. Nevertheless, it seems clear that something significant occurs between the two in the woods–even if only in Boy's imagination. He repeatedly speculates on the scenario, asking himself, "Was *he* [Follie] what Christy hunted for in the woods, going with his birdbag and his gun and returning with bird's blood on him and a chatelaine of slain birds girdled round his hips?" (121). If Folner has indeed been Christy's sexual prey in the woods, then the intentions of Christy's subsequent invitations for Boy to go there with him become increasingly suspect. With these invitations Christy may merely seek to establish more firmly Boy's position within homosocial realms typified by hunting. Or, as in the cases of the hunting trip and the day of swimming with Berryben, Christy again may be manipulating these same-sex interactions to allow an arena for expressions of his gay desire. That is, Christy may use the supposedly nonsexual fraternal bonding of the hunt to have sex with his nephew as he has possibly done with his brother.

At this point, before the two ultimately fateful trips to the woods with Christy, Boy remains simultaneously confused, frightened, and intrigued by his elder uncle and his mysterious ways. Christy "would go off hunting (in Folner's same woods)," Boy recalls, consistently promising his nephew, "One day when you're old enough I'll take you huntin with me, we'll go huntin, Boy." When Christy returns from his forays, Boy senses the brutality that Christy has unleashed. He would "then come back to us as though he had been in some sorrow in the woods, with birds' blood on him and a bouquet of small, wilted doves hanging from his waist over his thigh, or a wreath of shot creatures: small birds with rainbowed necks, a squirrel with a broken mouth of agony." Boy is not, however, wholly repulsed by these artifacts of Christy's violence. Rather, although hesitant, he thrills when Christy "would come to me and speak, for he had found words, 'Listen Boy, listen; come out to the woodshed with me quick and let me show you somethin, come with me, quick; by Gum I've got somethin.'" "What would he show me if I went?" (159), the titillated Boy ponders.

Twice Boy succumbs to his curiosity and goes into the woods with Christy, investing each time with significant albeit not always fully understood meaning. In the first instance, even the ostensible reason for the trek into the woods–to hunt for a mother possum and her babies–works to create an exclusively male sphere. The hunt for the possum and her young is to culminate with the eradication of the female and the results of procreation. That this sphere is to be exclusively male does not, however, foreclose circulations of eroticism. Rather, Goyen's diction almost immediately begins to establish the sexual charge to the homosociality and, somewhat later, offers a coherent symbol of homosexual interactions. "I trembled to go, and slipped away and met him," Boy remembers. "I saw him waiting for me (like a lover) . . . We rejoiced (without words) at our meeting secretly" (163-164). Thus, like lovers, the uncle and nephew embark and soon after begin the work of excavating the young possums from a stump. While Goyen's earlier conflations of Christy's violence and sexual desire help his ferocious chopping to assume sexual overtones, the symbolism needs little deciphering. As Christy hacks at the stump, he unintentionally strikes Boy and thus comes painfully close to a brutal penetration of the boy: "Because I came too close to him once he came down on my thigh with his axe–so gently that he only cut a purple line under the skin and no blood came." Even though this penetration is ultimately checked, thus revealing Christy's ambivalence about engaging in such sexual acts, his actions nevertheless traumatize him: "Christy wept and begged me not to tell anyone and tied his bandanna tightly round the wound and hugged me and trembled; and I have never told" (164). At least for the moment, despite his crystalizing desire for Boy, Christy cannot consummate the relationship sexually.

In contrast to Christy, whose frantic demands for silence about the incident betray its illicitness, Boy reacts not with terror or hysteria but rather with an elation comparable to that of his first orgasm. "I almost fainted and fell to the ground," he recalls, "but did not cry" (164). Indeed, he appears thrilled to bear the proof of his uncle's physical violation and, like Christ to His doubting disciples, does not hesitate to display his marked body: "I have carried on my thigh the secret scar he left (O see the wound on my thigh left by that hunter's hand!) and have never told" (164). Yet, as with his first orgasm, Boy remains confused about the meaning of this mark and the significance of Christy having given it. Boy senses only that the episode is not finished and that Christy is likely to be centrally involved in its culmination. "After that, there was a long time of waiting in which I knew there was a preparation for something," Boy reflects. "Within this waiting (was Christy waiting too?) we looked at the map together or I watched him make the ship in the bottle or heard the frenchharp in the woodshed" (164).

The long anticipation does end, however, and Boy confesses his epiphany as abruptly as he has it: "And then one summer night I learned his truth (and mine)" (164-165). Squatting outside his uncle's window, Boy sees Christy asleep, naked and aroused, and is transfixed by the beauty of his uncle's virile body, "hairy with a dark down, and nippled, and shafted in an ominous place." Instantly and, for the first time, fully aware of his desire for another man, Boy immediately articulates his embracing of this desire–"I whispered to myself 'Yes!'–as though I was affirming forever something I had always guessed was true"–and envisions a scenario in which the desire is not only mutual but acted upon. He recreates the laconic Christy's earlier beckonings and adds to them an explicitly sexual charge: "From where I watched him from below it seemed he might at some moment dive down to me and embrace me and there speak and say, 'Listen Boy, listen, let me tell you something . . .'" (165). "After that," Boy recalls, "I knew how beautiful he could be" (166).

Boy's opportunity to act on these desires, to "*fill the world with our sighs of yes! and make it sensual*" (167), arises when Christy again invites him into the woods, for the novel's–if not necessarily Boy's–climax: "And then, finally, it was the time Christy has whispered about" (168). And yet, when this scenario is set, Boy is not nearly so eager as when he is the voyeur safely distanced from his object of desire. That this very person may gratify these desires thrills him, and he recalls, "For a time he was leading me like a piper to the river; and for a time I was following in a kind of glory, and eager, and surrendered, and wanting to follow–just as he was, in his own dumb sorcery and splendor, leading me, victor, proud, like a captive." At the same time, however, "the uncaptured, unhypnotized part of me was afraid, wanting to run home (where was home to turn to, towards where?); for I knew he was leading me to a terrible dialogue in the deepest woods. All his hunting, all his shooting and gathering up of shot birds was a preparation . . . in which he would tell me some terrible secret" (171). Only slowly does Boy realize the actual source of this anxiety. He, already the youthful image of Folner, is about to become a literal surrogate for the person whom the family, Charity, and, perhaps most importantly, Christy reviles. Although mute at the time, looking back Boy imagines he could now name the anticipated interactions with Christy: "'Yes that's what Folner did and you despised him,' I would answer him if we could have a conversation now" (172).

Irony thus permeates this culminating scenario. On the one hand, Boy fears that sexual interactions with Christy will dictate for him an identity like Folner's: passive and effeminate and therefore subject to familial and communal ridicule and rejection. On the other hand, Christy, functioning out of a radically different logic, initiates these actions to prevent Boy from becoming like the detested Folner. If Christy's indulgent mothering of Folner, that contingent on Christy's sacrifice of masculinity, supposedly causes–or at least is a significant factor in–Folner's problematic effeminacy, then Christy's antithetical treatment of Boy may possibly insure Boy's acceptable masculinity. Since violence and sex have been such an effective means of eradicating the feminine, as symbolized in the mother possum, it provides for Christy the most likely method to squelch whatever burgeoning displays of femininity Boy may make. Thus, for Christy, Boy's indoctrination into homosexual sex within an exclusively masculine realm will 'save' him from replicating Folner's transgressive performances of gender. Because Christy understands gayness to be contingent on transgressive performances of gender rather than same-sex activity, Boy's literal rather than symbolic penetration will, as Christy reflects, "keep him from the fruits like Follie, my own brother" (174). According to this logic, Christy can quite frankly fuck the gayness out of Boy.

This logic is not, however, coherent even for Christy, and it is his own ambivalence, that already marked on Boy's body with the scar of Christy's axe blow, which ultimately prevents the sexual consummation of the relationship. For all his thrill at maleness engaged in violent sexual acts, Christy falls back upon the puritan notion that all sex, regardless of the object choice, is corrupting. Just as he honors the virginity of Otey Bell, his by-then drowned wife, he feels he must not violate his nephew. "Boy, Boy you are so good, what made you so good?" he wails to himself. "I am spoiled and he is clean; O I am vile, a shitten lamb. I will corrupt him, do not let me corrupt him when we get to the thicket. I didn't spoil Otey, I let her wait . . . But I never touched her" (184).

Christy cannot negate his desire for Boy, however, by an act of will. Physical urges counter well-meant resolutions, and the possibilities for pleasure offered in Boy's body tantalize Christy as incessantly as his naked body has done Boy earlier. As the two walk deeper into the woods, Christy fantasizes about both of their bodies, focusing specifically on their genitals: "O myself, how splendid myself, good as a stallion, and pretty, and circumcised (is he?), for who, who got me?" And, just as Boy's fantasies bring the two bodies together, so too do Christy's. "Does he do it?" Christy asks himself. "How will I ask him? (If your Uncle Jack was on a mule and couldn't get off would you help your Uncle Jack off?)" (184). For all of Christy's anxieties about corruption inherent in sexual interactions, he acknowledges the pull of the sadomasochistic pleasures they offer: "For I knew, even then, that we all have got somethin in us that will give pain, that will make somebody go *uhuh uhuh uhuh* and wag's tongue and roll's eye and breathe as though he is gaspin or suffocatin with the croup, or say *whew! whew!* as though he is burnt; and almost die. To give this pain, and to get it, we will do almost anything" (176). To consummate the relationship with Boy thus seems doubly attractive. The sexual union will not only arrest his further evolution towards Folner's gender transgressiveness but also provide Christy the release of orgasm.

When the men reach the woods, these conflicting circulations of desire and anxiety almost overwhelm each of them. They desperately crave sexual interaction yet fear its consequences. For Christy, while the interaction will not necessarily call Boy's masculinity into question, it will forever spoil his presumed virginity, while for Boy the acts will validate a gay identity that offers ridicule, alienation, and ultimately suicide. Not surprisingly then, the climax of *The House of Breath* is without actual climax. When Christy pauses in his preparations for the symbolic penetration, Boy flees: "Yet some enormous tenderness was rising out of him. His look asked for something that I could not give because I had not learned how to give it. I backed away, backed away and he sat still on the stump. He pointed his gun at me to shoot me like a bird; and I backed away. And then he lowered his gun and watched me and let me get away; and then I ran" (185).

While this flight leaves Christy sexually frustrated but nevertheless relieved of the anxiety prompted by Boy's approaching defilement, his escape does not resolve Boy's uncertainty about his desires and the identity he holds to be contingent upon these desires. Christy does not shoot Boy and therefore, in Goyen's symbolic order, sexually penetrate him; nevertheless, Christy unwittingly sets into play a ritual that functions comparably for Boy. A yoke of birds shot by Christy beats against the fleeing Boy's body, and, when he eventually pauses, he imbues the wounds they have inflicted with enormous significance: "I ran on again with his yoke of birds swinging against me, Christy's message to me. I ran blessed with his yoke of loves, or words, his long sentence of birds, bloody and broken and speechless, sentences of his language shot out of his air and off his trees' boughs that were his words' vocabulary" (186). For Boy, the wounds mark Christy's desire, and he knows now that he "really *loved* Christy, longed for him, calling to him" (187). Indeed, this love is so intense that Boy feels he should have succumbed to the intuited sexual advances. "I betrayed Christy!" Boy thinks. "That I failed him in the woods, he who gave me all these gifts of birds, who spoke for the first time to me and waited for me to answer!" (187).

To the frustration of Boy and readers, Goyen ends this facet of the relationship between the uncle and nephew here. When Christy eventually returns from the woods, there is no mention of the events that take place there. "No one even seemed to know that I had even been away," Boy remembers, "and Christy never mentioned it. We never went hunting again" (189). The novel ends a scant five pages later, with Boy's outcome uncertain. Goyen never clarifies whether or not Boy assumes the transgressive gender performances of Folner. All that is clear is that, in his reflections on his two uncles, it is not Folner's model and expressions of desire that Boy recalls. Rather, it is Christy's, and in vivid contrast to the conclusion of *Other Voices, Other Rooms*, *The House of Breath* ends with Boy's hymn to his masculine uncle: "O Christy, our great lover! Reach down your birdbloodied hand to me, you who decorated me with your garland of news, crowned me with your birdbays of love, blessed me with the flowers and the songs of our woods, hung me with the trappings of our woods to send me, wrought like a frieze with all this beauty, all this knowledge" (191).

With this concluding image, Goyen again establishes how his understanding of the gendering of male homosexuality diverges from Capote's. Espousing a Foucauldian model, Capote collapses male same-sex desire and gender transitivity. In *Other Voices, Other Rooms* gay identity is contingent upon an inversion of gender in which performances of femininity take precedence over those of masculinity. On the other hand, Goyen allows for the existence of a masculine man who, like the effeminate one, can physically act upon gay desire. In fact, like Halperin, Goyen posits this figure as the cultural ideal of male homosexuality. And yet, *The House of Breath* crucially offers two coexisting and competing models of gayness and foregrounds the conflicting understandings that Boy and Christy hold about the relationship of same-sex physicality and identity. Scripted as such, Goyen's novel escapes the reification of homosexuality that Sedgwick identifies in both Foucault's and Halperin's theorizations; instead, *The House of Breath* anticipates Sedgwick's demands to interrogate "the gaps *between* long-coexisting . . . understandings of same-sex relations." Goyen thus not only queers Twain's famous tale of adolescent boyhood but also forcefully destablizes 'the' homosexuality of 'the' American South at midcentury, calling into question the paradigms that Capote offers as immutable in his own "fairy *Huckleberry Finn*."

WORKS CITED

Capote, Truman. *Other Voices, Other Rooms*. New York: Random House, 1948.
Clarke, Gerald. *Capote: A Biography*. New York: Simon & Schuster, 1988.
Fiedler, Leslie. *Love and Death in the American Novel*. 1960. New York: Doubleday, 1992.
Foucault, Michel. *The History of Sexuality*. Vol. 1. 1976. Trans. Robert Hurley. New York: Random House, 1978.
Goyen, William. *The House of Breath*. New York: Random House, 1950.
Halperin, David M. *One Hundred Years of Homosexuality and Other Essays on Greek Love*. New York & London: Routledge, 1990.
Phillips, Robert. *William Goyen*. Boston: Twayne, 1979.
Sedgwick, Eve Kosofksy. *Epistemology of the Closet*. Berkeley & Los Angeles: U of California P, 1990.

Inscribing a Lesbian Reader, Projecting a Lesbian Subject: A Jane Rule Diptych

Marilyn R. Schuster
Smith College

SUMMARY. This diptych represents two takes on the short fiction of Jane Rule, the Canadian lesbian novelist whose 1964 novel, *Desert of the Heart*, was markedly different from other lesbian fiction available at that time. Traveling through time, theory, and texts, I approach Rule's fiction from two directions. First, using feminist

---

Marilyn R. Schuster received her BA in French from Mills College in 1965 and her PhD in French language and literature from Yale University in 1973. She has been on the faculty at Smith College since 1971 and is now Professor of French and Women's Studies. Her scholarly work has been in the areas of curriculum transformation (bringing ethnic studies and feminist scholarship into the liberal arts curriculum and classroom), women's studies, French, and comparative literature. She edited her first book, *Women's Place in the Academy: Transforming the Liberal Arts Curriculum*, with Susan Van Dyne in 1985. Her second book, *Marguerite Duras Revisited*, was published in 1993 in the Twayne World Authors series. She is now working on a volume for New York University Press tentatively called *Passionate Communities: Reading Jane Rule*. She has also written articles for journals such as the *Harvard Educational Review*, the *French Review*, *Nineteenth-Century French Studies*, and *Feminist Studies* on curriculum transformation and on writers such as Arthur Rimbaud, Marguerite Duras, Monique Wittig, and Jane Rule. Correspondence may be addressed: Neilson Library, Smith College, Northampton, MA 01063. E-mail: mschuste@sophia.smith.edu

[Haworth co-indexing entry note]: "Inscribing a Lesbian Reader, Projecting a Lesbian Subject: A Jane Rule Diptych." Schuster, Marilyn R. Co-published simultaneously in *Journal of Homosexuality* (The Haworth Press, Inc.) Vol. 34, No. 3/4, 1998, pp. 87-111; and: *Gay and Lesbian Literature Since World War II: History and Memory* (ed: Sonya L. Jones) The Haworth Press, Inc., 1998, pp. 87-111; and: *Gay and Lesbian Literature Since World War II: History and Memory* (ed: Sonya L. Jones) Harrington Park Press, an imprint of The Haworth Press, Inc., 1998, pp. 87-111. Single or multiple copies of this article are available for a fee from The Haworth Document Delivery Service [1-800-342-9678, 9:00 a.m. - 5:00 p.m. (EST). E-mail address: getinfo@haworth.com].

maps for (re)reading, I show how "Dulce" inscribes a lesbian reader. Second, tracing the steps of lesbian and queer theorists, I show how "Home Movie" projects a lesbian subject. Taken together, these readings seek to shed light on lesbian creative practice in the homophobic climate of postwar North America. *[Article copies available for a fee from The Haworth Document Delivery Service: 1-800-342-9678. E-mail address: getinfo@haworth.com]*

Poetry and fiction can sometimes do what theory has not yet learned: to speak a language of desire where there had been only silence or denial. Adrienne Rich has taught us that; as have Audre Lorde and Monique Wittig and many other writers who refused to be silenced long before the current wave of queer writing. Jane Rule's fiction–and the ways it has been received and ignored–provides a rich ground for exploring the creation of a language of desire in a context of denial.

Born in New Jersey in 1931, Jane Rule matured as a woman and a writer in the decade following World War II. The postwar effort to restore order on the home front included a campaign to define healthy femininity as heterosexual, monogamous, and reproductive. At the same time, as Jennifer Terry and other queer theorists have amply demonstrated, homosexuality was intensely pathologized. Medical and psychological discourses categorized "homosexual" as sick and were joined by the politics of McCarthyism that marked "homosexual" as traitor. Kinsey was denounced in the early fifties for proposing a continuum of sexual practices and desire rather than an opposition between the healthy, reproductive heterosexual and the sick, degenerate homosexual.

Literary texts were bound up in the same models of deviance. The lesbian fiction available to Rule as a young writer was self-punishing like *The Well of Loneliness*; or formulaic, requiring "heterosexual recuperation" at the end (the lesbian loses "the girl" or is killed off, marriage and nature triumph over deviant desire); or highly coded like Gertrude Stein.

Jane Rule's work, formed in that hostile climate, reveals strategies of resistance and subversion. In the two essays that follow, the first on "Dulce" from *Inland Passage* and the second on "Home Movie" from *Outlander*, I propose a diptych of readings, approaching these short stories from two directions and considering what it was to read then and to read now, to write then and to write now. The first excursion represents an effort, using feminist maps of (re)reading, to uncover in Rule's work strategies for *reading queerly.* Reading queerly reveals the ways in which sexualities produce, repress, disguise, substitute for each other in language and in desire. The second part of the diptych traces the steps of lesbian and queer theorists to explore the strategies Rule devises for *writing queerly.*

Rule's work goes beyond the representation of lesbian identity or the inclusion of lesbian themes. She explores sexuality in language; her discursive explorations inscribe a desiring lesbian subject.

Further, Rule's texts create a special bond of reading between reader and writer. Read in the context of nineties queer provocations in theory, literature, and film, Rule's stories may seem understated. But along with increased queer visibility in recent years, there has been a return of pathologizing discourses that echo the medical and political languages of the fifties. Discourse about AIDS, and religious and political campaigns to explain, contain, or excise queer sexualities in the body politic bear an uncanny resemblance to the languages about deviance in the fifties. Rule's strategies of resistance and subversion continue to be useful to a population at risk. The enthusiastic reception of the Canadian documentary film *Fiction and Other Truths: A Film about Jane Rule*, released in 1995, has shown this to be true.

SAILING TO GALIANO: JANE RULE AT HOME

The journey to Galiano cannot be rushed. To get to the ferry at Tsawwassen–a spit of land that separates Boundary Bay from the Strait of Georgia–requires three city buses from my temporary home on the University of British Columbia campus in Vancouver. I tuck *Inland Passage* back into my bag as the bus pulls up to the ferry dock. On this sunny June day, foot passengers with backpacks and cars with camping equipment wait for the boat that will take them to the Gulf Islands for a holiday weekend. First stop, Galiano Island, where Jane Rule and Helen Sonthoff will meet me at the Sturdies Bay dock.

Crossing Over

I've been traveling for much longer than the two hours on buses. Along with many other readers, I first met Jane in *Lesbian Images*, herself a reader of lesbian writers, holding her own story up to the stories available. In that book, as in her own fiction, Rule was charting new territory: reading as a writer, but also as a lesbian looking for stories that would help her map what it means for a woman to love women and to articulate that desire in language. Her readings of other lesbians in that book led me to her own writing, which had been unknown to me before. I turned to *Desert of the Heart* and then was given a worn photocopy of *This Is Not for You*, out of print but passed around from woman to woman, a silent community of readers finding, at last, stories to give shape and meaning to our lives.

For nearly twenty years I've been meeting Jane in her books, then in letters, and once, two years ago, in person. This, my second sailing to Galiano, is a return to territory now more familiar. I've been living with her letters, college papers, unpublished stories, manuscripts, photographs, rejection notices, and, finally, reviews in dozens of boxes at the University of British Columbia archives. She is the only company I've kept for two weeks. Moving back and forth in time, I try to piece together her childhood, her first loves, her persistence as publisher after publisher turned down *Desert of the Heart.*

As I returned to the late fifties in her papers I asked myself the questions I'd asked when I first read *Desert of the Heart*: How did this middle child of an American middle-class family become Canada's most public lesbian? How did she find a way to write stories of lesbian lives that weren't punishing or tortured? stories that echo Yeats (as in the title of her novel *The Young in One Another's Arms*, taken from "Sailing to Byzantium") and *Pilgrim's Progress* (in the quest allusions of *Desert of the Heart*) more than Radclyffe Hall's *The Well of Loneliness* or pulp fiction. And how could it be that a writer so vitally important to readers throughout North America has been ignored by the professional arbiters of literary reputation–academics, literary critics, and now, queer theorists?

Taking a seat by a window in the ferry, I wait for the horn to sound the beginning of the hour-long voyage through the Strait of Georgia. Strange waters, these: the border between Canada and the United States follows a quirky, jagged line between the Gulf Islands in British Columbia and the San Juan Islands in Washington state, Canada as often to the south of the United States as to the north.

As the ferry pulls out of the dock I think about my first trip to Galiano two years ago, a vacation with Susan, partner in life and work, to celebrate the completion of book manuscripts about other women writers. The closer we got to the island, the more apprehensive we became. How much of Jane's life entered her fiction directly? Would Helen, our mothers' contemporary, who graduated from Smith College years before either of us was born (and where we both now teach), turn out to be the model for Constance in *Memory Board*, lovable but without any short-term memory? I kept looking at a picture of Jane on the back of *Contract with the World*, taken when she was the age I was that summer; what would she look like now, twelve years my senior, but suffering from arthritis of the lower spine that sometimes nearly cripples her? What a risk they had taken, we thought, to invite us in as houseguests for several days rather than take the ferry ride themselves to the city. Or, simply, to decline an invitation from strangers. Later, when we confessed these apprehensions over one of many glasses of Scotch, Helen said (in full command of her short-term memory), "It's difficult for Jane to travel because of her arthritis and we've found through experience that you can put up with almost anyone for two days." A welcome and a warning that made us all laugh.

On that trip, we had driven off the ferry to follow the directions to their house. There is only one main road the length of Galiano. We drove through an Emily Carr landscape of fir trees and red-barked arbutus, with occasional glimpses of the water. Later we'd explore traces of Indian middens on the beaches of this tiny island where the past and present mingle, but no landfill, no savings and loan, no gas station have brought the most visible signs of the late twentieth century. Without their careful directions we would have missed the house–a cedar cabin tucked into a hillside, modest and unassuming from the road, protecting the privacy of Helen's flower garden and Jane's pool.

They greeted us like old friends and after settling into our room, we joined them for sherry before lunch. Gradually we discovered the signs of other presences–little drawings and paintings by Elizabeth "Hoppy" Hopkins, Gerard Manley Hopkins's niece, who had been their neighbor and whose grave they visit on walks to the sea. "The Poseurs," a portrait of cats preening hangs next to a painting of foot passengers in bright summer gear descending from the ferry at Sturdies Bay. Dozens of Indian baskets hang in the living room, traded for trout caught by Jane's namesake great-grandmother, Jane Vance, in the Eel River in the Northern California redwoods early in this century.

We wondered when we made that journey–Susan a reader of American women poets–if Galiano were like Emily Dickinson's room. Did the island shut out the world, but open up the freedom to create? When Jane and Helen moved there permanently in 1976, Jane had imagined long stretches of uninterrupted time to write. She was forty-five and had published dozens of stories, three novels, and most of a fourth, but she dismissed these as "apprenticeship novels" and looked forward to writing the works of her creative maturity. But even so, she didn't ever close the door of that house to the outside world. Every afternoon in summer she invited all children, permanent residents and visitors alike, to swim in her pool while she kept watch. Every winter she and Helen would travel to family and warmer weather in California to ease her arthritis and keep the elaborate networks of their friendships and kinships alive. Island living, yes, but isolation, no. Once in Galiano they took an active role in island life, acting as the "Bank of Galiano," making loans so that neighbors could start businesses or buy houses. It was after moving to Galiano that Jane assumed her most public political voice, writing a column, "So's Your Grandmother," for *The Body Politic*, the gay liberationist newspaper in Toronto.

The freedom to write that moving to the island promised didn't last, however. A short time after Jane and Helen moved to Galiano, Jane's arthritis was diagnosed and started to worsen. Although she would write three more novels and publish three collections of stories and essays, Jane had constantly to choose between pain and writing: the pain killers prescribed for her illness blocked the concentration needed for writing. On that earlier visit, I was only vaguely aware of these circumstances. Jane's hospitality and kindness require her to shield her guests from her own discomfort. As we sipped after-dinner Scotch one night, I asked what she was working on now. It had been three years since *After the Fire* and I was eager for her next book. "I've retired," was the unequivocal answer; further discussion was not invited. Her decision, while clear, had not been easy.

The foreclosure of future texts made me want all the more to return to Rule's early work. Crossing over to Galiano Island, I think about the twenty years that I've been reading Rule and about the ways I have learned to "read queerly." What did it mean then, what does it mean now, to be a lesbian writer–or reader?

Reading Then, Reading Now

What it means to me now to be a *lesbian* reader is informed above all by *feminist* ways of reading. Reading "queerly" is inseparable in my practice from reading "as a woman." Two maps for reading queerly have emerged for me in the last twenty years, each predicated on affinity and difference, identification and separation between the writer and the reader. The first is the model for feminist reading developed by Adrienne Rich in her foundational 1976 essay about Emily Dickinson, "Vesuvius at Home: The Power of Emily Dickinson." Traveling to Dickinson's home at a century's remove even as I am traveling to Rule's home at a generation's remove, Rich clearly stakes out the importance of recovering the cultural and geographic context of the woman writer and the equal importance of clarifying her own cultural location as reader. The affinities she senses with Dickinson as a poet writing against the expectations of her time and place are neither more nor less important than the differences that separate the two women, the two historical moments in which they think and write. Patricinio Schweickart returns to Rich's essay in 1986 to propose a paradigm for feminist readings of women writers that Rich illustrates in her reading of Dickinson. Schweickart pays as much attention to the rhetorical strategies of Rich's text as she does to its content, especially the use of a personal voice and Rich's choice of images to articulate her relation to her subject.

Schweickart focuses on Rich's organizing metaphors–of witness, travel, and "trying to connect"–arguing that the images delineate a process for feminist reading. "The first," explains Schweickart, "is a judicial metaphor: the feminist reader speaks as a witness in defense of the woman writer" (46). The second, travel metaphor, points to the importance of uncovering the writer's historical and cultural context. The third image–"an insect against the screens of an existence which inhabited Amherst, Massachusetts"–acknowledges that reader and writer are both separated and united by the text between them (47).

As I think about reading and rereading Rule, first as a stranger and then as someone I've gotten to know through texts and conversation, I think about our affinities and am reminded of our differences. Lesbians looking to literature to make sense of our lives, we came of age in different cultural contexts. Rule began her teaching career in the McCarthy years; pressure was exerted on schools to require faculty to sign a loyalty oath that implicitly, if not explicitly, exacted allegiance to heterosexuality as well as the American flag. In that climate, Rule left behind her United States citizenship and moved to Canada in 1956. Rule came of age as a writer at a time when Radclyffe Hall and Beebo Brinker were the most visible literary lesbians; in that literary context, Rule sought to map out new ways of writing lesbian desire.

Having come to adulthood and professional maturity in the post-Stonewall, queer-friendly decades of the seventies and eighties, I've been nourished not only by a political climate distinctly less hostile than the climate Jane left when she went to Vancouver, I have something she didn't have–her fiction. And yet the assertions of queer pride in the nineties have not replaced the verbal and physical bashing of the fifties; they barely cover over continuing fear and loathing of sexuality not contained by heterosexual reproduction. The rantings of McCarthy have been taken over by talk radio, and the repercussions, less public but no less real, are felt in the daily lives of gays and lesbians who may or may not see themselves represented in Queer Nation. The space between the rhetoric of talk radio and the rhetoric of queer power may be, precisely, the space occupied by much of Rule's fiction and many of her readers. It is this space that I hope to explore in reading Rule: in part because she has been passed over by many other professional readers but also because she has been important in an intensely private way to me and to many other readers.

As Schweickart says of Rich's essay, a feminist reading of a woman writer weaves–but does not blend–"the context of writing and the context of reading" (54). I understand that to mean that the feminist reader does not appropriate a woman's text or use it to authorize or validate her way of reading, but looks at the interaction of these different but mutually illuminating contexts, making clear her own stakes as she proposes an interpretation that accounts for the text she's reading and, ideally, can be extended (tactfully) to other readings.

The model for feminist reading provided by Rich and analyzed by Schweickart is complemented in my mind by the *bond of reading* between women writers and readers that Shoshana Felman proposes in *What Does a Woman Want? Reading and Sexual Difference.* Felman's book brings together readings she had done over many years, primarily of texts by Balzac and Freud, but newly framed in her book by readings of texts by women–Woolf, Rich, de Beauvoir. Felman discovers her own presence in her earlier reading, her personal stakes in interpretation visible only in hindsight and illuminated by later reading of women writers. She explains that in her experience as a critic "[f]eminism . . . is indeed for women, among other things, reading literature and theory with their own life–a life, however, that is not entirely in their conscious possession" (13). Her goal is to unsettle apparent certainties about autobiography and personal writing that have become commonplace in recent years. She asserts that "*none of us, as women, has as yet, precisely, an autobiography*" (14, emphasis hers). Positioned as "other," women don't have a story, but must become a story, through the *bond of reading.*

Felman is primarily concerned with *sexual difference*, what it means to be(come) a woman and to read as a woman, which for Felman means to read as a feminist. Her insights, however, translate very usefully to thinking about *different sexualities*. Felman, like Rich, is interested in reading practices, specific engagements with texts. She focuses on the negotiation that constitutes the subjectivity of *both* the writer and the reader, an act of newly gendered reading that extends deconstructionist methods. She looks at what it means to *assume* one's sexual difference in the act of reading: "assuming, that is, not the false security of an 'identity' . . . but the very insecurity of a differential movement, which no ideology can fix and of which no institutional affiliation can redeem the radical anxiety, in the performance of an act that constantly–deliberately or unwittingly *enacts* our difference yet finally escapes our own control" (10).

The potential implications of Felman's effort to read sexual difference for specifically *lesbian* writers and readers become clearer as she turns to Simone de Beauvoir's reading of herself as a feminist writer. Felman cites an interview de Beauvoir did with Jean-Paul Sartre three decades after writing *The Second Sex*. Sartre misreads de Beauvoir by telling her: "You became a feminist in writing this book." De Beauvoir counters by saying "But I became a feminist especially after the book was read, and started to exist for other women" (11). The book, Felman argues, is the site for a negotiation through which both the writer and the readers constitute themselves. Felman says "feminism comes to be defined here almost inadvertently as a bond of reading" (12). "The bond of reading," argues Felman, "constitutes a renewed relation to one's gender" through a relay of "becomings." "*Becoming* a feminist is undertaking to investigate what it means to *be* a woman and discovering that one *is* not a woman but rather *becomes* (somewhat interminably) a woman; discovering, through others' reading and through the way in which other women are *addressed* by one's own writing, that one is not born a woman, one has become . . . a woman" (12, emphasis hers).

If one were to substitute "lesbian" for "woman" in the above passage, the allied projects of writing and reading queerly can be seen to participate in a similar bond of writer and reader, made possible, but not wholly contained by, the text. When resituated in the cultural context of North America from the late fifties through the eighties, the bond of reading enabled by a writer who *becomes* a lesbian in her fiction and, more importantly, through the ways her fictions are read, can be understood as doubly confirming–confirming the legibility of sexual difference *and* of different sexuality. Multiple bonds of reading in which difference is confirmed and conferred can be seen in readings of African-American women writers and by other groups read as *other* or as *different* by the (falsely) unified white, masculine, heterosexual mainstream.

I know from letters I've seen in the archives, written to Jane over the last three decades, that other readers, like me, have read her fictions "with their own lives." Rule's fictions have enabled them to take their lives more into their "conscious possession."

Reading Queerly

On this return trip, as the ferry continues its slow but certain crossing, my mind filled with unsorted fragments of memory and manuscripts (published and unpublished) from the archives, I open *Inland Passage* to "Dulce," a story about subjectivities (and sexualities) redefined through bonds of reading. Jane had told me once that she particularly loved this story; she loved it because it didn't come easily, but when she'd written it she liked what she found there. I return to that story first, to meet Jane again in a literary landscape she had worked hard for and that had worked for her.

Inland Passage, like most of Rule's collections of stories and essays, invites a consideration of what it means to read at different historical and political moments, specifically, what it means to read (and write) sexuality. Published by Naiad in 1985, *Inland Passage* contains twenty-one stories, some of which were written as early as 1963. Some belong to a series Jane dismisses as her "Anna and Harry stories," stories of straight domesticity intended for mainstream women's magazines. At least four in the collection were first published in the Canadian women's magazine *Chatelaine*.

"Dulce," previously unpublished, opens the collection. The story can be read as a parable for reading; its placement in the collection leads me to reconsider the other stories, to read against the grain of the middle-class domesticity of the women's magazine stories. Like many of Rule's stories, this one contains a number of autobiographical lures, bits of her own story reconfigured in a character who is, nonetheless, clearly not her: Dulce lives in Vancouver, graduated from Mills College as an English major (shunning the courses in child development and dietary science designed to resocialize women after the war), studied Shakespeare, like Jane as a young student, at Stratford. Dulce becomes in the story a model reader of texts, though not a writer; a listener who asks the right questions, but not a speaker. The autobiographical details seem almost an effort to throw the reader off. The character is so clearly not Rule, that she seems only to be teasing with the surface references. In another way, though, Rule demonstrates in this story Shoshana Felman's observations about women, memory, and autobiography: "women's autobiography is what their memory cannot contain" (Felman 15). The story is about secrets and silences and learning to read oneself by reading others. It is also about false keys to meaning, about not rushing to an interpretation that suggests that a single key will unlock the full range of possible meanings the story might generate.

Dulce presents herself at the beginning of the story as a twenty-one-year-old orphan whose desire is to give herself away "having no use of my own for it." Claiming her orphan status is a way of drawing close to her older, childhood friend Wilson, orphaned very young, her only close friend. A poet, Wilson plays the role of brother, teacher, and intellectual mentor to Dulce in the story. He dedicates books and poems to her, he's an absent friend who provides heterosexual protection by correspondence when she is at college and uninterested in the advances of the boys around her. Even Dulce believes in this screen romance, so when Wilson decides to move permanently to England, discovering he was "born on the wrong continent," she asks rather plaintively, "What about me?" Wilson can only say, "I'm sorry" (13). Later, Oscar, a sculptor who is a mutual friend, reveals to Dulce in starkly homophobic terms, that Wilson is not a "real man": "He's a faggot . . . A queer, a homosexual" (14). Oscar then takes it upon himself to initiate Dulce into the pleasures of heterosexuality. She seems more an observer than a participant in their affair and even as it progresses, she rereads Wilson's poems and discovers meanings she hadn't been able to read before:

> I took down Wilson's first volume of poems and turned to the love poems which had always bewildered me. What I thought had been about unrequited love was instead forbidden, I could quite clearly see, but nothing prevented the reader from supposing the object to be female, married or otherwise lost to him. It was not, however, a better explanation. Had they been, in a perverse way, poems also for me, the only way Wilson knew how to tell me that he was incapable of loving me? (15)

Dulce is learning to "read queerly," to read encoded desire. But she is also learning that the gay subtext coexists with the heterosexual screen, props it up, speaks multiple desires rather than a single love story. She rethinks the names that Oscar has given to Wilson, names she'd heard before but never considered seriously. Wilson might be a "faggot," but he is also "entirely masculine." What Oscar takes as the definitive key to the meaning of Wilson's poetry, Wilson's homosexuality, is, rather, a key to understanding Oscar. He projects his own reductive understanding which occludes any other adjacent readings. Dulce understands that her new knowledge adds layers of meaning without erasing what had been there before. She can understand the coexistence of forbidden and unrequited love where she'd only met confusion. She can even read in the text some of her own story with Wilson, or at least the language doesn't exclude it.

Dulce also sees Oscar's sculpture differently now. "Compared to Wilson, Oscar was transparent, his work hugely, joyously sexual, his needs blatant, his morality patriarchal" (16). The gay text is multilayered, resists as well as invites interpretation, is darkly attractive. The (anxious) heterosexual male text is transparent, imposing; it reproduces the dominant morality which, in turn, reaffirms the artist. Ultimately, Dulce loses interest in the art and the man. When asked to choose between her dog and Oscar, she chooses her dog.

Just as Wilson's poems become less bewildering but more complex when Dulce reads beyond the heterosexual pretense, her own desire becomes more legible when she has an affair with Lee, another would-be writer, this time a young woman, who, with her daughter, moves in with Dulce. Dulce uses the same language to describe her sexual discovery with Lee that she used to describe her textual discovery in Wilson's poems: "my sexual bewilderment and constraint left me" (26). As with Oscar, however, the insight outlasts the relationship, and for essentially the same reason: just as Oscar projected his loathing of "queers" onto Wilson and confirmed his own heterosexual desirability with Dulce, Lee has internalized society's fear of "preying lesbians" and uses Dulce to exorcise her fear. While Oscar uses disgust of gays to prop up his own seemingly uncomplicated heterosexuality, Lee becomes suicidal with internalized homophobia. Only through a novel that misrepresents her affair with Dulce can she write that homophobia out of her system and out of her future texts.

Lee's novel provides an opportunity for Rule to represent Dulce again as a reader of fiction, of sexuality, and of herself. Having apprenticed herself as a reader with Wilson's poetry and her own life, Dulce is a more suspicious, more canny reader of Lee's novel. Wilson's poetry had taught her to break through heterosexual codes to a gay subtext. Lee's novel teaches her that certain figures of lesbian desire are also part of heterosexual codes (like Oscar's insults), written to reassure heterosexual readers rather than to express lesbian desire. Dulce recognizes a misspelled, partial translation of herself in the villainous character named Swete. The writing of the novel allows Lee, more than her psychoanalysis or her brief marriage to her psychiatrist, to purge herself of the suicidal self-hate provoked by her lesbian affairs. After this first novel, Lee divorces her shrink and matures as a writer, eventually becoming "one of Canada's best known lesbians" (31). To unmask Swete as Dulce doesn't reveal who Dulce is, it reveals Lee's struggle as a lesbian writer in a society and language that only validates heterosexual romance.

The story concludes with Dulce, now Dulcinea to a whole generation of poets in Western Canada who dedicate their work to her, as an old woman who prefers art to artists, the representation of passion to love itself. The last sentence of the story–that Rule worked so hard to create and that speaks to her still–is a metaphor for the lesbian reader, whose story can be told, but at a distance, and not without traces of sorrow: "My real companions, in my imagination, are my counterparts throughout history and the world who, whatever names they are given, are women very like myself, who holds the shell of a poem to her ear and hears the mighty sea at a safe and sorrowing distance" (32). Dulce provides a model for reading queerly that demonstrates how reader and writer constitute each other through the bond of reading. As the consummate reader of texts, Dulce by the end of the story becomes a generatrix of the texts of others.

Dulce's character, particularly in the context of the other stories in *Inland Passage* provides not the autobiography of Rule it teasingly seems to promise in the beginning, but an autobiography of reading queerly.

Through Oscar's insult, Dulce learns to read Wilson. Through her affair with Lee–and the contrast it provides with Oscar–she learns to read her own desire. In neither case does she arrive at a totally clarifying, adequate reading; the texts, like these lives, are distorted by heterosexual anxiety. Rule shows that the negotiation between writer and reader, the bond of reading, is always in process, always inflected by the time and place of both writer and reader; meaning is never fixed or finalized or possessed in the way that Oscar thought he had fixed the meaning of Wilson's poems.

In addition to learning that reading queerly doesn't lead to closure but to an opening up of layered, sometimes contradictory meanings, Dulce gradually learns the curious interdependence of heterosexual and queer meanings. The series of displacements and discoveries (textual and sexual) Dulce experiences as reader of Wilson and Lee and lover of Oscar and Lee shifts the erotic and linguistic balance conventionally assigned to heterosexuality and homosexuality. Heterosexuality is defined against homosexuality, it depends on exclusivity, the radical separation of sexual meanings. If Wilson is queer, that is all his poems can mean, according to Oscar. Homosexual desire, on the other hand, can incorporate, coexist with and illuminate heterosexual desire (and fear). The queer text (and queer sex) is not imitative and reductive, but a more complex, inclusive paradigm that does not depend on expulsion of an opposite, an other.

Rule shifts the erotic and linguistic balance in a series of relays, as Felman would say. The apparently uncomplicated confidence of Oscar's sexuality–and art–is supported by his defensive condemnation of "faggots." After revealing Wilson's guilty secret, Oscar confirms his own sexuality with Dulce. And yet it is after her heterosexual initiation with Oscar, that Dulce is better able to know and name her own lesbian desire. Having written out her internalized loathing to an assumed heterosexual audience, Lee is able to become a leading lesbian writer, embarrassed by her earlier detour of denial. Dulce, meanwhile, reads beyond the pretense of the demonized lesbian to see a reflection of Lee's struggle rather than a distorting representation of herself. In each case, heterosexual imposition is the illusion, the incomplete, false, or falsifying reading, the source of pain. Rather than represent homosexual texts or desire as imitations or as pale reflections (not real men) Rule's story represents heterosexual readings as partial and heterosexual desire as anxiously supported by the phantom of the homosexual other.

This Not Quite Promised Land

As I finished "Dulce," I thought back to early, unpublished (Rule has said, "unpublishable") manuscripts I had read in the archives. *Desert of the Heart* was not Rule's first novel; she spent years working through other manuscripts for novels and short stories before she wrote the characters of Evelyn and Ann with such unapologetic clarity. In fact, *Desert of the Heart* was her third or fourth novel, depending on how you count multiple, radical revisions of novels she titled *Who Are the Penitent*, *This Not Quite Promised Land* (in two entirely different versions), and *Not for Myself Exactly* (an alternate title for *This Not Quite Promised Land*) among other heavily reworked manuscripts. The negative titles would be echoed later in the 1970 novel that followed *Desert of the Heart*, *This Is Not for You*, in which Rule portrays from within a tortured lesbian subjectivity defined through internalized homophobia and denial. Thematically the traces of condemnation and repentance in these early manuscripts signal the struggle of the young Rule to break through literary and social restrictions to speak a different kind of desire.

Like Wilson's early poems in "Dulce," these fictions represent unrequited, forbidden, or dangerous heterosexual desire. The romance plots often stage uncertainty about gender performance, most frequently as lonely efforts by male characters to define manhood. In psychological isolation, feeling inadequate, these characters resist or conform to what they perceive as restrictions imposed by gender expectations. While male characters struggle with the exigencies of masculinity, female characters often recognize strength in each other. A few flashes that hint at the quality of Rule's later fiction capture this recognition between strong female characters. For example, one male character observes: "There can be, between two women, a sudden intimacy of direct recognition that, in comparison, makes even lovers seem remote from each other" (box 11, folder 2, 100). Reading forty years later, I can't help but wonder if crises of masculinity sometimes stand in for crises of femininity; the erotic charge of the "intimacy of direct recognition" seems barely disguised.

Gender transpositions and encoded desire in these manuscripts lead to insoluble technical problems concerning point of view and plotting. The various versions of *This Not Quite Promised Land* center on the thwarted love story of an Englishman (Derek Good) and an American woman. The woman character is suggestively named Page Benjamin, combining the youngest child and the beckoning page, the site of the writer's desire and struggle. In one version, their story is told (improbably) in a long retrospective narrative by Page's eventual, British husband (Peter Sargent) from their Vancouver home decades later. One of the many problems with the narrative is that there is no plausible reason why Derek and Page's affair should be forbidden, much less why Peter should know such intimate details about it. Page fears she would have to "give up conventional security" if she married Derek, but her family has already been described as vaguely nomadic and unconventional.

Rule's experimental manuscripts show a young writer trying to find ways to express sexual desire and discovering the imbrication of body and language, sexuality and social codes. In a sexual initiation scene, for example, Rule imagines erotic violence that merges pleasure and disgust, masculine aggression and female masochism: "Derek used Page's body with lust and brutality which she received, exalting in pain. He named her the foulness of his despair, and in those names she felt a wild joy. It was a shocking and magnificent night, out of which they came exhausted and free of any fear of separation" (box 11, folder 2, 27). In the margin, Rule has penciled "rewrite."

Using the map for rereading suggested by "Dulce," the struggle of lover and mistress, writer and blank page staged in this initiation yields multiple interpretive possibilities. The easiest way to read (and dismiss) these efforts would be to assume that heterosexuality is an imperfect, distorting disguise. We would assume that Rule is hiding the "real" lesbian subject behind a heterosexual screen in order to write for a mainstream audience. In fact, this reading resolves one of the major flaws of the text: once Derek is read as the literary cross-dressing of a lesbian lover for Page, the forbidden aspect of their love becomes plausible. But this reading mimics Oscar's reading of Wilson: once you have the key, the text becomes transparent. If we imagine coexisting, layered sexual meanings (such as Dulce discovers in rereading Wilson after Oscar's revelation) we can understand the sexual initiation scene in a more complex way. If we imagine that Rule is simultaneously staging anxious heterosexual desire and forbidden lesbian desire, a relay of associations emerges. First, we can discern a model of a heterosexual erotic based on a coupling of male aggression (*lust and brutality*) and misogynist anxiety (*the foulness of his despair*) with female passivity (*she received*) and masochism (*in those names she felt a wild joy*). When read as a displacement, this masculine, pornographic model of heterosexual desire fades into a model of lesbian desire that is infected and inflected by heterosexual disgust. This reading acknowledges the heterosexual screen, the lesbian subtext, and their imbrication. The lesbian aggressor, assuming Derek's role, uses Page sexually and speaks the sexual insults that name lesbian desire. She violates sexual taboo even while speaking the words that have always named it as taboo, foul, and forbidden. "Derek" uses the (blank) "Page" to claim the foul, despairing words that "name" lesbian desire in an erotic economy that only validates heterosexual desire. The misogyny of the heterosexual coupling transmutes into homophobia in the lesbian coupling.

Reclaiming the demonizing language releases the shocking, wild joy that Page experiences; the union realized in this struggle is verbal as well as physical: (re)possessing language as well as possessing bodies. Whether the language has been reclaimed or merely repeated is moot in this early effort. Rule's injunction to herself to rewrite reveals how important she thought this passage was, but reminds her (and us) that it was not yet resolved.

If we reread *This Not Quite Promised Land* as about *both* heterosexual initiation *and* lesbian love in an anxious, homophobic culture we can see the ways that heterosexual anxiety and lesbian denial inform each other. Further, we can imagine that lesbian desire is about more than the forbidden (*the foulness of despair*) even while marked through and through by the forbidden and by the violence of denial.

Rule arrived at the language of *Desert of the Heart* only after having navigated through the codes and detours of these first literary efforts. The first readers of *Desert of the Heart* in 1964, trapped in the unexamined contradictions of anxious homophobia Rule tries to unravel in the early manuscripts, responded to the first published novel with charged ambivalence. Readers reading in public, in the mainstream press for example, were able to see only what they could already recognize: demonized lesbian characters and a reincarnation of Radclyffe Hall. David Benedictus in the *Sunday Telegraph* (February 9, 1964) provides an exemplary reading of this type: "the relationship between the two principals is a tortuous and tormented one. Nevertheless, this is a literate, compassionate and bitter book, a sort of well, well, well, of loneliness." Benedictus fails to engage the text and can only see a repetition of his own expectations. He forces Rule into a figure of the lesbian writer that doesn't, in fact, fit.

Readers reading in private, with their own lives, resembled Dulce rereading Wilson; they found a more complexly layered text and traces of their own story. One woman, writing from England, said: "having only just discovered your novel *Desert of the Heart* I find that you have written my book for me. Oh not the same place, the same time or the same people. But it's the same sense, the same significance and the same expression. I have read and reread it about twenty times and you used all the words I would have used if I could have" (box 19, folder 9, 1971). In this more intimate bond of reading, Rule is constituted as *a* lesbian writer not assimilated to a single model of *the* lesbian writer; in the same movement, her reader finds the words to speak her own life and therefore to possess it more fully.

* * *

The ferry horn sounds and cuts short my imaginary voyage through Rule's early work. "Dulce," then, will be my guide through the rich but unsorted, contradictory papers from Rule's experimental years. As I raise my eyes from the pages of *Inland Passage*, Sturdies Bay comes into view. Waiting for the ferry to release its travelers, I strain to see the islanders awaiting the boat. Towering over the heads of the crowd, two tall women greet their neighbors and scan the crowd of foot passengers. I wave to them, Jane and Helen, welcoming hostesses, good neighbors, gentle survivors in their adopted land.

JANE RULE'S "HOME MOVIE": PROJECTING A LESBIAN SUBJECT

In a writer's notebook from 1967, Jane Rule wrote "Problem about short stories: I don't want to write thin magazine stories. That's why I start out without a story, just a tension or circumstance. Then I can catch a language, but without a direction I can't write a story. But impatience to get something on paper produces dutiful, dull totally discovered ideas or moments, suggestive scenes without point. I've got to get the 2 together, be willing to sit with a note book until I am ready out of a rich world to say something" (box 18, folder 14, June 14, 1967). Rule's desire to make *discursive exploration* the heart of her project rather than repeat "dutiful, dull . . . discovered ideas" prefigures current thinking about lesbian subjectivity. Rule's work bears out Monique Wittig's contention that when the lesbian writer enters language, she unwittingly reveals the unspoken heterosexual contract that shapes meaning in language and exerts material power in society. Confronting the heterosexual contract, lesbian critics and now queer theorists have moved in the last fifteen years from denouncing stereotypes and defining positive lesbian identities to the current discussion of subject positions and the desiring subject as markers of sexuality in language and literature. Efforts to theorize the lesbian writer and the lesbian reader/critic suggest new approaches to reading Rule's work.

Queer Theory: From Stereotype to Subject Position

In her introduction to *New Lesbian Criticism*, Sally Munt (1992) details the specific knot of anxieties that inhibit the lesbian critic or theorist as she tries *first* to characterize the current state of lesbian studies and *second*, her own position within this growing, shifting, sometimes treacherous field. Located in the territory where queer studies, women's studies, and critical theory overlap, lesbian studies is invigorated by current theoretical debates. But, as Munt points out, lesbian studies is not just another mode of poststructuralist practice. Lesbian criticism's "multi-discursive character" is also a product of many years of "reading between the lines, from the margins, inhabiting the text of dominant heterosexuality even as we undo it, undermine it, and construct our own destabilising readings" (xiii). The lesbian reader/critic has developed multidiscursive strategies by appropriating or adapting current theoretical models but, just as important, by recovering lesbian writers, like Rule, who have negotiated social and literary discourse in their efforts to open up lesbian subject positions. The lesbian reader/critic, like the lesbian writer, may, on the one hand, occupy a heady theoretical or imaginative position but she is inevitably also located in social and institutional environments that continue to be misogynist and homophobic. The tensions that inhibit the lesbian critic and writer, however, are also the ground of her creativity. In Rule's terms, what begin as inhibitions become "a rich world" from which to speak.

Bonnie Zimmerman has noted (Munt 6) that much lesbian theorizing has continued the work of 1970s lesbian feminists (Bunch, Frye, Rich) who figured lesbianism as an attack on the patriarchy and male-defined heterosexuality. In a groundbreaking article in 1993, Shane Phelan demonstrated the ways in which this form of lesbian feminist opposition, by continuing to focus on patriarchy and heterosexuality, risks bearing out the lessons of Lyotard and Foucault that: "being in opposition is one of the modes of participation within a system" (776).

Phelan argues further that recent lesbian theorists who retain "lesbian as a meaningful category" have begun to imagine a way out of this critical and political impasse. Citing Gloria Anzaldúa, Diana Fuss, Judith Butler, and Teresa de Lauretis, Phelan shows that these diverse theorists are moving "toward views of lesbianism as a critical site of gender deconstruction" (766). Having passed through Foucault, among others, these theorists are more concerned with finding effective strategies for representing subjectivity than with naming truths, what Rule might call "discovered ideas."

In Teresa de Lauretis's landmark article from 1990, "Eccentric Subjects: Feminist Theory and Historical Consciousness," she elaborates her concept of an "eccentric subject" as a "remapping of boundaries between bodies and discourses, identities and communities" (138), developed primarily by feminists of color and lesbian feminists. She says "such an eccentric point of view is necessary for feminist theory at this time, in order to sustain the subject's capacity for movement and displacement. . . . It is a position of resistance and agency, conceptually and experientially apprehended outside or in excess of the sociocultural apparatuses of heterosexuality, through a process . . . that is not only personal and political but also textual, a practice of language in the larger sense" (139). De Lauretis prefaces this discussion with a reading of a text that leads to the knowledge that stable notions of self and identity rooted in the past, in "home," are "based on exclusion and secured by terror" (136). Home must eventually be given up, replaced with an unstable but more dynamic notion of "community."

To shift discussion of Rule's work from a focus on stereotypes, or identity, to subject position, as queer theorists propose, allows for a more productive look at the creative process and the ways that language, gender, and sexuality shape each other. Rule is a self-consciously intertextual writer, drawing on canonical and noncanonical frames of reference, questioning or confirming ideas about meaning and literary form. Faced with an absence of literary foremothers or with lesbian texts that merely repeat the terms of the unwritten heterosexual contract, Rule has tried from her earliest work to create a poetics of possibility that refuses a fixed lesbian subject, whether demeaning or celebratory. Language, as the passage from her notebooks I quoted in the beginning demonstrates, is her testing ground; her goal is "to catch a language" rather than "tell" an already determined story.

"Home Movie": To Catch a Language

"Home Movie," a short story first published in *Sinister Wisdom* in 1980 and then reprinted in the collection *Outlander*, published by Naiad Press in 1982, provides a good point of departure for discussing Rule's effort "to catch a language" to create a lesbian subject formed within language but also in tension with it. Situated in Greece, marked as an originary site for lesbian subjectivity, the story centers on a North American woman, Alysoun, who is an artist and an outsider like many of Rule's characters. As a musician she interprets musical scores, "repeating" the music she is given, but "interpreting" it through her own talent and sensibility. As a visiting foreigner (on tour as a soloist, a clarinetist), she observes a society whose rules are familiar and yet different from the ones that formed her. She also looks back on her own formation with the perspective that distance and displacement allow. Through an act of literal and figurative "translation," she imagines her own desire for a Greek woman.

A series of projected images in which Alysoun is both spectator and spectacle articulate the formation of a lesbian subject. The projections begin with home movies glimpsed through an open window in Greece that trigger uncomfortable memories of home movies from her childhood in

America. Home movies she accidentally witnesses and then remembers capture images that are distorted, exaggerated, repeated, reversed, fragmented, and reassembled; the relatively crude apparatus of the hand-held camera, the repeated rituals of family holidays and the games families play by reversing the projector, zooming in to exaggerated close-up, speeding up and slowing down, all underscore the arbitrary, cliché character of the medium and, by extension, the limits and conventions of growing up middle class, white, and female in mid-twentieth-century America. The story ends with a televised performance that carries Alysoun's adult face back "home" while publishing her features throughout the world.

I will organize my discussion around the opening paragraph of the story that defines Alysoun's dilemma, the means Alysoun finds in the story to articulate herself as a desiring subject, and the triumphant final image of the story. The story follows a trajectory in which Alysoun moves from embarrassed passive spectator of herself as a child (framed in her father's home movies) to the confident active image of a successful artist beamed around the world. The primitive technology of home movies and the sophisticated high tech of satellite transmission each signal in different modes the ways in which a lesbian subject negotiates the languages of "home" and of the street, of family and culture, of the intimate and the performative.

> Alysoun Carr sat at a table in a street cafe in Athens drinking ouzo. Directly across from her, through an open window and onto a far wall, a "Home Movie" was being projected. A young couple grew larger on the wall. Suddenly the enormous head of a baby filled the whole window, as if it were going to be born into the street. Alysoun, careful in a foreign country never to make so melodramatic a gesture as to cover her eyes if she could help it, looked away. She added water to the ouzo and watched what had been clear, thick liquid thin and turn milky. She did not like the licorice aftertaste, but she liked the effect, which was a gentling of her senses so that she could receive things otherwise too bright or loud or pungent at a level of tolerance, even pleasure. In another ten minutes, if the movie lasted so long, she could watch it without dismay. (3)

Isolated in a public place, Alysoun is portrayed as a fascinated if embarrassed voyeur. The fantastic image of a baby in a home movie (who risks being born into the street) becomes a reflection/reminder of her own overexposed childhood; her first gesture is to look away, to numb or "gentle" her senses hoping to tolerate the spectacle/memory or even take pleasure in it. Significantly, the "ten minutes" needed for the ouzo (clear turned to murky) to take effect take the reader into Alysoun's reverie about her own childhood, and though we return only briefly to the spectacle on the far wall of the stranger's home, we do watch the home movies of Alysoun's memory, an internalized projection. The "young couple" of the first paragraph has been reduced to "her father" in the second, the mother eclipsed by the father's framing of Alysoun's childhood.

The technology of home movies (capturing holidays, creating an illusion of reversed action as the projector seems to pull a diver up through the water and back to the board) is understood as reactionary by Alysoun. The moment of unbearable intimacy and exposure she turned away from in the first paragraph takes her to the most dreaded moment in the childhood viewings–"when her own baby face would fill the frame." Alysoun is distinguished from the other family spectators in at least two ways. What provokes giggles in her siblings (the technological tricks of the camera and projector) creates alarm for Alysoun. Reversing the action (or the viewer's expectations) may be a game for her siblings, but Alysoun knows by the ways she has disappointed her father in adult life that one doesn't counter paternal expectations with impunity.

Further, she is her father's favorite ("Alysoun was the prettiest baby I ever saw"), perceived as beautiful in the family films even as she offers up a "silent snort" instead of a smile, but she knows she has disappointed him by growing up into an adult who, unlike her siblings, has "failed" to reproduce. Her siblings took pleasure in tricks that turned visual expectations inside out in the father's home movie, but Alysoun creates disappointment by living against paternal expectations as an adult. The split between the cherished, paternal image of herself as a baby and her perplexed adult self is unsettling. "Only the camera could give him back that pretty baby who, snorting out at her adult self, made Alysoun feel as disoriented as if she had been physically dragged by the camera back up out of the water and onto the spring board." In the story, Alysoun has learned that only by reproducing the heterosexual parents' scenario is the child allowed to become an adult, to move beyond the frame of the family of origin into a family of her own that reproduces the home movie in a new generation.

In the present moment, a glimpse back at the Greek home movie across the way shows Alysoun a remarkably bad representation of a flower garden. She is led to remark on the universality of cliché–rather than the universality of great art. "People talked about the universality of great art, but far more universal is the mark of the amateur, trapping all he loves in the cage of his unpracticed seeing. . . . " It is the clichés of family photos, the conventions of middle-class life that repeat themselves endlessly across cultures and borders, capturing the loved one in the prison of the familiar. Alysoun would remain stymied by the language of cliché if it weren't for other languages she learns to use, gifts from other female characters: the languages of flowers, music, and desire. These female characters (an unstable but dynamic community of sorts) assist Alysoun to project a lesbian subject rather than turn away from the image of a presexual, subjected child.

In a gesture that reverses the Lacanian model of the child moving into the Symbolic Order as he separates from the prelinguistic bond with the mother, Alysoun remembers when she learned to name the world around her as her mother taught her the language of flowers. In the story, Alysoun retrieves this language at the invitation of Constantina, a Greek translator who, like Alysoun, is thirty. Constantina, comfortable in her Greek homeland, rescues Alysoun from her awkward isolation and from overbearing male colleagues as she asks for Alysoun's help in translating a Eudora Welty story into Greek.

Because she has paid attention to Alysoun, Constantina knows her most important secrets: that she doesn't have a mysterious lover (an excuse to keep men at a distance) and that she knows the names of flowers. She offers her the opportunity to use this gift–to exchange that knowledge for a pleasant escape from the loneliness and tensions of being on tour. Alysoun, usually self-protective, is pleased to be known in this way, on her terms. In contrast to the alarm she recalls when thinking back to her father's home movies, Alysoun remembers learning about flowers from her mother: "she had learned the names of flowers very early in her vocabulary, where they stayed certain and bright, a gift from her mother. . . . In memory no film had ever picked from her, Alysoun, not much more than flower-high, walked with her mother naming the last of the Daffodils–Carlton, King Alfred–and the early tulips–White Triumphator, General de Wet. . . . She was walking, nearly hidden in the rhododendrons, saying, 'Unique, Pink Pearl, Sappho . . . ' when she slept. It was noon when she woke" (7). The flowers become real to Alysoun in language, signaling that nature itself is a product of discourse, or at least that nature becomes accessible through the mother tongue. In a state of dreamy half-sleep, Alysoun moves from early to late spring, from military masculine names to sexualized feminine names "pink pearl, Sappho." Her mother's garden thus leads her back to Sappho, giving her a world she can offer Constantina in language as well as a means to name herself.

Constantina also awakens other memories: of her best friend (Bobby Anne) who played the clarinet, marked in the story as a "masculine" instrument in contrast to the violin, piano, flute, or the overly feminine harp. Alysoun has become a professional clarinetist because she wanted to be like her friend and discovered that it was the instrument she loved rather than the girl. Her father disapproved the choice because "he never liked influences on his children other than his own" (9).

Alysoun and Constantina spend the afternoon before Alysoun's concert walking among flower vendors, creating what they call a "Eudora Welty bouquet" as Alysoun identifies the flowers from the story Constantina is translating. With this exchange of words and flowers their friendship is established and they walk arm in arm as Alysoun muses: "accompanied by a man, [she] felt not so much protected as invisible, and she sometimes wondered if her need to vomit or scream was a fear not of the dangers of the street but of obliteration. With Constantina she had the odd, light-hearted sense of being conspicuous and safe" (11).

Three other moments in the story delineate Alysoun's newly created subject position in a language she at once remembers, offers up, and claims as her own. First, alone in her hotel room, arranging the magnificent bouquet they acquired, Alysoun imagines herself confessing another secret to Constantina: she had loved a woman long ago who has since become unreal to her. As she plays out a fantasy conversation with Constantina in her mind, "Fear woke in her womb, feeling so like desire that if someone very loving, very skillful had been there at that moment to hold her, to touch her, she would not have been resisted. Constantina" (13). A repressed memory that had turned to fear is transformed back into desire through her fantasy seduction by Constantina.

The second moment that marks Alysoun's new knowledge involves another fantasy exchange with a woman. She begins a letter to Eudora Welty. She knows she won't send the letter, but it is the gesture of writing, of putting words to her new knowledge that is important. After trying to explain the pleasure thinking about her story has brought, Alysoun writes about what the story has taught her: "I've discovered that fear is desire, not shame or guilt or inadequacy or any of those other things. The question to ask about fear is not what are you afraid of but what do you want. If you know what you want and you can have it, then fear doesn't seem like fear at all . . . " (13).

Finally, after a successful concert, Alysoun is taking her bow when she becomes aware of "the cameras." This time, her father is a mute spectator as her concert is beamed via satellite around the world. Transforming the confining childhood memories of the opening paragraph, Alysoun looks into the camera "and for one dangerous second she was tempted to snort before, instead, she smiled her full . . . professional smile through a rain of flowers her mother had taught her to name" (14).

Languages learned and practiced in a shifting community of women allow Alysoun to break out of the infantilizing frame of unmet heterosexual expectations and to claim an articulate lesbian subjectivity. Significantly, Rule invents a character whose sexuality is defined less by the object of her desire than by the desiring subject. The seduction by Constantina is imagined but not realized, the letter to Welty is composed but never sent. Constantina is not so much the object of her desire as a means for her to name it, to become a desiring subject. The final image not only transforms the opening image of which Alysoun is an unwilling spectator into a triumphant projection in which Alysoun is a confident performer, it also signals the inevitable coexistence of the intimate and public, the personal and social aspects of sexual subjectivity. Alysoun's claiming of an adult, lesbian subjectivity is not just a private matter, a hidden hotel fantasy. It entails public scrutiny–but whether or not her family of origin will "see" the full meaning of the image on their television screen, Alysoun is ready to project it.

WORKS CITED

Benedictus, David. Rev. of *Desert of the Heart*, by Jane Rule. *The Sunday Telegraph* 9 February 1964, n.p.

de Lauretis, Teresa. "Eccentric Subjects: Feminist Theory and Historical Consciousness." *Feminist Studies* 16 (1990): 115-150.

Felman, Shoshana. *What Does a Woman Want? Reading and Sexual Difference*. Baltimore and London: The Johns Hopkins UP, 1993.

Munt, Sally, ed. *New Lesbian Criticism: Literary and Cultural Readings*. New York: Columbia UP, 1992.

Phelan, Shane. "(Be)coming Out: Lesbian Identity and Politics." *SIGNS* 18 (1993): 765-790.

Rich, Adrienne. "Vesuvius at Home: The Power of Emily Dickinson." *Parnassus: Poetry in Review* (1976); in *On Lies, Secrets, and Silence*. Adrienne Rich. New York: W. W. Norton & Co., 1979. 157-184.

Rule, Jane. *After the Fire*. Tallahassee: Naiad Press, 1989.

______. *Contract With the World*. New York: Harcourt, Brace, Jovanovich, 1980; Tallahassee: Naiad Press, 1982.

______. *Desert of the Heart*. Toronto: Macmillan, New York: The World Publishing Co., London: Secker & Warburg, 1964; Tallahassee, Naiad Press, 1983.

______. *Inland Passage*. Tallahassee: Naiad Press, 1985.

______. *The Jane Rule papers* in the University of British Columbia Library, Special Collections and Archives Division include 36 boxes (6.1 m.) acquired from 1988 to 1993. The collection includes notes, manuscripts, drafts, galleys, and correspondence relating to her published and unpublished novels and short stories; biographical and autobiographical material, nonfiction manuscripts, and personal and professional correspondence; reviews of her work and audio recordings of interviews and readings.

______ . *Lesbian Images*. Toronto and Garden City: Doubleday, 1975.

______ . *Memory Board*. Tallahassee: Naiad Press, 1987.

______ . *Outlander*. Tallahassee: Naiad Press, 1981.

_____ . *This Is Not For You*. New York: McCall Publishing Co., 1970; Tallahassee: Naiad Press, 1984.

______ . *The Young in One Another's Arms*. Garden City and Toronto: Doubleday, 1977; Tallahassee: Naiad Press, 1984.

Schweickart, Patricinio P. "Reading Ourselves: Toward a Feminist Theory of Reading." *Gender and Reading: Essays on Readers, Texts, and Contexts*. Ed. Elizabeth A. Flynn and Patricinio P. Schweickart. Baltimore and London: The Johns Hopkins UP, 1986.

Terry, Jennifer. "Theorizing Deviant Historiography." *differences: A Journal of Cultural Studies* 3.2 (1991): 55-74.

Wittig, Monique. "The Mark of Gender" in *The Straight Mind and Other Essays*. Boston: Beacon Press, 1992. Originally published in 1985.

Built Out of Books: Lesbian Energy and Feminist Ideology in Alternative Publishing

Kate Adams

Allan Hancock College

SUMMARY. This paper chronicles the birth of lesbian-feminist publishing in the 1970s, a significant but often overlooked chapter of American alternative publishing history, and one that would help create the circumstances supporting a flourishing lesbian and gay literature in the 1980s and 1990s. Between 1968 and 1973, over 500 feminist and lesbian publications appeared across the country, and what would become an organized network of independent women's bookstores began to appear. In 1976, a group of feminist tradeswomen–printers, booksellers, and others–would meet in the first of a series of Women in Print conferences that would give a name to the fledgling alternative press movement. Fueled by the energy of the women's movement, lesbians were instrumental actors in a variety of feminist publishing enterprises that, taken together, constituted a

Kate Adams has a PhD in American Studies from the University of Texas at Austin, where she wrote a dissertation entitled "Paper Lesbians: Alternative Publishing and the Politics of Lesbian Representation in the United States, 1950-1990." She has published essays of lesbian literary and cultural studies in *Radical Revisions: Lesbian Texts & Contexts* (NYU, 1990), *Listening to Silences: New Essays in Feminist Criticism* (Oxford, 1994), and *Tilting the Tower: Lesbians Teaching Queer Subjects* (Routledge, 1994). She teaches English at Allan Hancock College. Correspondence may be addressed: English Department, Allan Hancock College, Santa Maria, CA 93454. E-mail:kate_adams@telis.org

[Haworth co-indexing entry note]: "Built Out of Books: Lesbian Energy and Feminist Ideology in Alternative Publishing." Adams, Kate. Co-published simultaneously in *Journal of Homosexuality* (The Haworth Press, Inc.) Vol. 34, No. 3/4, 1998, pp. 113-141; and: *Gay and Lesbian Literature Since World War II: History and Memory* (ed: Sonya L. Jones) The Haworth Press, Inc., 1998, pp. 113-141; and: *Gay and Lesbian Literature Since World War II: History and Memory* (ed: Sonya L. Jones) Harrington Park Press, an imprint of The Haworth Press, Inc., 1998, pp. 113-141. Single or multiple copies of this article are available for a fee from The Haworth Document Delivery Service [1-800-342-9678, 9:00 a.m. - 5:00 p.m. (EST). E-mail address: getinfo@haworth.com].

unique brand of print activism that illuminated and revised categories of identity; empowered individuals to overcome social isolation and discrimination; and informed nascent lesbian and feminist communities about strategies of resistance. *[Article copies available for a fee from The Haworth Document Delivery Service: 1-800-342-9678. E-mail address: getinfo@haworth.com]*

> I had worked in the civil rights movement; I had worked against the war; but prior to women's liberation, it had simply not occurred to me to miss myself in all the books I plowed through.
>
> –Melanie Kaye/Kantrowitz[1]

In an essay-memoir cataloguing the changes brought on by "the sixties"–that constellation of forces originating in the civil rights movement, the new left's activism against the Vietnam war, the women's liberation movement, and a host of related, countercultural challenges to the United States of the Cold War 1950s–Kirkpatrick Sale uses a metaphor that captures a central apprehension of many Americans who were changed by that decade of popular protest and challenge. He writes that in his apartment there are two bookshelves; one is filled with books "from and about the 60's" whose publication was vital to him and for which he feels, "the word comes to me, affection"; still, he rarely looks at or consults those volumes. On another shelf, above his desk, are the books he often consults and rereads, most of them published well after the 1960s had ended:

> And yet, there is not one book on that second shelf, I think, that could have been conceived or written without the sequences of events, feelings, insights, connections, and associations known as the 60s . . . [without] the ideological, political, psychological reorientations that a small number of people provoked at that time within a great many millions . . . not merely in those who in fact became "radicalized" (letting that phrase stand for a lot of things) but in those many others whose lives today would have been literally unthinkable fifteen years ago.[2]

The popular protest movements that so changed the United States in the second half of the century were built upon the activism of tens of thousands; they were built upon the bodies of men and women marching, boycotting, sitting at lunch counters, or not sitting in buses. But in another sense that Sale captures here, the '60s revolutions were built out of books. Millions were inspired to activism by the words and ideas delivered by a rapidly expanding alternative press. The books, newspapers, and journals of the alternative press did indeed change many lives, and among them were lesbians whose lives today would be unthinkable, in Sale's phrase, if not for the profound impact on the national life that the alternative press was able to effect.

The "underground" or "counterculture" press has had its share of chronicles, but the histories that they produce often fail to consider that the same years that produced an alternative press organized around left politics and countercultural rebellions also saw the creation of a staggering array of publishing activities specifically devoted to the projects of women's liberation.[3] These new lesbian and feminist papers–and the journals, presses, radio programs, bookstores, and other alternative media outlets that would follow them in the decade to come–were supported by a readership that found in their pages inspiration for and evidence of the dramatic social and political changes being wrought by the activism of the women's liberation and nascent gay liberation movements. The "necessary bread" of these popular protest movements was published in literally hundreds of new newspapers and journals. Some short-lived and parochial, some with more lasting and more national influence, these papers and journals espoused revolutionary social change that affected millions of women. The "visionary tradeswomen"[4] who founded presses and printshops and bookstores, many of them lesbian, created a lasting network of institutions, many of which would survive through the 1980s era of backlash to stand as an important monument to the creative and political potential of cultural feminism.[5]

Different chroniclers mark the beginnings of women's movement publishing with different symbolic moments. David Armstrong points to a 1965 document informally distributed among women activists in the Civil Rights Movements and the New Left. The document, "Sex and Caste: A Kind of Memo," was the work of Mary King and Casey Hayden, white southerners working with SNCC in Mississippi, who had links as well to the New Left. Written as an extension of the informal conversations the author had been having with "other women in the peace and freedom movements," the memo has been seen as "a catalyst to feminism," in Sara Evans's words, articulating the frustrations that women, especially white middle-class women, were feeling in the predominantly male-led and increasingly nationalist SNCC.[6] Others point to another informally distributed but very different document–"The SCUM Manifesto"–mimeographed and handed out on New York City street corners in 1967 by its author Valerie Solanis. Still others point to the first issue of the first women's liberation newsletter, *Voices of the Women's Liberation Move-*

ment, published in March 1968 in Chicago, or to the antisexist pamphleteering of NOW activists in Pittsburgh and New Jersey who founded both KNOW, Inc, the first feminist press in the country, and WOWI (Women in Words and Images), whose best-selling pamphlet *Dick and Jane Were Victims* took on the sex-role stereotyping in children's textbooks in 1969. Many point to 1970 as the watershed year, which saw a number of watershed publishing events: the first distribution of the Radicalesbians' influential essay, "Woman-Identified Woman"; the takeover of *Rat*, a left alternative newspaper in New York City, by its women staff and the publication therein of Robin Morgan's "Goodbye to All That"; the sit-in by 100 feminists at the offices of the *Ladies Home Journal* as well as the class action suits brought against *Newsweek*, *Time*, *Life*, *Fortune*, and *Sports Illustrated* for sex discrimination.[7]

Perhaps a more useful symbol for what would come to be called the "Women in Print Movement" is not a particular year or publication, but a purchase. When in 1969, the first investment of a new organization called D.C. Women's Liberation was a mimeograph machine,[8] it was a symbol of how central to feminist activism alternative publishing would be. Feminists took seriously A. J. Leibling's well-known adage: "Freedom of the press is guaranteed only to those who own one." Women's liberation activists brought with them from the civil rights and new left movements "a growing tradition of politically radical self-publishing," in Shirley Frank's phrase, leading two early chroniclers of women's publishing, Polly Joan and Andrea Chesman, to assert that "more than any other movement in history, feminism has been identified with publishing."[9]

That identification would have a consequent, far-reaching effect on the possibilities of lesbian self-representation in U.S. culture. Women's liberation would open unprecedented space for the expansion of paper lesbianism, and much of the alternative publishing work it created would be supported by lesbian energy. Particularly in the 1970s, the paper lesbian was a paper feminist; that is, lesbian women helped shape the voice and politics of feminism by devoting their creative and entrepreneurial energies to the production of feminist alternative media enterprises.

THE MAILING ADDRESS OF THE MOVEMENT

> I wrote a letter asking for some literature of the Women's Liberation Movement that I could read. It was for a social studies report that never materialized. But that is irrelevant like school is. The important thing is I read the stuff and immediately agreed with everything.
>
> –Connie Dvorkin, 1970[10]

In the latter part of 1969, the mainstream media seemed to discover overnight the groundswell growth of feminism. Suddenly, press coverage of the women's liberation movement increased tenfold. The *New York Times*, whose coverage of women's issues in 1966 had resulted in only 168 stories, published 603 stories in 1970 and triple that many in 1974. Television stories on the movement tripled from 1969 to 1970 as well.[11]

Then the anthologies of feminist writings began to be published. Not unlike the "instant books" that suddenly appear in airports and grocery stores hoping to cash in on some national fad, crisis, or disaster, best-sellers like *Sisterhood Is Powerful* and less well known but popular titles like *Radical Feminism*, *The New Woman*, and *Liberation Now!* appeared, all from mainstream, corporate presses–Random House, NYT/Quadrangle, Bobbs-Merrill/Fawcett, and Dell. But a quick look at the acknowledgments pages of these early anthologies reveals their prehistory: much of their contents had their origins in the growing left and countercultural press underground and in the pages of the small, independent feminist newspapers and magazines that were springing up all over the country. For example, the articles in *Sisterhood is Powerful* were drawn from both the left alternative press (*Ramparts*, *Rat*, *Leviathan*) and the new radical feminist periodicals (*Voices of the Women's Liberation Movement* and *Women: A Journal of Liberation*). Most of the material in *Radical Feminism* was first published in *Notes from the First Year*, an annual journal that appeared three times and was published by New York Radical Feminists. *The New Woman* was actually a reprint of an issue of *motive* magazine, whose publisher, the United Methodist Church Board of Education, was dumbfounded by editor Charlotte Bunch-Week's special double issue and amazed by its sales–60,000 copies–and the controversy that it created.[12] The editors of *Liberation Now*, who culled the pages of *Up From Under* and *Women: A Journal of Liberation* among other early papers for their selections, marked their difference from the mainstream publishing establishment by intentionally omitting their names from their book's cover, so as not to "distort the fact that the book was made possible by the efforts of every woman whose work appears herein," not to mention the work of the unnamed editors, typesetters, and printers who first brought their work to print.[13]

Before the *New York Times* or Random House discovered them, unnamed and unnumbered writer-activists and activist-publishers of the women's movement had been collaborating in small groups and collectives for several years, inventing and then filling the pages of new feminist periodicals, the paper samizdats with names like *off our backs*, *It Ain't Me, Babe*, *Lavender Woman*, *New Directions for Women*, *Lesbian Tide*, *The*

Furies, *The Kalamazoo Woman*, *Point Blank Times*, and dozens of others. In fact, just as the mainstream media was discovering feminism, radical feminists were debating the merits of publishing with or boycotting the mainstream in favor of establishing and supporting the new alternative media. Early on, feminists worried about the power of the mainstream press to co-opt the women's liberation movement or to misrepresent it, and different feminist groups asserted different strategies to avoid such results, such as allowing only female reporters from the mainstream press to cover movement news stories.[14] Toby Marotta notes in his *The Politics of Homosexuality* that by the fall of 1969, "avoiding the established media had become a tenet of Radicalesbian operating procedure." Two of the most prominent of the New York-based Radicalesbians, Rita Mae Brown and Martha Shelley, asserted "that in order to avoid being co-opted radicals should publish only in alternative journals like *Rat* and *Come Out!*" (248). As a result of such tactics, between March 1968 and August 1973, over 560 new publications produced by feminists appeared in the United States,[15] each one serving as a mailing address for the movement.

The regional newspapers–some of them no more than 6-page mimeographed newsletters in the beginning–were where tens of thousands of women could find the women's liberation movement in their own communities. Before there were women's centers or bookstores, health clinics or credit unions, the newspapers represented a place where women could put a face on the ideas and experiments of feminism by joining with other women to read and write and talk about them. Most often established in larger cities and college towns, following the pattern of left/political and countercultural alternative papers, the local women's paper meant that the movement had arrived, *here*–wherever here was: Chicago, Kalamazoo, Sacramento, Houston, Pittsburgh. Thousands of women took their first step toward joining the women's liberation movement simply by finding it–in newsprint. In the pages of the paper, women found instructions for setting up a CR group, or ads for roommates; they found Marxist, socialist, and anarchist analyses of women's condition, and deeply personal accounts of individual writers' lives and struggles. Readers found event calendars, discussion group announcements, and other kinds of encouragements to join in a movement, including regular invitations to come down to the office and help put out the next issue of the paper, a staple feature of most women's liberation periodicals, since most were always chronically underfunded and reliant on volunteer labor for their continued existence.

Many of the common features of women's liberation newspapers can be found in the pages of *It Ain't Me, Babe*, a regional paper serving the Bay

Area of California. Established in Berkeley by Alice Malloy, who would later help start the Oakland women's bookstore, A Woman's Place, with her lover Carol Wilson, *It Ain't Me, Babe* began publishing in 1970, about the same time that *off our backs*, founded by Marilyn Webb in Washington, D.C., began appearing. While *off our backs* gained national prominence and is still publishing, and *It Ain't Me, Babe* remained more local in influence and lasted only a few years, both newspapers served similar purposes in their early years and codified features that would be imitated in later, more well known feminist periodicals such as *Ms.*

The pages of *It Ain't Me, Babe* reflect the early years and emphases of women's liberation in a regional context. When the first issue hit the streets of Berkeley in January 1970, its front page featured a photo of a crowd of women at a protest, their clenched fists upraised, and a line drawing of a long-haired figure clothed in a martial-arts workout costume, her body tensed forward in posture of readiness. The three front-page articles recounted the events of the previous week, surrounding U.C. Berkeley's offering of a new P.E. course that quarter, Karate 1–for men only. In protest, 60 women showed up to pre-enroll for the course, chanting "Self Defense for Women Now!" and passing out pamphlets explaining "the importance of self-defense as it related to the daily oppression of women" and asserting that "women's physical weakness and its psychological consequences can only be overcome through developing their bodies." The P.E. department "not only refused to let them pre-enroll but called in the cops who threatened the women with arrest." The front-page focus on ending gender-based discrimination in the university continued inside the paper, where an article addressed simply to "Sisters" folded out into a two-page spread, listing demands made of the U.C. chancellor that included curriculum revision and expansion; admission and hiring programs that would result in a student body and faculty at least 50% female; birth control information on demand at the student health center; maternity and paternity leave for all students and employees; and an immediate end to "housing regulations and all dormitory rules relating to women" that took for granted the university's *in loco parentis* role in the private lives of its female students.[16]

Not all of the paper's reporting was centered on Berkeley or the university, however; *It Ain't Me, Babe* also contained articles on national and international news stories of interest to women, based on reporting from the major dailies or wire services, or from the Liberation News Service or the Underground Press Syndicate, alternative organizations created by and for the operators of underground left and countercultural papers.[17] Or the alternative press itself would be the focus rather than the provider of articles and stories: *It Ain't Me, Babe* ran several stories, including one in cartoon form, about the women staffers of the New Left paper *Rat*, who, tired of the patronizing attitude of its male editors toward women's liberation stories, staged a takeover of the magazine and put out their own issues. Still, the primary focus of *It Ain't Me, Babe* was on raising consciousness close to home; it served readers in the Bay Area, with distribution points in Berkeley, Oakland, San Francisco, and San Jose, among others. Even the "Female Liberation Almanac," a quasi-regular feature of the paper, expressed a regional slant and a penchant for exalting both the famous and the unknown: the February 1970 almanac, for example, celebrated both the date of Susan B. Anthony's birth in 1820 and the day in 1965 that "Mona Hutchins (then a 19-year-old student at U.C. Berkeley active in the Free Speech Movement) became the first woman to ride on the outside steps of a San Francisco cable car," challenging the often-enforced but unwritten rule that women must ride inside.[18]

The assumption that given the necessary information, women would come to understand and resist their oppression in both private and public life is the primary editorial principle of women's liberation newspapers like *It Ain't Me, Babe*. The slow, accretive rhythm of the consciousness-raising group and its transformations of individual lives permeates the newspaper, especially in those features that focus on women's relationships with men and other women. One senses it in the regular cartoons of comic book artist Trina Robbins, which featured the continuing saga of "Belinda Berkeley," a young woman beginning to perceive that working as a secretary to support her "old man" while he writes his novel is not what she anticipated doing with her B.A. in English. One perceives it in the rough, barely edited personal narrative called "Sex: An Open Letter from a Sister," in which a woman haltingly, but with growing boldness, recounts how she began talking to other women about the "myth" of the vaginal orgasm:

> I've talked to eighteen women so far (not counting my mother) and all but two are exactly as I am. Clitoral-manual [sic]. When I asked open ended questions most women hemmed and hawed. But when I put the matter straight, made my own confession like at the beginning of this article I heard "yes, yes me too." And were they relieved.[19]

The work of women talking honestly to each other across differences and divisions undergirds as well the frustrated voice of the pseudonymous author of "Consciousness for What?" as she critiques women's liberation in general and the CR group particularly for disdaining and dismissing the interests of married women with children; the same theme is elaborated in Susan Griffin's magnanimous rebuttal to it:

> I had a child so that I would be a "woman" and not just a "girl." I wanted big hips, big breasts full of milk, I wanted to be Sophia Loren. Some woman ten years younger than me comes along. She's free I say to myself. . . . She says, why don't you come to meetings, and I give her a blank stare and point to my daughter and she says "That's just a cop out," and I want to kick her in the ass. . . . Now in a more calm moment, when my kid is in daycare and I'm in front of the typewriter, I can be generous with the seventeen year old . . . [her] shrillness is part of her survival cry against the entire weight of Western civilization, a civilization bent on putting her in the kitchen and making her pregnant.

The CR group is central as well to the widely reprinted article by Judy Grahn that originally appeared in *It Ain't Me, Babe* under the title "Lesbian as Bogeywoman," an early response to the growing gay/straight split that so vexed women's liberation activities:

> One night at my regular women's liberation group meeting one of the women said, "You know, the first night you told us you were a lesbian, I sat in terror for the rest of the meeting, waiting for you to attack me or something."[20]

The risk of turning one's own individual coming-to-consciousness into speech and then into action is acknowledged, encouraged, and celebrated in the newspaper. Indeed, the newspaper is in a sense a movable, newsprint CR group, expanding participation in that patient, primary, grassroots form of activism to anyone who reads its pages. Turning the slow dawning of consciousness–that "click" of understanding that *Ms.* magazine made so famous and that was the engine of the CR group–into a larger conversation among women about their cultural and social roles was the inspiration that undergirded the feminist alternative press.

THE LAVENDER PRESENCE

> Walking to graduate school classes at the university in North Carolina, I put the width of the sidewalk between me and the woman sitting at the literature table in front of the library. The pamphlets and two-cent newsletters–*Research Triangle Women's Liberation Newsletter*, August 11, 1969–were loose on the cardboard table and were not safely *in* the library.
>
> –Minnie Bruce Pratt[21]

Newspapers like *It Ain't Me, Babe* and *off our backs*, although founded by lesbians and significantly influenced and supported by lesbian women, were not specifically lesbian-feminist in their editorial outlook. Lesbian presence in the women's liberation movement was one among many issues debated and discussed in their pages, along with reproductive freedom and abortion rights, the ERA, job discrimination, the economic inequalities of marriage, etc. Both *It Ain't Me, Babe* and *off our backs* defined themselves as women's liberation or feminist periodicals, not lesbian-feminist ones. Yet lesbians were just as central in the production of these general interest feminist newspapers as they were in more specifically lesbian-feminist ones, such as *Lavender Woman* in Chicago and *Lesbian Tide* in Los Angeles.

Certainly for lesbian women, the mere existence of a women's liberation newspaper in their community brought the promise of life-altering possibilities and goes a long way toward explaining the overrepresentation of lesbian women in the founding and running of newspapers, journals, bookstores, and publishing houses. For older generations of lesbians, the local paper meant diminishing isolation, if they should wish it; it meant heretofore undreamed-of possibilities for connection with others.

For most lesbians through the 1960s and into the 1970s, the possibilities for active, out participation in American culture were just as bleak as they had been in the 1950s. Foraging through secondhand bookstores and prowling libraries for traces of the paper lesbian continued to be the staple, time-consuming, and furtive tools of consciousness-raising for scores of individual lesbians in the years before the women's liberation movement and the alternative press opened up the discourse. Judy Grahn, a working-class lesbian student at Howard University in the early 1960s, remembers that when she went to the Library of Congress looking for information about lesbian existence, she was confronted with locked stacks accessible only to those with expert credentials. Carol Seajay, who hunted down secondhand lesbian pulps as a Michigan high school student in the late 1960s, trained herself to read them only up to the last twenty pages, to avoid sharing the lesbian protagonist's inevitable tragic end. Kay Tobin, an isolated lesbian working as a researcher for the *Christian Science Monitor*, was troubled that what little material she could find about lesbianism was filed under "perversions" at her place of work, but it was there that she found a copy of well-known psychiatrist Robert Robertiello's *Voyage from Lesbos*, his account of the successful cure of a lesbian patient. She made an appointment with him, drove from Boston to New York to keep it, and after making a few open-ended queries, "came to the real question: 'How do I meet others?' " Much to her surprise, he gave her an old issue of *The*

Ladder and Tobin "drove back to Boston on a cloud," making plans to join the D.O.B. and change her life:

> I can meet other women. I will join this group and I will work in it until I find somebody. If I join the New York chapter and don't find anybody there, I'll go to Chicago and join the Chicago chapter. If I don't find anybody there, I'll go to San Francisco.[22]

It is almost inconceivable from a contemporary vantage point that only three decades ago, a trained researcher's only entree into lesbian conversation and community depended on the casual knowledge of a curing psychiatrist, or that a lesbian student would be locked away from the books in which her culture examined her.[23] The point is that for lesbian women coming of age in the 1960s and for those even younger, lesbian visibility within the women's liberation movement meant a tremendous paradigm shift; the presence of a more open, available, and various discourse about lesbian existence outside the pages of pulp fiction and pulp psychology fundamentally altered their experience of their sexuality relative to the majority culture and relative to the experience of lesbians before them.

Tobin, Seajay, and Grahn are unique lesbians of their generation in that they would all go on to play significant roles in the lesbian-feminist alternative publishing movement of the 1970s. Tobin would use the D.O.B. and *The Ladder* as her springboard into political activism, and she would edit one of the first anthologies of gay/lesbian coming-out stories, *The Gay Crusaders*, in 1972. Seajay would found the San Francisco women's bookstores, Old Wives' Tales, and publish *Feminist Bookstores Newsletter*, which would become a bible for the feminist bookstore business, serving to link the growing number of women's bookstores and publishing houses. Grahn's self-publication of her own prose and poetry would lead her to found The Women's Press Collective in 1978, an important early publisher of the work of Pat Parker, Alta, Susan Griffin, and others. Yet the experiences that inspired them to these efforts–coming out into an information vacuum, being cut off from access to information about themselves–were completely common to lesbian life throughout the United States before the women's liberation movement and the explosion of paper lesbianism the feminist alternative publishing inspired. The debilitating effects of their invisibility in the American mainstream go a long way toward explaining why so many lesbians found themselves actively engaged in constructing a network of alternative media that could announce their presence to the culture at large.

That the culture at large did not and would not recognize lesbian existence in positive terms unless forced to do so by lesbians themselves was the lesson of *The Ladder* and its assimilationist politics. The lesbian bookwomen of the 1970s, however, pursued a different relation to the mainstream: confrontational and, to varying degrees, separatist, the paper lesbians of women's liberation were more interested in bringing down the establishment than in assimilation on the establishment's terms. Whereas *The Ladder* often published generally positive articles commenting on mainstream media's attention to lesbian and gay existence, even when that attention was blatantly homophobic in nature, lesbian-feminist journals of the 1970s were much more apt to excoriate, subvert, or ignore the mainstream media's construction of lesbianism in pursuit of their own radical rather than assimilationist agendas. For example, in 1964 *The Ladder's* "Cross Currents" column praises *LIFE* magazine for publishing "humorous anecdotes about Gertrude Stein and her friend Alice B. Toklas" in an excerpt from Hemingway's recently published *A Moveable Feast*; with anticipation and enthusiasm, the article goes on to commend *LIFE* for interviewing some San Francisco D.O.B. members for a future article about homosexuals. In contrast, in 1973, three lesbians calling themselves "Collective Lesbian International Terrors"–Maricla Moyano, Susan Cavin, and Marcia Segerberg–and organized specifically "to counterattack recent media insults against Lesbians" began publishing a series of statements in the feminist media. Collectively known as the C.L.I.T. Papers, these statements encouraged "strong militant Lesbian voices" to counter "media infractions" and support lesbian-feminist media:

> to halt co-optation of Lesbians by the media [we] ask that all Lesbian-feminist writers and readers not . . . publish in, read, or buy the straight press. The reason behind this request is to prevent the straight media from taking our ideas under their liberal umbrella. It is a misuse of our issues and energy. Buying the straight media, we become paralyzed by the hopelessness of the world situation as presented to us by the Male News Front.

The C.L.I.T. Papers were widely reprinted in lesbian and feminist papers across the nation, beginning with *off our backs* and *Majority Report.* Eleven years after *The Ladder* praised *LIFE* for mentioning Gertrude Stein and interviewing lesbians, the C.L.I.T. papers appeared once more in a lesbian-feminist quarterly that would use *LIFE* magazine's distinctive cover design–a black-and-white cover photo under its block-letter logo: white capital letters boxed in red–for its own photo cover design. In this case, though, the white capital letters inside the red box at the top left of the cover spelled out *DYKE* rather than *LIFE*, and under the quarterly's name was a full-page photograph of three young, white lesbians, grinning into the camera, dressed in swimsuits and cutoff shorts and looking as if they had just waded out of the lake.[24]

The lesbians of *DYKE* and the lesbians who wrote the C.L.I.T. papers; the lesbians who, like Carol Seajay and others, were creating alternative publishing institutions with their energy; the lesbians who, like Judy Grahn in the west and Rita Mae Brown in the east, were providing the theoretical essays and poems and novels for those new institutions to print–all of these women were engaged in activities that would significantly alter paper lesbianism. Whether the battleground was the editorial offices of *Rat* or *The Ladies' Home Journal*, lesbian activists were pushing both the mainstream and progressive media's perception of the lesbian. The paper lesbian was becoming a radical, confrontational, nonassimilationist freedom fighter, often styling herself as the advance guard in the feminist war on patriarchy.

THE INTRICATE WEBBING OF WOMEN'S PUBLISHING

> The effort to make the statement, the grit necessary for women writers to overcome the years of patriarchal rejection, to get angry enough to say I AM I AM by publishing a book, starting a women's press, all converged into that magical moment sitting in someone's kitchen or living room surrounded by brown cardboard boxes. . . .
>
> –Polly Joan/Andrea Chesman[25]

The editors of *It Ain't Me, Babe* printed in every issue a boxed sidebar entitled "Read." Inside the margins of its black borders was a short bibliography of books, pamphlets, articles, and journal titles. Among the dozen or so books listed were Betty Friedan's *The Feminine Mystique*, Doris Lessing's *The Golden Notebook*, Simone de Beauvoir's *The Second Sex*, and Eleanor Flexner's *Century of Struggle*. For these, the editors listed no publisher's names or prices: these books, already in paper covers for the most part, were easily available from mainstream presses and bookstores. Among the articles and pamphlets listed were Anne Koedt's "The Myth of the Vaginal Orgasm," Juliet Mitchell's "Women: The Longest Revolution," Marge Piercy's "Grand Coolie Dam," and Pat Mainardi's "The Politics of Housework." Some journals were listed as well: *Women: A Journal of Liberation* from Baltimore; *No More Fun and Games* from Massachusetts; *Tooth and Nail* from Berkeley's own Women's Liberation Basement Press. Following each of these titles was an address, a name, and a price: for a dime or a quarter, sent to a post-office number or to someone's apartment mailbox in cities all across the nation, one could receive the first pioneer publications of a movement that would be called "Women in Print."

By 1973, all but seven states could boast some feminist alternative media outlet–a newsletter, a newspaper or magazine, a journal–that served as a mailing address for the movement.[26] More importantly, feminist presses were being established–small operations that for less than a dollar and the price of postage would send you their latest pamphlets and off-prints, and larger, more ambitious undertakings that began publishing hardcover and papercover books. Some of these larger presses supported their lesbian and feminist publishing projects by running full-service print-shops–doing the pasteup and layout for small businesses or for local lesbian-feminist journals or newspapers; donating labor or materials to other feminist groups; wrestling with a recalcitrant offset that its new owners were still learning to operate, and always struggling under the burdens that undercapitalized small businesses face.

And to sell and distribute the steadily growing stream of lesbian and feminist books, newspapers, and magazines, a new kind of capitalist enterprise was popping up as well in neighborhoods across the nation: the women's bookstore. In 1973, there were 9 such stores; in 1976, the number had grown to 44; in 1978, 60 bookstores were surviving. Each one served as meeting place, cultural center, and information clearinghouse for its community, and most survived through the 1970s and into the 1980s, long after other kinds of community space–women's centers and buildings, for example–had disappeared.

In the early 1970s Carol Seajay had discovered the women's liberation movement in the pages of her hometown newspaper, *The Kalamazoo Woman*. By that time she had reread–all the way to the last page–a friend's used copy of *The Price of Salt*, and had begun to imagine that her own future as a lesbian could be something other than irredeemably tragic. By 1976, after attending college, she had moved to San Francisco and was doing regular volunteer shifts at A Woman's Place in Oakland, the women's bookstore established by Carol Wilson and others in 1973, where Seajay found two whole shelves of books and magazines focusing on lesbian life and thought, more than she had known existed, most of which had been brought to press by lesbians themselves. She loved working at the bookstore, in spite of the 90 minutes she spent on various buses between Oakland and San Francisco, where she lived, and in spite of the fact that she did it for no pay. Her work at A Woman's Place fed her fantasy that she might at some point in the future be able to open a similar store in San Francisco.

Like thousands of her contemporaries, Seajay's perception of her future was being changed by the challenges of women's liberation. The possibility of starting another bookstore was one path. Another was the "women in the trades" movement. Since 1974, Seajay had been working to get the city of San Francisco to fund and support an electrician's apprenticeship program for women, a first step toward breaking down the barriers that had traditionally kept women from pursuing male-dominated trades work. Seajay imagined that an apprenticeship program could be her foot in the door, an opportunity to pursue a more lucrative field of work than those traditionally open to women, and perhaps a way to finance a bookstore in the future. She and her lover were talking seriously about such a project, and had even applied for a start-up capital loan at the San Francisco Feminist Federal Credit Union.

A Women's Place, like other women's bookstores of the era, served as meeting place and cultural center to its community, and it often sponsored readings by women authors. One night in early 1976, Carol Seajay found herself in a group of women at the Bacchanal, an Oakland women's bar, continuing a conversation that had begun in the bookstore after a reading by novelist June Arnold. Arnold was a cofounder of Daughters, Inc., a Vermont-based lesbian-feminist publishing house that would publish many important lesbian novels, including Arnold's own *The Cook and the Carpenter* and *Sister Gin*, Bertha Harris's *Lover*, and Rita Mae Brown's first two novels, *Rubyfruit Jungle* and *In Her Day*. Brown's first novel, published in 1973, had achieved enormous sales through word-of-mouth advertising (60,000 copies by 1975), and the sale of its paperback reprint rights to Bantam for $250,000 and the publicity associated with the sale helped to make Daughters, Inc., one of the best known of the early presses.

The conversation was good that night at the Bacchanal, and although it may have looked purely social in its setting and tone to a casual onlooker, it was a vital part of the work these women had set themselves to do. The informal, fledgling network of individuals and collectives running newspapers, presses, and bookstores across the nation relied on conversations just like this one to trade information and ideas. As they traveled from one part of the country to another, lesbians engaged in the alternative press movement inspired each other with new ideas and new information; a lesbian author or editor from Massachusetts might arrive in Maryland with a carton of books or a stack of newspapers to sell on consignment at a women's bookstore in Baltimore; the feminist newspaper she picked up there and carried home might inspire an article or an action in New Haven.

An idea debated and picked over in a conversation over beers in Boston might become, in an amazingly short period of time, the inspiration for a feature essay appearing in a lesbian-feminist journal in Los Angeles or Las Cruces.

The brainstorming that night in the Bacchanal led to events that would make the essential but informal networking between lesbian bookwomen a little less informal and haphazard but even more vital. June Arnold suggested that the book publishers, the bookstore people, the press operators, the magazine producers should all get together in one place to trade information, to distribute their books and newspapers, to ask each other questions. The idea led Arnold to organize the first Women in Print Conference, held that summer in Omaha, Nebraska, and irregularly thereafter in various states.[27]

This first Women in Print Conference drew 130 women, all of them women in the publishing trades. The conference was not conceived of as a gathering for writers but for the tradeswomen who put out the papers, who called for submissions, who nursed secondhand Gestetners and Multiliths through printruns of 500 and 1,000, who collated and bound by hand, and who, more often than not, distributed their products via a casual system that depended on the backpacks and VW buses of sympathetic women, traveling from one part of the country to another, who were willing to drop off a carton of books or stack of journals to women's bookstores along their way. In the early 1970s, when feminist bookstores numbered in the dozens and feminist presses struggled to keep up with the demand those few bookstores created, distribution was the weakest link. Bookstore workers, corresponding with dozens of different small press operations, found out how labor intensive it was to get a single title from a single press. Keeping the bookstore shelves stocked was time-consuming and expensive. Distribution and availability was even more difficult in areas where there was no women's bookstore. In Houston, for example, where there was no women's bookstore in the early 1970s, Pokie Anderson, the editor of the local women's newspaper, *Point Blank Times*, took it on herself to buy books from Daughters, Inc., and to keep them in her garage, along with other pamphlets and materials that she thought women in her community should have access to.

In 1973, Helaine Harris and Cynthia Gair founded WIND (Women in Distribution), a distribution company that specifically served the lesbian and feminist alternative press community. WIND served as a central clearinghouse for the lesbian-feminist presses and journals: a bookstore could make one order to WIND rather than dozens to individual presses.

Seajay's attendance at the Omaha Women in Print conference was a turning point for her. On the first night, in a marathon session, each woman introduced herself and the organization she was representing. For the first time, women who had been reading and thinking about each other's work met face to face. Dozens of women printers met the publishers of journals and newsletters; women's bookstore owners–there were 18 to 20 in attendance–met the women who mailed them books. June Arnold, Parke Bowman, and Bertha Harris, publishers of Daughters, Inc., were there; Harriet Desmoines and Catherine Nicholson, editors of the brand-new journal *Sinister Wisdom*, attended, as did Dorothy Allison, Charlotte Bunch, Sonya Jones, Karyn Jones, and many others representing feminist journals, printers, and publishing houses. At one point Barbara Grier, who was there representing the newly established publishing house, Naiad, received a standing ovation from the gathering, recognition of what *The Ladder* had meant to lesbians before the women's liberation movement.[28]

As part of her introduction during that first session, each woman told the group what it was she had come to learn at the conference. Seajay's question was simple: was it possible to open a bookstore with $6,000, and could such a business support two people? The next day, a woman approached her and gave her an answer: yes, it was possible, the woman said. We did it in New York, with about that much money. The woman was Karyn London of New York's Womanbooks, one of about 20 bookstores represented at the conference, and one of the most successful and largest women's stores at the time. Seajay took London's answer home with her, where she discovered that while she was gone, she had been accepted into the electrician's apprenticeship program's first class for women, and the Feminist Credit Union had approved her loan. She decided to be a bookseller rather than an electrician; by October of that year, Old Wives' Tales opened at Valencia and 16th street, in a neighborhood near the Castro District that was home as well to a Marxist bookstore called Modern Times, the George Jackson Defense Fund office, a lesbian bar, the Tenants' Union, and a large co-op grocery store whose parking lot was littered every Saturday morning by the pamphlet- and flyer-filled information tables of dozens of progressive groups doing grassroots organizing. Seajay was 26 years old. She operated the bookstore, with the help of a changing collective, for the next ten years before passing it on to other women who kept it open for twenty years.

Besides Old Wives' Tales, Seajay founded another important institution that year: with the encouragement of the bookstore owners she had met at the Women in Print Conference, Seajay began publishing *The Feminist Bookstores Newsletter* (later called *Feminist Bookstore News*), an extraordinarily important resource assuring the growth and stability of women's bookstores over the next two decades. Using a borrowed typewriter, Seajay would type all the copy for each newsletter onto stencils, do her own layout, take the layout to the printer ("two buses unless I can get someone to loan me a car"),[29] and then address and mail each newsletter by hand. Working at the bookstore and keeping up with the 12- to 24-page newsletter led quickly to 70-hour weeks.

From the very first issues, published in late 1976 and early 1977, *FBN* became an important clearinghouse for information that rarely made it into the pages of *Publishers Weekly* or the ABA newsletters. All the small press and lesbian-feminist publishing ventures that women's liberation movement had spawned could use *FBN* as a kind of message board, alerting bookstore owners and collectives about what was available, what was in print. Bookwomen relied on *FBN* booklists, published in almost every issue of the newsletter, to bring to their attention new materials on special subjects: writing by and on behalf of women in prisons; regional actions and events sponsored by local activists; how-to manuals on everything from auto repair to cabin building to the legal procedure for keeping your maiden name after marriage; poetry by working-class Appalachian women; memoirs of women living in urban communes and rural collectives; homegrown, little-press, nonsexist children's books; poetry, fiction, and theory by lesbians. Even the newly reprinted anthologies of old *Ladder* material, edited by Barbara Grier and published by Diana Press, founded in 1972, the year that *The Ladder* quit publishing, were eagerly received by the readers of *FBN*.[30]

In the early years, most of those readers were bookstore owners and bookstore collectives, the lesbian bookwomen who founded and maintained undercapitalized, politically oriented small business against all odds and often with no experience. A good portion of each newsletter was devoted to their letters, in which they would ask each other questions, debate issues, and add their individual bits of information to the growing information bank. Their concerns ranged from where to find published resources on battered women to how to anticipate and order for Christmas and holiday sales. They mused aloud about the contradictions inherent in operating ideologically motivated businesses–whether they should carry the exploitative *The Joy of Lesbian Sex* simply because customers asked for it, or sell remaindered books knowing the authors would not receive royalties, or spend advertising dollars with publishers whose political and economic agendas offended them. They wondered if the standard ways of doing business employed by the mainstream publishing industry–bulk ordering rules, 60/40 split discounts, returns options–could be meaningfully changed to better serve their stores' needs. They spoke sardonically of the difficulties of doing business with "L.I.C.E."–Seajay's acronym for the "Literary Industrial Corporate Establishment," and counseled each other to "pay the feminist publishers first and let the straights [establishment publishers] wait!" at the end of each month's business. The bookwomen wrote of their struggles to keep stores open and stocked, with little money and a lot of passion and hard work.[31]

Perhaps the newsletter's most important service was its up-to-date listings of new books by and for women from both mainstream and feminist presses. Culled from correspondence sent to *FBN* by feminist distributors and publishers as well as from mainstream publishers' catalogues, press releases, *Publishers Weekly*, and other industry sources, the listings were enormously important to the women responsible for keeping their bookstores stocked, saving them time and energy and duplicated effort. Here in the closely typed, single-spaced pages one could keep up with the avalanche of new journal titles being founded in the new women's studies programs at universities; with the latest novels offered by Daughters, Diana, and Persephone, three of the largest and most important lesbian-feminist presses; with the new pamphlets and poetry from The Women's Press Collective, founded by Judy Grahn, Pat Parker, Susan Griffin, and Willyce Kim; with the latest "lost" women writers brought back into print by the activist American literature professors who had founded The Feminist Press in 1970. At some bookstores, each collective member or worker combed through the latest issue of *FBN* using different colored pens to mark news items or publishing notes that she wanted her co-workers to be aware of.[32]

The newsletter also alerted the bookstores to important books in danger of going out of print. In fact, *FBN* would often publish requests that bookstore owners blitz mainstream publishers with letters encouraging them to keep important but slow-selling books in print: one such campaign convinced Bantam to reprint Joanna Russ's lesbian-feminist science fiction novel, *The Female Man*; another saved *The Well of Loneliness* from going out of print during the 50th anniversary year of its original publication. The bookstores also had a hand in keeping Toni Morrison's early novels (*Sula*, *The Bluest Eye*) and Alice Walker's *Meridian* available, urging their mainstream publishers to get them into paperback. On another occasion, *FBN* subscribers helped Marge Piercy persuade Doubleday, the hardcover publisher of her second novel, *Dance the Eagle to Sleep*, to allow it to be published in paperback.[33]

The *Feminist Bookstores Newsletter* was vital to the business of keeping the women's liberation movement in print. For example, when Women in Distribution (WIND) declared bankruptcy in 1979 after five years in operation, many feminist bookstores and presses were left in immediate financial danger. A distribution company, if it fails, can bring down a lot of the small presses whose books it handles, as well as create havoc in the operations of all the bookstores who rely on them for ordering. Because WIND specialized in distributing lesbian and feminist press books and periodicals to lesbian and feminist bookstores across the nation, and because WIND had followed the revolutionary practice of stocking *every* title of *every* press it did business with, its existence was a central aspect of every bookstore's ordering procedures, and its failure was potentially disastrous. Seajay and her co-workers at the *FBN* devoted a week's worth of marathon work sessions to producing an emergency issue of the newsletter, addressed primarily to the women's bookstores who would have to learn how to do WIND's work virtually overnight. Working closely with Helaine Harris and Cynthia Gair of WIND, Seajay published listings of *every* lesbian and feminist publisher the WIND did business with, explaining the differing terms and transactions that each bookstore would confront when they began ordering from dozens of publishers rather than a single source.[34]

REVOLUTIONARY CAPITALISM?

> . . . media are not to be defined as major simply by their size. This is generally accepted of elite publications like *Foreign Affairs* or *The Economist* . . . but it is past time that it was also acknowledged to be an accurate assessment of a number, at least, of radical media.
>
> –John Downing[35]

For lesbian women themselves, pouring energy into the Women in Print movement was a life-giving, life-altering activity, creating positive change in individual lives. Hundreds of women all over the country enthusiastically made the mailing address of the movement their permanent address. But lesbian presence in the front lines of the women's liberation movement created controversy for feminism itself and flavored its portrayal in the mainstream media. The "gay/straight" split and other ideological battles were problematic constants in the women's liberation movement; in fact, the gay/straight split and other forms of factionalism were sometimes the motivating impulse behind lesbians creating new alternative media. The newspaper *off our backs*, for example, was founded by Marilyn Webb in 1969 when she was "purged" from D.C. Women's Liberation. Another group of lesbians in Washington, D.C., founded the short-lived but influential newspaper *The Furies* after a failed attempt to make coalitions with heterosexual feminists.[36] Pouring energy into building lesbian-feminist publishing institutions was often the cause of, or resulted in, fractious debate about lesbian separatism, among lesbians themselves as well as between lesbians and the larger feminist movement.

The revolutionary potential of lesbian-feminist bookwomen distributing their artistic and theoretical work across the nation can be perceived in the tone of a *New York Times Magazine* article about Daughters, Inc., an enormously successful lesbian-feminist press founded by June Arnold and her partner Parke Bowman in 1973. When Arnold and Bowman moved Daughters Inc., from Vermont to New York City in 1976, the event became an occasion for the *New York Times* to publish a fairly defensive and dismissive four-page article by Lois Gould entitled "Creating a Women's World." Laid out around four large photographs of the short-haired, denim-clad publishers unpacking boxes of books, or checking the stock at a women's bookstore, or standing dwarfed against a large printing press, the article focuses on lesbian-feminism's most threatening idea–separatism–calling it "another passing strangeness in a 'movement' some say is already tearing apart over strangenesses of one kind or another"(10). Throughout the article, Gould positions her relationship to her husband and male editors against Daughters' "woman identification"; she laments novelist Joanna Russ's failure to imagine a two-gendered egalitarian society in her feminist utopian novel *The Female Man* (which was not published by Daughters). She requires the women she interviews–Bertha Harris, Charlotte Bunch, June Arnold, and Parke Bowman–to defend themselves against unnamed critics who say they're merely playing at publishing, that the press is simply a "toy," a diversion, and that the dream of a female culture is a misuse of their energy, a futile secession. In the context of this treatment, the publishers' message is hemmed in: that they are building what they see as a necessarily focused enterprise with exclusive interests that are aesthetically and ideologically motivated. Women's literary separatism is constructed in the article as startling, misguided, perhaps dangerous, but more probably nebulous, and definitely lesbian. The treatment is dismissive, setting it apart from that which might greet similarly exclusive and ideological publishing enterprises taken up by, for example, poets or pacifists or African-Americans.[37]

There were splits and controversy as well over economic politics. A debate over feminist businesses split women in lesbian and feminist communities along a continuum that has come to be defined at its endpoints by the terms "cultural feminism" and "radical feminism," and women operating bookstores found themselves directly implicated in those debates. For some in the movement, the growth of women's bookstores and presses, women's music companies and festivals, and other forms of "female culture" or "lesbian culture" represented a falling away from the radical feminist ideals of revolutionary change toward a kind of "settling" for a separate culture, limited in its ability to affect the larger culture. Some saw women's culture as the commodification of the movement by capitalist impulses. For others, the invention of alternative institutions was the necessary, separatist strategy that could free women to be and think for themselves, that would produce real change in the culture at large.

Alice Echols, a historian of the women's liberation movement, has argued that radical feminism was eclipsed by cultural feminism around 1975, a result of women's need to get beyond the "painful and often immobilizing discussions about women's differences" (254) that characterized activists' debates over class, race, sexuality, and ideological divisions. Echols characterizes "cultural feminism" as a tendency *away from* the sexism of the new left and its chronic failure to organize around women's issues, as well as the paralyzing schisms of gay/straight and other political divisions. At the same time, she sees cultural feminism as a tendency *toward* a monolithic, universalizing notion of womanhood, organizing political activity around essentializing notions of female values and female culture, and as a retreat from patriarchy rather than as a resistance to it (272-73).

The debate over feminist economics was played out in the pages of various movement journals and newspapers, during a time when a great deal of "trashing" of some movement leaders was taking place. Some of the discussion concerned the collective, nonhierarchical ideal of feminist organization and action, and the fear that such a model was not possible in small capitalist businesses. Echols sees the debate over feminist economics as part of the process by which cultural feminism, co-opted by the dominant culture, diluted the essence of radical feminism and settled for a reformist ideology that the mainstream could approve and that effaced women's real racial, sexual, and class differences.

But the legacy of perhaps the most successful kind of feminist business–those started by "the visionary tradeswomen" of the bookstores and publishing houses–transcends the cultural/radical debate. The bookwomen got the word out, and kept getting it out, even as the women's liberation movement waned. Sherry Thomas, a member of the Old Wives' Tales collective, remembers being in Nebraska visiting Catherine Nicholson and Harriet Desmoines, founders of *Sinister Wisdom,* when the news that WIND was filing bankruptcy came. The three women spoke well into the night about WIND, about how that last year of the decade had also seen the closing of Diana Press and of at least one major women's bookstore, reminding them all of "the fragility of institutions we've come to almost take for granted":

> . . . we may be entering a new period of difficulty, a time to reaffirm our commitment to keeping feminist theory, art, culture alive in the world. We felt a strong need, a hunger, to learn from the "failures," to understand patterns and problems that might keep the rest of us from similar fates. Is this the beginning of the end of feminist business strategy? Will inflation, recession, repression knock a hole in that effort? "What made us think they'd *pay* us to make a revolution, anyway?" Harriet asked.[38]

The Women in Print movement was closing out the decade in more danger than it had begun it; the 1980s would see the rise of Reagan and Reaganomics, as well as a significant neoconservative backlash against the feminist ideologies that had motivated the women's liberation movement. But through that coming decade, lesbian bookwomen would continue to flourish, weathering conservative retrenchment from the culture at large as well as backlash from both inside and outside of feminism.

As Desmoines suggests, there was never any reason to assume that women's bookstores or a network of feminist alternative media would be able to survive the chronic problems of insufficient access to capital, yet they did. In 1992, Carol Seajay, who still publishes *Feminist Bookstores Newsletter*, wrote in *Ms. Magazine* that "financially speaking, *none* of the first generation of bookstores or publishers should have survived" because "there simply weren't enough bookstores to sell enough books to make feminist publishing financially viable":

> But women kept opening feminist bookstores and publishing companies just the same, and kept them open as long as possible, until the time came when there *were* enough outlets to make feminist publishing viable and enough books to support feminist bookstores. (62)

Of the more than 100 feminist bookstores operating today in the United States and Canada, nearly 40 were open ten years ago; more than a dozen have been in continuous operation since the early 1970s. In the last decade of "post-feminist" backlash, feminist bookstores' sales have increased from $4 million to $30 million, with the largest stores stocking an impressive 15,000 to 18,000 titles. A good portion of that stock–as much as 40% in some stores, according to Seajay–is work by and for lesbians. This statistic alone marks a tremendous achievement: it is not possible any longer to imagine a young woman exploring her sexuality from within the information vacuum that lesbians faced before the women's liberation movement.

The Women in Print movement challenged the publishing establishment and in the process changed what counts as knowledge. In so doing, the movement created some of the most lasting alternative institutions of cultural feminism. For many lesbian-feminist artists and activists, building a female culture in the 1970s and 1980s meant refusing to assimilate–in the hopes that on the ground of that refusal, new understandings of the world could be devised. This work is central to the achievement of lesbian-feminist alternative publishing, an achievement that was inspired and supported by the separatism of cultural feminism. For the defining feature of separatism–the marking out of separate intellectual and literary space, and the building of separate institutions–is the essence of alternative lesbian-feminist publishing. And the literary and theoretical products of alternative lesbian-feminist publishing have been one of the richest and most lasting accomplishments of the women's liberation movement.

NOTES

1. Melanie Kaye/Kantrowitz, 9.
2. Sale, 331-332.
3. Treatises that focus specifically on the underground press of the 1960s often fail to incorporate the influence of women's liberation on the alternative press. See for example Learner, Glessing. More recent texts, such as Downing, also fail to analyze the impact of feminist or lesbian movement on the alternative press. John Tebbel, the dean of American publishing historians, tells us little about the underground press or the women's liberation press in his 1974 classic, *The Media in America*, nor in the more recent *The Magazine in America, 1741-1990*, which fails to list even *Ms*. in its index, and includes in its definition of "alternative magazines" *The National Review* and a Christian home-schooling periodical as well as *Ramparts* and *Rolling Stone*.

There are exceptions to this rule of general exclusion, however. One 1970s text that does incorporate the impact of the women's liberation press is Roger Lewis's *Outlaws of America*. David Armstrong's more recent *A Trumpet to Arms* includes a chapter on feminist publishing. See also Lauren Kessler's *The Dissident Press* and Abe Peck's *Discovering the Sixties*.

4. For the phrase "visionary tradeswoman" I am grateful to Carol Seajay.
5. Before the women's liberation and gay liberation movements began using the tools of alternative and underground publishing in the late 1960s, there were a few early and influential journals active in the late 1950s and early 1960s. What separated these "homophile-era" publications, such as *The Ladder*, from the lesbian-feminist publications that followed them after 1969 was a revolution–or

more precisely, the congruence of several revolutions. Political and cultural changes in the late 1960s and 1970s, leading to a host of literary and journalistic experimentations, expanded the scope and altered the look, feel, and editorial politics of alternative publishing enterprises like *The Ladder*. In the first decade of its existence, from 1955 to 1965, each issue of *The Ladder* arrived in readers' hands out of a virtual vacuum: with the exception of the male-oriented homophile publications *One* and *Mattachine Review*, there was no gay or lesbian alternative media. There was no feminist alternative media until the first newsletter appeared in 1968, and the "underground" newspapers such as *The L.A. Free Press*, *The Berkeley Barb*, and *The East Village Other* did not start publishing until late 1965. A central part of the mission of *The Ladder* in those early years was remedying the cultural invisibility and isolation of gay and lesbian people: it strove to support its primary constituency and to educate the public at large by providing both with the precious resource of information. But from 1967 to 1972, *The Ladder* became only one voice in a chorus of voices calling for an end to a variety of oppressions by challenging the dominant culture's authority to determine the limits of personal and political freedom for certain categories of citizens. In its last years, *The Ladder* was one publication among hundreds expanding the role of the alternative press in American culture. No longer was the paper lesbian contained by the pages of pulp paperbacks and psychological treatises, or by the limited editorial vision of a single lesbian magazine. In 1970, fourteen years into its existence, *The Ladder* was joined by the first of a new generation of alternative publications devoted to reporting and theorizing about gay and lesbian existence: in that year, the new organization New York Gay Liberation Front (GLF) began publishing *Come Out!* and in 1971, *Gay Community News* began publishing in Boston. *The Advocate*, which began publishing as a 12-page mimeographed newsletter in 1967, predates *Come Out!* and *GCN* by three years, but its content did not emphasize political/theoretical or lesbian issues. See John Tebbel, *The Magazine in America*, 255.

6. Armstrong, 226; Evans, 98-101.

7. Echols, 104-105, 214-215; Frank, 90, 102; Freeman, 109; Hole and Levine, 254-270.

8. Bunch, 139.

9. Frank, 89. On page 90 Frank quotes Joan and Chesman, who coauthored the 1978 *Guide to Women's Publishing*, published by Len Fulton's Dustbooks (Paradise, CA), the press he started in 1963 to publish the first of many annual editions of *International Directory of Little Magazines and Small Presses*. Hole and Levine make a similar point in *Rebirth of Feminism*, noting Kathie Sarachild's assertion that "putting out newspapers and knowing where to distribute them was second nature" to feminists who had participated in building "a network of underground papers" growing out of "the black and student movements"(270). In relation to the lesbian movement, the point is made most comprehensively by Alisa Klinger, who argues in her dissertation *Paper Uprisings: Print Activism in the Multicultural Lesbian Movement* (U of California, Berkeley, 1995) that North American lesbians used "literature as a locus for political organization" (1), "cultivat[ing] the printed page to foster their grassroots struggle for self-determination" (2).

10. In 1971, Connie Dvorkin was a high school student from New Jersey who refused to take Home Economics and integrated her high school's all-male shop class instead. See Connie Dvorkin, "The Suburban Scene," *Sisterhood is Powerful*, ed. Robin Morgan (New York: Random House, 1971): 362-366.

11. Ferree and Hess, 75; Freeman, 114.

12. Sponsored by the United Methodist Church and read by students at Methodist colleges, *motive* magazine published its special double issue on women in March 1969. It was edited by Joanne Cooke, a new employee of the magazine, and by Charlotte Bunch-Weeks, who suggested that the issue be organized around the women's liberation movement. Controversy arose before the magazine even appeared when the Methodist Publishing House "refused to run the machines to print the issue" (12) because of four-letter words used in some articles. After its publication, unprecedented numbers of calls, letters, and visits to the *motive* office in Nashville, Tennessee, led to a second printing of the issue and in 1970, its republication as *The New Woman* by Bobbs-Merrill, followed by Fawcett paperback reprinting. In the book version, the editors printed a number of the letters that *motive* received; responses included praise, angry subscription cancellations, and the demand that *motive* "stop sending this Garbage to the students in our colleges. Good for outhouses in the mountain country" (170).

Thirty years old when the controversy arose, *motive* magazine stopped publishing in 1972. Both issues published in that year were special-topic numbers on homosexual liberation. Charlotte Bunch-Weeks, Joan E. Biren, Rita Mae Brown, and Coletts Reid coedited the lesbian-feminist issue, the final issue in *motive*'s history.

13. *Liberation Now! Writings from the Women's Liberation Movement*. New York: Dell, 1971, n.p. The statement appears between the acknowledgments pages and the table of contents.

14. Freeman, 111-116.

15. Mather, 82. Mather notes that "most of these were newsletters, although there were also 60 newspapers, nine newspaper/magazines and 72 magazines and journals. They appeared in all but seven states."

16. *It Ain't Me, Babe*, 15 January 1970: 1, 4-5.

17. For the role of both the Liberation News Service and the Underground Press Syndicate in the growth of the countercultural press, see Leamer, 42-48, 85-80, 116-123.

18. For national and international news stories drawn in part from other news sources, see "The Pill?" and "Sexist Job Listings Challenged in Federal District Court," *It Ain't Me, Babe*, 29 January 1970. See also Leamer on the workings of both the Liberation News Service and the Underground Press Syndicate, 42-48, 113-128.

19. "An Open Letter from a Sister," *It Ain't Me, Babe*, 29 January 1970.

20. "Consciousness for What?" *It Ain't Me, Babe*, 11 June 1970; Susan Griffin, "Single or Schizoid," 1 July 1970: 6; Judy Grahn, "Lesbian as Bogeywoman," 11 June 1970.

21. Pratt, "Identity: Skin Blood Heart," 40.

22. Grahn; Carol Seajay, Interview, 16 May 1993; Kay Tobin, interview with David Marcus, *Making History*, 110-111.

23. The question of "locked stacks" confronting gay and lesbian researchers that Judy Grahn raises is not confined to the 1960s or the Library of Congress. It wasn't until 1976, for example, that gay and lesbian student activists at Stanford University successfully lobbied the libraries there "to place materials on homosexuality in the open stacks. Works on the subject in the HQ76 Library of Congress classification had previously been held in locked stacks, where library patrons could consult them only upon special application to the loan desk." See Koskovich.

24. "Cross Currents," *The Ladder* 8, 8 (May 1964): 11. "C.L.I.T. Papers, C.L.I.T. Statement #1," *DYKE* 1, 1 (winter 1975-76): n.p. A later statement (#2) has been reprinted in Hoagland and Penelope, 357-366.

25. Quoted in Frank, 90. The phrase "the intricate webbing that is women's publishing" comes from Joan and Chesman, 105.

26. Mather, 82.

27. Interview with Carol Seajay, 16 May 1993. Personal conversation with Susan of Bookwoman, Austin, Texas, 19 October 1993. For an alternative reading of June Arnold's sponsorship of and relation to the Women in Print Conference, see Bertha Harris's Introduction to her novel *Lover*.

28. Interviews with Carol Seajay (16 May 1993) and Barbara Grier (1 May 1993).

29. *Feminist Bookstores Newsletter* 1, 5 (1977): 1.

30. *Feminist Bookstores Newsletter* 1, 3 (January 1977): 7-9.

31. *Feminist Bookstores Newsletter* 1, 4 (1976): *FBN* 1, 9 (1977): 3; *FBN* 2, 1 (1978): 5, 7.

32. Interview with Carol Seajay (9 May 1993). During a three-month cross-country trip in 1978, Seajay was buoyed by visiting women's bookstores and hearing stories like this: they often helped her to keep the crushing double workload at Old Wives' Tales and *FBN* in perspective.

33. *Feminist Bookstores Newsletter* 2, 1 (1978): 9; *FBN* 2, 2 (1979): 2; *FBN* 3, 2 (1979): 11. Notes on this issue appear throughout *FBN*'s first three years.

34. *Feminist Bookstores Newsletter* 3, 3 (1979).

35. Downing, 352.

36. Echols, 1988.

37. Lois Gould, "Creating a Women's Culture." *New York Times Magazine*. 2 January 1977: 10-12, 38.

38. "More on WIND'S Closing" *Emergency F.B.N.* 3, 3 (1979): 2-3.

WORKS CITED

Adam, Barry. *The Rise of a Gay and Lesbian Movement*. Boston: Twayne/G. K. Hall, 1987.

Anderson, Pokie (Houston activist). Phone Interview. 8 August 1993.

Armstrong, David. *A Trumpet to Arms: Alternative Media in America*. Boston: South End Press, 1981.

Buch, Charlotte. "Feminist Journals: Writing for a Feminist Future." *Women in Print II*, ed. Joan E. Hartman and Ellen Messer-Davidow. New York: Modern Language Association, 1982, 139-152.

Carden, Maren Lockwood. *The New Feminist Movement*. New York: Russell Sage Foundation, 1974.

Damon, Gene (pseud. of Barbara Grier). "The Least of These: The Minority Whose Screams Haven't Yet Been Heard." *Sisterhood is Powerful*, ed. Robin Morgan. New York: Random House, 1970, 297-306.

Douglas, Carol Anne. *Love and Politics: Radical Feminist & Lesbian Theories*. San Francisco: Ism Press, 1990.

Downing, John. *Radical Media: The Political Experience of Alternative Communication*. Boston: South End Press, 1984.

Echols, Alice. *Daring to Be Bad: Radical Feminism in America, 1967-1975*. Minneapolis: U. of Minnesota Press, 1989.

Evans, Sara. *Personal Politics: The Roots of Women's Liberation in the Civil Rights Movement and the New Left*. New York: Vintage, 1979.

Faderman, Lillian. *Odd Girls and Twilight Lovers: A History of Lesbian Life in Twentieth-Century America*. New York: Columbia University Press, 1991.

Ferree, Myra Marx, and Beth B. Hess. *Controversy and Coalition: The New Feminist Movement*. Boston: Twayne, 1985.

Frank, Shirley. "Feminist Presses." *Women in Print II: Opportunities for Women's Studies Publication in Language and Literature*. Joan E. Hartman and Ellen Messer-Davidow, eds. New York: Modern Language Association, 1982, 89-116.

Freeman, Jo. *The Politics of Women's Liberation*. New York: Longman, Inc., 1975.

Gould, Lois. "Creating a Women's Culture." *New York Times Magazine*, 2 January 1977, 10-12, 38.

Glessing, Robert J. *The Underground Press in America*. Bloomington: Indiana University Press, 1970.

Grahn, Judy. *Another Mother Tongue*. Boston: Beacon Press, 1984.

Grier, Barbara. Phone Interview. 1 May, 1993; 11 and 18 July, 1993.

Harris, Bertha. *Lover*. Daughters, Inc., 1976. Introd. Bertha Harris. New York: New York UP, 1993.

Hoagland, Sarah Lucia, and Julia Penelope, eds. *For Lesbians Only: A Separatist Anthology*, London: Only women Press, 1988.

Hole, Judith, and Ellen Levine, eds. *Rebirth of Feminism*. New York: Quadrangle/ New York Times Books, 1971.

Joan, Polly, and Andrea Chesman. *Guide to Women's Publishing*. Paradise, CA: Dustbooks, 1978.

Kaye/Kantrowitz, Melanie. "On Being a Lesbian Feminist Artist," *Heresies* 3 (1977). Reprinted in *We Speak in Code* (Pittsburgh: Motheroot Publications, 1980), 9.

Kessler, Lauren. *The Dissident Press: Alternative Journalism in American History*. Beverly Hills: Sage Publications, 1984.

Klinger, Alisa. "Paper Uprisings: Print Activism in the Multicultural Lesbian Movement." Diss. U of California, Berkeley, 1995.
Koedt, Anne, Ellen Levine, and Anita Rapone, eds. *Radical Feminism* [An anthology drawn largely from the feminist annual *Notes from the Revolution*]. New York: Quadrangle/New York Times Books, 1973.
Koskovich, Gerard. "Out on the Farm: The Gay & Lesbian Rights Movement at Stanford, 1968-1978." Stanford, CA: Gay and Lesbian Alliance, 1988.
Leamer, Laurence. *Paper Revolutionaries: The Rise of the Underground Press.* New York: Simon & Schuster, 1972.
Lewis, Roger. *Outlaws of America: The Underground Press and Its Context.* Middlesex: Pelican, 1972.
Marcus, Eric. *Making History: The Struggle for Gay and Lesbian Equal Rights.* New York: Harper Collins, 1992.
Marotta, Toby. *The Politics of Homosexuality.* Boston: Houghton Mifflin, 1981.
Mather, Ann. "A History Of Feminist Periodicals." *Journalism Quarterly* 1, 3 (1974): 82-85; 1,4 (1974/75): 108-111; 2, 1 (1975): 19-23+.
New York Times. *A Gay News Chronology, Jan 1969-May 1975.* New York: Arno Press, 1975.
Peck, Abe. *Uncovering the Sixties: The Life and Times of the Underground Press.* New York: Pantheon Books, 1985.
Pratt, Minnie Bruce. *Rebellion: Essays, 1980-1991* Ithaca: Firebrand Books, 1991.
Sale, Kirkpatrick. "A Matter of Influence." *Sixties Without Apology*, ed. Sohnya Sayres et al. Minneapolis: University of Minnesota Press, 1984: 331-332.
Seajay, Carol. "20 Years of Feminist Bookstores." *Ms. Magazine*, July/August 1992, 60-63.
______ . Phone Interview. 9 May 1993; 16 May 1993.
Tebbel, John. *The Media in America.* New York: Mentor Books, 1974.
Tebbel, John, and Mary Ellen Zuckerman. *The Magazine in America, 1741-1990.* New York: Oxford University Press, 1991.
Tobin, Kay, and Randy Wicker. *The Gay Crusaders.* New York: The Paperback Library, 1972.
Tuchman, Gaye. "Women's Depiction by the Mass Media." *Signs* 4, 3 (1979): 528-542.
Wandersee, Winifred D. *On the Move: American Women in the 1970s.* Boston: Twayne Publishers, 1988.
West, Celeste, ed. *Words in Our Pockets.* Paradise, CA: Dustbooks, 1985.
Zimmerman, Bonnie. *The Safe Sea of Women: Lesbian Fiction, 1969-1989.* Boston: Beacon Press, 1990.

Bertha Harris's *Lover*: Lesbian *and* Postmodern

Amanda C. Gable
Georgia Institute of Technology

SUMMARY. This article argues that the 1976 novel (reprinted in 1993) *Lover* by Bertha Harris, though receiving little critical attention in the past, can be considered an exemplary novel within discussions of both postmodern fiction and lesbian (or queer) theory. The article analyzes in particular the novel's self-consciousness as manifested by characters who cross-dress and who are artists (including the writer of the novel we are reading). The article calls for Harris to be added to the group of writers such as Wittig, Anzaldúa, Lorde, and Winterson, who are discussed within the context of a postmodern lesbian narrative. *[Article copies available for a fee from The Haworth Document Delivery Service: 1-800-342-9678. E-mail address: getinfo@haworth.com]*

Amanda C. Gable received her PhD in American literature and feminist studies from Emory University. She has an article, " 'Women Ran It': Charis Books and Atlanta's Lesbian-Feminist Community, 1971-1981," co-authored with Saralyn Chesnut, forthcoming in an anthology on southern lesbian and gay history, *Carryin' On in the Lesbian and Gay South,* edited by John Howard. Amanda Gable also writes fiction; her stories have been published in *Other Voices*, *The Crescent Review*, *Sinister Wisdom*, *The North American Review*, and elsewhere. She has taught creative writing and literature at Denison University and currently coordinates a graduate writing program at Georgia Institute of Technology. Correspondence may be addressed: 420 Oakland Street, Decatur, GA 30030.

[Haworth co-indexing entry note]: "Bertha Harris's *Lover*: Lesbian *and* Postmodern." Gable, Amanda C. Co-published simultaneously in *Journal of Homosexuality* (The Haworth Press, Inc.) Vol. 34, No. 3/4, 1998, pp. 143-154; and: *Gay and Lesbian Literature Since World War II: History and Memory* (ed: Sonya L. Jones) The Haworth Press, Inc., 1998, pp. 143-154; and: *Gay and Lesbian Literature Since World War II: History and Memory* (ed: Sonya L. Jones) Harrington Park Press, an imprint of The Haworth Press, Inc., 1998, pp. 143-154. Single or multiple copies of this article are available for a fee from The Haworth Document Delivery Service [1-800-342-9678, 9:00 a.m. - 5:00 p.m. (EST). E-mail address: getinfo@haworth.com].

Originally published by Daughters Press in 1976, Bertha Harris's third novel, *Lover*, an erudite, metafictional,[1] lesbian narrative, has received surprisingly little critical attention.[2] Reprinted in 1993 by New York University Press with an introduction by the author, *Lover* may now begin to take its place as an exemplary novel within discussions of postmodern fiction and lesbian theory.

Though the novel has received mention in important articles,[3] no full-length article on Harris or the novel has appeared. It is unlikely that the relative scarcity of the text alone limited critical work: a perhaps greater factor was the timing of the novel's initial publication. The narrative structure of *Lover* didn't fit within the norm of the midseventies post-Stonewall lesbian fiction,[4] and the lesbian content of *Lover* didn't fit within the norm of a predominantly male heterosexual postmodern fiction of the time.[5] In short, *Lover* significantly challenged both literary categories to which it most obviously belonged. By breaking the structural conventions of a more realistic lesbian fiction, Harris provides a self-conscious narrative which can playfully examine different angles of lesbian identity construction. By inserting the lesbian and the lesbian writer into an existing body of metafiction, Harris adds to that genre a missing critique of gender and sexual identity. In its theoretical concerns *Lover* anticipates by a decade or more the interests of contemporary feminist critics such as Judith Butler, Diana Fuss, and Teresa De Lauretis, and the development of lesbian (and queer) theory.[6] In its stylistic concerns the novel clearly fits into an ongoing critical discussion of metafictional (or postmodern) texts begun as early as 1979 by Robert Scholes and continued more recently by Patricia Waugh, Brian Stonehill, and Brian McHale.[7]

One of the most obvious bridges between the two critical discussions–lesbian (and queer) theory and postmodern (and meta-) fiction is the novel's obsession with cross-dressing and the creation of art (including the writing of the novel itself). These aspects of the novel serve to highlight issues of representation in language and in art–concerns of postmodern fiction–and representation of "the" lesbian–a concern of lesbian and queer theory. The recurring instances in the novel of cross-dressing call into question fixed gender and sexual categories, and the characters producing art call attention to the novel as a construction. Therefore, an analysis of the novel's self-consciousness, both through its instances of cross-dressing and art production, will help demonstrate the novel's relevance to the discussion of postmodern literature in general and lesbian theory in particular, and hopefully will begin a more wide ranging discussion of the novel in these contexts.

Bertha Harris's novel *Lover* is a metafictional text, that is, it draws attention to itself as a work of fiction[8] and in doing so also calls attention to the problems of "representing" the lesbian, particularly the lesbian writer or artist and lesbian literature. In fact the novel is about a lesbian writing a novel and painting forgeries and putting on plays in drag and coming of age and becoming a lover. Harris's metafictional narrative structure highlights the problems of defining the term lesbian but also points to the possibilities that the figure of the lesbian gives to those who want to question the dominant conceptual framework that establishes "normal" binaries (male/female, homosexual/heterosexual, etc.). This type of questioning, in fact, is a defining trait of postmodern literature. According to Linda Hutcheon, "it seems reasonable to say that the postmodern's initial concern is to de-naturalize some of the dominant features of our way of life; to point out that those entities that we unthinkingly experience as 'natural' . . . are in fact 'cultural'; made by us, not given to us" (2). Lesbian (and queer) theory, too, is poised to scrutinize what is considered natural, both within the dominant discourse and within lesbian and gay discourse. The self-conscious use of the word queer in "queer theory" shows the double intent. As De Lauretis writes in *differences: Queer Theory Issue*, " 'Queer Theory' conveys a double emphasis–on the conceptual and speculative work involved in discourse production, and on the necessary critical work of deconstructing our own discourses and their constructed silences" (iv). In *Lover* the concerns of representation of art and the writing of a novel are intricately tied to "the" lesbian and constructing a complicated identity for her. In her 1993 introduction to the novel, Harris says she wrote the novel as a "pleasure dome" for the sexual subversives of the feminist movement (xxi). But she also says that "[a]lthough *Lover* is presumed to be a 'lesbian' novel, and it is, the sexual subversives I put in it are not always, nor necessarily, lesbian. I am no longer as certain as I used to be about the constituents of attraction and desire; the less certain I become, the more interesting, the more like art-making, the practice of love and lust seems to me . . . " (xxi). Implicit in this description by Harris of her novel is an eschewing of fixed categories or a notion of an "essential" lesbian identity; explicit is her assertion that the complications and complexities of art and sexuality go together.

CROSS-DRESSING

The beginning of the novel, a witty synopsis of the comic opera *Der Rosenkavalier*, brings up gender trouble and ultimately lesbian fun and play.[9] (Pastiche is also a common characteristic of postmodern fiction.) *Der Rosenkavalier* begins with Octavian (the mezzo-soprano dressed as a young man) in bed with an older woman, the Marschallin; they have just finished making love when the curtain rises. Literally what the audience is aware of is that two "women" are in bed together and the comedic farce begins. Soon in this same scene Octavian must cross-dress as a maid to avoid detection as the Marschallin's lover. In the plot of the opera Octavian is a young man, and the other characters respond to him as such–however, the audience "sees" a woman dressed as a man dressed as a woman–an effective doubleness in a novel about the construction of gender and the representation of the lesbian.

Harris's use of cross-dressing in the novel allows her to expose the seams of the fictional process and to raise issues of representation and identity. In her use of the frame of the plot of *Der Rosenkavalier* she not only alludes to the farcical nature of her work but highlights the issue of cross-dressing–that what you "see" depends on what you expect to see. From a heterosexist point of view we expect a "man" to be in bed with the Marschallin; from a lesbian point of view we see two women in bed together–the character is the same. But Octavian is actually another figure as well, the figure of the transvestite. This figure not only helps mark the lesbian, but also signifies problems of "true" representation and "clear" gender categories. Marjorie Garber in her 1992 book *Vested Interests: Cross-Dressing and Cultural Anxiety* acknowledges that the transvestite has often been interpreted as a figure for one of the "two" genders. She asserts, however, that the transvestite should be viewed as a third figure who puts into question binary pairings of all kinds but most specifically gender and sexual orientation pairings. Garber argues that "*transvestism is a space of possibility structuring and confounding culture*: the disruptive element that intervenes, not just a category crisis of male and female, but the crisis of category itself" (17). A category crisis results in the breakdown of boundaries between binary oppositions which causes "cultural, social, or aesthetic dissonances," and the transvestite is often a marker of the dissonances that arise around "categories" of race and class, as well as those around gender and sexual definition (10-17). In order to break down gender and sexual boundaries, Harris transports cross-dressing from another narrative (*Der Rosenkavalier*) as well as having her own characters, both male and female, cross-dress. She also uses the theatricalness of cross-dressing to give *Lover* the atmosphere of a performance.[10]

Practically speaking, cross-dressing allows Harris's women characters, as historically it did for real women, to function in traditionally male roles or in traditionally male spaces. In other words it allows them to cross boundaries that otherwise would have inhibited their movements and actions. For instance the character Veronica is described as cross-dressing as a male novelist. Samaria's mother works as a prostitute; her aunt cross-dressed and worked as a man on the docks. An orphanage director interestingly thinks that the mother both cross-dresses *and* is a prostitute. I think Harris adds this touch because both activities call attention to sexuality and historically were two of the few ways women could work outside the home and become financially independent. Both these activities, cross-dressing and prostitution, also place the women alone walking in the dock area, which is normally off-limits to women. Veronica also cross-dresses as a Hollywood-type producer, Mr. Horoscope, to entice her sons Bogart and Boatwright to perfect their "doll" and to go over Niagara Falls in a barrel. Her "performance" emphasizes the stereotypical notions of gender that the boys have, and she, as Mr. Horoscope, ironically out-mans them.

In other scenes various characters engage in cross-dressing behavior which in part signifies them as lesbians. When Flynn pauses on the stairs, "straightens her tie (she will do anything for love) and goes down to eat" (55), she is not dressed to pass as a man. She is dressed in her Etonian necktie as a lesbian (54). In another scene between an anonymous narrator (the lover) and her beloved in New York City, Harris carries cross-dressing to a farcical extreme.

> It is hard to dress because she doesn't know who she will be tonight. She could be Queen Elizabeth the Second if she had time to do her hair in pin curls, if she owned something simple and fuschia-colored, with a bolero jacket, if she had a pearl necklace. She thinks of T. S. Eliot; but her jock strap is at the laundry and her lips are too full. She wants to wear a stained trench coat and be a detective. She wants to squire this broad to a blue-plate special, then back to her place or her place.
>
> But the beloved is pounding the mattress and yelling, "Empty! Empty!" so the lover makes the simplest choice. She becomes a drag queen named Roman. She laces white shoe skates with red pompoms to her feet and circles her recumbent beauty, flashing her brawny black-haired legs. She spins like a top. (63)

Harris here is acknowledging the transvestite figure as the signifier of the lesbian, but does not use a figure of a woman cross-dressing as a man. Instead the lover decides to cross-dress as a drag queen. This allows Harris to break multiple categories; the drag queen stereotypically functions to mark the homosexual (gay or lesbian) or to call attention to the construction of the female gender. But she disrupts the categories; drag queens are "supposed" to be men. By showing the transvestite as not-lesbian (since the lover has to impersonate the drag queen) and showing a transvestite that calls attention to the construction of male gender, Harris effectively shows how the transvestite creates dissonance while also producing a truly comic moment. She takes her farce even further though; as the lover leaves to go to the restaurant with her lover she "hooks her pepper-and-salt beard behind her ears" (63). Now, this lesbian lover dressed as a man dressed as a woman, redressed as a man, "is ready" to go out into public. In Harris's novel cross-dressing functions both to show the lesbian and to show how categories of gender and sexual identity ultimately fall apart and become absurd.

Another important cross-dressing scene in Harris's novel takes place within a theater setting which adds complexity to the idea of cross-dressing as a critique of "true" representation. The Veronica and Samaria lesbian clan put on plays as a type of profit-making venture, and through the vehicle of these plays, Harris shows how costuming can create a new identity but never completely disguise what is under it. The main performance discussed in the novel is *Hamlet*; in their production Flynn ends up agreeing to play Gertrude and Veronica is Hamlet.[11] Harris's references to cross-dressing within the theater call attention to the general "impersonation" that goes on in theater, and this particular scene illustrates that costuming cannot totally mask or transform the body which it covers. In the theater scenes, as in the scene between the lover and the beloved, Harris moves the cross-dressing beyond the edge of what we expect. The costuming does not impersonate but rather creates another third self. Flynn as Queen Gertrude is "[n]aked–but for the black beard so long it hangs beyond that deep place between her breasts" (74). Veronica as Hamlet approaches her in a "white wedding dress" (74). Veronica says to Samaria in between the passages about the production of *Hamlet*: "I know all that. I know about costumes. Daisy has a princess costume. And kings and queens and spies and angels, and God more than anyone, go in disguise. You all wear costumes so that we won't know you. There are many old stories about you, and you can't fool me because I know all the stories" (73). Costumes seem to be alternate selves in this passage; rather than covering up a self, they create another layer of self. Though in one sense costumes are an attempt to disguise their wearers, they are never quite successful.

THE ARTIST–THE FORGER

In addition to cross-dressing, the novel *Lover* is obsessed with how the products of the other creative arts blur the boundaries between concepts of original and reproduction, and real and imagined. For instance, forgery, Veronica's occupation, illustrates the problem of distinguishing the original from the reproduction and the real from the imagined. Samaria says:

"Forgery . . . is not an act of art. It is like an act of God because, in the hands of the great masters, the forgery is no different from the real thing. Veronica is a great master, perhaps the only one left alive and she is no specialist, she has done it all. Forgery means that the art is not real but that no one, not even the forger (like in Veronica's case) can tell the difference between the first and the second . . . " (109).

In the realm of literature the novelist becomes the forger, creating a written version of stories taking place around her. These written stories would become indistinguishable from the real "original" stories.[12] The written stories are another level of representation of life; representations of other representations and so forth. In this way literature could be considered parallel to Veronica's profession as a forger. Flynn says to Samaria in the same passage: "Now she [Veronica] is a *belles-lettrist*, she is writing a novel that is not a novel–to please you, I guess, because you like to read" (110). The novel that Veronica is writing is called *Lover*–in all likelihood the novel we are reading. That it is a novel which is not a novel may mean that it is not a typical novel, or because Veronica is writing it, it could be a forgery of a novel. Veronica tells us, "I am always exactly the work I am presently engaged in painting–I mean, there is no difference between me and my painting during my dream, and I am not afraid of that" (117). Harris's insertion of "Bertha" into her novel as a character and the details which lead us to associate Veronica with Bertha Harris, the author, play out the idea that the author is one with her novel. The novel is not a fictionalized version of the author's life or ideas but in a sense *is* the author and her ideas as they happen.[13]

The twins Rose and Rose-lima tell Flynn toward the end of the novel: "If you understood life, if you had experience, you'd know it's all done with mirrors–just like everything else" (198). What we know in our "real" life is just as refracted and constructed as what we read in a novel. Rose-lima tells Flynn, "Let me remind you that the human nervous system can hardly tell the difference between its acts of imagination and its acts of reality" (200). Rose-lima is contradicting what Flynn has believed, that is, that the brain would be able to speak the truth. Traditionally reality is considered true and the imagined is considered fiction, the forgery. But Harris wants her readers to consider a framework where the forgery is the true. Harris wants her readers to question the "truths" we hold about fiction, gender, authors, and lesbians–she wants us to question how it is that people and things get represented in visual art and through language.

A central passage of the novel connects Harris's questioning of the categories of the real and the imagined with what happens when one becomes a lover. The following passage, which questions the categories of real and imagined, is presented by an unidentified narrator who is ostensibly describing how one becomes a lover.

> But one is very much like the other, anyway. And if you can't discern difference between the original and the reproduction, then difference does not exist: they are the same, although they take up separate blocks of time and space and may change one's ideas about the course of history. She reminds me of a character in the early fiction of a minor American novelist. Indeed, as far as I'm concerned, there is no difference between the two–between the living and the written–between the idea, the fantasy, and she who walks up and down on the wooden floor, shaking it with her heavy step, above me. No matter where I turn, I find a total disregard for the truth. (60)

According to this point of view, literature (or language) creates identity as much as it imitates identity. What she finds in her apartment with her beloved is a disregard for categories which is "normally" what passes for the truth. The rest of this short chapter tells of the lesbian lover and her beloved's evening. In a way it is a visualization of the construction of the lover who at one point becomes indistinguishable from the beloved. What can be imagined, Harris seems to argue, is as true as what we see across from us in the room, and is as true as what we "say we see" across the room.

Harris's novel repeatedly shows us it is impossible to find the "difference" between binary oppositions. The character Flynn is intrigued with the possibility that if the head is separated from the body the head will speak only the truth. Even though she got her ideas from a science fiction movie, she seems to pursue some experimentation in earnest. Predictably her experiment is a failure and the rabbits she has been using all die. Through Flynn, Harris seems to be saying that to gain the truth requires a separation of elements, like the head from the body, which, once accomplished, destroys the reason for finding the truth in the first place. Flynn, however, is looking for *the* truth; I believe Harris would accept the idea of "truths," if truths were simultaneously many-sided and many-voiced.

By naming her primary artist figure, Veronica, which means "true image," Harris makes a good joke and sets up a serious critique of the pursuit of *the* truth.[14] Veronica's forgeries end up being "true images." Veronica also is the author of *Lover*, which becomes then both a forgery and a true image.[15]

> "So it is left up to me," Veronica wrote, "to be the one to tell the truth–and the truth being that this fiction, like all before it, ends with the lovers . . . "
>
> One thing leads to another: when a novelist falls in love with the

> painter, then her novel becomes a forgery of paintings–she is hoping to screen her quick-change acts behind a confusion of forms, and ever deny them change. . . . (208)

Much of *Lover* plays with the notion of what is real and what is imagined to show that what we believe to be real can be a sleight of hand, a mask–still real, but not in a fixed state. So too the lover, the lesbian is, like everything else in the novel, constantly changing–changing her clothes, her appearance, her identity, and her location. If Harris shows us in *Lover* that lesbian identity is a problematized category, she also shows us that the lesbian as category calls into question all other categories–the ultimate forger. Instead of being in trouble, Harris shows us the lesbian is making trouble–and having a pretty good time of it.

CONCLUSION

In a 1994 anthology, *The Lesbian Postmodern*, edited by Laura Doan, several of the writers frame their essays around the issue of whether and in what way the two words–lesbian and postmodern–go together. Robyn Wiegman in the introduction asks: "What, in other words, can the lesbian–as a politics, discourse, identity of bodies, subjectivity, and sexual practice–mean and be within the critical context of the postmodern?" (5). Later in the anthology Judith Roof states: "The problem of postmodern flux versus epistemological certainty that characterizes criticism of the work of such overtly lesbian writers as Monique Wittig and Nicole Brossard reveals a critical anxiety about the relationship between the lesbian and the postmodern" (54). Ultimately what I argue in this article is that Bertha Harris's novel *Lover* is also grappling with these theoretical issues, and was doing so well before the current discussion. I would like to see Bertha Harris's name added to the group of writers most often discussed within the context of a postmodern lesbian narrative–writers such as Monique Wittig, Nicole Brossard, Gloria Anzaldúa, Audre Lorde, and Jeanette Winterson. Particularly with her notion and use of the concept of forgery–women as the originals, lesbians as the forgery–Harris presents a different angle on the "problem" of identity category and perhaps from this angle she also allows for the anxiety about the relationship between the lesbian and the postmodern to be reduced. In her introduction to the new edition of the novel, Harris joins lesbian and postmodern in a section subtitled "*Lover* Enjoys Postmodernism" and thereby declares a pleasure from the union, not an anxiety. Finally it may be the great humor of the novel *Lover* that will contribute the most to the theoretical discussion of the lesbian postmodern.

NOTES

1. Within what I view as the larger category of postmodern fiction, Harris's text *Lover* has the particular characteristics of metafiction as defined by Patricia Waugh in *Metafiction: The Theory and Practice of Self-Conscious Fiction* (New York: Methuen, 1984)–"fictional writing which self-consciously and systematically draws attention to its status as an artifact in order to pose questions about the relationship between fiction and reality" (2).

2. Harris's first and second novel were *Catching Saradove* (1969) and *Confessions of Cherubino* (1972) published by Harcourt. *Confessions of Cherubino* was reprinted by Daughters Press in 1978.

3. See Catherine Stimpson, "Zero Degree Deviancy: The Lesbian Novel in English," *Critical Inquiry* 8 (2) (winter 1981): 363-379; Julia Penelope Stanley and Susan J. Wolf, "Consciousness as Style; Style as Aesthetic," *Language, Gender, and Society*, ed. Barrie Thorne (Rowley, MA: Newbury House, 1983) 125-139; Sally Robinson, "The 'Anti-Logos Weapon': Multiplicity in Women's Texts," *Contemporary Literature* 29 (7) (spring 1988): 105-124; and Bonnie Zimmerman, "Feminist Fiction and the Postmodern Challenge," *Postmodern Fiction: A Bio-Bibliographical Guide*, ed. Larry McCaffery (New York: Greenwood, 1986) 175-188.

4. Another Daughters Press lesbian novel published in 1973, *Rubyfruit Jungle*, perhaps epitomizes more the dominant midseventies lesbian narrative. Though stylistically realistic narratives about lesbians (predominantly white) who were coming of age and coming out provided a welcome relief to a negative and pathological view of lesbians, as a group they had limitations. (Few Black lesbians were published during this time; Pat Parker and Audre Lorde, both poets, were exceptions.) In terms of style and plot the books were often predictable. Bertha Harris, in her essay, "What We Mean to Say: Notes Toward Defining the Nature of Lesbian Literature," *Heresies* (fall 1977): 5-8, in part, addresses these issues: "[T]o those acquainted with reading . . . what is being called lesbian literature these days is sheer winkieburger . . . [and] [m]ost lesbians (like everybody else) would rather feel than read; they thus achieve their most longed-for goal: to be like everybody else" (5-6).

5. Such writers as Pynchon, Barth, Barthelme, Coover, and Reed are often cited as postmodern (and metafictional) writers. In fact, Gass is reported to have first coined the term "metafictional" in a 1970 essay. See M. H. Abrams, *Glossary of Literary Terms* (Orlando, FL: Harcourt, Brace College Publishers, 1993) 135; and Brian McHale, *Postmodern Fiction* (New York: Routledge, 1989).

6. See Judith Butler, *Gender Trouble: Feminism and the Subversion of Identity* (New York: Routledge, 1990); Diana Fuss, *Essentially Speaking: Feminism, Nature and Difference* (New York: Routledge, 1989); Diana Fuss, ed., *inside/out: Lesbian Theories, Gay Theories* (London: Routledge, 1991); Teresa De Lauretis, guest ed., *differences* special issue, *Queer Theory: Lesbian and Gay Sexualities* 3 (2) (1991); and Teresa De Lauretis, "Sexual Indifference and Lesbian Representation," *Theatre Journal* 40 (2) (May 1988): 155-177.

7. Robert Scholes, *Fabulation and Metafiction* (Urbana: University of Illinois Press, 1979); Brian McHale, *Postmodernist Fiction* (London: Routledge, 1991); Brian Stonehill, *The Self-Conscious Novel: Artifice in Fiction from Joyce to Pynchon* (Philadelphia: University of Pennsylvania Press, 1988; and Patricia Waugh, *Metafiction: The Theory and Practice of Self-Conscious Fiction* (London: Methuen, 1984). See also David Harvey, *The Condition of Postmodernity* (Cambridge, MA: Blackwell Publishers, 1989).

8. As Patricia Waugh explains in her book *Metafiction: The Theory and Practice of Self-Conscious Fiction* (New York: Methuen, 1984), metafiction calls attention to the "rules" of fiction and the "rules" of language which allow us to construct meaning of our experience in the world. Rather than reinforce a feeling of reassurance that the boundaries between the real and the fictive are permanent and definite, metafiction tries to show/expose the underpinnings (the rules) of how a certain reality is constructed. By doing this, metafiction suggests that as the rules change so the "reality" changes. See also Linda Hutcheon *Narcissistic Narrative: The Metafictional Paradox* (New York: Methuen, 1980 & 1984).

9. Harris also used this type of frame in *The Confessions of Cherubino*, in which the *Marriage of Figaro* by Mozart (with its "trouser role" for Cherubino) sets the stage for gender intrigue.

10. In the introduction to the new edition Harris writes: "*Lover* should be absorbed as a theatrical performance. *Lover* has a vaudeville atmosphere" (xix).

11. Harris alludes here to a tradition of women playing male Shakespearean roles. Garber discusses the phenomenon in her book *Vested Interests* and points out, for instance, Sarah Bernhardt's famous portrayal of Hamlet (37).

12. This idea is very close to Roland Barthes's idea of the author as scriptor from his essay "Death of the Author."

13. Harris writes in her introduction, "As I wrote, I had in mind some of the most intellectually gifted, visionary, creative, and sexually subversive women of our time. I got to know nearly all of them within the women's liberation movement . . . In no particular order, the real life lurking behind *Lover* was: Jill Johnson, Eve Leoff, Jenny Snider, Esther Newton, Jane O'Wyatt, Phillis Birkby, Carol Calhoun, Joanna Russ, Yvonne Rainer, Valerie Solanas, Smokey Eule, Mary Korechoff, Kate Millet, Louise Fishman, and myself. Books by Virginia Woolf, Gertrude Stein, Jane Ellen Harrison, and Valerie Solanas show up on a bookshelf in *Lover* as my own *objets de virtu*" (xxiv-xxv), and "I wrote *Lover* to seduce Louise Fishman. It worked" (lxxviii). Louise Fishman is a lesbian painter–see Ginny Vida, *Our Right To Love: A Lesbian Resource Book* (Englewood Cliffs: Prentice Hall, 1978) 261-263.

14. The last chapter of the novel begins with an epigraph explaining the story of Veronica who gave her handkerchief to a suffering person and after the face was wiped the handkerchief retained the image of the face. Harris does not include in her epigraph that St. Veronica was said to have specifically given her handkerchief to Christ on his way to his crucifixion. The word "vernicle," the epigraph explains, means true image (207).

15. In the section of her introduction titled "*Lover* Enjoys Postmodernism," Harris says of a main character Veronica–"[w]hen . . . [she] isn't writing the fiction I'm supplying her with, she's forging masterpieces and salting archaeological digs with fakes. Forgeries, I'm suggesting, are aesthetically at a further remove from usefulness and meaning than their originals. As mirror-images, duplicates, twins, of the originals, they are better art. Within the secluding perimeters of *Lover*, women are the originals, lesbians are the forgeries" (xxvi).

WORKS CITED

Doan, Laura, ed. *The Lesbian Postmodern*. New York: Columbia University Press, 1994.

Garber, Marjorie. *Vested Interests: Cross-Dressing and Cultural Anxiety*. New York: Routledge, 1992.

Harris, Bertha. *Lover*. Plainfield, Vermont: Daughters Press, 1976.

______. Introduction. *Lover*. 1976. By Harris. Forward. Karla Jay. New York: New York University Press, 1993.

______. "What We Mean to Say: Notes Toward Defining the Nature of Lesbian Literature," *Heresies* (fall, 1977): 5-8.

Hutcheon, Linda. *The Politics of Postmodernism*. London: Routledge, 1989.

Breaking the Silence, Dismantling Taboos: Latino Novels on AIDS

Alberto Sandoval Sánchez

Mount Holyoke College

SUMMARY. As AIDS has ravaged the world in the last two decades, literature has played an important role in giving testimony of the epidemic. According to different communities and particular experiences, AIDS literature can offer ways of coping and surviving. In the last few years the U.S. Latino/a population has been highly affected by AIDS. The first genres to register AIDS were poetry and theatre. In this essay I examine how AIDS is represented in the first four Latino novels to deal with the subject matter: Ana Castillo's *So Far from God*, Daniel Torres's *Morirás si da una primavera*, Elías Miguel Muñoz's *The Greatest Performance*, and Jaime Manrique's *Latin Moon in Manhattan*. My critical reading centers on how AIDS

Alberto Sandoval Sánchez is Professor of Spanish at Mount Holyoke College. He received his PhD in 1983 at the University of Minnesota. He is both a creative writer and a cultural critic. He has published numerous articles on Latin American colonial theatre, U.S. Latino/a theatre, issues of migration and identity, and the representation of AIDS in Latino culture. He is recently working on two books: *José Can You See? Essays on Theatrical and Cultural Representations of Latinos/as* and *Stages of Life: Latinas in Teatro* (in collaboration with Nancy Saporta Sternbach from Smith College). The author would like to thank his sister Milagros for inspiring him to write this essay after she read *Latin Moon in Manhattan*. Correspondence may be addressed: Department of Spanish, Mount Holyoke College, South Hadley, MA 01075.

[Haworth co-indexing entry note]: "Breaking the Silence, Dismantling Taboos: Latino Novels on AIDS." Sánchez, Alberto Sandoval. Co-published simultaneously in *Journal of Homosexuality* (The Haworth Press, Inc.) Vol. 34, No. 3/4, 1998, pp. 155-175; and: *Gay and Lesbian Literature Since World War II: History and Memory* (ed: Sonya L. Jones) The Haworth Press, Inc., 1998, pp. 155-175; and: *Gay and Lesbian Literature Since World War II: History and Memory* (ed: Sonya L. Jones) Harrington Park Press, an imprint of The Haworth Press, Inc., 1998, pp. 155-175. Single or multiple copies of this article are available for a fee from The Haworth Document Delivery Service [1-800-342-9678, 9:00 a.m. - 5:00 p.m. (EST). E-mail address: getinfo@haworth.com].

constitutes a new articulation of identity, particularly gay and ethnic identity. Most importantly, I propose that these novels contribute to dismantling homophobia and compulsory heterosexuality, deconstructing sexual and cultural taboos, and breaking the silence on AIDS/SIDA. *[Article copies available for a fee from The Haworth Document Delivery Service: 1-800-342-9678. E-mail address: getinfo@ haworth. com]*

AIDS has infiltrated all kinds of literary genres and discursive formations around the world. Since its identification in the early eighties, the epidemic has moved from being primarily a medical crisis to a crisis of signification as a sociocultural construction. Among U.S. Latinos/as most of the literary representations of AIDS have been confined to poetry and theatre. These literary representations of AIDS register the poetic personal response to the plague and the urgency through theatrical sketches to educate communities on prevention, safe sex, and usage of clean needles. Slowly, but significantly, in the nineties the novel is a genre that has started to break the silence on AIDS in Latino/a literature.

In this essay I shall analyze how AIDS is articulated and discursively constructed in the following novels: Ana Castillo's *So Far from God*, Daniel Torres's *Morirás si da una primavera*, Elías Miguel Muñoz's *The Greatest Performance*, and Jaime Manrique's *Latin Moon in Manhattan*. I shall concentrate on how AIDS intersects with sexuality, specifically with homosexuality. Breaking the silence on AIDS means breaking cultural and sexual taboos in Latino culture. As AIDS continues its rampage, the protagonists have to accept the fact that currently there is no cure. This tragic reality which imminently culminates in a horrific death contributes to the identity formation of the characters in the age of AIDS. No one can escape AIDS in the literary domain: neither those that are infected, nor those that are affected. Nor can the reader avoid being trapped in the devastating effects of the plague.

In Castillo's novel *So Far from God* La Loca, who had already died at the age of three and miraculously resurrected, dies for a second time of AIDS. La Loca inhabits a world of imagination and solitude after dying as a child because she developed a phobia of people and was repulsed by the smell of humans. She exiles herself from society and people start calling her La Loca. Her only refuge is an acequia near the house where she meets a spirit, La Llorona, from the underworld. After losing weight her jeans get looser, and her mother calls the family doctor to treat her daughter who had never been sick before. At the end of the novel, she is diagnosed with AIDS. Her mother cannot accept the fatal diagnosis because there was no way sexually or intravenously that she could have contracted the virus: La

Loca had never left home and had never had a social life. The young woman could not be saved from AIDS, even when the family doctor exercised his own alternative tratamiento, and later some healers tried in vain to alleviate her illness, "because this was a time in which the cure was as mystifying to all of society as was the disease. Even as wise a doctor as el Doctor Tolentino knew that although sometimes a disease could be stopped, death ultimately could not be" (229).

Clearly Castillo's message is that anyone can contract AIDS. The fact is that AIDS is a reality within the magical realist world of the novel and in the real world of the reader. La Loca's first contact with AIDS needs no explanation, rationalization, nor justification, but just like her first death and resurrection must be taken as a mystery. It is up to the reader to accept both deaths: one as a supernatural intervention, the other one as a catastrophic collapse of the human immunological system. Also, it is the reader who must negotiate with La Loca's retardation or mental illness, and her supernatural powers of foretelling the future. In this way the author confronts the reader with the tragedy of AIDS without making it an issue of contraction. AIDS can affect the most innocent victims like La Loca; however, that does not matter, what really matters is that there is no cure and that with AIDS human beings are at the mercy of the "terrible enfermedad." Can La Loca's death mean that human beings with AIDS are "so far from God" as long as there is no cure? Does La Loca's death emblematize martyrdom after so much suffering and pain? Is she a role model to AIDS victims, or to society at large which is always discriminating and instigating prejudices against AIDS carriers? Whatever AIDS means in this text, it cannot be argued that La Loca's dying of AIDS is a marker that functions as a recognition of the epidemic and as a tribute to people with the immunodeficiency virus who finally in the literary world have a patron saint in La Loca Santa herself, "Patrona de las Enfermedades Misteriosas." Castillo makes readers think about AIDS. She confronts them with a tragic death in order to raise consciousness: AIDS can happen to anybody, even to the most innocent literary character in a world of magic realism.

If in *So Far from God* AIDS hits home unannounced and unexpected, in Daniel Torres's novel *Morirás si da una primavera* AIDS is a presence which is even inscribed in the title. The author plays semantically with the signification of AIDS. Although the translation into English is awkward and impossible, the title reads "You shall die if you should get it in the springtime" and/or "You shall die of AIDS during the springtime." AIDS is once again emphasized with a dedication: "Y a todos los que luchan por no morirse en primavera"/"For all of those who struggle for not dying of AIDS." Torres has explained the title in the following terms:

> Please notice that "si da" is a phrase with double meaning: "if you get it," and also the acronym of AIDS in Spanish: SIDA. The hedonistic element appears in the last part of the title, the springtime as the season of blooming and optimism. How could we talk about the crisis and spring at the same time? Well, because there is always hope in every given problem and because it is a Puerto Rican "¡Ay bendito!" attitude: if you have life, there is hope until the very last minute. (179)

As a matter of fact, the novel's title and dedication indicate a horizon of expectations for the reader within the isotopic narrative of AIDS; however, once the reader enters the fictive world of the protagonist, Papo, AIDS is slippery, evasive, unnamed. It is an absent presence, a present absence, a supplement. What the reader encounters is a postmodern narration which is ambiguous, porous, fragmented, heterogeneous, multiple. When AIDS appears in the text, it is registered specially through the color red and its association with blood and AIDS. In the opening paragraph the protagonist is positioned in a red circle from which there is no escape: "Claro que no importan los tiempos en los que se tome tu vida porque todo describe en ella la fascinación de un círculo rojo del que nunca se sale" (14-15). The image reads: red circle = blood = AIDS. Located in a space of redness/blood, later in the novel, Papo circulates indefinitely in the redness of an elliptical spiral that has no center: "Ya no te encierran los círculos. Ahora parece que son elipsis sin centro alguno donde circular en rojo eternamente" (57). The subject navigates in a continuous state of hemorrhage as AIDS contaminates his body.

Morirás si da una primavera is the coming-out story of a Puerto Rican in the age of AIDS. He narrates his sexual needs and encounters on the Island and in New York City. The novel starts with a one-night stand in a hotel room (#754) with a foreigner, Alejandro, who later takes Papo to New York. As Papo's relationship with him comes to its end, he finds out about his HIV status. Papo reminiscences about his past gay experiences, his life as a prostitute, and friends (including his pimp and his mentor). Through memories and conversations Papo takes the reader to a series of encounters in the streets, in the bars, and even with his first lover (Rafael) who was a closet case.

Rafael is a basket case of internalized homophobia and paranoidal closeting: "Tener un amante, lo que se dice tener un amante, con Rafa era prácticamente imposible . . . El pobre Rafa tenía la responsabilidad por los padres que tú detestabas, esos que se dan a la vida sin piedad por la bendita institución familiar" (35). In fact, Papo left Rafael because their relationship was never going to materialize. When he decides to contact him again, it is too late. Rafael has died of AIDS. At this point the text and Papo are marked by AIDS. In a letter that is never sent (or written) Papo confesses to Alejandro his HIV-positive status: "no te canso con mis problemas, pero dar positivo en la prueba no es nada fácil–el mundo se te llena todo de calles sin salida alguna: bueno voy a lo que quería decirte, o a lo mejor no quiero decir nada: un patuleco al que le va mal no tiene derecho ni a escribir ni a hablar a desatiempo . . . " (43). At the end of the letter Papo insinuates his future death in the spring: "no me olvides, porque sólo eso sería suficiente para que las noches que me quedan hasta esta primavera sean tan oscuras como estos días vacíos con los que no sé qué hacer sin ti" (43-44).

The novel closes with Papo's state of suspension between past and present, experience and fantasy, life and death, loneliness and companionship, in San Juan and/or New York. Papo is left alone inhabiting his own writing and what is left with him is the vacuum of having AIDS: "Y se te va quedando el vacío de que morirás si da una primavera" (77). Papo has no place to return to, not even to his own writing because he has only told half the truth: "Una topografía irregular donde perdiste siempre los rumbos que indicaban una posible vuelta, pero adonde exactamente . . . Nunca supiste a ciencia cierta" (78).

Torres's novel is the first openly gay novel on AIDS in Puerto Rican literature. The other writer who dealt with homosexuality explicitly was Manuel Ramos Otero who died of AIDS in 1990. *Morirás si da una primavera*, like Ramos's short stories and poetry, dares to articulate a Puerto Rican gay identity. Coming out constitutes an act of liberation as the protagonist breaks away from sexual taboos, moral impositions, and Catholic restrictions. He speaks out explicitly about his sexuality. Coming out rescues him from a life imprisonment which he compares to the experience of being pulled out of a well: "pero te sacaban de un pozo sin fondo llevándote lentamente a la superficie y mostrándote por dónde se sale definitivamente del closet" (18-19). After coming out, Papo must escape from the homophobia perpetuated by the family, the church, and the state in Puerto Rico, and internalized by closeted gays. Papo's only alternative is to migrate to New York City where he is free to come out and realize his sexual fantasies. Puerto Rico only entails stagnation and closetness: "Como siempre en Borinquen bella donde no pasa nada (cuando estás a pié, sin carro, pelao y jodío)" (34); "donde la gente se muere de puro aburrimiento porque no pasa absolutamente nada" (58).

Papo's new gay consciousness cannot tolerate the marginalization and oppression of homosexuals in Puerto Rico. In consequence, once he moves to New York, cruising, sexual encounters, and erotic pleasure determine his gay life away from the Island's homophobic environment.[1] On the Island there was no social space for queers. Neither was there a possibility to construct a gay identity, and for this reason Papo was at odds with Puerto Rican homophobic discrimination: "En la isla nunca te había ido muy bien que se dijera. Como que todos los hombres estaban ya cogidos de antemano por todo el mundo. Además, una gran mayoría de los maricones lo escondían todo y a ti ya no te interesaba jugar al esconder. Te gustaban los hombres y eso hacía tu gran diferencia" (41).

New York means a scandalous and promiscuous liberation of the body and the mind: Papo is free to be gay, to have gay sex. In fact, migration is the factor that makes possible the construction of a gay identity and facilitates writing on a subject which is a social, cultural, and sexual taboo. (In a similar way, Papo, Torres, and Ramos Otero as openly gay writers do their gay writing in the United States.) Nevertheless, freedom has its price. This new gay identity intersects with an ethnic identity and an AIDS identity. Papo must negotiate with the Anglo world as well as with AIDS. He is aware of stereotypes of Puerto Ricans in the United States as gang members of *West Side Story*: " . . . hasta que llegaba la famosa preguntita que nunca falla: WHERE ARE YOU FROM? A lo que invariablemente contestabas FROM PUERORICO, I AM PUERORICAN, para apresurarte a añadir que sólo hacía año y medio que estabas aquí, con lo que te evitabas a toda costa, según tú, que te confundieran con uno de la claque del *West Side Story* y compañía con lo de I WANT TO LIVE IN AMERICA, I WANT TO LIVE IN AMERICA" (26). On the one hand, Papo's negotiation with ethnic prejudices, stereotypes, and racism in the United States produces a subjectivity in process where identity is constantly reshaped and redefined. On the other hand, his gay identity will be affected by AIDS. Given that Papo does not practice safe sex, it is inevitable for him to contract the virus. Once he finds out that he is HIV-positive, his gay identity will be altered.

The problem is that Papo does not have the language and psychological tools to construct a new Puerto Rican gay identity with AIDS/SIDA. Papo cannot even pronounce the word AIDS. For example when his first lover Rafael died of AIDS, AIDS remains unnamed: "Fue lo último que supiste de tu Rafa hasta la otra llamada, cuando ya no estaba y era irremediable" (37); "intenté con Rafa pero no hubo respuesta, ya había muerto" (43). Papo's denial of AIDS leads him to an erasure of the epidemic: he cannot accept it as a reality in gay life, naming it would signal its acceptance and the need to modify his sexual behavior: "La cosa era cogerte lo que fuera cuando quisieras, con quien fuera y cuando pudieras. Así pensabas. A la verdad que sobre eso no te habías enterado demasiado, pese a las reuniones aquellas de emergencia en el grupo al que asististe una época en Santurce para crear un centro de ayuda a las víctimas. De eso hace relativamente poco tiempo, pero te parece mucho más del que parece. De todas maneras, eso lo borraste totalmente y como que no existe, no es verdad" (24-25). Clearly Papo's denial of the AIDS epidemic is not ignorance or misinformation. His fear of having to change his sexual life contributes to the total erasure of AIDS up to a point that he has sex without a condom: "habías mamado sin condón" (30). What is worse is that he cannot return to Puerto Rico because he is not willing to go back into the closet. Besides, returning with AIDS would complicate all matters because eventually his body would be marked by AIDS. In a Catholic homophobic society, having AIDS and being gay would be for Papo a death sentence and it would mean having to give up his gay identity. For this reason, he remains suspended at the end of the novel. In his memory Papo is trapped in a "tapón" in Santurce: gay life in Puerto Rico is stagnant, a no-exit situation. Indeed, there is no possibility of return until Papo accepts his AIDS condition and makes a political decision and commitment to being a migrant gay Latino with AIDS in New York City.

The truth is that Papo is politically naive. His only political act in his life was his desire to come out in Puerto Rico, but this act of consciousness forces him to migrate. His political decision is limited and constricted because he does not have a sense of community nor any participation in political activism. His only way to cope and survive with his gayness and AIDS is through his fantasies and campiness. One of his fantasies is his fascination with wearing a dress: " . . . donde se te encajó el ruedo del vestido que nunca tuviste" (13). That same fantasy of cross-dressing is performed by a transvestite friend of Papo whose hemline is unfinished before a drag show: "¿Qué tal, cómo quedé? Regia, ¿no te parece? Eres perversa, pero hermosa. El traje al ponérmelo me luce que, no, francamente no te gusta. ¡Pero queda el ruedo por coger! Maldita sea, ¡coño!" (52-53). Ironically, for both the hemline is unfinished. For Papo life becomes more complicated with AIDS: he will never be a woman dressed to the nines, nor will his life be completed because of AIDS. In this context, the hemline is a supplement for what he lacks.[2]

The incomplete hem ultimately reveals his unwillingness to make a decision, to come out with AIDS. Papo is not ready yet to make a decision; consequently his future is uncertain. Ironically, this dress, like his life, is not finished: it is unfulfilled and happiness is unreachable even within his fantasies. His life is condemned to errancy in the streets, in his fantasy, and in his writing. He searches for an encounter with that special person that he has never met, always wearing the dress with an unfinished hemline: " . . . buscándolo sin sentido. Para qué, si no estaba precisamente ni en San Juan ni en Nueva York: todo sucedía en un punto intermedio en el cual se confundían los dos espacios" (68). After migration Papo has been exiled from his place of origin; after AIDS his gay lifestyle (and identity) has been exiled from his body. His exiled existence causes an existential crisis of unaccomplishment which materializes in the dress that he never got to wear: "Encuentras sólo la soledad cuarteada por el uso inmisericorde del pasado, aquél que no tuviste, como el dichoso vestido del cual no diste nunca la más mínima pista a tus amigas para que te lo consiguieran y tal vez fueras feliz en esta historia maltrecha de locas, educación sentimental de paterías, mojiganga de voces discordantes" (36). Being exiled, totally frustrated, and with a feeling of underachievement, Papo's campiness is his only strategy of/for survival. The novel itself is a "patería," a queer act of experimental narration and a performance of postmodern narrative voices that register the history/story of his gay life before and after AIDS in exile.

Precisely it is exile, not metaphorical but political exile, at the center of Elías Miguel Muñoz's novel *The Greatest Performance*. Two exiles recount their past lives and vicissitudes of being gay and lesbian in a Cuban homophobic environment. Through a series of conversations, flashbacks, and memories motivated by photos, Mario and Rosa reexamine their lives as they grew up in Cuba in a repressive society where gender roles unceasingly reinforced compulsory heterosexuality. Their families perpetuate gender attributes and roles and have no room for children with sissy or tomboy inclinations. Both characters share their secrets and intimate life with each other (and the reader) in order to reaffirm their gay/lesbian identity. They constantly emphasize the discrimination, prejudices, and marginalization against homosexuals in Cuba, especially against Mario who is humiliated by being called derogatory names. For example, Rosa's father forbids her to be in Mario's company: "Can't you tell he is a pájaro?" (16). In his dialogue with Rosa, Mario confronts her father's homophobia with a new ironic perspective: "Pájaro. Bird. One of the words Cubans used in those days (still today?) to denigrate a gay man. What were some of the other ones? Ah yes, Duck, Butterfly, Inverted One, Sick One, Broken One, Little Mary, Addict, Pervert" (16). Obviously this is a very political novel of exile, and Castro and communism must be targeted and blamed for homophobia. When seen with more objectivity, however, homophobia is everywhere and not limited to revolutionary Cuba.

As the novel develops it becomes a coming-out story. Their childhood secrets and fantasies once shared in the conversation/reencuentro are revealed directly. Mario retells in graphic detail his sexual encounters with other young men and his fear of gay bashing. In his first sexual experience with another man Mario plays the role of the passive partner who pleases the active macho: "If you touch me just a little, I swear I'll do anything for you, boy. Leave your hand there for a while, yes, like that. Now you can move it inside. The fly is open, try it. Put your hand inside, that's good. It's hard, isn't it? Let's bring it out . . . I'll pull the skin all the way back, look how it moves, and then the head gets bigger; it swells up. You lick it with your tongue, like you're tasting mercocha . . . what a nice little tongue you have . . . " (37). By remembering, Mario is breaking the silence, breaking sexual taboos. By doing so, he also condemns the abuse and exploitation experienced by gay boys, including his friend Antonio's gay bashing, a brutal act where he hits his face and kicks him: "I told you to leave me alone! . . . I told you to get out of my way. Go find yourself another macho to fuck you. You faggot!" (41).

On the other hand Rosa, who went to Spain in exile, was molested by her uncle and almost raped until she decided to fight back. She led her uncle into a trap making him believe that she would have sex with him. When they got close she kicked him in the balls putting an end to his molestation. After Spain Rosa was granted a visa to rejoin her family in the United States. Her new home is in California where her Americanization and assimilation take place. She never comes out to her family but she has a lesbian lover and a gay life on the side. Rosa passes as straight with her family that insists on her future marriage. She introduces her lover to her family as her roommate in order to please them.

Mario's gay experience is totally different. He becomes sexually active and openly gay. Sexual life is pure fun and promiscuity is a component of urban gay life in California, until AIDS makes its presence felt. If exile meant sexual liberation and the freedom to articulate a new gay identity, exile also forces Latinos/as to construct a new U.S. Cuban identity. This new identity requires constant negotiations with the past, their present "gusano" condition, and their inclusion into a Hispanic ethnic minority in the United States. It is Rosa who decisively rejects the past in her yellow brick road to assimilation: "I need to stop living off memories the way my parents do, I said to myself. I began to see nostalgia as my enemy. And the images of my homeland that I carried inside as an obstacle for my success. I stashed my Spanish albums away, my photos, my letters, my Cuban mementos in the closet" (84). Indeed, Rosa is doubly closeted: her ethnicity is in the closet and her sexuality is in the closet. This double life makes her move far from home to go to college, and after college she moves to an apartment with her lover, the so-called "roommate."

Mario's experience is different: he has an affair with a Puerto Rican in New York City whose former lover has died. AIDS enters the text silently, unnamed: "And now his friend is gone forever" (102). Eventually AIDS touches Mario: he must be tested. It is at this point that his friendship with Rosa becomes stronger and reaffirmed. She becomes his inseparable companion and family for a week while they wait for the results. It is at this period of time that they renegotiate with their past culture and Cuban identity: "We played all your oldies, Los Memes, Los Bravos, Manzanero, Massiel, Raphael. The music that I had forgotten or that I never knew. We danced and sang all week . . . You cooked black beans and pork and fried plantain and you made my favorite Cuban dessert, mercocha" (127). When the moment of truth arrives, Mario is speechless: "I had no words, no thoughts, no feelings. I was a vacuous form where nothingness lived. How could I tell him [the doctor] who I was. Did I know? Do you know, Rosi, who am I?" (129). Mario's self-definition with AIDS has reached a state of crisis. AIDS places Mario at an intersection where recovering the past–Cuban, sexual, and life in exile–is the ultimate self-examination and evaluation of identity. Given that his ethnic identity has already been recovered and reactivated during a week of anxiety, fears, and hope, now he must tell the doctor about his sexual habits: "So I spill my guts out. A benevolent and sexless voyeur, he watches me as I give myself to maleness; as I swallow and eat and choke and rim and fuck and get fucked and fucked and fucked again. And when the orgy ends, when nothing is left of all the bodies but a mound of ashes in his carpet, he rises . . . " (129).

In fact, AIDS is the catalyzing agent that produces a reevaluation and reconstruction of Mario's and Rosa's identities. In Mario's life AIDS terminates his sexual freedom, and exile becomes a confrontation with death. His exile, initially conceived as an "escape to a land where dreams become reality" (15), becomes a rendezvous with Thanatos.

AIDS has not only affected Mario physically but it has affected Rosa emotionally. She must accept that her best friend is dying and encourage him to never give up: "We're gonna fight this off, Marito! We're going to fight it off and win!" (136). At the end they share a series of fantasies and recollections where Mario reaffirms his gayness. In these fantasies Mario is strong enough to challenge his homophobic father and Cuban society. In their final shared fantasy Mario plays the role of the Carnival Queen, a game that he used to play with Rosa in their childhood. He has finally become who he really wants to be. This is his greatest performance and their friendship is stronger than ever: "we found each other: a refuge, a song, a story to share" (149). In this never-never land, which truly is a deathbed scene, Mario and Rosa long for utopia and freedom. Although it could be interpreted as a strategy for/of survival, their ultimate utopian world erases the past and draws the line on the absurd: "we were made in test tubes and we were able to choose, as adults, the identity and gender that we fancied. Then we were free until the moment of our deaths (painless deaths) to change from man to woman, from woman to man, from tree to flower, from ocean water to ivy . . . We never heard of Castro. (Not even Castro Street.) Nobody hides, waving a dagger in the air, behind the mask of God. A plague hasn't broken out" (150). They inhabit a space which positions them in prerevolutionary Cuba and pre-AIDS. Their reactionary politics locates them at a crossroads where nostalgia and utopia intersect. This is an ahistorical space which erases all contradictions and negotiations especially with AIDS: "Yes. I will create this place where you can be who you've always wanted to be, Marito. Where You and I have become the same person. This moment of greatness. I will create it. When the performance ends. And life begins" (151). What is at stake here is that after AIDS their freedom has come to its end. The only way to survive is to escape by erasing history.

If with AIDS death is inevitable and it is inevitable that after AIDS sexual freedom, and all freedom, is terminated in their political exile, their only refuge is utopia. Rosa and Mario, utopian refugees, exile themselves to a world where AIDS does not exist. In this utopian world there is no possibility for articulating a gay identity with AIDS. Both the past and the present must be erased, and even death must be denied to make room for utopian freedom. In this world of freedom there are no political commitments: not even a commitment to fight AIDS and to survive with AIDS; there is no space to construct a gay identity with AIDS. The very real threat and existence of AIDS is totally exiled from their lives.[3]

In its concerns with identity formation after AIDS and commitment to making political acts of intervention to create solidarity with AIDS infected people, Jaime Manrique's novel *Latin Moon in Manhattan* is the most complex and politically committed when compared to the novels analyzed above.

The protagonist of the novel, Santiago, who lives in Manhattan, goes back home to visit his mother in Queens. Going home is becoming more Colombian, as he says: "I began to metamorphose; the closer I got to my mother's house, the more Colombian I became" (4). Nonetheless, going home generates a crisis of identity. Sammy struggles between two cultures and two languages, between nationalism and assimilation, between past and present. This crisis gets worse because of his sexual preference. He is gay and he is going home to visit his gay friend, Bobby, who is dying of AIDS: "I had decided to visit my friend Bobby. Perhaps this was the main reason for my trip to Queens this weekend. Bobby was deteriorating very fast and he was dying" (16). In this way, sexuality and ethnicity are the main factors that articulate Sammy's identity in the novel.

Sammy is in the process of coming out to his mother but he still is in the closet. Although she is an understanding and compassionate woman, she insists on Sammy marrying. She even visits Bobby and educates his mother on issues of AIDS: "Did you know she refuses to touch him? She won't even go into his room. She stands by the door, with her hands behind her back . . . I tried to explain to her that AIDS can't be caught by casual contact. To show her, I sat on Bobby's bed and combed his hair and arranged his pillows" (21-22). His mother's fear of Sammy catching AIDS forces her to shift her topic of conversation when she asks Sammy to marry Claudia: "Why don't you get married? Why don't you marry Claudia?" (22). The mother's insistence on marrying her son to his childhood friend registers the always present homophobia and compulsory heterosexuality in Latino culture. Her fear of AIDS forces her to impose on her son a heterosexual lifestyle and "matrimonio de apariencias": "Although Mother knows perfectly well what my sexual preference is, ever since Bobby had come down with AIDS she started an insane campaign to try to get me married to my childhood friend Claudia Urrutia, hoping perhaps I'd be spared Bobby's fate" (22). At this point in the novel, Sammy is not willing to break the silence, contributing in this way to perpetuating sexual taboos in Latino culture. Although he has broken the silence on AIDS, he still is not prepared to come out publicly. As a result, he is trapped into playing his mother's game, even with her Colombian friends. He is forced to visit her friends who also insist on his marriage to Claudia. The irony is that Claudia is a lesbian, as Sammy says when thinking out loud: " 'Mother, Claudia is a . . . ' dyke, I was going to add, but I knew this would just make matters worse" (22), and with the mother's friends he explains to the reader his silences: "I figured it would be better to play along than to go into long explanations about my and Claudia's sexuality" (29). Silence is the way out for Sammy in order to survive at home among the Colombian migrant community in Queens.

Sammy's visit to Bobby is a political act of intervention. His visit provides the reader with the opportunity to face AIDS. Given that Bobby is in his final days, his deathbed scene is tragic and horrendous. Sammy describes meticulously Bobby's grotesque appearance: "He was beginning to look like a recently excavated mummy. The skin between the eyebrows and eyelashes has sunken even further than the last time I had seen him, so that even in repose his eyes bulged like golf balls. The skin that covered them seemed translucent and thin like a spider's web. The eyes remained opened a third of an inch, so that only the white of his eyes showed. His entire face, including his parched lips, was peeling off in white, crispy flakes. He had become a monster" (44-45). For Sammy, facing Bobby means confronting AIDS and his homosexuality.

Bobby had moved from Colombia to the States to escape intolerance and homophobia. Indeed, Bobby was Sammy's role model in his construction of a gay identity. In fact Sammy moved out of his mother's home after reconnecting with Bobby: "when Bobby appeared again in my life I understood that I had to move out of my mother's house if I was ever going to accept my sexuality. His example was very important to me in this respect" (45).

Sammy assists Bobby in his final hours. In their last conversation Bobby performs a campy act in which humor is a strategy of/for survival: "This queen is dead" (50) he says wittily. He alternates hilarious lines with serious statements which forge the foundations for Sammy's gay political consciousness: "I remember how I used to despair thinking I would never get away from that dreadful macho town. I knew I had to get away from there and become the gorgeous queen I was meant to be" (49). It is through Bobby that Sammy realizes his need to come out and to face his sexuality: "Only recently had I realized that it wasn't so much AIDS I was afraid of, but of being sexually intimate with another person" (50).

Bobby expires after having his last Colombian dinner with Sammy. For Sammy it was easier to deal with Bobby's death than with his hysterical mother. The woman loses control and accuses Bobby's lover of her son's death: " 'You killed my son. Murderer. Murderer. You killed my son. Goddam you for turning Bobby into a homosexual. Bobby was no maricón. Not my son! I hate all homosexuals!' she screamed, turning to face me accusingly. 'I hate them all! I hope they all die of this plague!' " (54).

That night Sammy and his mother go to the Saigon Rose, a nightclub in Queens, where his sister Wilbrajan, a singer, was going to perform. There he also meets with Claudia and friends. Wilbrajan sings a tango in memory of Bobby who is the topic of conversation that night: " 'Tonight,' she went on, 'is a very sad night for me. A fellow compatriot, and dear friend of the soul, Bobby Castro, died this afternoon. To his memory I shall sing "Volver" ' " (65). " 'I shall always think of Bobby when I sing "Volver," ' Wilbrajan said. 'Tango is about pain' " (69). In their conversations at the nightclub both AIDS and homosexuality are silenced.

Back home in his room, Sammy feels Bobby's presence. Such an appearance functions as a reminder to Sammy to break the silence on his homosexuality. Bobby's death provides Sammy with the courage to come out to his mother. Under these circumstances, Sammy is not afraid any more to confess his sexuality to his mother who insists on marrying him to Claudia. He refuses to play the game: "Because I'm a homosexual and Claudia is a lesbian, that's why. Because I'll never love a woman that way" (83). Sammy is breaking the silence:

> But the word homosexual had never been spoken, never been said in her presence, not in connection with me. It was as if as long as it was unspoken there was still room for things to change some day, to declare that everything had been a passing fancy. As long as I didn't admit to it, there was hope that I would eventually marry like all good Colombian boys. Bobby used to say that the main difference between Colombian and American men was that all Colombians were gay until they married, whereas most Americans first married and then came out. (83)

Sammy's attack on Latin American homosexual practices between men before marrying are brought into the open without hesitation. In this sense machismo is deconstructed and compulsory heterosexuality is demythified. After coming out to his mother, Sammy must return home to Manhattan. His mother accepts his sexuality but still refuses to talk about it. However, her greatest fear is that Sammy could contract AIDS like Bobby. After coming out for good, Sammy feels "freer, more liberated" (84). He is ready to start a new life, a new life where Bobby serves as a role model and an inspiration to disclose his sexuality without fear or repression.

In the first part of the novel Sammy struggles to come out until he finally accepts his sexuality and tells his mother about his sexual preference. Bobby's death plays an important function as Sammy searched for ways to articulate his gay identity. Because of the homophobia in Latin American culture, he has not been able to express his sexual desires and erotic pleasures. Such desires have been repressed in favor of compulsory heterosexuality. Indeed, according to his account of his first sexual experience, Latin American societies find it more acceptable to have sex with an animal than with another man. This is clearly exposed when his uncle takes him to initiate Sammy into sex by having intercourse with a donkey. Ironically, during this rite of initiation into manhood, Sammy is fixated on his uncle's erected penis:

> I saw Uncle Hernán unzip his pants. With his huge dick sticking out, he approached me. Not understanding what was happening . . . Soon,

> Uncle Hernán was in frenzy, eyes closed, his buttocks pushing in and out, in and out; he moaned and cried in pleasure when he finished . . . He remained that way, panting, until he stepped backward and collapsed on the grass, his penis limp but still large, . . . I walked over to the burra he had just fucked, and what seemed like large quantities of semen oozed out of her vagina. Becoming aroused, I put my hard cock inside her. (12-13)

What excites Sammy is his uncle's penis, its huge size, and his semen. As he gazes at his uncle's penis, Sammy reveals his homosexuality not yet materialized. Furthermore, this sexual act of bestiality transgresses "normal heterosexual intercourse" by becoming a parody of heterosexuality and a demythification of masculinity. On the one hand, Sammy's gaze subverts heterosexual intercourse by exposing his homoerotic desire as he gazes at his uncle's penis and semen. On the other hand, his uncle implicitly initiates him into homosexuality (through an ambiguous incestuous relationship). This scene is a powerful revelation of Sammy's homosexual desire as he witnessed his uncle's kinky and unnatural sexual act. In short, this grotesque deformation of heterosexuality constitutes the foundational scene of Sammy's future gay life based on voyeurism.

If the first part of the novel is structured around Bobby's death, the second part centers on his relationship with his cat, Mr. O'Donnell. Indeed, the cat replaces Bobby's body and duplicates his illness. Furthermore, it has a heart condition that is fatal, just like Bobby's AIDS condition. Bobby was described as follows: "I was astonished at his weightlessness, and when I placed my hands under his armpits, his arms were thin and light, like breadsticks" (47). They are so similar that the cat descriptively resembles a body living with AIDS: "As I picked him up, he felt lighter, bonier, as if he had lost weight over the weekend. On the spot where he had been lying remained thick chunks of his hair. In the summer O'Donnell shed copiously, but the way he was shedding lately he'd soon go bald. As I ran my fingers over his stomach, I noticed his coat of hair had lost all luster. Overnight, Mr. O'Donnell had become old" (96). The comparison is fully achieved when the cat has a sudden death like Bobby.

The reader immediately realizes that Manrique constructs the novel around two deaths: Bobby's and the cat's. Both deaths result in an ontological and existential crisis for Sammy: "How can one be happy in the face of death surrounding us? I said thinking about Bobby's death and the approaching demise of Mr. O'Donnell. How can one pursue happiness as a main goal in life when there's so much pain and suffering everywhere? It makes for a nation of blind people. People who search for what doesn't exist" (124). In this philosophical way Sammy calls attention to AIDS and the true meaning of life, compassion, happiness, death. The irony is that the cat's death has made him aware of Bobby's death. Still, in the face of losses, Sammy has to go on with his crisis by working as an interpreter in court and by relating to eccentric friends.

Sammy suffers a radical transformation in the second part of the novel: "In the past couple of weeks, though, I've felt as if my life were going from monochrome into color" (160). There is no doubt that Bobby's death has affected him profoundly, as in a moment of solitude he thinks: "I thought of Bobby, and I thought of how he was dead and it was almost as if he had never existed and that somehow did not seem right. It occurred to me that I had known Bobby for most of my life, and I had no tangible memento of him, not even a photograph, just memories, which time would eventually distort and flatten out . . . Then I felt Bobby's presence next to my bed . . . 'I surrender,' I said. 'You can talk to me, Bobby, if that's what you want.' Then I fell asleep" (180).

If Bobby's presence assists Sammy in constructing his sexual identity, Mr. O'Donnell's death makes Bobby's death from AIDS more present:

> His eyes were very yellow like lighted lanterns, and they expressed horror. I thought of Bobby, of the last look he had given me, and at that moment I understood one of the differences between man and cat: man knows he's going to die, so he can get ready and be willing, even eager, to go. A cat knows the end is near, but that's all. He can't accept death: he can't trust in it, cats are perhaps too metaphysical an entity to need to believe in the idea of a beyond; a cat is his own god and man his creation. (183)

With both deaths, but particularly with Bobby's death, Sammy has learned to understand the meaning of life. AIDS has given him an understanding of mortality and friendship. Death is part of life, and Bobby has really taught him how to die and to make choices in life. The ultimate irony is that humankind can feel more compassion toward a cat than toward a friend with AIDS. If so, a cat's death may even have more recognition than a human being's death. In these terms, as Sammy walks though Times Square, he reads the flashing news: "I read: MR. O'DONNELL, THE MOST WONDERFUL CAT OF FORTY-SECOND STREET, DIED TONIGHT, AUGUST 2, 1990" (185). The message is clear and loud: humankind cares more about the death of a cat than the death from a gay human being. Ironically, Bobby's death from AIDS remains ignored and silenced. Between the lines Manrique is raising consciousness: AIDS is a taboo and silence = death.

In the last chapters, Sammy's relatives and Claudia visit him at his place in Manhattan. The visit turns into Mr. O'Donnell's wake. This celebration contrasts sharply with Bobby's death. It seems as if Bobby's death must be erased, silenced. There is no room for a proper funeral for Bobby, a gay man who dies with AIDS. In contrast, the cat who died a natural death deserves a ritualistic ceremony. In this context, it is obvious that within the Colombian national collective imaginary, homosexuals and people with AIDS are exiled. They prefer to mourn a cat than a "maricón." Although "It's very Colombian to celebrate someone's passing" (188), the death of a "maricón" with AIDS is no reason for celebration or mourning within the Colombian nationalist homophobic discourse. Indeed, it is Sammy's mother who observes their lack of humanity: "I can't get over we have a wake to Mr. O'Donnell and not to Bobby who died a few days past and now is like he never was alive" (206). In solidarity his sister says: "Let's have a minute of silence for Bobby who can't be physically here, although he's with us in spirit" (206). Still this final tribute is marked by silence. Still there is no language to talk about homosexuality and AIDS in Latin American/Latino culture. Both homosexuality and AIDS are taboos. Manrique himself has commented on this matter in an article on AIDS and Manuel Puig: "Although he officially died of a heart attack . . . I began to hear stories that he had been ill with AIDS. Some of the people close to him reluctantly began to admit it, while others denied it vehemently, as if having the disease would somehow make him a lesser man and tarnish his achievements. After all, if homosexuality is the greatest taboo in Hispanic culture, AIDS is the unspeakable" (26).

The novel closes with Sammy coming to terms with his homosexuality. Bobby's death, indeed, has liberated him by making Sammy confront both his sexuality and mortality. Sammy recognizes his sexual needs and homoerotic desires. As a result, he invites his neighbor over, a gay exhibitionist who has exposed himself to Sammy on various occasions in his window. Finally, Sammy accepts his sexuality and overcomes his fear of having sex. He invites Reinhardt over: "It was the wildest and the tenderest act I had ever engaged in" (211). At this moment Sammy remembers once again his role model, his confidant, Bobby: "Did the fact that we had been to bed mean that he was now my boyfriend? Would we ever do it again? I didn't have a clue about any of these things. I wish Bobby was still alive and I could call him and ask him these questions" (211). Although Sammy is on his own, he has learned how to configure a gay identity through Bobby.

At the end of the novel Sammy is determined to articulate a gay identity and to express his sexual desires and erotic pleasures: "my life was about to change. I didn't know what any of it meant; but for the first time ever, I felt grown up, ready to leave behind the shackles of the past" (211). Sammy does not only have a sexual partner but a cat enters into his apartment, probably Mr. O'Donnell's offspring. This is a new beginning for Sammy who has learned from the death of his best friend from AIDS to construct a gay identity, to give new meaning to life after coming out, and to express his sexual desires, needs, and pleasure, even in the age of AIDS.

* * *

Latino novels on AIDS speak of the tragedy of the epidemic in our communities. According to the *HIV/AIDS Surveillance Report* in June 1996 there were 78,926 cases of AIDS among U.S. Latinos/as. AIDS is not affecting just the gay community but the population at large. AIDS is just one more oppression in the history of exploitation, disfranchisement, marginalization, and silencing of U.S. Latinos. When AIDS intersects with ethnicity, class, migration, race, and sexuality, as in the case of many Latinos/as, life gets more complicated. For some Latinos/as, it is not simply a matter of articulating a gay sexual identity, but having AIDS materializes the construction of a subjectivity in a process that allows for the questioning of sexual taboos and the breaking of silence at home on homosexuality and AIDS. Through literature Latinos/as negotiate with AIDS in their efforts to understand and cope with the epidemic, with death, with the community, with the family, with friends, and with the self. Undoubtedly the gay response to AIDS dominates the writing on the subject since they were the first high-risk group affected by the syndrome.

After AIDS and confronting death, what is there to lose? AIDS has opened the doors for Latinos/as to come out of the closet, to put to work a politics of affinity and survival, and to turn literature into an act of intervention and survival. Latino/a AIDS literature embodies an act of self-affirmation in order to live and die with dignity among relatives and friends. Eventually as AIDS spreads among the Latino/a heterosexual population, especially among women of color and children, literature will bear witness and testimony, intervene, and give voice to experiences. For now, writers such as Castillo, Torres, Muñoz, and Manrique are breaking the silence once AIDS hits home. Silencio = muerte.

NOTES

1. Torres has stated: "The key element in this AIDS narrative is homoeroticism: sex and pleasure, desire and its consequences in this dangerous era. The exploration of the AIDS crisis is limited to the HIV status, one of the first stages in the chain of humiliations that each individual has to suffer in struggling with the

disease. For Papo, knowing that he is going to be ill is like a dead-end street with no exit. His attitude exemplifies the situation of having no real option . . . The only possibility for Papo is sexual fantasy as a way to fight death with the simple notion of hedonism, that is, the doctrine that pleasure and happiness are the highest good, the devotion to pleasure as a way of life" ("Hispanic Literature" 6).

2. See Manzotti for an excellent critical reading of the novel, which centers on Papo's postmodern identity and postcolonial difference. According to Manzotti, Papo's hybrid condition installs him within the margins and Otherness that defines colonial subjectivity.

3. For a critical reading of the theatrical version of the novel, entitled *The Last Guantanamera*, see Manzor Coats. Her interpretation of the play's ending is primarily centered on the utopian aspect: "friendship and mutual comprehension and understanding are offered as the starting points for any utopian project. Similarly, the need to undress and to get rid of our repressive and homophobic monsters also seem to be a key prerequisite" (760). I totally agree with this reading, but the ahistorical and apolitical aspects of utopia should also be considered.

WORKS CONSULTED

Alonso, Ana María, and María Teresa Koreck. "Silences: 'Hispanics,' AIDS, and Sexual Practices." *Differences*, 1,1 (1988): 101-124.

Boffin, Tessa, and Sunil Gupta, eds. *Ecstatic Antibodies: Resisting the AIDS Mythology*. London: Rivers Oram Press, 1988.

Carter, Erica, and Simon Watney, eds. *Taking Liberties: AIDS and Cultural Politics*. London: Serpent's Tail, 1989.

Castillo, Ana. *So Far from God*. New York: W. W. Norton & Company, 1993.

Crimp, Douglas, ed. *AIDS: Cultural Analysis/Cultural Activism*. Cambridge, MA: MIT Press, 1989.

Crimp, Douglas, and Adam Rolston, eds. *AIDS Demographics*. Seattle: Bay Press, 1990.

HIV/AIDS Surveillance Report. U.S. Department of Health and Human Services. 8,1 (1996). Atlanta: Centers for Disease Control and Prevention.

Manrique, Jaime. *Latin Moon in Manhattan*. New York: St. Martin's Press, 1992.

______ . "Manuel Puig: The Writer As Diva." *Christopher Street*, 203 (July 1993): 14-27.

Manzor Coats, Lillian. "Performative Identities: Scenes Between Two Cubas." *Michigan Quarterly Review*, special issue *Bridges to Cuba/Puentes a Cuba*, 33, 4 (fall 1994): 748-761.

Manzotti, Vilma. "Rolando Morelli, Daniel Torres y sus desacatos a lo 'idéntico.' " Apropaciones, identidades y resistencia desde los márgenes. Ed. José Maristany. Montreal: Université de Montréal, 1994. 29-38.

Miller, James, ed. *Fluid Exchanges: Artists and Critics in the AIDS Crisis*. Toronto: University of Toronto Press, 1992.

Muñoz, Elías Miguel. *The Greatest Performance*. Houston: Arte Público Press, 1991.

Murphy, Timothy F., and Suzanne Poirier, eds. *Writing AIDS: Gay Literature, Language, and Analysis*. New York: Columbia University Press, 1993.

Nelkin, Dorothy, David P. Willis, and Scott V. Parris, eds. *A Disease of Society: Cultural and Institutional Responses to AIDS*. Cambridge: Cambridge University Press, 1991.

Nelson, Emmanuel S., ed. *AIDS: The Literary Response*. New York: Twayne Publishers, 1992.

______ , ed. "AIDS and the American Novel." *Journal of American Culture*, 13, 1 (spring 1990): 47-53.

O'Connell, Shaun. "The Big One: Literature Discovers AIDS." *New England Journal of Public Policy*, special issue on AIDS, 4, 1 (winter 1988): 485-506.

Pastore, Judith Laurence, ed. *Confronting AIDS Through Literature: The Responsibilities of Representation*. Urbana: University of Illinois Press, 1993.

Preston, John, ed. *Personal Dispatches: Writers Confront AIDS*. New York: St. Martin's Press, 1990.

Román, David. "'It's My Party and I'll Die If I Want To!': Gay Men, AIDS, and the Circulation of Camp in U.S. Theatre." *Theatre Journal*, 44 (1992): 305-327.

______ . "Performing All Our Lives: AIDS, Performance, Community." *Critical Theory and Performance*. Janelle G. Reinelt and Joseph R. Roach, eds. Ann Arbor: University of Michigan Press, 1992. 208-221.

______ . "Fierce Love and Fierce Response: Intervening in the Cultural Politics of Race, Sexuality, and AIDS." *Critical Essays: Gay and Lesbian Writers of Color*. E. S. Nelson, ed. New York: Harrington Park Press, 1993. 195-219.

______ . "Teatro Viva! Latino Performance and the Politics of AIDS in Los Angeles." *¿Entiendes? Queer Readings, Hispanic Writings*. Emilie Bergmann and Paul Julian Smith, eds. Durham: Duke University Press, 1995. 346-369.

Román, D., and A. Sandoval. "Caught in the Web: Latinidad, AIDS, and Allegory in *Kiss of the Spider Woman, The Musical*." American Literature, 67, 3 (September 1995): 553-585.

Sandoval, Alberto. "A Response to the Representation of AIDS in the Puerto Rican Arts and Literature: In the Manner of a Proposal for a Cultural Studies Project." *Puerto Ricans and AIDS: It's Time to Act, Centro de Estudios Puertorriqueños*, 6, 1 and 2 (spring 1994): 81-186.

______ . "Dios bendiga nuestro hogar." *Piso 13 Gay* (Puerto Rico), 2, 3 (Sept.-Dec. 1993): 13.

______ , ed. *Ollantay Theater Magazine*, special issue on AIDS and Latino Theatre, 2, 2 (summer/fall 1994).

______ . "So Far From National Stages, So Close to Home: An Inventory of Latino Theatre on AIDS." *Ollantay Theatre Magazine*, special issue on AIDS and Latino Theatre, 2, 2 (summer/fall 1994): 54-72.

______ . "Staging AIDS: What's Latinos Got To Do With It?" *Negotiating Performance: Gender, Sexuality, and Theatricality in Latin/o America*. Ed. Diana Taylor and Juan Villegas. Durham: Duke University Press, 1994. 49-66.

Singer, Merrill et al. "SIDA: Economic, Social, and Cultural Context of AIDS

Among Latinos." *Medical Anthropology Quarterly*, 4, 1 (March 1990): 72-114.

Torres, Daniel. *Morirás si da una primavera*. Miami: Iberian Studies Institute, 1993.

______ . "An AIDS Narrative. *Puerto Ricans and AIDS: It's Time To Act." Centro de estudios puertorriqueños*, 6, 1 and 2 (spring 1994): 178-181.

______ . "Hispanic Literature and Writers in the U.S. Today." [Achieving Success as a Latino in the U.S.A. or 'Represento a los que llevan la música por dentro' (I represent those who carry music inside them)]. Manuscript. 1995.

Watney, Simon. *Practices of Freedom: Selected Writings on HIV/AIDS*. Durham: Duke University Press, 1994.

Worth, Dooley, and Ruth Rodriguez. "Latina Women and AIDS." *Radical America*, A special issue: Facing AIDS, 20, 6 (1987): 63-67.

Nietzsche, Autobiography, History: Mourning and *Martin and John*

John Champagne
Penn State University, Erie, The Behrend College

SUMMARY. How might gay and lesbian literature be read not as a mimetic representation of homosexuality, but as an activity linked to problems of subjectivity and historiography? Reading Dale Peck's novel *Martin and John* alongside passages from Friedrich Nietzsche's "On the Uses and Disadvantages of History for Life" and Sigmund Freud's "Mourning and Melancholia," this essay argues for an understanding of Peck's text as an attempt to link two apparently different processes of import to contemporary gay male subjects in particular: the writing of what Nietzsche terms "critical history," and the mourning of those lost to HIV disease. It concludes by linking *Martin and John* to feminist critiques of identity and traditional historiography, as well as noting the connection between these two critiques. *[Article copies available for a fee from The Haworth Document Delivery Service: 1-800-342-9678. E-mail address: getinfo@haworth.com]*

John Champagne is Assistant Professor of English at Penn State University, Erie, The Behrend College. The author of two novels, *The Blue Lady's Hands* (Secaucus, NJ: Lyle Stuart, 1988) and *When the Parrot Boy Sings* (New York: Meadowlands Books, 1990), Champagne's most recent book is *The Ethics of Marginality: A New Approach to Gay Studies* (Minneapolis: University of Minnesota Press, 1995). Personal essays have appeared in John Preston's *Hometowns: Gay Men Write About Where They Belong* and *A Member of the Family*. Correspondence may be addressed: Penn State Behrend, Station Road, Erie, PA 16563-1501. E-mail: jgchampgne@aol.com

[Haworth co-indexing entry note]: "Nietzsche, Autobiography, History: Mourning and *Martin and John*." Champagne, John. Co-published simultaneously in *Journal of Homosexuality* (The Haworth Press, Inc.) Vol. 34, No. 3/4, 1998, pp. 177-204; and: *Gay and Lesbian Literature Since World War II: History and Memory* (ed: Sonya L. Jones) The Haworth Press, Inc., 1998, pp. 177-204; and: *Gay and Lesbian Literature Since World War II: History and Memory* (ed: Sonya L. Jones) Harrington Park Press, an imprint of The Haworth Press, Inc., 1998, pp. 177-204. Single or multiple copies of this article are available for a fee from The Haworth Document Delivery Service [1-800-342-9678, 9:00 a.m. - 5:00 p.m. (EST). E-mail address: getinfo@haworth.com].

A *New York Times* review of Dale Peck's 1993 experimental novel *Martin and John* cited on the novel's cover refers to it as "an indelible portrait of gay life during the plague years." Clearly, this is one way to understand the relationship of this novel to recent historical events. That is, it is possible to minimize some of the formal difficulties of the novel, and treat it chiefly as a series of short stories chronicling gay (white urban middle-class) life in the age of AIDS. In attempting to chart the relationship between "history" and Peck's novel, one might, then, praise (or fault) *Martin and John* in terms of the "accuracy" of its representation of contemporary gay life.

This kind of mimetic criticism has, however, been under attack for some time. For example, Christine Gledhill's 1978 essay "Recent Developments in Feminist Criticism" argued persuasively the limitations of a criticism concerned primarily with delineating "positive" and "negative" images, one of Gledhill's important points being that "there is no simple alternative reality to fill the gap and displace" representations thought to be stereotypical or inaccurate (822). Gay and lesbian critics in the academy in particular have often followed feminism's lead, arguing, for example, that different political constituencies have conflicting understandings of what might constitute a "positive" image of a gay or lesbian person (Morton). These critiques suggest that we must find another way to read the relationship between "history" and "fiction" in Peck's novel, a way that might move beyond a simple concern with the accuracy of its representation of the "plague years."

I'd like to use this essay as an opportunity to meditate on some admittedly very broad questions concerning the relationship between "history," cultural marginality, and *Martin and John*. Reading Peck's novel alongside passages from Friedrich Nietzsche on history and Sigmund Freud on mourning, I will conclude by raising the question of how culturally marginalized peoples write themselves into their own historical narratives. My use of Nietzsche is idiosyncratic, perhaps even promiscuous. I am not suggesting that Nietzsche's (and, later, Freud's) work contains the key with which to unlock the secrets of *Martin and John*. Nor am I making the simple-minded assertion, often erroneously attributed to poststructuralism, that fiction and history are the same thing. In his meditation, Nietzsche defines what he calls "three species of history"–the monumental, the antiquarian, and the critical. Each of these implies a different conception of the past, and, as a result, serves a different purpose. In the last chapter of *The Ethics of Marginality*, I suggest some of the hazards of monumental and antiquarian approaches to histories of (homo)sexuality. I'd like to take this argument in a slightly different direction here, mentioning briefly some of the problems with these modes of history, but concentrating primarily on a discussion of *Martin and John* as putting into play a critical sense of history. Each of Nietzsche's three modes of historiography makes a different affective and aesthetic appeal to its readers. My argument assumes that Peck's novel shares with Nietzsche's critical historiography a similar appeal. Placing an account of this appeal alongside a discussion of mourning and HIV, I want to think, in what in a piece like this can only be very provisional ways, about history, mourning, and identity "during the plague years." Before doing so, however, I will introduce Peck's novel to readers unfamiliar with it, and say a bit more about a particular moment that emblematizes *Martin and John*'s refusal to respect the usual distinctions drawn between history, autobiography, and fiction.

In "Fucking Martin," the second to the last chapter of *Martin and John*, a character named Susan addresses the chapter's narrator, a character named John, as "Dale" (219). More precisely, she whispers the name as a question in response to what is apparently a pause in their lovemaking. This slip of the tongue is a remarkable moment, even in a novel such as *Martin and John*, in which proper names never seem to find a stable referent.

Specifically–up until this point in the novel, the majority of the chapters in *Martin and John* have been narrated in the first person by a character named John.[1] The name "John," however, does not necessarily refer to the same character from chapter to chapter. The same is true for the names of a number of the other characters in the novel, including Susan, Martin, Bea, and John's father, who in the first chapter is named Henry.[2]

While the use of these various names seems at first random, over the course of the novel, a pattern emerges. Martin is always the object of John's desire; Bea and Henry are usually parental figures; Susan is always a friend, and sometimes one with whom John has a sexual encounter. In addition to these repeated names, a number of motifs occur in more than one chapter: a disfigured hand, a facial scar, beer, a rattle, two men seated at a piano, a number of devices from *The Wizard of Oz*. Given the way these motifs resurface in stories not causally connected with one another, the reader might note something almost obsessive in their repetition. These enigmas are somewhat resolved, however, by the novel's concluding chapter.

Martin and John is divided into alternating chapters, the first set in italics, the second in plain text.[3] Read by themselves, the italicized chapters create a coherent narrative that we might label the "history" of John's life up until the novel's present. Written in the first person as a kind of truncated autobiography, they tell the story of John, a young, presumably white gay man who escapes his widowed abusive father by running away from Kansas to New York. There, he falls in love with Martin, who eventually dies of AIDS. The final italicized chapters recount John's efforts at mourning, something I will discuss in detail later in this essay. Significantly, the novel begins and ends with italicized chapters.[4]

In the last (italicized) chapter of the novel, we also surmise that, if the italicized chapters represent John's "history," or some "factual" attempt such as autobiography to represent his life in words, the nonitalicized chapters are the stories John tells about his life, his attempt to revise and rework its horrors. In this final chapter, John practically tells us as much. He confesses that, as a child, he made up "happy" stories to counter the hardships of his life. "Soon," however, "the stories I imagined were as horrible as the one I lived. I found a power in it, and the power increased as the imagined horror became more and more like the events of my life" (224). This seems an appropriate description of the novel. Both the italicized and nonitalicized sections are filled with what might appropriately be termed "horrors"–scenes of family violence, adolescent prostitution, unhappy love affairs, gay bashing, the devastating effects of HIV disease on the body. Given a certain repetition of motifs between the italicized and nonitalicized stories, it thus seems plausible that the nonitalicized chapters in particular might represent the stories John invented.[5]

Also significant is the fact that the nonitalicized chapters are generally longer than the italicized ones, and resemble more traditional short stories. The italicized chapters contain fewer of the qualities we often associate with well-crafted stories–less "development," more of a certain immediacy. In the nonitalicized chapters, the narrator takes some time to explore some of the origins of the horrors that lurk beneath the surface of the everyday. When the violence finally erupts, it is almost expected. This is not the case in the italicized chapters, in which the violence seems more random, immediate, and unexplained.[6] These chapters are sometimes written in the present tense, and have a certain "personal" quality resembling journal entries or autobiographical ruminations.[7]

Later in the final (italicized) chapter, John makes the connection between the italicized and nonitalicized chapters even more explicit. Quoting himself, he cites the first sentence of the first nonitalicized chapter and implies that this chapter is in fact a story in which he recounted "something that hadn't happened" (225). "Everything's been a little confused since then, what's real and what's invented," he tells us, "but it all seems to make more sense too." Also of pertinence is the fact that these revelations occur in the novel's final chapter, thus resolving one of the novel's most persistent enigmas. Taken together, then, the italicized and nonitalicized chapters constitute a kind of memoir, a hybrid genre that uneasily combines "true" stories from John's life with (fictional) stories that reveal the "truth" of that same life.

In these final pages of the novel in particular, however, John suggests that there is no clear line to be drawn between "fiction" and "history." While the pattern of italicized and nonitalicized chapters attempts to stabilize one as "imagination" and the other as "truth," John's confession deconstructs this binary, planting the seeds of doubt in the reader's mind as he or she attempts to interpret recursively this "disturbing" novel. The italicized chapters become contaminated with the possibility that they are as "fictive" as the stories John creates. If John can no longer tell what's real and what's invented, how can we? Complicating this of course is the reader's awareness that *Martin and John* is a novel, that even its "truth" is a fiction, and, conversely, that, given certain Western notions of the aesthetic, "fiction" might still embody "truth." Significant here is the novel's high modernist experimental form. This arguably sets it apart from much gay fiction, which, like much popular fiction in the United States, is written in a predominantly realist vein.[8] In other words, in its initial chapters, Peck's novel announces itself as "art," and thus bears the burden of a history in which art is thought to exist in a privileged relationship to truth.

Martin and John's pattern of italicized "truth" and nonitalicized "fiction" is further complicated by the moment in which Susan addresses John as "Dale," the first name of the "real" novel's author. "Dale" is a name that is not used in any of the other chapters. The novel makes no attempt to explain why Susan refers to "John" as "Dale"–an unusual gesture for one of the nonitalicized chapters in particular, even in this novel in which names are used so promiscuously. Instead, following Susan's question, "John" (or "Dale")–the character in a story invented by John–apparently begins to speak of himself in the third person, describing John and Susan continuing to make love, as well as John's thoughts of Martin. However, following this paragraph, the narrator, while continuing to describe John and Susan's lovemaking, now refers to himself as "I," and tells the reader that John's face "is just a mask for mine" (220). All of this suggests that "I" is perhaps "Dale" and "John" is perhaps someone else, a character the narrator ("Dale"?) has invented in order to allow him to tell his story. This reading is supported by the conclusion of this chapter, in which "Dale" (?) admits, "I thought I'd controlled everything so well, the plants, Martin, John, Susan." The chapter ends with two sentences, each its own paragraph: "In this story, I'd intended semen to be the water of life. But, in order to live, I've only ever tasted mine." Who here is the "I"? Not the "real" John; as he tells us in the next and final (italicized) chapter, he has HIV. Not "John"; as the narrator has already told us, this name is a mask for "mine." According to the logic of the novel, then, in the chapter "Fucking Martin," "John" is (initially) a mask for "Dale" who is perhaps a character created by John who is a character created by Dale (Peck).

Because the "Dale" is posed as a question, however, we are left with another possibility: perhaps the novel in its entirety–italicized and non-italicized chapters–is "really" the work of "Dale" and not John, who may or may not be Dale. In this second to the final chapter,[9] the possibility arises that the "John" in both the italicized and nonitalicized chapters is the invention of a character named "Dale" who is himself the invention of a "real" "historical" novelist named Dale. In other words, perhaps we have been fooled all along: "John" and John are both actually masks for "Dale," who is a mask for Dale (Peck). Through the use of this single unexplained name, the novel blurs not only the lines between two fictional worlds–John's "real" life and the life he recreates for himself through his fiction–but also between "fiction"–the novel *Martin and John* and, perhaps, "history"–in the form of an autobiography of sorts of author Dale Peck. *Martin and John* is thus actually "Dale's" story, which may or may not be Dale's story, although, given the popular tendency to read all fiction (and first novels in particular) as in some sense autobiographical, for some readers, "Dale" will be Dale.

And if in fact John and "John" are "Dale," and "Dale" is Dale, why is it Susan who reveals this to us? What does it mean that a character in Peck's novel says what the novel's apparent narrator–and possible author–will not or cannot? Is the fictive Susan the only one able to tell the "literal" truth here? It is almost as if Susan has somehow forgotten the rules of the game and taken on a reality of her own–a reality which also happens to be our own in that it includes a real person named Dale (Peck). The fact that the name is posed as a question, and Susan's question in particular, however, leaves open the door for still another reading: perhaps Susan simply made a mistake, committed the unforgivable but, ironically, familiar sin of calling her lover–and in the heat of passion–by the wrong name. Perhaps she herself is not sure if John is "John" or "John" is "Dale" or "Dale" is Dale.

As a matter of convenience, I will now bracket off considerations of "Dale," and refer to the narrator of the italicized passages as John, and the narrator of the nonitalicized passages as "John." Perhaps, following the example of Virginia Woolf, I should invite the reader to call the narrator "any name you please–it is not a matter of any importance" (732). In any case, I want to turn now to Nietzsche's "On the Uses and Disadvantages of

History for Life" in order to think about what kind of "history" is represented in Peck's novel.

HISTORY AND MARTIN AND JOHN

> History pertains to the living man in three respects: it pertains to him as a being who acts and strives, as a being who preserves and reveres, as a being who suffers and seeks deliverance. (67)

Nietzsche begins his "Untimely Meditation" on the uses of history with an assertion that we need history "for the sake of life and action," and not for its own sake (59). According to Nietzsche, too much of the historical sense paralyzes our ability to act in the present: "Forgetting is essential to action of any kind" (62). He thus invites his reader to meditate upon the proposition that "*the unhistorical and the historical are necessary in equal measure for the health of an individual, of a people and of a culture*" (63).

According to Nietzsche, monumental history uses the greatness of the past to inspire action in the present. It looks to the past to provide "models, teachers, comforters" (67) for contemporary subjects. As Nietzsche defines it,

> That the great moments in the struggle of the human individual constitute a chain, that this chain unites mankind across the millennia like a range of human mountain peaks, that the summit of such a long-ago moment shall be for me still living, bright and great–that is the fundamental idea of the faith in humanity which finds expression in the demand for a *monumental* history. (68)

Nietzsche is careful to warn, however, that if the monumental mode of understanding history rules over the antiquarian and the critical, "the past itself suffers *harm*: whole segments of it are forgotten, despised, and flow away in an uninterrupted colourless flood"(70-71). Interested only in preserving the greatness of the past, monumental history risks degenerating into "free poetic invention" (70). In order to produce a sense of the past as elevated and noble, worthy of preservation, it must necessarily overlook a great deal, and risks becoming a means of ignoring the vitality of the present.

Unlike monumental history, which approaches the past selectively, antiquarian history attempts to tend with care all that has existed from old

(72-73). Conservative and curatorial, it treats all of the past as equally worthy of preservation. Like the monumental historical mode, it too risks stifling the present, for the antiquarian mode "knows only how to *preserve* life, not how to engender it" (75). When the antiquarian mode of regarding the past dominates the monumental and the critical, "[t]he fact that something has grown old now gives rise to the demand that it be made immortal," and historiography becomes a matter of mummifying the past rather than salvaging it for use in the present.

Though it, too, hazards certain dangers, the critical mode of history is perhaps the most useful mode of history for life. As Nietzsche argues, "If he is to live, man must possess and from time to time employ the strength to break up and dissolve a part of the past: he does this by bringing it before the tribunal, scrupulously examining it and finally condemning it; . . ." (75-76). The critical historical mode invites us to contemplate the past only until we have reached the point at which we might free ourselves from it. At this point, "life alone, that dark, driving power that insatiably thirsts for itself" (76), demands that we "take the knife" to the roots of the past and destroy it. As my epigraph to this section reminds us, according to Nietzsche, the critical historical sense understands the human subject as "a being who suffers and seeks deliverance" (67) and who specifically seeks deliverance from that suffering through the act of thinking historically.

One way to make sense of *Martin and John* is to read it as the attempt by John to engage with Nietzsche's critical historical mode, and, as a result, free himself from the terrors of his past. In the (autobiographical) italicized chapters in particular, John breaks up and dissolves a part of his past by "scrupulously examining it and finally condemning it" (Nietzsche 75-76). In the final (italicized) chapter, John recalls lying in bed one day with Martin, trying to figure out how he'd gotten there. "Not just to Martin's bed, but to that place in my life" (Peck 225). He begins to narrate to Martin some of his memories. Hearing these memories, Martin asks John if he has ever thought of writing his memories down, "a piece at a time if I had to, and putting those pieces in order. . . . " One way to read these italicized chapters, then, is as John's attempt to write himself into a critical history, to tell the story of his past so that he might live and act in the present. While the initial impulse was to free himself from his history "before" Martin, by the conclusion of the novel, following the trauma of Martin's suffering and death–described in harrowing detail in the italicized chapters entitled "Circumnavigation" and "Lee"–John also must necessarily move beyond the pain of losing Martin to HIV disease.

This (autobiographical) critical history is itself interrupted, however, by John's fiction, the interruption paradoxically serving to make John's autobiography "more" "real." After insisting that one has to start over sometimes (223), John explains that this might involve telling oneself new "fictional" stories: "in your mind there's a battle as it tries to find something to grab on to, whether it's a memory of something that happened or a memory of something you imagined, a story you told yourself" (224). Recall John's contention that he found power in imagining stories that were as horrible as the ones he'd lived, "and that power increased as the imagined horror became more and more like the events of my life." If the autobiographical chapters represent John's (critical/historical) act of remembering, perhaps the stories he tells represent that other act Nietzsche notes as necessary for life: the act of forgetting. It might in fact be argued that *Martin and John* is an extended deconstruction of the binary "remembering/forgetting." Throughout Peck's novel, John moves back and forth between a kind of willful forgetting necessary for life and the attempt to employ a critical historical mode. The two, however, are not easily disentangled: in order to forget, he must remember. In order to be delivered from his suffering, he must first recall in detail the events of the past; but in order to remember his past–and thus destroy it in the service of living–he must forget it through the fictions he writes. The "fictional" (non-italicized) stories, employing as they do tropes from John's "history," are thus paradoxically acts of forgetting which can only come to fruition through an act of remembering.

While this deconstruction of the binary "remembering/forgetting" is played out across the surface of the novel as a whole, one chapter in particular stages this deconstruction in some relief. In the midst of the (italicized) chapter entitled "Tracks," while critically examining an event from his "real" life–his initial flight to New York following a brutal beating by his father–John tells us, "Because there was nothing left of me, I went with him. [John is speaking here of a young runaway he meets in Port Authority.] The world accumulated history as each second passed, but I sloughed it off as though my body were coated in wax. I wanted to remember nothing, foresee nothing, there was nothing I wanted to know about myself" (112). Here, John cannot possibly say what he means, nor mean what he says. If there was nothing left of him, then "he" could not have gone with the runaway–there would be no "I" remaining. More importantly, if in fact he had "sloughed off" history as he says he did, he would not be able to narrate this moment from his past. Without a knowledge of his past, there could be no "Tracks" (nor would any "tracks" or traces be left through which to reconstruct John's autobiography). The precondition of John's narrative is thus its inability to mean what it says.

The value of this deconstruction of "remembering/forgetting" is that it prevents us from falling for the lures of the monumental and antiquarian modes of historical thinking. For neither of these other modes moves toward what Nietzsche understands as the life affirming "destruction" embodied in the critical mode. While the monumental mode necessarily forgets the unpleasantness of the past, such forgetting is not strategic, but inadvertent. Monumental history is made possible by a failure of memory, but, according to its own logic, that failure of memory is an error, a refusal to recognize, for example, the blunders of the past. The antiquarian mode by contrast makes no room for forgetting whatsoever. It insists that all of the past is worthy of preserving in its entirety. Only the critical mode moves toward a deconstruction of the binary "remembering/forgetting," forgetting enough of the past to make life in the present possible, and, as Nietzsche explains in a passage on the dangers of the critical approach, remembering enough to insure that life in the present will flourish with a (perhaps modest but crucial) sense of history.

The dangers the critical historical mode confronts are substantial; owing to their pertinence to a discussion of *Martin and John*, I cite them at some length.

> For since we are the outcome of earlier generations, we are also the outcome of their aberrations, passions and errors, and indeed of their crimes; it is not possible wholly to free oneself from this chain. If we condemn these aberrations and regard ourselves as free of them, this does not alter the fact that we originate in them. The best we can do is to confront our inherited and hereditary nature with our knowledge of it, and through a new, stern discipline combat our inborn heritage and implant in ourselves a new habit, a new instinct, a second nature, so that our first nature withers away. It is an attempt to give oneself, as it were *a posteriori*, a past in which one would like to originate in opposition to that in which one did originate:–always a dangerous attempt because it is so hard to know the limit to denial of the past. . . . (76)

In its eagerness to destroy the past, the critical historical mode risks failing to take sufficient account of the ways in which the past might continue to exert an influence on life in the present. It threatens to suggest that subjects are "free" to rid themselves of the burden of history at will. In the face of this danger, Nietzsche suggests a critical practice in which one attempts to confront one's own historicity, and to use the knowledge gained in such a confrontation to provide for oneself a "new" way of being.

I don't find it particularly helpful to read Nietzsche here as if, in attempting to chart how we might free ourselves from an overly burdensome past, he were engaging in some kind of "essentialist" argument regarding human nature. His prose demands a more careful reading. The condition of possibility of a first nature "withering away" is its historicity. Such a nature cannot by definition be natural. If human nature is that which is essential or fundamental to all human beings, then there can be no such thing as a "second" nature. Both "new instinct" and "second nature" are oxymorons. Nietzsche's prose here acknowledges its own impossibility. Further evidence is provided in a subsequent passage in which he argues the seemingly impossible proposition that "this first nature was once a second nature" and that "every victorious second nature will become a first" (77). I thus read this passage as an attempt to save critical history from a simpleminded historicism by acknowledging its conditions of (im)possibility. In this formulation, historiography is not the empiricist project of writing down "what really happened." It is, rather, the attempt to confront historical knowledge with its own impossibility–while still striving to know. In this passage, Nietzsche is putting into play an anti-historicist historicism, an attempt to undermine a simpleminded historicism (emblematized in such phrases as "our inherited and hereditary nature"), while simultaneously acknowledging the hold of that "chain" of "aberrations, passions, errors, and crimes" we call history.

Taken in its entirety, *Martin and John* might represent an attempt by John to engage in the critical activity Nietzsche describes in this passage. Throughout the course of writing these two sets of texts, italicized autobiography and nonitalicized fiction, John is attempting to free himself from the chains of his past while simultaneously acknowledging the limits of such an activity. The combination of "autobiography" and "fiction" is crucial to this project. A simple, straightforward retelling of one's life would suggest that one were merely the outcome of the past, unable to do anything more than preserve, as the antiquarian historian might, the details of one's history. Obviously, autobiography doesn't "really" work this way; it is always more than a value-neutral and objective portrait of a life. I am suggesting, however, that, in its "initial" use of the genre, the novel deploys this commonsense understanding of autobiography. In its concluding chapter in particular, through John's insistence that "what's real and what's invented" is no longer clear to him, *Martin and John* undermines even this naive sense of autobiography, raising the possibility that John's "history" might be contaminated by "fiction."

An exclusively "fictional" retelling of one's life, on the other hand, would suggest that one could in fact free oneself easily from the chain of history. *Martin and John* undermines such a suggestion in at least two ways. First, as I have already implied, John's autobiography supplements, in the Derridean sense of the term, the fictional stories, both supplying what is missing from them–their "cause," as it were, John's "real" life–as well as adding something to them in excess of John's life. Particularly significant here is the intrusion of the name "Dale" in the final (nonitalicized) story, as it both seems "excessive," even in an experimental novel such as this one ("Dale" is too much here) and threatens to supply the "key" to deciphering the novel's enigmas in the form of Dale (Peck's) "fictional" memoir (Dale is too much here). Second, the novel insists that John's invented stories be at least as "horrible" as the life they supposedly re-present. They come dangerously close to repeating rather than escaping from John's history. On a formal level, then, *Martin and John* "enacts," albeit "fictively," Nietzsche's critical mode of history. The act of writing both autobiography and fiction–"contaminated" as they both are in this novel by "history" and "invention"–allows John to forge for himself a "second" nature, while still remembering the fact that he "originates" somewhere else–in some mysterious and complicated combination of the two, in "Dale's" imagination, in Dale's imagination. The name "Dale" appears, after all, in what is ostensibly John's "last" story. John must know he might not be John. In one of his stories, he has "John" say, " . . . I feel like my old self again, though which self that is I don't know" (105).[10]

Additionally, several passages in the novel illustrate John's attempts both to "break up and dissolve" a piece of his past through his writing, while simultaneously confronting the fact that it is not possible to free oneself wholly from the chain of history. As he writes in the final chapter, "I tell myself that by reinventing my life, my imagination imposes an order on things and makes them make sense" (224)–suggesting that his fiction can in fact free him from the horrors of his history. But John immediately follows this statement with his confession that "sometimes I think that horror is all I know and all I'll ever know, and no matter how much I try to loose my mind from the bonds and the boundaries of the events of my life, it returns to them always, obsessively, like a dog sniffing for a bone it buried too deep and now can't find." What John here casts as an obsession we might call, after Nietzsche, the necessary attempt to understand the past's hold on the present. A similar instance occurs in "Tracks." Of his cryptic explanation for how his father's boot had crippled his hand, he notes, "The only answer I could give, as free of history as possible, it still contained a force that stunned me, propelled by the weight of everything I'd lost, and hinting, somehow, at things I had yet to gain" (114). Although John begins this chapter telling us about his desire to flee from history, in this passage, he confesses that such attempts necessarily fail. He is necessarily the outcome of his father's aberrant behavior, and must find a way to cope with this.

HISTORY, MOURNING, AND MARTIN AND JOHN

Nietzsche's description of critical history, with its emphasis on the attempts of human beings to use history to deliver themselves from suffering, bears a resemblance to the now familiar account of mourning provided by Freud in his 1917 essay "Mourning and Melancholia." According to Freud, the work of mourning involves a testing of reality. In mourning, the recognition that the loved object no longer exists leads to a situation in which the libido is necessarily withdrawn from its attachments to the object (165-66). However, a struggle arises: "man never willingly abandons a libido-position, not even when a substitute is already beckoning to him" (166). In what Freud terms the normal outcome of mourning, the object is ultimately abandoned, but not without a great deal of effort:

> The task is now carried through bit by bit, under great expense of time and cathectic energy, while all the time the existence of the lost object is continued in the mind. Each single one of the memories and hopes which bound the libido to the object is brought up and hyper-cathected, and the detachment of the libido from it accomplished. . . . when the work of mourning is completed the ego becomes free and uninhibited again. (166)

Like the critical historian, then, the mourner subjects the past–in the form of memories of the loved object–to an extended examination that ends in its destruction–in the form of the reattachment of the libido to a new object. Freud's account of the fierceness with which the mourner's libido is bound to the memory of the lost object suggests something of Nietzsche's understanding of the human subject as "chained" to its past. The difficulty with which mourning is accomplished parallels that involved in the historical subject's attempt to combat his or her "first nature" in an effort to free him- or herself from the residual influence of "earlier generations." For both writers, a destruction of the past–through the work of mourning, through a critical historiography–is vital for the continuation of life.

One of the important differences between Freud's account of mourning and Nietzsche's account of the work of the critical historian is that Freud is explaining unconscious processes, while Nietzsche is presumably writing of willed activity. The question of the unconscious is one which I deliberately leave behind here. My own use of Freud in this essay will thus strike some readers as particularly idiosyncratic, selective, perhaps even downright "wrong." Douglas Crimp's "Mourning and Militancy" makes clear some of the difficulties of attempting to use Freud's analysis to discuss mourning as a conscious activity. As I have already suggested, shoring up the truth claims of psychoanalysis is not one of the goals of this essay. Rather, I am interested in seeing how Nietzsche, Freud, and Peck share–albeit unevenly–a certain discursive conception of mourning (or, at the very least, the seeking of deliverance from suffering). My account of mourning in *Martin and John* will thus not focus on John's unconscious processes. Rather, I will stress from Freud the sense of mourning as an activity, though I will consider it as a "conscious," or at the very least "willed" one, and read the novel as an attempt to put into play a discourse around mourning as an activity.

Given the reading of the novel with which I have been working, we might understand the book as a whole as an instrument of John's mourning–for his father, for his mother, for Martin. In the (autobiographical) italicized chapters in particular, John recounts scenes of his life with his mother and father as well as both the happy and difficult memories of loving Martin. Of particular pertinence here are not only the later chapters that describe in some detail John's interactions with Martin–in these instances, the strength of John's libidinal attachments to Martin is fairly self-evident–but also the many moments in the initial chapters in which some kind of incestuous attachment, fantasy, or wish linking John and one or both of his parents is presented. For example: in the very first (italicized) chapter, the familiar Oedipal triangle appears in a slightly unusual configuration: a frustrated mother calls her husband at work when her baby boy won't stop crying. "Ain't nothing wrong with John. Ain't nothing wrong with *my son*," he tells her, suggesting she has implied the opposite (3). When he returns home–the baby finally quiets down just as he arrives–the mother worries that the father will take out his anger on her. It is as if the parents are competing for the son's love. While this first italicized chapter appears to be narrated by the mother, it is actually narrated by someone else, as suggested by the fact that it is surrounded by quotation marks; in all likelihood, this narrator is John.

The second italicized chapter depicts an almost prototypical primal scene. Sleeping on the beach with his parents, the child wakes to see them making love. He tries to rise, but his father holds him down. He falls asleep again, and wakes for a second time. This time, as his father continues to hold him down, he fantasizes that his father is drowning both mother and child. The third (italicized) chapter describes the love John feels for his father despite the brutal ways he is treated by him; in the fourth, in which John is savagely beaten by his father after confessing to having given his first blow job, John compares aloud his trick's dick to both his own and his father's (85). In the italicized chapter "Lee," John recalls his mother's gaze, "those eyes which looked at me, which accused me, which told me more plainly than words, You are his son" (195).[11] All of these passages suggest, as Freud might, that John's autobiographical ruminations make possible the de-cathecting of his libido from memories of his (beloved and hated) father and mother.[12]

Taken together, then, the italicized chapters would thus represent John's attempts to de-cathect his libido, through autobiography, from three of the primary love objects of his life—his mother, his father, and Martin. As Freud suggests, this involves a kind of careful and deliberate recounting of memories of the lost object. Beginning as they do in medias res, and shorn of details that might help the reader place them in terms of time, space, and even character, many of the italicized chapters indeed have the quality of recounted memories.

John, however, reminds us that while memory is his only possession, "it resists ownership" (225). Because the line between "what's real and what's invented" is confused, it is not enough simply to de-cathect from his memories. He must also leave behind all the stories he has told himself throughout his life, from the time he was a child, "kept awake by the sound of my parents fighting in the other room," (224) to the stories he wrote presumably as a way of coping with Martin's death. Given the slippage in the novel between "reality" and "invention," the nonitalicized stories might themselves be read as "memories" of sorts (screen memories?) recounted in the wake of "fucking Martin." Also significant is the almost obsessive repetition of names and motifs. This repetition suggests something of the "great expense of time and cathectic energy" (Freud, "Mourning," 166) required by mourning. As Freud suggests, the progress of grief is slow and gradual (177). Perhaps his autobiographical sketches do not provide John with a sufficient means of de-cathecting; they must be supplemented by his fiction.[13]

As might be surmised, the final (italicized) chapter in particular makes clear the relationship between John's writing and mourning. In addition to describing the circumstances under which he began to write, and the complicated relationship between his "memory" and stories, this final chapter informs us that, at the novel's conclusion, "it's a year since Martin died" (223), the novel itself constituting a kind of record of John's mourning. This chapter also implies that John is coming to the end of his mourning process.[14] In the last paragraph of the novel, John tells us that he has spent his life swaying between the two high points of a pendulum, between "love and hate, rage and joy, terror and numbness" (227); this, however, has changed recently. "Everything tells me that if I want to survive I have to find a middle ground," he confesses (228). The writing of this "novel" has allowed him to leave behind his history (with his mother, with his father, with Martin) and to move toward some kind of "normalcy," at least as John himself might define it.

A number of the chapters in the novel–both italicized and nonitalicized–suggest that sex might play a particular role in John's mourning.[15] The third- and second-to-the-last chapters of the novel–the first, italicized, the second, not–contain what are some of the most explicit and, for some readers–my undergraduate students, for example–disturbing depictions of homoerotic sex. These chapters, coming as they do near the end of the book, one right after the other, suggest that, as John's mourning increases in intensity, so do his attempts to use sex to assist him in that mourning.

"Lee," the second to the last "autobiographical" chapter, is apparently named after an older man with whom John has sex. Interestingly, it is the only chapter that combines italicized and nonitalicized passages. The italicized passages, written in the present tense, describe their sexual encounter. The nonitalicized passages are written in the past tense and interrupt the italicized passages; they, too, appear to be autobiographical–one of them makes reference to John's "broken hand" (195). The first one is a somewhat humorous account of a sexual encounter; it allegorizes the fine line between sexual pleasure and pain. The other nonitalicized passages describe extremely painful moments in John's life: what are apparently three encounters with Martin in which the agony of his illness leads him to treat John with deliberate cruelty, and a fourth passage, in which John describes the accusing gaze of his mother, her body wracked by bruises and broken bones delivered by her husband.

During the course of the sexual encounter described in the italicized passages, John screams at Lee to "fuck me harder" (190) and then "hit me" (191). He convinces Lee to insert a gun into John's anus, and eventually asks him to "pull the trigger" (196). Apparently shocked and obviously unwilling to comply with John's request, Lee loses his erection, grabs his clothes, and runs out of the room, leaving John. ". . . I hear myself sob aloud and I think that at last I've succeeded," he tells us, "for I cry only for myself."

The next chapter, "Fucking Martin"–the final nonitalicized chapter–presents in some detail a sadomasochistic sexual encounter between "John" (who in this same chapter, you will recall, is referred to by Susan as "Dale?") and Henry. John begins the particular passage by telling us that "[t]here was a time when I'd wanted to be powerless, and have sex. I wanted to lose control" (206). During the course of their sexual encounter, Henry collars, leashes, gags, ties up, and hoods John, and subjects his body to a number of devices–ball stretchers, nipple clamps, and hot wax among them. This chapter also contains accounts of John's lovemaking with Martin. As explicitly described as the scenes with Henry, their lovemaking is nonetheless more conventionally romantic and sensual. They kiss, laugh, hold one another.

In both of these chapters, it is made clear that John orchestrates these encounters. John begins his description of sex with Lee by suggesting that he himself has put "a layer of space between us" (190). "He couldn't possibly understand why I ask him to do these things," John confides. About Henry, John tells us, "It was not, I think, in Henry's nature to hurt anyone" (206). He assumes that, left to his own devices, Henry would have preferred "vanilla" sex with perhaps a few toys thrown in. "But," John tells us, "I insisted, and he knew what to do" (206-07). In both of these chapters, then, John is engaged in activities he himself has sought out and chosen. In other words, he is not acting unreflectively, but is rather someone who is pursuing conscious desires.

The novel also makes clear the relationship between these sexual activities and mourning. In the middle of his encounter with Lee, John tells us he wants to scream, in what is apparently a response to his memory of Martin, "Will nothing make you go away?" (193). Also of obvious importance is the fact that the narrative describing their sex is literally interrupted by John's memories of his family and Martin. Near the end of "Fucking Martin," John tells us that the day Martin died was the day he sought out Henry. In this chapter, John makes clear the relationship between his s/m encounter with Henry and mourning: "S/M, if you let it, or if you can't stop it, delivers what it promises: pain that transforms" (207). In the middle of the sex, John apparently fantasizes that Henry cuts off his head and holds it above his body so he can look at himself. This allows John to achieve a kind of "normalcy": "My mind bounced too, from memory to memory, and all of them seemed somehow transformed into visions that, no matter how painful they might have been once, were now ecstatic, and it was wonderful, a kind of freedom from the past–it was what I wanted" (208).

Some psychoanalytically inclined critics might suggest that, in both of these stories, John's mourning begins to take on the character of what Freud terms "melancholia."[16] Rather than discuss John's behavior in terms of individual pathology and unconscious processes, however, I would like to conclude this essay by suggesting briefly how we might think through another connection between history, mourning, and *Martin and John*. In order to make this case, I will have to turn briefly from the novel to "the real" (as perilous as such a turn might be) as well as to a brief discussion of recent debates in historiography, before returning again to Peck's novel.

CONCLUSION: GAY MEN, MOURNING, HISTORY, AND FICTION

A number of gay male critics–Douglas Crimp, Michael Moon, and Jeff Nunokawa among them–have written recently on mourning, gay men, and HIV disease. All three of these particular writers refer in varying degrees to Freud's account of mourning, although there is no consensus among them concerning the overall usefulness of this account. Moon complicates Freud's account of mourning by calling into question its reliance on a sense of "normalcy" historically denied to gay men (cited in Crimp, 235-36); Crimp defends Freud from Moon's critique, insisting that, in Freud, the achievement of "normalcy" is always precarious and provisional; Nunokawa only mentions Freud in passing. All three critics, however, make important contributions to our understanding of the extreme difficulties facing gay men today as they attempt to mourn the loss of their lovers and friends from HIV disease. The media's continuing demonization of gay men as "AIDS carriers"; the cultural vilification and degradation of gay male sexuality; the necessity of abandoning or at least modifying long cherished forms of sexual expression; continuing concerns around one's own HIV status; internalized homophobia; news of yet another friend's seroconversion, or fall in t-cell count, or death; the sense of immediate relief that often accompanies the death of a long-suffering loved one; subsequent survivor's guilt; the sheer number of deaths many gay men have had to face–all of these necessarily inhibit the conclusion of mourning, characterized as it is by a return to some kind of "normal" life as it was defined prior to the death of the loved one. One of the important contributions of Freud's account of mourning in this context is its insistence that the work of mourning is "absorbing"; again, as Freud suggests, "progress" in mourning "is slow and gradual" (177). For Freud, mourning is neither simply an emotion nor an activity, but a combination of the two, a psychosocial process requiring, under the best of circumstances, a great deal of time and psychic energy. We still understand very little of its "economics." Many gay men today thus face a set of historical and cultural circumstances that make the successful completion of mourning nearly impossible.

If, as Nietzsche suggests, a critical historical approach allows us to free ourselves from the past while still recalling that small part of it to which we are necessarily still chained, perhaps gay men need to approach mourning as the critical historian might. That is, we need to cultivate ways both to remember and forget those whom we have lost from HIV disease (as well as to cope with all the other losses alluded to above that have accompanied AIDS). In doing so, however, we face another set of problems, problems related to historiography. Specifically: how do marginalized subjects formerly "hidden from history" write themselves into a historical narrative? What are the means at hand whereby those whose lives have been overlooked or omitted by traditional historiography might interrupt this omission? At least one historiographical method involves using the protocols of orthodox historiography in the name of the Other. As Michael S. Sherry suggests in an issue of *Perspectives*, the American Historical Association Newsletter, gay and lesbian history, for example, need not represent any threat whatsoever to established ways of "doing" history. Lest historians worry that recent work in gay and lesbian history might challenge established methods of historiography, Sherry assures them that "far from shattering a synthetic view of history," new fields such as gay and lesbian history "offer fresh ways to make something whole of it" (6). Interestingly, Sherry makes a point of reassuring other historians that gay and lesbian history is easily accomodatable to a history course structured around such traditional notions as "the American experience." In Sherry's account, gay and lesbian studies offers little critique of "business as usual" in the university–or at least in History departments. Concerning pedagogical approaches to gay and lesbian history, Sherry confesses, " . . . I try to be conventional in a course whose subject is novel and charged. Students get a familiar chronological structure and formal lectures. . . . I give them conventional structures and methods not to mainstream the subject–not to make it like other history in every way but one–but to empower students: to let them know that even an atypical history is knowable, within their grasp" (8). Absent here is any critique of the power/knowledge nexus as it necessarily informs the writing of a history of a marginalized group in particular. Apparently, Sherry has taken Jean Baudrillard at his word, for here is a version of gay and lesbian studies in which its practitioners have in fact "forgotten" Michel Foucault's warnings concerning the hazards of disciplinarity and the establishment of "new" objects of knowledge. Sherry's lessons for teaching gay and lesbian history evidence the historically familiar (imperialist) desire to know the Other, here disguised as a kind of benevolent concern for students, the language of empowerment obscuring the fact that such desire is never disinterested.

Arguing a position which by implication is highly critical of Sherry's, feminist historian Joan W. Scott has noted the ways in which the critical thrust of some recent histories of difference has been seriously weakened by their continuing reliance on the epistemological framework of orthodox historiography (24). These histories of difference take as their project the making visible of formerly neglected historical subjects. According to Scott, such histories often rest their claims to legitimacy on "the authority of experience, the direct experience of others, as well as of the historian who learns to see and illuminate the lives of those others in his or her texts." Scott argues that such well-meaning histories of the Other "lose the possibility of examining those assumptions and practices that excluded considerations of difference in the first place. They take as self-evident the identities of those whose experience is being documented and thus naturalize their difference" (24-25). As a result, rather than using the alterity of the Other as a lever with which to challenge, for example, normative structures of knowledge, the historian of difference simply enlarges the view offered by traditional history–much the way Sherry's gay history class simply includes homosexuals in the story of the American experience. Banished, for example, in this particular instance is any attempt to understand something like the relationship between the construction of the modern "American" and the modern "homosexual," the points of convergence and conflict between these two discourses of identity, and the ways in which such groups as "Queer Nation" might or might not be linked to the ongoing ideological project of constructing that fictive collectivity called "America."

In an essay arguing a position similar to that of Scott's, Christina Crosby has critiqued the "empiricist historicism" of U.S. women's studies in the name of a more radical historiography. According to Crosby, a historiography that takes as its goal the simple description of minority experience according to the protocols of traditional historiography is inadequate. Such description necessarily remains in what she terms "the circle of ideology" (136). When feminist historians believe that all that is necessary is the making visible of a previously neglected historical subject–"woman," now conceived, under the rubric of "difference," in all her diversity–"[t]he *relationship*, . . . between 'the real' and knowledge of the real, between 'facts' and theory, history and theory is occluded even as women's studies seeks to address the problem of theoretical practice." According to Crosby, rather than a simple inclusion in history of "the reality" of the female subject, as "inclusive" and "multicultural" as that reality might be, what is instead required is an exploration of the ways that " 'history,' the 'real,' even 'the fact of difference' necessarily reflect the conception of knowledge by which they are available to thought . . . " (137).

In an effort to write the subaltern subject into history, a number of "postcolonial" novelists in particular have attempted to include in their fiction what are ostensibly historical events. Toni Morrison, Mahasweta Devi, Chinua Achebe, Ngugi wa Thiong'o–the list could be extended in a number of different directions. These novels provide a possible alternative to orthodox histories of the Other. However, if such novels are read "mimetically," as if they simply make visible, through fiction, a "real" subject previously hidden from history, they necessarily fall into the traps described by Scott and Crosby. That is, they fail to interrogate the *discursive* production of the subaltern subject, for instance, dehistoricizing and mystifying the production of the Other as other, and occluding the ways in which the reality of the real is itself an ideological effect. Additionally, such a reading suggests too simplistically that "fiction" is identical to "history." While a number of interesting critiques of traditional historiography have attempted to deconstruct the binary "history/literature," such a deconstruction–like all such deconstructions–can never fully succeed. As Gayatri Spivak has argued, in the wake of such a deconstruction,

> That history deals with real events and literature with imagined ones may now be seen as a difference in degree rather than in kind. The difference between cases of historical and literary events will always be there as a differential moment in terms of what is called "the effect of the real." What is called history will always seem more real to us than what is called literature. Our very uses of the two separate words guarantees that. (243)

I want to conclude by reading *Martin and John* strategically as a kind of (fictive) critical history. Clearly, I am not attempting to draw an exact homology between the events depicted in the novel and the real. In fact, as I've already suggested, the formal difficulties of the novel make such a reading perilous, if not actually impossible. While I have not read the novel as history, I have attempted to draw some kind of relationship between its discursive strategies and "events" in the real. Continuing in this vein, I would provisionally suggest that *Martin and John* gives concrete expression to gay men's mourning as a form of critical history in the "plague years" in particular. If it provides a historical record of anything, it is the record of a historically and culturally specific affect–the agony involved in the mourning of those who have died from HIV disease, and the difficulties gay men face as they try to mourn their loved ones in a rabidly homophobic culture. Peck's novel is a historically specific critical response to the work of mourning. Even as a piece of fiction, it deploys neither a monumental or antiquarian sense of history, nor an aesthetic that corresponds to either of these modes. Unlike, say, *New York Times* obituaries, memorial cover stories featured on such tabloids as *People* magazine, or movies of the week, it does not celebrate the life of a "great" person who has died of HIV disease. Nor does the novel act as an antiquarian historical response to HIV might, recording in loving detail the everyday events of either Martin's or John's life, or John's process of mourning. Unlike, say, the Names quilt project or Paul Monette's *Borrowed Time*, *Martin and John* does not preserve and revere either the loved one or the grief of his mourner. Significant here is the fact that, even within its own fictional world, *Martin and John* does not heroicize either character. In neither the italicized nor nonitalicized chapters could either one be said to function unambiguously as some kind of "positive" role model. The "real" Martin is in fact largely absent from the italicized "autobiographical" chapters of the novel in particular. The most precise picture we get of him occurs in "Circumnavigation," in which he is almost literally reduced to an anus leaking shit and blood. In the nonitalicized chapters, there is little that connects one "Martin" to the next, other than that he is the (apparently always "lost") object of John's desire. As for John, the formal difficulties of the novel, including the insertion of the name "Dale" in the crucial second last chapter, render it nearly impossible to create a coherent sense of who he is as a character–the difficulty in fact "increasing" as the reader proceeds through the novel and its formal pattern becomes clearer. Nor does the novel portray John's act of mourning as worthy of imitation. Considered in this light, "Lee" and "Fucking Martin" are crucial chapters, in that they refuse to provide "positive" models of mourning. These chapters complicate the attempt, however benevolent, to read the novel as simply "breaking the silence" around gay men and mourning. One would be hard-pressed to read *Martin and John*, then, as some kind of noble tribute to the person who has died of HIV disease, or a monument to mourning today. Unlike both the monumental and antiquarian modes of history, it moves toward "destruction" rather than "conservation," to the forgetting of the past rather than its remembrance–while still invoking that small amount of memory required to understand one's having been produced in the present as the outcome of a past. This dialectic of remembering and forgetting is richly emblematized in a series of questions "Dale"/John asks himself in "Fucking Martin": "How can this story give Martin immortality when it can't even give him life? Now I wonder, Has this story liberated anything but my tears? And is that enough? I want to ask. To which I can only answer, Isn't that enough?" (220-21). "Dale's" refusal to answer these questions keeps in play that precarious and (im)possible deconstruction of remembering/forgetting and foregrounds the uneasy relationship between the writing of ("fictive," critical) history and mourning.

In its obsessive use of names that seem never to refer to the same person, as well as its insistent stagings of John's unsuccessful attempts to "find" himself, *Martin and John* also problematizes "essentialist" understandings of identity, suggesting that identities are provisional and precarious, produced by a set of forces we might refer to catachrestically as "history," and subject to shifting definition. The novel seems committed, both thematically and formally, to an interrogation of identity. Linked to this interrogation of identity is the novel's multi-leveled deconstruction of the binaries "history/literature"–through the alternating of the "autobiographical" italicized and "fictional" nonitalicized chapters, through its discussion of the shifting line between "history" and "stories." The insertion of the name "Dale" in particular is crucial in that it brings these two gestures together: further complicating our understanding of the narrator's identity in particular, it also opens the novel up to the "outside" world through its invocation of the first name of the book's historical author, and thus further de-stabilizes the line we draw between "history" and "fiction." In this single moment, then, the novel is in fact suggesting that the critique of identity and the deconstruction of the binaries history/literature are in fact not unrelated.

In reading *Martin and John* as a kind of critical history alongside Scott's and Crosby's critiques of "orthodox" histories of the Other, I want to laud the novel's formal innovation as an attempt to interrupt historiographical approaches such as those suggested by Sherry. Interestingly, both Scott and Crosby also draw a connection between a critique of essentialist identities and traditional historiographic approaches, Scott arguing that "experience" based histories of the Other necessarily re-inscribe essentialist understandings of identity, and Crosby noting that to specify one's identity through such declarations as "I am a gay white middle-class man" is not necessarily to historicize the production of that identity and the reality-effect it induces. I would not take this comparison too far; Scott and Crosby are, after all, writing about history, and not about fiction. Theorists like Spivak, Scott, and Crosby, however, have suggested specific ways in which history and fiction might productively "interrupt" one another, allowing us to read how truths are produced, and not simply revealed, in both. The citation of Virginia Woolf earlier in this essay was thus not intended merely to be clever; in *Martin and John*, Peck writes fiction that interrogates the possibility of identity and historiography; in "A Room of One's Own," Woolf writes a history that uses fiction to complicate identity. In words similar to John's, she tells us, " 'I' is only a convenient term for somebody who has no real being. Lies will flow from my lips, but there may perhaps be some truth mixed up with them; it is for you to seek out this truth and decide whether any part of it is worth keeping" (732). In her 1971 essay "When We Dead Awaken: Writing as Re-Vision," Adrienne Rich reads "A Room of One's Own" as indicative of a certain failure of nerve on Woolf's part. Arguing that Woolf is painfully aware in the essay of being overheard by men, Rich suggests that the "dogged tentativeness" of Woolf's tone, its refusal of a certain authority, indicates that she is "a woman almost in touch with her anger" (466). Another way of reading Woolf, however, one that ties her project "historically" to Scott's, Crosby's, Spivak's, and perhaps even Peck's, is to see this gesture of a refusal of identity and the authority a stable identity brings as a powerful and important one. As Jane Gallop has suggested in her reading of Lacan, "the phallic illusions of authority" can only be called into crisis from within a discourse of authority (20)–much the way Woolf, I would argue, does in her essay. As Gallop suggests,

> To speak without authority is nothing new; the disenfranchised have always so spoken. Simply to refuse authority does not challenge the category distinction between phallic authority and castrated other, between "subject presumed to know" and subject not in command. One can effectively undo authority only from the position of authority, in a way that exposes the illusions of that position *without renouncing it*, so as to permeate the position itself with the connotations of its illusoriness, so as to show that *everyone*, including the "subject presumed to know," is castrated. (21)

(Interestingly, Gallop's position here is similar to Crosby's contention that we must learn to read how truths are produced, "including the truth one holds most dear," not simply to abandon the search for truth but rather in an effort to sustain "a critique of something which is both dangerous and indispensable" (142)–Crosby's words themselves a paraphrase of Spivak.)

I would suggest that, rather than attempt, as Rich does, to psychoanalyze Woolf's intentions through a reading of her correspondence (476 n. 5)–as if such letters simply made available for discovery the "real" Virginia Woolf–we read Woolf's remarks as a strategic attempt to take up a position of authority without merely repeating phallocentrism's demand that the subject be in a position of mastery over her own discourse. One of the things that links *Martin and John* and "A Room of One's Own," then, is an effort to use fiction to write into history a subaltern subject without simply extending the sovereignty formerly granted to the privileged white heterosexual male to the Other. While it is perhaps premature–and, given the fact that this is the closing line of my essay, too late–to suggest that Peck's novel is a "feminist" one, perhaps the critique of traditional historiography is an important site in which feminism and "queer" theory /gay and lesbian studies might come together as allies.

NOTES

1. Even the first chapter, a passage in which John's mother, Bea, appears to be speaking, seems actually, for reasons I will discuss shortly, to have been recounted by John.

2. For example, in the chapter entitled "Blue Wet-Paint Columns," Bea, John's mother, dies and is survived by her husband; in a subsequent chapter, entitled "Transformations," it is John's father, Henry, who dies, leaving behind his wife Bea; in another chapter, "The Search for Water," Bea is John's stepmother, Henry is Martin's lover, and John's father remains unnamed. In a chapter entitled "Driftwood," Martin is an adolescent drifter John first meets when he is sixteen; in "Transformations," he is John's stepfather and lover; in "Always and Forever" he is a rich school teacher John meets at "Sue's" party.

3. Throughout this essay, whenever I cite any of the italicized passages from the novel, I omit the italics. Instead, I indicate in the passages that precede the citation whether the selection appears in italics or plain text.

4. Also of pertinence is John's remark, in the final chapter, that, since Martin's death, he writes everyday, every afternoon. "Martin told me to," he tells us (224). Given the placement of these words near the conclusion of the novel, we are led to believe that these italicized chapters might be examples of this writing. Finally, in this same chapter, John recalls telling Martin about a series of memories–"about my hand, and about a man named Harry, and about a warm November day at the beach" (225)–all of which appear in the italicized chapters entitled "Given This and Everything," "Someone Was Here," and "The Beginning of the Ocean" respectively.

5. For example, in an italicized chapter entitled "Tracks" located in roughly the middle of the novel, the narrator, identified by another character as "John," describes the facial scar of a young man he meets at Port Authority. This scar "ringed his left eye" (112). Later in this chapter, he confesses, " . . . his eye haunts my stories" (115). In fact, "Driftwood," one of the earliest nonitalicized chapters of the novel, is narrated by a character named John who has a "crescent-shaped scar" that curls around his right eye (37). The repetition of this motif, and its transformation–from "left" to "right" and from the young man to the narrator–perhaps suggests to the reader that some kind of imaginative alteration of the "reality" documented in "Tracks" has occurred in the "fictional" "Driftwood."

6. For example, in the italicized "The Beginning of the Ocean," we sense from the very first paragraph the fear of the five-year-old who has been asked to hold his father's beer as he drives. "I'm not supposed to let it spill," the child tells us fearfully, the father smacking his hands away when he clings to the can too tightly (32). Within the first few sentences of "Lee," John is telling his trick, "I want it to feel like rape" (190).

7. For example, characters are mentioned briefly–"David," for example, in the chapter entitled "Given This and Everything"–and then dropped.

8. Rather than engage in a long discussion of whether or not there is such a thing as "gay fiction"–a question that risks being answered with reference to idealist categories–I would refer (not unproblematically) to the Library of Congress Cataloging-in-Publication Data printed in the novel, the first two headings of which read "1. AIDS (Disease)–Patients–United States–Fiction. 2. Gay men–United States–Fiction."

9. Interestingly, this chapter is titled "Fucking Martin," the title under which the novel was published in Great Britain–thus suggesting the importance of this particular chapter to the novel as a whole. Also worth noting is the fact that "fucking" in this context can be either a gerund or an adjective–further adding to the "undecidability" of the novel.

10. Significantly, in the last few lines of the (italicized) chapter prior to the one in which "Dale" appears, John describes "a name that remains unconnected to any identity no matter how many times it is assumed. And that name, I must remind myself, is my own: John" (197).

11. For reasons I will discuss shortly, these words appear in plain text rather than italics.

12. In noting this correspondence between John's feelings of love for his father and his feelings toward Martin, I'm not drawing any conclusions about the etiology of his homosexuality, I am not suggesting that there is something pathological in John's attachment to his father, and I am not suggesting that the reader is to assume that "real" incest has taken place between John and his father. Regarding the first proposition: such a conclusion would require one to engage in a form of extremely specious psychoanalytic criticism. Characters are not people, and homosexuality is not a pathology that needs to be explained. Regarding the second proposition, I would only want to note that, according to Freud, a negative Oedipus complex is not only "normal," but necessary for the development of the male child's ego. According to Freud, abandoned love objects form the basis for future identifications. See in particular "The Passing of the Oedipus-Complex." Regarding the third proposition: there does not appear to be sufficient textual evidence to determine whether or not John and his father actually had sex of any kind.

13. Mourning is in fact a thematic concern of many of the nonitalicized chapters of *Martin and John*. In "Blue Wet-Paint Columns," a son recalls the progression of his mother's fatal illness; his father mourns his dead wife by dressing in her clothes. In "Driftwood," a family mourns a brother killed in a drowning accident. In "Three Night Watchmen," Martin and John mourn the death of their rela-

tionship, and the dreams they had of escaping from their dusty small-town life to New York. In "Fucking Martin," John mourns Martin's death.

14. He tells us that he writes "because I can't stop," suggesting that the mourning process has both "accelerated" and gotten easier over time (224). Also significant is his recent conclusion that his writing is "not enough. Already I feel myself becoming bored," again implying that his mourning process is coming to an end (227).

15. Two of the earlier nonitalicized chapters make this connection between sex and mourning. In "Driftwood," the family mourns its drowned son by transferring their libido to a new object–Martin. "My mother cooked him food, my father tried to boss him around," their adolescent son John tells us (56). John's efforts at mourning?–he and Martin make love. In "Transformations," Henry's wife and son mourn his death by sharing the same lover.

16. According to Freud, melancholia replicates the symptoms of grief, the one most notable exception being that the melancholic experiences "an extraordinary fall in his self-esteem, an impoverishment of his ego on a grand scale" (167). I will not make the connection between *Martin and John* and melancholia, and for a variety of different reasons. As Freud suggests, "melancholia is in some way related to an unconscious loss of a love-object, in contradistinction to mourning, in which there is nothing unconscious about the loss" (166). In *Martin and John*, John's losses are conscious–so much so that he enters into certain activities–writing and sex foremost among them–that he hopes will allow him to cope with those losses. More to the point: as I've already suggested, I am not interested in this essay in, say, subjecting John to therapy. According to Freud, unlike mourning, melancholia is a pathology. In order to determine if John is a victim of this pathology, one would have to determine if his behaviors are symptomatic of this impoverishment of the ego. Some might be led, too quickly, I would add, to conclude that his sexual behaviors in particular do in fact evidence this. This is too simplistic a reading of the dynamics of s/m, particularly as they are portrayed in this novel. We might also wonder if Peck and Freud place the same value on the ego, given the ways in which *Martin and John* valorizes a certain freedom from identity.

WORKS CITED

Champagne, John. *The Ethics of Marginality*. Minneapolis: U of Minnesota Press, 1995.

Crimp, Douglas. "Mourning and Militancy." In Russell Ferguson, Martha Gever, Trinh T. Minh-ha, & Cornel West (Eds.), *Out There: Marginalization and Contemporary Culture*. New York: New Museum of Contemporary Art, 1990. 233-45.

Crosby, Christina. "Dealing with Differences." In Judith Butler & Joan W. Scott (Eds.), *Feminists Theorize the Political*. New York: Routledge, 1992. 130-43.

Freud, Sigmund. "Mourning and Melancholia." In General *Psychological Theory*. New York: Macmillan, 1963. 164-79.

______ . "The Passing of the Oedipus-Complex." *In Sexuality and the Psychology of Love*. New York: Macmillan, 1963. 176-82.

Gallop, Jane. *Reading Lacan*. Ithaca: Cornell University Press, 1985.

Gledhill, Christine. "Recent Developments in Feminist Criticism." In Gerald Mast & Marshall Cohen (Eds.), *Film Theory and Criticism*. New York: Oxford University Press, 1985. 817-45.

Monette, Paul. *Borrowed Time*. San Diego: Harcourt Brace Jovanovich, 1988.

Moon, Michael. "Memorial Rags." In George E. Haggerty and Bonnie Zimmerman (Eds.), *Professions of Desire: Lesbian and Gay Studies in Literature*. New York: MLA, 1995. 233-40. Cited in Crimp.

Morton, Donald. "Birth of the Cyberqueer." *PMLA* 110, no. 3 (May 1995): 369-81.

Nietzsche, Friedrich. "On the Uses and Disadvantages of History for Life." In *Untimely Meditations*. Translated by R. J. Hollingdale. Cambridge: Cambridge University Press, 1983. 59-123.

Nunokawa, Jeff. " 'All the Sad Young Men': AIDS and the Work of Mourning." In Diana Fuss (Ed.), *Inside/Out, Lesbian Theories, Gay Theories*. New York: Routledge, 1991. 311-23.

Peck, Dale. *Martin and John*. New York: HarperPerennial, 1994.

Rich, Adrienne. "When We Dead Awaken: Writing as Re-Vision." In David Bartholomae & Anthony Petrosky (Eds.), *Ways of Reading: An Anthology for Writers*. Third Edition. Boston: Bedford Books, 1993. 463-77.

Scott, Joan W. "Experience." In Judith Butler & Joan W. Scott (Eds.), *Feminists Theorize the Political*. 22-40.

Sherry, Michael S. "Teaching Lesbian and Gay History." *Perspectives* 31, no. 8 (November 1993): 1; 6-9.

Spivak, Gayatri. "A Literary Representation of the Subaltern: A Woman's Text From the Third World." In *In Other Worlds*. New York: Routledge, 1988. 241-68.

Woolf, Virginia. "A Room of One's Own." In David Bartholomae & Anthony Petrosky. *Ways of Reading: An Anthology for Writers*. 731-58.

Resources for Lesbian Ethnographic Research in the Lavender Archives

Alisa Klinger

Arizona State University

SUMMARY. The problematics of undertaking lesbian ethnography and cultural history are related in part to the dearth of printed records lesbians kept or preserved for posterity. Technological, financial, and security considerations typically made it necessary for them to operate more informally and inconspicuously, hand-to-hand and by word-of-mouth. Lavender archives, nonetheless, are the repositories of lesbian cultural history. This paper preoccupies itself with the pragmatic issues of developing and maintaining accessible research venues from which to cultivate the study of multiracial and multiethnic lesbian lives. I provide a survey of available resources for doing lesbian scholarship, addressing some of the ethical issues involved with lesbian ethnographic research. *[Article copies available for a fee from The Haworth Document Delivery Service: 1-800-342-9678. E-mail address: getinfo@haworth.com]*

Alisa Klinger recently completed her dissertation, "Paper Uprisings: Print Activism in the Multicultural Lesbian Movement" (University of California, Berkeley, 1995). She is Assistant Professor of Women's Studies at Arizona State University. She has published pieces on lesbian movement politics, multiracial and multiethnic lesbian print culture, and lesbian, gay, and bisexual campus activism. Correspondence may be addressed: Women's Studies Program, P.O. Box 873404, Tempe, AZ 85287-3404. E-mail: aklinger@asu.edu

[Haworth co-indexing entry note]: "Resources for Lesbian Ethnographic Research in the Lavender Archives." Klinger, Alisa. Co-published simultaneously in *Journal of Homosexuality* (The Haworth Press, Inc.) Vol. 34, No. 3/4, 1998, pp. 205-224; and: *Gay and Lesbian Literature Since World War II : History and Memory* (ed: Sonya L. Jones) The Haworth Press, Inc., 1998, pp. 205-224; and: *Gay and Lesbian Literature Since World War II: History and Memory* (ed: Sonya L. Jones) Harrington Park Press, an imprint of The Haworth Press, Inc., 1998, pp. 205-224. Single or multiple copies of this article are available for a fee from The Haworth Document Delivery Service [1-800-342-9678, 9:00 a.m. - 5:00 p.m. (EST). E-mail address: getinfo@haworth.com].

> As you open this book and begin to read, I would like you to hold an image in your mind. . . . millions of letters and diaries of women, famous or obscure, going up in flames, sifting to ash; library stacks of biographies which do not tell the truths we most need to know; hundreds of the private papers of women acclaimed for their public contributions, sealed and placed under lock and key, or doled out by literary executors to those scholars who will accept censorship; dissertations, the work of years, which are forbidden to be published, read or quoted. As you read the stories in this book I would like you to think of those piles of ash, those cages behind which women's words, lesbian words, lie imprisoned, those shelves of life-histories gutted of their central and informing theme.
>
> –Adrienne Rich[1]

> If all your time and energy has to go into defending yourself, into surviving oppression, there's not going to be much left over for building libraries.
>
> –Noretta Koertge[2]

Paper is perishable. It is easily mislaid, forgotten, shredded, burned. It fades with wear; it disintegrates over time. Paper, despite its debility, has been the primary currency of North American lesbian cultural exchange throughout most of the twentieth century. As electronic technology is swiftly rearranging our relationship to print, it seems particularly apropos to ask: what happens to the reams of paper–the novels, the newspapers, the notebooks, the order books, the letters–that have circulated lesbian culture from person to person, town to town, generation to generation? In this discussion, I follow the trail of paper created by lesbians to account for the proliferation of lesbian community archives alongside lesbian-feminist alternative publishing ventures and literary projects. Additionally, I suggest how students, community researchers, and scholars can access, respect, and preserve the traces of lesbian life that contain our individual and collective histories.

If lesbians have historically been "hidden from history," then their books, papers, and artwork–the records of their existence and resistance–have been no more secure.[3] Books with lesbian content are regularly left off reading lists, banned from school libraries, and turned back at borders. While these routine kinds of censorship are detrimental, the availability and safety of lesbian materials is even at risk in research libraries. Take for instance the recent, egregious example of censorious vandalism at the

Zimmerman Library at the University of New Mexico. In November 1994, it was discovered that a shelf of bound periodicals, comprising thirty gay literature and women's studies journals valued at over $25,000, had been defaced with swastikas and obscenities. In addition, the complete run of the *Journal of Homosexuality* and several women's studies titles (classed in the HQ1101-HQ1236 section) were reported missing, and books on the Nazi party were found misshelved in the women's studies subject section of the library.[4] Although an extensive search of the library–a 300,000 square foot facility with over 900,000 volumes–did not recover the missing materials, they were later found concealed atop the highest shelves, behind other volumes, in a remote part of the library where discontinued volumes are stored. Such acts of vandalism particularly and the threat of textual terrorism generally make the lavender stacks an endangered community resource.

While the vulnerability of lesbian materials to bias crimes accounts in part for the creation of lesbian community-based archives, mainstream institutional disinterest, neglect, and dissimulation have contributed significantly to lesbian endeavors to conserve their history in community archives of their own making and under their own control. When *The Radcliffe Quarterly*, for example, included an extensive feature commemorating the Schlesinger Library's fiftieth birthday, "demonstrating that women have a history" and that women can no longer be treated as an undifferentiated group, it was regrettable but not surprising that no reference to lesbianism was made (Press 1). Although photographs of both Gertrude Stein and Adrienne Rich appear on one page, the conspicuous omission of specific references to the Schlesinger Library's resources for lesbian studies effectively constitutes a roadblock for students and scholars attempting to reclaim lesbian history.

Whether they choose to publicize their collections or not, university and public libraries are increasingly developing their lesbian holdings by lining their shelves in the first instance with the books and periodicals published by and readily available from academic and mainstream presses. Because lesbian materials historically have been independently rather than mass produced, the college-affiliated scholar or community researcher seeking the more ephemeral yet still consequential traces of lesbian history and culture than scholarly holdings include will more readily find them at a variety of community archives.[5] According to the Gay and Lesbian Task Force Clearinghouse of the American Library Association (ALA), there were in fact more than 110 such collections by 1993 (Owens 86).[6] Brooklyn's Lesbian Herstory Archives, the June L. Mazer Lesbian Collection in West Hollywood, and a host of other lesbian-specific and co-gender gay archives across North America (including the ONE Institute/International Gay and Lesbian Archives in Los Angeles with its new "ONE Lesbian Collection," the Gay and Lesbian Historical Society of Northern California Archives, the Archives gaies du Québec, and the Canadian Lesbian and Gay Archives in Toronto) are devoted to the collection, preservation, and dissemination of an enormous range of resources essential for undertaking lesbian historical and ethnographic study.[7] As the academic institutionalization of lesbian studies becomes more secure, the value of community-based archives like these and the preservation work that they perform will become more obvious to the scholars who rely on them to provide the raw materials that their studies require. At the same time, these community-based outposts of lesbian print activism will be required to meet new demands and challenges as they renegotiate their relationship to academic institutions.

The archives' collections of community-based publications, providing the most consistent coverage of lesbian personalities, establishments, and accomplishments, are indispensable for chronicling lesbian book history and cultural formation. The minutiae of lesbian existence are recorded in manuscripts, books, periodicals, essays, speeches, pamphlets, leaflets, brochures, letters, unpublished papers, visual and audio works, newspaper clippings, memorabilia (including matchbook covers, lapel buttons, bumper stickers, posters, flyers, and costumes), and ephemera. The Mazer Collection even sports retired softball and baseball uniforms from the 1940s, 1950s, and 1960s, donated by former professional softball player Mary Rudd (Wolt 1). In addition to their special holdings, the lesbian archives own complete sets or substantial runs of both their organizational newsletters and the fleeting and more established lesbian and/or feminist and gay newsletters, periodicals, and newspapers that are often omitted from academic library collections.[8] Germane resources, particularly for a study of lesbian discursive production, include *Black/Out* (the magazine of the National Coalition of Black Lesbians and Gays), *Common Lives/Lesbian Lives*, *Feminary* (one of the only publications devoted specifically to Southern literary concerns), *Feminist Bookstore News*, *Gay Community News* (a Boston-based weekly), *Lambda Book Report: A Review of Contemporary Gay and Lesbian Literature*, *Lesbian Connection*, *Lesbians of Color Caucus* newsletter, *Matrices: Lesbian Feminist Resource Network*, *Motheroot Journal: A Women's Review of Small Presses*, *New Directions for Women*, *off our backs*, *Out/Look*, *Publishing Triangle News*, and *Sojourner, A Third World Women's Research Newsletter.*[9] Given North American lesbians' tremendous penchant for paper, however, it is ironic that there are not more traces of print, other than the published materials themselves, to testify to the reams of paper produced by the women in print movement.[10] In her history of *Lavender Women*, Michal Brody notes that "[i]t seems we couldn't take ourselves seriously as a business, but we understood the seriousness of being a printed medium" (171). Her pithy observation about how the cultural devaluation of women's work has been internalized by lesbians perhaps best explains why there are so few extant organizational records either for the Chicago lesbian newspaper collective that published 26 issues of the paper from 1971 to 1976 or for the Women in Print movement generally.

Despite the overall paucity of records that have survived from now defunct lesbian-feminist print shops, publishing collectives, and bookstores, several regional archival collections house crucial materials for piecing together the history of American lesbian cultural investments and enterprises. For instance, numerous filing cabinet drawers at the Mazer Collection are teeming with Diana Press's production lists, job files, and meeting minutes. The Mazer Collection also has more than 1,000 periodical titles and about 3,000 books, including Barbara Grier's forty-year collection of lesbian periodicals and the papers of the Daughters of Bilitis, in its modest rent-free space in the City of West Hollywood.[11] The operational records of the Women's Press Collective, a conglomerate of three women-owned printing companies (Up Press, the Women's Press Project, and Women's Press) in the San Francisco Bay Area during the 1970s and 1980s, are preserved at the Gay and Lesbian Historical Society of Northern California Archives ("Women's Press Records Preserved" 14). In addition, the GLHS has acquired the records from A Women's Place Bookstore (Glass 12) and Oracle Books, a feminist bookstore operated by lesbians from 1973 to 1980 (Chandler 6). The letters, photographs, and papers belonging to influential Bay Area poet Elsa Gidlow and her lover Isabel Quallo, and such African-American lesbian newspapers, magazines, and journals as *Azalea*, *Aché*, and *Black Lesbian Newsletter*, are also part of the GLHS collection.[12] Audre Lorde, cofounder of Kitchen Table Women of Color Press, donated a portion of her personal papers and manuscripts to the Lesbian Herstory Archives. Moreover, Barbara Grier and Donna McBride, cofounders in 1973 of the first and largest lesbian publishing house in the world, have made a gift of their extensive collection of books and periodicals, formerly the Lesbian and Gay Archives of Naiad Press in Tallahassee, Florida, to the San Francisco Main Public Library for their Gay and Lesbian Center.[13] The nine-thousand-volume collection, amassed by Grier and McBride since 1950–well before the first lesbian or women's presses made their mark on the publishing world–is "the most complete personal library of lesbian and gay books in the

English Language."[14] The pulp novels and Daughters of Bilitis and Mattachine Society publications that make up the Grier-McBride Collection will be the cornerstone of the new Gay and Lesbian Center, the first such center to be made part of a public library, sharing quarters with the archives of filmmakers Peter Adair (*Word Is Out* and *Absolutely Positive*) and Rob Epstein (*Common Threads: Stories from the Quilt* and *The Times of Harvey Milk*), and journalist and author Randy Shilts (*And the Band Played On* and *The Mayor of Castro Street: The Life and Times of Harvey Milk*).

Many community archivists, scholars, and activists contend that the control of lesbian and gay archives must reside with lesbian and gay people themselves rather than with governmental, civic, or academic institutions. The community-based, perhaps separatist, rationale for such libraries as the Gay and Lesbian Historical Society of Northern California Archives, the Lesbian Herstory Archives, and the June Mazer Lesbian Collection was devised precisely to create a "safe-space" for lesbians and gay men and to prevent their culture from being submerged through bureaucratic (fiscal or philosophical) fiat, proxy, or neglect. By and large, the lesbian archival collections subscribe to the feminist principles and goals expressed in the Mazer Collection's mission statement:

> we are committed to seeking out and including materials by or about lesbians of all backgrounds and experiences, especially those who are not usually seen or heard. We are committed to keeping the Collection open and available to every woman, without examination, credential, or fee. ("Our Commitment" 8)

Prioritizing issues of security and accessibility, Bill Walker of the Gay and Lesbian Historical Society of Northern California Archives argues that

> [t]he experience of the lesbian and gay movement has repeatedly shown that we can never rely on simple promises to preserve our rights or serve our interests. Homophobia and bigotry are deep and hardy forces, and rhetoric and good intentions are not effective instruments against them. ("Historical Society News" 5)

Despite the indisputable technological advantages, the Lesbian Herstory Archives in New York, like the Mazer Collection and the Gay and Lesbian Historical Society, is extremely wary about ensconcing its history in public or academic institutions. The Lesbian Herstory Archives was conceived in 1973 by a group seeking to represent lesbian and gay students and instructors at the City University of New York. Some of the lesbians who had been out before the second wave of the women's movement were alarmed that their prefeminist lesbian culture had suffered erasure. Their fear that the historical suppression of lesbians might repeat itself, despite the strides made in lesbian liberation during the 1970s, motivated twenty-five women to initiate the Archives project.[15] While the founding group members eventually dispersed, Deborah Edel and Joan Nestle, lovers at the time, took on the enormous commitment of creating and housing the Lesbian Herstory Archives in their apartment. From 1974 until 1992, the "community's memory" resided in Joan Nestle's West Side apartment and storage facilities (Brandt 43). In an interview with Beth Hodges, Deborah Edel and Joan Nestle defend their decision to keep the Archives a lesbian grassroots and unaffiliated organization, unencumbered by the protocols that invariably accompany government funding or academic support:

> *Deborah:* It's been important that we take our time to build up trust, knowing that the money will come when we need it and when we can handle it, and that we spend our time now building a base that isn't dependent on governmental funds, but is built on what women can give of their own lives. We always need money, but we want it to come from women who believe in our work.
>
> *Joan:* Something we need to free for ourselves–and this is a controversial issue–is the hold of academic institutions over cultural collections. We must not be tempted to take money from them, not be tempted to install the collection on a university, even if it's a woman's university. We must not be fooled into forgetting that these institutions, which seem to be devoted to learning, are part of the military industrial complex that makes the world impossible for most people, as well as for lesbians. (qtd. in Hodges 101-2)

With the 1992 relocation to its permanent home in Brooklyn's Park Slope district, the Lesbian Herstory Archives (registered as the Lesbian Herstory Educational Foundation, Inc.) attained its greatest measure of independence. The three-story townhouse housing the Archives cost $600,000, purchased with a $300,000 down payment amassed entirely from individual donations. Joan Nestle maintains that the property acquisition, the culmination of a twenty-year dream, creates a unique "place where women from all over c[an] come and be in a place that is just about our history as lesbians. Not a revisionist version, but the history of lesbians as they experienced it, wrote it, lived it" (qtd. in Brownworth 73).[16]

Ironically, some of the greatest research challenges facing patrons of the Lesbian Herstory Archives stem from its radical feminist political commitment to accessibility and collectivity. One of the Archives' first principles, for instance, is "'giving access without judgement (sic). . . . No woman is refused and no woman's work is refused'" (Nestle qtd. in Hodges 102). Consequently, the collection presently comprises more than "10,000 books, 12,000 photographs, 200 special collections, 1,400 periodical titles, 1,000 organizational and subject files," as well as a plethora of nonprinted matter (Brownworth 73). The Archives' refusal to implement a selection policy ensures an incredible diversity of cherished, provocative, and revealing materials, yet the lack of comprehensive cataloguing or trained librarians forestalls the unearthing of many buried treasures. The "How To Use The Lesbian Herstory Archives: A Pathfinder for Research" (1993), an introductory informational sheet distributed to patrons, recognizes the challenges facing researchers when it warns that conducting searches at the Archives is a labor-intensive and largely self-reliant task: "Our volunteers here at the Archives can assist you by pointing you in the right direction, but it is up to you to dig into the files, periodicals, newsletters, and books to uncover those little gems you are seeking."

It is undeniable and understandable that the grassroots lesbian archives, dependent entirely upon community donations for their financial solvency, do not provide the hours of operation, the regularity of services, the level of organization, or the technological resources consistent with public or academic library practices. The impediments to research notwithstanding, the independent lesbian organizations maintain the autonomy to perform the exceedingly crucial social function of community cohesion in addition to the historical enterprise of document collection. That the photocopier at the Lesbian Herstory Archives sits alongside the kitchen sink and that organizational meetings are held at the kitchen and dining-room tables, best illustrate how lesbian archives attempt to perform simultaneously the multiple functions of a library, a community center, a museum, and a household. It is a sobering reality that, in the wake of the Reagan/Bush/Mulroney era, the Mazer Collection–an archive–remains the only "Lesbian-only-identified resource" in the entire city of Los Angeles ("Mazer to Host Community Meeting" 7). The dire shortage of space and funds that threatens the survival of even this small facility is perhaps best symbolized by the bathtubful of posters, paintings, and signs that are stored in the Collection's bathroom.

The issue of whether to struggle to subsist as an endangered community repository or to be integrated in a more financially secure general library collection is particularly acute for the Gay and Lesbian Historical Society of Northern California. With the creation of the celebrated James C. Hormel Gay and Lesbian Center of the San Francisco Main Public Library, the Society had to reconsider its own goals and determine its future direction. Questions about the "control of the collections and the Center over time" were of greatest concern to the Society during negotiations between the two facilities ("Historical Society News" 5).[17] After three years of discussions, the community-based organization and the public institution signed their 1996 agreement that

> while the material will be housed in state-of-the-art archival vaults in the new main library, accessed through the library's catalogues and other finding aids, available to the public whenever the library is open, and cared for by a professional staff, the material nevertheless belongs to the GLHS and is merely on deposit with the library. ("GLHS & The SFPL Sign Historic Agreement"11)

Similarly, McBride and Grier decided that it is under the stately protection of the San Francisco Public Library that their collection can best endure, achieving the greatest accessibility at no charge to the widest range of individuals. The bequeathing of materials from the private domain to the public (civic) sphere makes the collection available to patrons using wheelchairs and public transit. (The Lesbian Herstory Archives, located on bus and subway lines, is also wheelchair accessible.)[18] From an archivist's or a researcher's perspective, the greatest benefit of housing a lesbian and gay collection in a public library facility is that there are the technological and financial resources for acquisitions, preservation (especially deacidification), cataloguing, electronic communications, and photocopying.[19] The San Francisco Public Library, according to Sherry Thomas, will first treat the paper of 2,000 lesbian pulp paperbacks. The preservation and restoration of these paperbacks, some dating back to the 1940s, is expected to cost $17,000. Subsequently, "the library will copy all of the books, letters, and periodicals onto CD-ROM (compact disk, read-only memory) so that they can be accessed by all library users in San Francisco and from other remote libraries via computer transmission" (Thomas qtd. in Brown 25). The decision to stack materials belonging to the Gay and Lesbian Center with other collections on shelves throughout the library rather than to isolate them in the Gay and Lesbian reading room strategically ensures that the materials will be visible even to patrons who do not specifically choose to visit the Gay and Lesbian Center. This organizational strategy designates lesbian and gay materials as a legitimate branch of knowledge and experience at the same time that their relevance to other subject fields is recognized. The San Francisco Public Library has thus attempted to negotiate between community demands for exclusive lesbian and gay collections and equally persuasive arguments for incorporating lesbian and gay sections in general libraries.[20]

The dichotomous logic of exclusivity versus integration that often justifies whether a library's or a bookstore's lesbian collection remains autonomous or affiliated–a version of the "same versus different" and "single-issue or coalition" debates that tend to pervade virtually all areas of queer thinking and organizing[21]–perhaps best indicates that lesbians should not view the aggregation of their history as an either/or proposition. Rather, we must recognize that there is a dire need for a range of places committed to the preservation of lesbian history, from the drawer in someone's office, to the vertical files in the school library, to community facilities, to national and academic research libraries. As Degania Golove, coordinator of the Mazer Collection, remarked to a news reporter after visiting the new home of the Lesbian Herstory Archives:

> none of the archives are in competition with each other. Not everyone lives on the East Coast, and it's safer to have several collections. We need to have lesbian archives in as many places as we can. ("Mazer Collection Seeks to Buy Building" 73)

One of the most pressing concerns for community and professional librarians, archivists, and historians should be developing racially diverse collections in whatever venues, public or private, that are available outside the urban centers of the Atlantic Northeast, San Francisco, and Los Angeles. The hinterlands, where geographic isolation and limited demographics are acute factors, have a compelling need for the collected remnants that stitch together lesbian history. Bloomington, Indiana's The Shango Project: National Archives for Black Lesbians and Gay Men, a recent arrival in the world of lesbian and gay archiving, is a particularly promising and necessary initiative in the effort to record queer history. The Shango Project and newsletter, *Purple Drum*, is a "newly conceived effort to collect, preserve and maintain materials of historical interest which document aspects of African-American Lesbian and Gay existence in contemporary and historical society."[22] Lesbians, moreover, need to appreciate the legitimate archival value of the odds and ends of their daily lives. Since retrievable aspects of our histories, especially our literary and print histories, are encoded on even the most seemingly insignificant dust jacket, bookmark, and handbill, we must safeguard our legacy and resist the forces that seek to render us invisible by donating our published and unpublished papers, photographs, videos, and memorabilia to libraries and resource centers.

Lacking the sexuality-specific focus of lesbian and gay community archives and such public library collections as those found at the New York Public Library's Gay Information Center Archives and the Eureka Valley Harvey Milk Memorial Branch Library in San Francisco, institutional collections in academic and corporate libraries (including the Kinsey Institute), are nonetheless fertile and largely unexamined repositories for lesbian print materials. Yale University's Beinecke Rare Book and Manuscript Library, the Human Sexuality Collection at California State University, Northridge, and Cornell University's Human Sexuality Collection, as well as academic libraries at Boston University, Rutgers, the University of California, at Los Angeles and at Berkeley, Columbia, Tulane, Michigan State, and the University of Texas at Austin, are establishing and expanding important research, historical, literary, and archival collections "documenting the social prominence of gay and lesbian issues" (Owens 86). With increasing frequency, lesbian and gay organizations are securing the value of their organizational papers, correspondence files, memoranda, publications, galleys, and promotional materials for posterity by making donors' arrangements. For example, in 1994 the Duke University Special Collections Library became the repository for the records of *LGSN: The Lesbian and Gay Studies Newsletter*, a publication of the Gay and Lesbian Caucus for the Modern Languages. During the previous year, the National Gay and Lesbian Task Force decided to donate its project files, reports, publications, and correspondence from its first twenty years of existence to Cornell University's Human Sexuality Collection.[23] The Collection, established in 1989 with financial backing from *The Advocate* publisher David B. Goodstein, is considered to be the "most established and well supported archival program" in the United States.[24] Although academic collections are typically better furnished with gay male rather than lesbian materials, Duke University's collection is particularly strong in lesbiana, as is the Schlesinger Library at Radcliffe College that holds the papers of such eminent lesbians as pacifist feminist leader Barbara Deming and poet Adrienne Rich.

Yet, to continue to expand our vision of how lesbian life has been differently composed and framed at a variety of historical moments, by little-known as well as celebrated individuals, in a range of geographic and social locations, we must comb more thoroughly through the nondiscursive and printed artifacts housed in our community archival collections. The community-based archival work undertaken by Esther Newton for *Cherry Grove, Fire Island: Sixty Years in America's First Gay and Lesbian Town* is an impressive model of how social constructionist logic can best be grounded in the specifics of a particular time and place.[25] Similarly, Elizabeth Lapovsky Kennedy and Madeline D. Davis provide a compelling example of historically specific and community-based research in *Boots of Leather, Slippers of Gold: The History of a Lesbian Community*. Such scrupulously researched projects as Kennedy and Davis's thirteen-year compilation of materials and oral histories for their study are unquestionably time consuming and expensive (*Boots of Leather, Slippers of Gold* xii). When such research is conducted on women's lives, particularly if they are lesbians and/or women of color, it is also subject to the abiding, prohibitive cultural logic that devalues and underfunds women's work.

The global economic recession and the drastic fiscal consequences for higher education spending, at the same moment that the fledgling field of lesbian and gay studies is itself emerging, have no doubt discouraged some scholars from undertaking ethnographic research and contributed to the proliferation of theoretical treatments of sexuality in recent years. Scholars from such traditional humanities disciplines as literature, history, and philosophy, who have had an undeniably formidable role in the development of lesbian, gay, bisexual, and transgender studies and queer theory, are rarely party to the scale of research funding more customarily available to scholars in the social sciences. When compared to the major funding required to do ethnographic or historical field work, the more economical price tag on the production of queer theories, work that typically requires the consideration of printed and visual texts rather than relies extensively on travel, archival searches, and subject interviews, perhaps suggests why queer theoretical discourse, at least at this historical moment, seems to be growing exponentially. For innumerable graduate students, community researchers, and senior scholars, text-based scholarship rather than the study of human subjects has in fact become an economic necessity. In making such an observation, I am not assuming an antitheoretical position or disparaging the growing and important body of theoretical work to emerge in recent years. Rather, I am registering a disciplinary concern that the present, partially market-driven predilection for theory threatens to eclipse some of the still much needed investigation of the traces of lesbians' lived experiences that line the shelves and fill the drawers of our community archives.

If scholarly neglect of community archival resources is detrimental to the disciplinary development of lesbian studies, it also threatens the survival of lesbian archives themselves. Lesbian community archives, like women's bookstores and feminist publishing houses, are entirely dependent upon user support to remain operational in adverse political and economic climates. That support, although essential to the endurance of lesbian community archives, is only the first step lesbian studies scholars must take to protect our cultural resources and to pursue an ethical research methodology.[26] The very conditions that have made it necessary for lesbians to collect and conserve their own history outside of mainstream institutions pose special considerations for researchers. For instance, how can scholars abide by the lesbian community's unwritten rules of discretion when the academy insists that they identify the sources of their information? Scholars who utilize the lavender archives must be especially attentive to issues of discretion since much of the material they find there is personal in nature, relating to lesbians' coming out, intimate relationships, and sexual practices. It is therefore particularly important that scholars demonstrate their respect for the privacy of women who are mentioned in private documents (unpublished journals, letters, and diaries) or who appear in photographs by gaining permission from the appropriate sources for the materials they wish to use.

My own desire to treat equitably and responsibly the materials I discovered in community archives, has made me consider ways to scale the wall of authority–of discourse itself–that separates the academy from the communities that surround it and from which the lesbian "paper uprisings" I study emerged. Lesbian studies scholars might resist the historic tendency to silence lesbians by encouraging their research subjects, when possible, to speak for themselves. The increasing number of interviews and oral histories being collected by independent researchers and community organizations, such as the ongoing oral history project of the Gay and Lesbian Historical Society of Northern California, also offer scholars a wealth of firsthand materials to cite in their work. Lesbian studies scholars, moreover, might contemplate seriously how to make their research readily available to the communities that engender it. The lesbian community archives encourage researchers to donate copies of their published and unpublished materials to the collections, ensuring that interested community members can access them free of charge.

The vulnerability of lesbian cultural institutions to insolvency, censorship, and vandalism, however, argues for extending the reach of reciprocity beyond the printed page. Scholars can strengthen the relationship between the academy and the community not only by financially contributing to nonprofit community research facilities, but by sharing their time and skills with the volunteer labor force that maintains community collections. Scholars can also encourage further lesbian ethnographic research by introducing students to the alternative resources for scholarship available outside the academy. Hence, the survival of the lavender archive can best be safeguarded by patrons who invest their own resources in as well as entrust their words to lesbian community institutions.

NOTES

1. Foreword, *The Coming Out Stories*, xi-xii.

2. *Who Was That Masked Woman?* 179.

3. I borrow the term from the title of Martin Duberman, Martha Vicinus, and George Chauncey's collection of essays, *Hidden from History: Reclaiming the Gay and Lesbian Past*. The editors' introduction to the work provides a concise treatment of the relationship between historical research and lesbian and gay studies (1-13).

4. Jane Hood, one of the speakers at a rally held at the University of New Mexico, Albuquerque, condemning what has been designated "a hate crime against gender studies," claims that the periodicals included *Signs*, *Gender and Society*, *The Women's Review of Books*, and *Lesbian Ethics*. In her Internet report, she notes that "[o]n the empty shelf was a note that said, 'Where is your bitch propaganda?' Some books were left around with swastikas scrawled on them, and over the contents page of a journal on lesbian ethics was scrawled, 'God made women for men' (WMST-L, 28 November 1994)." Stephen Rollins, Associate Dean, General Library, University of New Mexico, reports that *Feminist Studies*, *Frontiers*, *Gender and Society*, *New Directions for Women*, *Signs* (current 10 years only), *Women*, *Women's Studies*, *Psychology of Women Quarterly*, and *Women and Politics* were also targeted (QSTUDY-L, 10 December 1994). The sheer number and weight of volumes involved, and their discovery within the library facility itself, suggests not only that numerous people were involved in moving and hiding the books, but also that the "theft" was an inside job performed when library patrons were not around to witness the perpetrators.

5. In 1979, Stuart Miller of the Social Responsibilities Round Table of the Gay Task Force of the American Library Association issued *Censored, Ignored, Overlooked, Too Expensive? How to Get Gay Materials into Libraries: A Guide to Library Selection Policies for the Non-Librarian*. Although the modest document is now dated, it provides historic insight into the issues at stake for lesbian and gay library patrons and administrators and a good deal of rudimentary information about library book selection procedures that is still relevant. See also Joan Ariel's "The Library As A Feminist Resource," for a pragmatic discussion of how users can best access the materials available from public, school, and academic libraries. Ellen Broidy's "Cyberdykes, or Lesbian Studies in the Information Age" provides an interesting discussion of the ramifications of technology and poststructuralism for library science, offering strategies for identifying relevant lesbian resources in technologically advanced libraries. She argues that

> [t]he central questions for today's librarians and researchers have ceased to revolve around the ability or desirability of isolating a single inoffensive yet definite word or term [for Library of Congress subject heading status]; critical theory and information technology (the ideal postmodern marriage) have combined (or conspired) to create the need first to conceptualize and then to describe bibliographically increasingly complex social and sexual constructs. (203-4)

6. For comprehensive address lists of national and international lesbian, gay, and bisexual archives and a reference guide to relevant periodicals, see Linda Garber, Alan V. Miller, and Stuart Miller. Stan Leventhal's "Starting A Gay Library," includes a list, organized by region, of gay and lesbian archives and libraries throughout the United States, Canada, and Mexico, as well as a brief history of New York's Pat Parker/Vito Russo Center Library (14-15). Useful information about using and starting lesbian and gay library collections is contained as well in the encyclopedic *Gay and Lesbian Library Service*. The edited reference volume treats pragmatically issues from library techniques to censorship. James A. Fraser's and Harold A. Averill's *Organizing an Archives: The Canadian Gay Archives Experience*, although dated particularly with regard to advancements in information and preservation technologies, is also a concise and comprehensive guide to operating a multimedia lesbian and gay archives. The work discusses the intricacies of choosing a name, developing a statement of purpose, designing organizational and administrative structures, handling acquisitions, organizing and indexing materials, maintaining records, and promoting an archive.

7. Founded in 1973 as the Canadian Gay Liberation Movement Archives before changing its name to the Canadian Gay Archives, the Canadian Lesbian and Gay Archives (CLGA) underwent its most recent name change in March 1994. The new name more accurately reflects the nature of the growing accessions, as well as the communities of patrons who utilize the collection. The Archives gaies du Québec (AGQ), a charitable organization, also underwent considerable changes in recent years. Ten years after its founding in 1983, the AGQ moved into its first office facility. The organizational papers of Labrys and Montréal Gay Women, of particular interest to lesbian researchers, are part of the collection. For a brief update on the holdings and operational interests of CLGA and AGQ, see "More Out and About" (6-7).

8. In addition to the newsletters I refer to in this discussion, it is worth consulting the irregularly published, but tremendously informative, *Gay Archivist: Newsletter of the Canadian Gay Archives*. Issue Number 10 (November 1992) is a particularly useful reference, containing an extensive list of Canadian feminist, lesbian, and gay newspapers and periodicals in the microfiche collection of the national, co-gender Canadian Lesbian and Gay Archives.

9. Clare Potter's *Lesbian Periodicals Index* provides reliable citations for over forty lesbian periodicals in circulation during the 1970s. Linda Garber's *Lesbian Sources*, with 162 subject headings, is a more recent source covering materials not included in Potter's work.

10. The Women In Print movement, or WIP, gets its name from lesbian publisher June Arnold of Daughters, Inc. who called the First Women in Print Conference in 1976. About 130 women came from all over the United States to attend the first event of its kind–an event that heralded the beginning of the North American lesbian publishing and bookselling boom. Participants included such writers, publishers, and booksellers as Dorothy Allison, Barbara Grier, Carol Seajay (who launched *Feminist Bookstore News* following the first WIP Conference), Parke

Bowman, Bertha Harris, and Harriet Desmoines and Catherine Nicholson (founders of *Sinister Wisdom*).

11. One of the Mazer Collection's primary goals is to raise funds to purchase a permanent home. See "Mazer Moves Forward," "Mazer to Host Community Meeting," and "Mazer Collection Seeks to Buy Building." The latter article sketches briefly the history of the Collection, from its founding as the West Coast Lesbian Collections in Oakland in 1981, to its 1987 relocation to Connexxus (a lesbian social services agency in West Hollywood), to its move to a private residence before arriving at its present West Hollywood location in 1989.

12. See Eric Garber's "A Different Kind of Roots: African-American Resources in the Archives," for a description of the GLHS lesbian and gay holdings.

13. According to Patricia Holt, "[t]he price tag for the Gay and Lesbian Center is $1.6 million, $1 million of which has already been raised" (59). The construction of the Center is funded by a $109.5 million bond issue approved by San Francisco voters in 1988. The additional $23 million required for equipment, interior furnishings, and books and periodicals is being raised through private donations from lesbian and gay community sources and gay positive national foundations (59). It is a sobering exercise in economies of scale to compare, for example, the budget of the publicly housed collection to the community-based Mazer Collection. The entire annual operational budget for the Mazer Collection amounts to ten to twelve thousand dollars. While the facility is rent-free and the labor is volunteer, the Collection must nonetheless cover its substantial and costly insurance bills as well as equipment and utility expenses (Cotter 35). What it is unable to pay for regrettably is the very level of community outreach and document preservation that is crucial to the expansion and continuance of the Collection.

14. San Francisco City Librarian Ken Dowlin's comment was included in "The Main Campaign: The Campaign for the New Main of the San Francisco Public Library" publicity statement, "Library Gay and Lesbian Center Accepts Major Gifts," for release following the April 23, 1992, groundbreaking ceremonies for the New Main Library (the first national archive of lesbian and gay books, magazines, films, and videos in a public library in America). For information about the Gay and Lesbian Center at the San Francisco Main Public Library, which opened in 1996 with a research center for lesbian and gay culture, contact Curator Jim Van Buskirk, San Francisco Public library, 100 Larkin Steet, San Francisco, CA 94102; (415) 437-4853.

15. For discussions of the Lesbian Herstory Archives see Deborah Edel's "The Lesbian Herstory Archives: A Statement of Cultural Self-Definition"; Beth Hodges's "An Interview with Joan [Nestle] and Deb [Edel] of the Lesbian Herstory Archives" and "Preserving Our Words and Pictures"; and Joan Nestle's "The Will to Remember: The Lesbian Herstory Archives of New York" (a revised, updated version published in this volume).

16. The top floor of the building has been made into a private residence as a security measure to ensure that the collection is not left unattended.

17. The pressure experienced by archives with substantial lesbian and gay holdings to relinquish their independence is not uncommon. In July 1992, the Canadian Women's Movement Archives/Archives canadiennes du mouvement des femmes (CWMA/ACMF) joined the Archives/Special Collections department of the Morriset Library, University of Ottawa. After operating as "independent, non-profit, community-based, and collectively run archives," for a decade, "[l]evels of funding and staffing required for the operation of the Archives had grown precipitously" ("More Out and About" 6).

18. For a treatment of the zoning complexities involved with installing the $35,000 wheelchair elevator outside of the Archives building, see Brownworth (73).

19. There are numerous Internet newsgroups and discussion lists related to various aspects of lesbian research; one of the most active is the Queer Studies List at the University of Buffalo (Ellen Greenblatt, Listowner, QSTUDY-L, listserv@ubvm.cc.buffalo.edu). In "A Quick Tour of Major Lesbian and Queer Resources on the World Wide Web," Ellen Greenblatt provides an excellent survey of lesbian and queer Web sites. The June L. Mazer Lesbian Collection recently launched its home page on the World Wide Web (Wolt "Mazer Merges Onto The Information Superhighway!"): http://home.earthlink.net/~labonsai; or http://www.lesbian.org/mazer

20. A related, but perhaps more pressing concern for archivists, librarians, and activists is how to make the co-gender collections, in both general and specialized libraries, equally responsive to and representative of the experiences of lesbians and gay men. Sherry Thomas, the director of development for special gifts for the Gay and Lesbian Center and publisher of the former Spinsters Press in San Francisco, notes that it was critical that lesbian materials be integral to the new center from its inception:

> We were particularly concerned about this since the majority of money would come from gay men. I'd known of Barbara Grier's work for years and years. It seemed to me necessary to have a stellar collection that had lesbian books at its core, and start with a center that was so strong in its lesbian representation so that there would never be a question as to what would be available to us. (qtd. in Brown 23)

21. Cruikshank discusses this phenomenon in *The Gay and Lesbian Liberation Movement* (67, 174-175).

22. According to The Shango Project's mission statement,

> [a] long-range goal of the project is to develop a resource center serving not only as archive but maintaining a database of all research and historical materials pertaining to Black Lesbian and Gay men in the African Diaspora. Such a central database will allow the use of a much-needed resource tool in exploring aspects of Lesbian and Gay male life and to further much-needed work on the multidimensional issues and problems faced by Lesbians and Gay men of African descent in society across the world. (WMST-L 25 June 1994)

The Shango Project also announces awards for work enhancing knowledge about Black lesbian and gay male culture and history. Two issues of *Purple Drum* are published annually. For information contact the project director or *Purple Drum* newsletter editor: The Shango Project: National Archives for Black Lesbians and Gay Men, P.O. Box 2341, Bloomington, IN 47402-2341; (812) 334-8860.

23. *LGSN* 21:1 (March) 1994: 12, citing *Chronicle of Higher Education*, 25 August 1993. See also announcement in *Chronicle of Higher Education*, 9 June 1993, A6.

24. See Brenda J. Marston's letter to the editor in *Out* 9 (Dec./Jan.) 1994: 14-15.

25. Esther Newton spells out some of the difficulties involved with undertaking the scale of community-based research she conducted for *Cherry Grove, Fire Island: Sixty Years in America's First Gay and Lesbian Town*:

> Most researchers in gay and lesbian studies are either independent scholars or carry big teaching loads at small colleges. As a result, we lack what scholars at big research universities take for granted: graduate student help, time off to do research, and financial support. Up to the present, few government or private foundations will fund intellectual projects concerning gays and lesbians. Very often I felt frustrated by how long the project was taking in between the demands of my full-time job, and by how much more research and interviewing I could have done with more resources. (xii-xiii)

26. Approximately five hundred people annually visit the June L. Mazer Lesbian Collection in West Hollywood, representing a very small fraction of the number of lesbians living in relative proximity to or traveling in the vicinity of the facility (Cotter 34). That the Collection is underused is especially unfortunate given the high density of colleges and universities in southern California. The Collection's future in fact depends on greater user involvement, particularly to assist with the listing and arranging of its holdings (Cotter 55).

WORKS CITED

Ariel, Joan. "The Library As A Feminist Resource." *Words In Our Pockets: The Feminist Writers Guild Handbook on How To Gain Power. Get Published & Get Paid*. Paradise, CA: Dustbooks, 1985. 286-295.

Brandt, Kate. *Happy Endings: Lesbian Writers Talk About Their Lives and Work.* Tallahassee, FL: Naiad, 1993.

Brody, Michal, ed. *Are We There Yet? A Continuing History of* Lavender Women: *A Chicago Lesbian Newspaper: 1971-1976.* Iowa City: Aunt Lute, 1985.

Broidy, Ellen. "Cyberdykes, or Lesbian Studies in the Information Age." *Lesbian Studies: Toward the Twenty-First Century.* Ed. Bonnie Zimmerman and Toni McNaron. New York: The Feminist Press, 1996. 203-207.

Brownworth, Victoria A. "Archives Gets a Home of Her Own." *Lesbian News* (March 1994): 73-74.

Brown, Katie. "Preserving Lesbian Literature." *Deneuve* 2.4 (July/August 1992): 23-25.

Chandler, Robin. "Archives Report." *OurStories: Newsletter of the Gay and Lesbian Historical Society of Northern California* 10.1 (winter 1995): 6.

Cotter, Katie. "The Future of Our Herstory." *Lesbian News* (September 1994): 34+.

Cruikshank, Margaret. *The Gay and Lesbian Liberation Movement.* New York: Routledge, 1992.

Duberman, Martin, Martha Vicinus, and George Chauncey, Jr., eds. *Hidden From History: Reclaiming the Gay and Lesbian Past.* New York: New American Library, 1989.

Edel, Deborah. "The Lesbian Herstory Archives: A Statement of Cultural Self-Definition." *Woman of Power*: "Revisioning History" 16 (spring 1990): 22-3.

Fraser, James, A., and Harold A. Averill. *Organizing an Archives: The Canadian Gay Archives Experience.* Toronto: Canadian Gay Archives Publication, 1983; fourth printing 1989.

Garber, Eric. "A Different Kind of Roots: African-American Resources in the Archives." *OurStories: Newsletter of the Gay and Lesbian Historical Society of Northern California* 10.1 (winter 1995): 4-5.

Garber, Linda. *Lesbian Sources: A Bibliography of Periodical Articles. 1970-1990.* New York: Garland, 1993.

"GLHS & The SFPL Sign Historic Agreement." *OurStories: Newsletter of the Gay and Lesbian Historical Society of Northern California* 11.1 (summer 1996): 11.

Glass, Christian. "Archives News." *OurStories: Newsletter of the Gay and Lesbian Historical Society of Northern California* 9.1 (spring 1994): 12.

Gough, Cal, and R. Ellen Greenblatt, eds. *Gay and Lesbian Library Service.* Jefferson, NC: McFarland, 1990.

Greenblatt, Ellen. "A Quick Tour of Major Lesbian and Queer Resources on the World Wide Web." *Matrices: A Lesbian and Lesbian Feminist Research and Network Newsletter* 11.2 (winter 1996): 8-9.

"Historical Society News: Lesbian and Gay Center of the San Francisco Public Library." *OurStories: Newsletter of the Gay and Lesbian Historical Society of Northern California* 7.3/4 (spring/summer 1992): 5.

Hodges, Beth. "An Interview with Joan [Nestle] and Deb [Edel] of the Lesbian Herstory Archives. (Part 1)." *Sinister Wisdom* 11 (fall 1979): 3-13.

______ . "Preserving Our Words and Pictures. Part Two of Interview with Joan Nestle and Deb Edel." *Sinister Wisdom* "Lesbian Writing and Publishing" 13 (summer 1980): 101-5.

Holt, Patricia. "A Room of One's Own." *10 Percent* (fall 1993): 58-59.

Hood, Jane. "Hate Crimes Against Gender Studies." *WMST-L* (28 Nov. 1994): n. p. Online. Internet. 28 Nov. 1994. Available FTP: wmst-l@umdd.umd.edu

Kennedy, Elizabeth Lapovsky, and Madeline D. Davis. *Boots of Leather, Slippers of Gold: The History of a Lesbian Community.* New York: Routledge, 1993.

Koertge, Noretta. *Who Was That Masked Woman?* New York: St. Martin's, 1981.

Leventhal, Stan. "Starting A Gay Library." *Lambda Book Report* 3.3 (March/April 1992): 14-15.

Marston, Brenda J. Letter. *Out* 9 (Dec./Jan. 1994): 14-15.

"Mazer Collection Seeks to Buy Building." *Lesbian News* 19.8 (March 1994): 73.

"Mazer Moves Forward." *In the Life: Newsletter of the June L. Mazer Lesbian Collection* 11 (summer 1996): 3.

"Mazer to Host Community Meeting." *In the Life: Newsletter of the June L. Mazer Lesbian Collection* 7 (summer 1994): 7.

Miller, Alan V., compiler. *Directory of the International Association of Lesbian and Gay Archives and Libraries*. Toronto: IALGAL, 1987.

Miller, Stuart. *Censored, Ignored, Overlooked, Too Expensive? How to Get Gay Materials into Libraries: A Guide to Library Selection Policies for the Non-Librarian*. Philadelphia, PA: Gay Task Force of the American Library Association, 1979.

"More Out and About." *CENTRE/FOLD: Newsletter of the Toronto Centre for Lesbian and Gay Studies* 4 (spring 1993): 6.

"More Out and About." *CENTRE/FOLD: Newsletter of the Toronto Centre for Lesbian and Gay Studies* 6 (spring 1994): 6-7.

Nestle, Joan. "The Will to Remember: The Lesbian Herstory Archives of New York." *Feminist Review.* "Perverse Politics: Lesbian Issues." 34 (spring 1990): 86-99.

Newton, Esther. *Cherry Grove, Fire Island: Sixty Years In America's First Gay and Lesbian Town*. Boston: Beacon, 1993.

"Our Commitment." *In the Life: Newsletter of the June L. Mazer Lesbian Collection* 5 (summer 1993): 8.

Owens, Mitchell. "Pump Up the Volumes." *Out* 7 (September 1993):85-87.

Potter, Clare. *Lesbian Periodicals Index*. Tallahassee, FL: Naiad, 1986.

Press, Aida K., ed. "Page One." *Radcliffe Quarterly* 79.4 (December 1993): 1.

Rich, Adrienne. "Foreword." *The Coming Out Stories*. Ed. Julia Penelope Stanley and Susan J. Wolfe. Watertown, MA: Persephone, 1980.

Rollins, Stephen. "Censorship of Library Materials–journals were defaced and removed from the shelves. . . ., *QSTUDY-L* (10 Dec. 1994): n. p. Online. Internet. 10 Dec. 1994. Available FTP: qstudy-l@ubvm.cc.buffalo.edu.

Shango Project. "Mission Statement." *WMST-L* (25 June 1994): n. p. Online. Internet. 25 June 1994. Available FTP: wmst-l@umdd.umd.edu

Wolt, Irene. "Take Me *Out* to the Ballgame." *In the Life: Newsletter of the June L. Mazer Lesbian Collection* 5 (summer 1993): 1+.

______, and Kati Newman. "Mazer Merges Onto The Information Superhighway!" *In the Life: Newsletter of the June L. Mazer Lesbian Collection* 11 (summer 1996): 1-2.

"Women's Press Records Preserved." *OurStories: Newsletter of the Gay and Lesbian Historical Society of Northern California* 7.1/2 (fall 1991/winter 1992): 14.

The Will to Remember: The Lesbian Herstory Archives of New York

Joan Nestle

Lesbian Herstory Archives

SUMMARY. This essay traces the history of the Lesbian Herstory Archives, one of the first lesbian-specific collections in the world, from its birth in the early 1970s to the present time. *[Article copies available for a fee from The Haworth Document Delivery Service: 1-800-342-9678. E-mail address: getinfo@haworth.com]*

Dedicated to the many co-coordinators and volunteers who make the ongoing activities of the archives possible.

> We should add that [she] draws less and less from [her] past. The colonizer never even recognized that [she] had one; everyone knows that the commoner whose origins are unknown has no history. Let us ask the colonizer [herself]: who are [folk] heroes? [her] great popular leaders? [her] sages? At most [she] may be able to give us a few

---

Joan Nestle, cofounder of the Lesbian Herstory Archives, is an author, editor, and retired teacher. An earlier version of this article appeared in the *Feminist Review*, no. 34 (spring 1990): 86-94. Correspondence may be addressed: 215 West 92nd Street, Apartment 13A, New York, NY 10025.

[Haworth co-indexing entry note]: "The Will to Remember: The Lesbian Herstory Archives of New York." Nestle, Joan. Co-published simultaneously in *Journal of Homosexuality* (The Haworth Press, Inc.) Vol. 34, No. 3/4, 1998, pp. 225-235; and: *Gay and Lesbian Literature Since World War II: History and Memory* (ed: Sonya L. Jones) The Haworth Press, Inc., 1998, pp. 225-235; and: *Gay and Lesbian Literature Since World War II: History and Memory* (ed: Sonya L. Jones) Harrington Park Press, an imprint of The Haworth Press, Inc., 1998, pp. 225-235. Single or multiple copies of this article are available for a fee from The Haworth Document Delivery Service [1-800-342-9678, 9:00 a.m. - 5:00 p.m. (EST). E-mail address: getinfo@haworth.com].

> names, in complete disarray, and fewer and fewer as one goes down the generations. The colonized seems condemned to lose [her] memory. (Albert Memmi, *The Colonizer and the Colonized*, 1967)

For many, remembering is an act of will, a conscious battle against ordained emptiness. For us, remembering is alchemy, transforming dirty jokes, limp wrists, wetted pinkies into bodies loved, communities liberated.

> The most searing reminder of our colonized world [the Sea Colony, a 1950s working class butch-fem in Greenwich Village] was the bathroom line. Now I know it stands for all the pain and glory of my time, and I carry that line and the women who endured it deep within me. Because we were labeled deviants, our bathroom habits had to be watched. Only one woman at a time was allowed into the toilet because we could not be trusted. Thus the toilet line was born, a twisting horizon of lesbian women waiting for permission to urinate, to shit.
>
> The line flowed past the far wall, past the bar, the front room tables and reached into the back room. Guarding the entrance to the toilet was a short, square handsome butch woman, the same every night, whose job it was to twist around her hand our allotted amount of toilet paper. She was us, an obscenity, doing the man's tricks so we could breathe. The line awaited all of us every night, and we developed a line act. We joked, we cruised, we commented the length of time one of us took, we made special pleas to allow hot and heavy lovers in together knowing full well that our lady would not permit it. I stood, a fem, loving the women on either side of me, loving my comrades for their style, the power of their stance, the hair hitting the collar, the thrown-out hip, the hand encircling the beer can. Our eyes played the line, subtle touches, gentle shyness weaved under the blaring jokes, the music, the surveillance. We lived on that line: restricted and judged, we took deep breaths and played.
>
> But buried deep in our endurance was our fury. That line was practice and theory seared into one. We wove our freedoms, our culture, around their obstacles of hatred, but we also paid our price. Every time I took the fistful of toilet paper, I swore eventual liberation. It would be, however, liberation with a memory. (Joan Nestle, *A Restricted Country*, 1988)

The Lesbian Herstory Archives of New York City, which began in 1973, grew out of a consciousness-raising group among the lesbian members of an organization called the Gay Academic Union. Concerned with the plight of gay students and teachers in high schools and colleges, the GAU was a rallying point for gay scholarship and battles against isolation and homophobia in the city's schools. Most of us were part of the city and state university systems, either as teachers, students, or support staff. Within a very short time, we split into the usual early seventies factions: sexist gay men, Marxists, and lesbian-separatists. I was a member of the latter two. Several of us in the CR (consciousness-raising) group who had come out before the Stonewall Rebellion and the advent of a formal feminist movement felt the need to establish a grassroots lesbian archives project. We remembered a world of lesbian culture that had nourished us but that was rapidly disappearing. We also knew, in this early day of lesbian publishing, that our presses and publishers were fragile creations, and we were concerned about preserving all their precious productions.

But the strongest reason for creating the archives was to end the silence of patriarchal history about us–women who loved women. We wanted our story to be told by us, shared by us and preserved by us. We were tired of being the medical, legal, and religious other. In 1974, the Lesbian Herstory Archives became a reality. In 1975, the archives took up residence in what was to become the home I would share with Deborah Edel, another member of the founding group whose dedication to the project has been unmeasurable.

From our newsletter, no. 1, 1975:

> The Lesbian Herstory Archives exists to gather and preserve records of lesbian lives and activities so that future generations will have ready access to materials relevant to their lives. The process of gathering this material will also serve to uncover and collect our herstory denied to us previously by patriarchal historians in the interests of the culture which they serve. The existence of these archives will enable us to analyze and reevaluate the lesbian experience; we also anticipate that the existence of these archives will encourage lesbians to record their experiences in order to formulate our living herstory.
>
> We will collect and preserve any materials that are relevant to the lives and experiences of lesbians: books, magazines, journals, news clippings (from establishment, feminist, or lesbian media), bibliographies, photos, herstorical information, tapes, films, diaries, oral herstories, poetry and prose, biographies, autobiographies, notices of events, posters, graphics, and other memorabilia and obscure references to our lives.

Early on in our organizing work, we realized that because the word "archives" sounded formal and distancing to many of the women we wanted to reach, we would have to dedicate many years to spreading the word about this new undertaking. At first, we carted samples of the archives' holdings to homes, bars, churches, synagogues, anywhere we were asked to speak. However, we soon realized that our copy of the first issue of *The Ladder* as well as other memorabilia would not survive these trips, and that more needed to be said than we could cover in the show-and-tell method. So we created a travelling slide show to bring home the message that all lesbians were worthy of inclusion in herstory, that as we have said a thousand times over, if you have the courage to touch another woman, you are a famous lesbian.

This slide show became our major organizing tool, our most powerful way to work against the feelings of cultural deprivation and personal isolation. It also allowed us to make our vision clear–what was a lesbian archives, how was it different from traditional archives, and how did it fit into the political struggles of our people? I would dedicate the presentation to lesbians who had sat next to me on the barstools of the Sea Colony, a working-class lesbian bar of the late fifties and early sixties. I always wanted to remind the progressively younger women in our audiences of the generations before them, of the different language and style of an earlier courage. I would say, "I am a femme of the fifties," or I would use the word "queer" to describe myself, the word into which I had come out. Particularly when I was speaking to lesbians in college settings or at women's conferences held at posh campuses or to gay and lesbian student groups on campuses like Yale or Harvard, it was very important for me to remind them that once I was a sexual criminal who stood on a bathroom line awaiting her allotted amount of toilet paper. I wanted the slide show to be seen as a challenge to whatever complacency the audience derived from their respectable surroundings, and I wanted the voices, the images, the ideas to make them proud of the complexity of the lesbian experience and sure that they had a place in it, no matter what kind of lesbian they were. Different settings, different presenters would change the introduction, but the core of the slide show stayed the same.

Our main task was to bring the collection alive, to show its inclusiveness, its respect for lesbians of all colors, classes, physical abilities, cultural backgrounds, and sexual styles. We had to clarify that our archives, our family album, our library, was not primarily for academic scholars but for any lesbian woman who needed an image or a word to survive the day. No letter of introduction was ever needed to gain access, browsing was as important as research, but we also had to convey the seriousness of our undertaking, why we should be trusted with the photograph of a dead lover or diaries that spanned twenty years. We had to combine passion with responsibility and openness with hard work. We had to be personal and public, political and confidential.

Always we were asked, but you don't mean my work, my poems, my letters, my photograph? Always there was incredulity at our assertion that the visitor's life was the important one. But I had known this deprivation so searingly in my own life that it was a question that brought out all my fire and love–Yes, yes, you are the lesbian for whom the archives exists, to tell and share your story.

From our visitors' book, 1979:

> For two days I have been thinking up wise and pithy things that I should include–no dice. So perhaps, Joan and Deb, the honest will work better. Only once before have I felt like I've come home. This is the second time. I never thought I would be that lucky again–and I realize it is my right to come home to the world. Thanks to you and all the lives in this room for showing me that right!

Judy

The slide show helped us make the point that one of our battles was to change secrecy into disclosure, shame into memory. We spoke of how families burned letters and diaries, how our cultural artifacts were often found on bargain tables or in piles of garbage. When we first started the archives, these were new ideas, but now with the international lesbian and gay archives movement, with the flourishing of a lesbian and gay social history movement, and with a raised consciousness about the importance of sexual choices in biographical studies, we hope the message has been given–no more pyres of same-sex love letters.

An excerpt from a love letter (c. 1920) found in a Greenwich Village gutter after the family had cleaned out the apartment of Eleanor C., a labor educator of the thirties and forties:

> This is a 'very quiet' letter, Eleanor dear, and you won't read it when you are dashing off somewhere in a hurry, will you–please.

Thursday night

Best Beloved

> I'm writing by the light of the two tall candles on my desk, with the flamey chrysanthemums you arranged before me. It's such a lovely

> soft glow and I'm glad because this is a 'candle light' letter. I wish you could know what a wonderful person you are, Eleanor darling, and what joy your letter written last night gave me. Not the part about me–that is pitifully wrong and only a standard for me to measure up to–but you make it all so wonderful and are clear about it. You know I feel terribly much the way you do about it all, but I could never say so, even in incoherent fashion, and so many times back of my nobler resolves I am just plain selfish about wanting you to look at and talk to . . . And I'm not afraid dear, I know our love will help–oh so much–and not hinder, it never does that, not even in my weakest moments . . .
>
> The candles are burning low, dear heart and the world is very still and beautiful outside. And I am so, oh so happy that I know you and love you. May God bless you through all time.
>
> Alice

The images in the slide show are as important as the words. They make the point that lesbians from different decades had different modes of self-presentation, that the collection represents lesbians from all ethnic and cultural backgrounds in their own image. Stone butches and lesbian separatists, leather women and Goddess-worshippers, passing women and lipstick lesbians, all carrying their other identities, look out at the audience, forming a mosaic of the lesbian community. A cross-generational, cross-cultural bridge is created, one that is of utmost importance if no one segment of our community is to be singled out for societal repression.

During the slide show, we stress the need to open the doors of the contemporary lesbian community to lesbians of difference, to passing women, to lesbian sex-trade workers, to an international and multilingual perspective. We try to avoid the hypocrisy of commemorating lesbians of the past while exiling their living representatives in the name of a selected herstory. Passing women, for instance, hold a great historical fascination, but as we explain the 'husband-wife' image on the screen–a *Daily News* centerfold photo from 1937–we stress the need to recognize the passing women of our own time. As we show the tattooed blue stars of the Buffalo working-class lesbian community of the forties, we make a plea for regional groups to start their own oral history projects to discover the lesbian folklore of their area. Always our goal is to connect the present struggles of lesbian women of all backgrounds to the past, to show the legacy of resistance and to give the keys needed to unlock the sometimes coded language of liberation battles of another time.

From our newsletter, no. 7, 1981:

> If we ask decorous questions of history, we will get a genteel history. If we assume that because sex was a secret, it did not exist, we will get a sexless history. If we assume that in periods of oppression, lesbians lost their autonomy and acted as victims only, we destroy not only history but lives. For many years, the psychologists told us we were both emotionally and physically deviant; they measured our nipples and clitorises to chart our queerness, they talked about how we wanted to be men and how our sexual styles were pathetic imitations of the real thing and all along under this barrage of hatred and fear, we loved. They told us that we should hate ourselves and sometimes we did, but we were also angry, resilient, and creative. We were part of a community that took care of itself. And most of all, we were lesbian women, revolutionizing each of these terms.
>
> We create history as much as we discover it. What we call history becomes history and since this is a naming time, we must be on guard against our own class prejudices and discomforts. If close friends and devoted companions are to be part of lesbian history, so must be also the lesbians of the fifties who left no doubt about their sexuality or their courage.
>
> We have shown the slide show now in hundreds of cities and towns in America, covering the span of our country; we have taken it to international audiences in Holland and England. We have shown it to an audience of one and to audiences of thousands. It has taken us to living rooms of rural homes, where we all had to take a pledge not to reveal any woman's identity, to social work training sessions, to bars where we competed with the ring of cash register and the dance music throbbing in the background. Always the message has been: "You, the women listening and watching are our lesbian herstory. You must send the photo, copy the letter, make the tape. You must cherish the courage of your own days, of your ways of loving, and not be intimidated by the thought of being part of a people's memory."

From our newsletter, no. 3, 1976:

> Summer was an interesting time for the archives with a record number of visitors including women from California, England and Italy. I found that whether I was talking with lesbians from Manhattan or Europe, the concern expressed for the preservation of our herstory creates an energy that whisks the archives from the past into our

> daily lives. There is motivation and activity everywhere. In London, women are producing street theater in the Punch and Judy tradition in support for Wages for Housework. In Italy, lesbian groups are beginning to meet in the high schools. Some of our visitors organized lesbian centers or were responsible for coordinating such notable events as the Lesbian Herstory Exploration near Los Angeles. Of course in many cases the enthusiasm was closer to home, taking the shape of an 'Hello. I just found out that the archives is a few blocks away and I'd like to stop by tomorrow.' This summer brought a feeling of universal lesbian power–women united in the celebration and adventure of pursuing our identity.
>
> Valerie

In order to survive in homophobic America as an archives, we have incorporated ourselves as a not-for-profit information resource center because the New York State Board of Regents maintains control over educational institutions and could therefore confiscate the collection for 'just cause.' In the same year we incorporated (1978), a law was pending in New Jersey recriminalizing homosexuality, and everyone knows criminals have no archives. We take no money from the government, believing that such an action would be an exercise in neocolonialism, believing that the society that ruled us out of history should never be relied upon to make it possible for us to exist. All the technology the archives has–the computer, the xeroxing machine–comes from lesbian, gay, feminist, and radical funding sources.

With its library of over 10,000 volumes, 12,000 photographs, 200 special collections, 1,400 periodical titles, 1,000 organizational and subject files, thousands of feet of film and video footage, art and artifacts, posters and T-shirts, buttons and personal memorabilia, the collection is now too large for its home of fifteen years, and we are trying to raise funds to purchase a building that will be a research center for lesbian culture with the archives collection at its heart. Our model for this is the Schomberg Center for Research in Black Culture which started as one black man's refusal to accept a teacher's edict that black people have no history.

The archives has never just been a home for the markings of the past. Our At-Home-With-the-Archives series allows lesbian cultural workers to try out first-time creations, gives space for open debates and discussions where women know that all are welcomed, and encourages political organizing. Our newsletter and displays in bookstores, libraries, and gay community centers, our participation in demonstrations and marches, all make clear that a lesbian archives is a participant in the creation of culture and social change as well as a preserver of our people's story.

From our statement of purpose, 1974:

1. All women must have access to the archives
2. The collection must never be bartered or sold
3. The collection must be housed in a lesbian community space and be staffed by lesbians

We, the founders of the Lesbian Herstory Archives, always took as our working principles that we were not interested in a role-model lesbian herstory, that we wanted the collection, and hence the record, to be as inclusive as possible. Since many of us who work with the archives are working-class women, we were not hampered by class censorship. We actively sort out documentation of the lives of lesbian factory workers, butch-femme communities of the forties and fifties, lesbian prostitutes and sex performers. Now hard hats and hobnail boots sit next to pasties and glossy prints of a famous lesbian stripper of the fifties. They, in turn, are joined by the lesbian-feminist artifacts of the seventies. We hope the discussion of lesbian strategies and identities that these objects represent will go on for generations to come, each decade adding its layer of complexity. The fullest record we can leave is the best legacy for the political and social survival of our lesbian daughters around the world. A simplified, homogenized past will not be rich enough in ideas, inspirations, actions, or images to nourish a diverse and embattled lesbian community of the future.

We also believed that we could go about our personal lives without harming the image of the archives in the community. I have worked very hard to make clear that what I write about as Joan Nestle, the femme, is not in any way the official voice of the archives, but as an archivist I have also made clear that the lives of all lesbian women are worthy of being documented. We have all put thousands of hours of work into the archives, many times not very glamorous work but as I have said before, there is a passion in what we do. For me, part of that passionate commitment to lesbian archiving is to say thank you to a generation of women who gave me love and showed me my first portraits of lesbian courage. Our archives belongs to no one group of lesbians and to no one selected image or formula for liberation; it will eventually pass into the hands of a new generation of rememberers who we hope will keep the door open to the multiplicities of lesbian identity. Our will to remember is our will to change the world, to continually reconstruct the words 'woman,' 'lesbian,' and 'gender' so they reflect the complex creations which we call our lives.

From the visitors' book, 1983:

> I am here among women
> who breathe softly in my ear
> who speak gently
> in a voice that will not be stilled.
> I am here in a cradle
> or a womb,
> or a lap,
> on a knee that is shapely
> under my thigh
> leaving the impression
> that I will never be alone.
>
> I am here
> to remember faces
> I have never seen before
> and I do
>
> love, Jewelle Gomez

IN A NEW HOME, SIX YEARS LATER

This article, a version of which was published in 1990, grows out of the first twenty-nine years of the Lesbian Herstory Archives' existence. Its language, its sense of embattlement, and its political vision have their roots in the American lesbian-feminist movement of the 1970s. Reading it from a more recent perspective, I can see how the discourse has changed in the intervening time. For instance, the word "identity," so popular in the seventies, is more complicated now, more diverse, more challenged in its implications. Transgender and passing women's history is no longer an orphan child of the movement, and no one need apologize any longer for an interest in butch-femme or leather communities. Working with the archives has given me the opportunity to understand the dialectical process close up, to see how each generation questions and adds to the ongoing cultural and, therefore, political discourse of a people. This public intergenerational dialogue is a gift of the twentieth-century American lesbian and queer movement to itself and to our national history.

In just six short years, tremendous changes have come to the archives itself, the most striking of which was our move in 1993 into a three-story limestone building in the Park Slope section of Brooklyn, New York. Over two hundred volunteers, including lesbian architects and carpenters, worked for close to a year to prepare the building for its new life. The core group of co-coordinators has expanded into approximately twenty women, many of whom are librarians and archivists and who have each marked the archives with their own special skills and insights. Polly Thistlethwaite, Lucinda Rhea Zoe, Paula Grant, Morgan Gwenwald, Amy Beth, Maxine Wolfe, and Desiree Yael Vester have made sure that the archives stays connected to the vital changes that are going on in the lesbian and queer communities. In June 1996, with our community, we celebrated the burning of our mortgage, the accomplishment of a grassroots miracle.

Not only has the interior world of LHA changed, but the social context has changed as well. Lesbian, gay, bisexual, and transgender history is now a thriving concern with both private and public institutions undertaking their own collections. The success of queer theory on academic campuses has ensured, at least for now, a continuing flow of ideas and new cultural works.

However, this recent respectability of queer archiving raises questions for the community at large and for the grassroots archives in particular. When the New York Public Library opened its gay and lesbian history exhibit last year in a cocktail party atmosphere, I knew our pioneering days were over. As I toured the exhibit, one that the Lesbian Herstory Archives had contributed to, I thought of all the years the library had been part of the problem–its card catalog a journey in self-hatred for a curious "homosexual." Our history with its documents and images is hot stuff now, capable of pulling in much-needed revenue, and it is true that these institutions have the staff and often the space for which grassroots archives have to beg. My heart lies with the lesbian and gay grassroots history projects and archives that risked all when the establishment would not go near queer material except as examples of pathology, but these are new times, and hopefully, our communities will be able to support differing visions of how memory is best cherished.

While things change, they also stay the same. In April of 1996, one of our coordinators, Alexis Danzig, donned her leather pants, made sure her motorcycle was all greased and ready, and took off on a whirlwind tour of over forty towns and cities, showing her new version of the archives slide show. Back in Brooklyn, we heard of her adventures through her weekly e-mails. This is a far cry from the time when Deborah Edel and I loaded up an old Volkswagen Beetle and sedately took off on the interstate highways, but the commitment that stretches over thirty years stays the same–to ensure that lesbian memory will live in this world with all its wonder, contradictions, and resilience.

Index

Abstract Expressionism, 7
Aesthetes, 7
African-American poets, 21
AIDS
effects on U.S. Latinos, 172
Latino novels on, 172
literature and, 156
AIDS poetry, 22-23
Alarcon, F. X., 21
Alternative press
feminism and, 116
feminist, 126-127
impact of, 114-115
Anderson, P., 128
Another Country (Baldwin)
politics of, 60-63
race and sexuality issues in, 53-57
as social protest, 63
structure of, 57-60
teaching, 51-53
Anthologies, 8
black gay, 19-20
feminist writings, 117
gay poetry, 10-11
gay poets-of-color movement, 21
queer poetry, 24-25
Antiquarian history, 183-184,186
Archives, lesbian, 2,207-208,
216-217
challenges of, 211-213
concerns of, 214-215
regional, 209-211
scholars and, 216-217
Arnold, J., 127,128,133
The Arno Press, 27-28
Art, creation of, in literature,
148-151
Baldwin, J., 54-57
Beat poetry movement, 7
Blackheart and Other Countries
collective, 20
Black male poets, 19-22
Black Mountain College writers, 7
Black nationalism, homosexuality
and, 54
Bookstores, feminist, 127,128,129,
134,135
Bookwomen, lesbian/feminist, 133
"Boston School" of poets, 15
Bowman, P., 133
Brown, R. M., 46,118,127
Capote, T., 72-75,86
Caribbean-American poets, 21
Castillo, A., 156-157
Catullus, 11
Christian iconography, 11
Christopher Street, 15
Cleaver, E., 54,63
C.L.I.T. Papers. *See* Collective
Lesbian International
Terrors C.L.I.T. Papers
Collective Lesbian International Terrors
(C.L.I.T.) Papers, 124-125
Conrad, F., 35,37-38
Cooper, D., 17-18
Cornwell, A., 46
Counterculture press, 115
Crimp, D., 190,194
Critical history, 184,186,189,197-200
Crosby, C., 196-197
Cross-dressing, 145-148
Cultural feminism, 134

Damon, G., *See* Grier, B.
Daughters, Inc., 127,133
Daughters of Bilitis (DOB), 7,209
  early days of, 30-31
  founding *The Ladder*, 29-30
  goals, 30
  research goal of, 35-37
De Lauretis, T., 104,145
Desert of the Heart (Rule), 99-100, 102
Diana Press, 209
Dillard, G., 16
Dixon M., 21
DOB. *See* Daughters of Bilitis (DOB)
"Dulce" (Rule), 96-99

East Coast Homophile Organizations (ECHO), 37
Eccentric subject, 104-105
Echols, A., 134
Edel, D., 211
Elegy poetry, 22-23
Epistemology of the Closet (Sedgwick), 67-68,71
Erotic gay poetry, 15-16

Fag Rag Poets, 15
FBN. See The Feminist Bookstores Newsletter (FBN)
Felman, S., 94-95
Feminism
  cultural, 134
  publishing and, 115-116
  radical, 134
Feminist bookstores, 127-129, 134-135
The Feminist Bookstores Newsletter (*FBN*), 129-132
Feminist bookwomen, 133
Feminist economics, 134
Feminist historians, 190
Feminist readings, 92-94
Ferguson, A., *See* Lyon, P.
Fiction, history and, 199-200
Forgery, the novelist and, 149
Foucault, M., 3,70-71
Freedman, M., 40-41
French decadents, 11
French symbolists, 11
Freud, S., 178
  study of mourning, 189-190

Gair, C., 128
Gallop, J., 200
Garber, M., 146
Gay, black writers, 20
Gay and Lesbian Historical Society of Northern California Archives, 209,210
Gay and lesbian history, 195-196
Gay and lesbian studies, 195
Gay Arts Movement, 18
Gay Beat period, 12
Gay ghettos, 7-8
Gay identity
  The House of Breath (Goyen) and, 75-86
  Other Voices, Other Rooms (Capote) and, 72-75
  Stonewall Riots and, 10
Gay Intelligentsia, The, 13-14
Gay literary magazines, 8
Gay newspapers, 8
Gay poetry. *See also* Literature
  anthologies for, 10-11
  cultural influences on, 12
  elegy, 22-23
  emerging trends, 23-25
  erotic, 15-16
  as field of study, 6
  following Stonewall Riots, 6
  during the forties, 12-13
  framework for critical inquiry of, 10
  Harlem Renaissance, 19-20
  Hispanic, 21-22
  mysticism in, 15-16

as performance, 13-14
small press movement and, 8
Gay poets. *See also* Queer poets
early themes of, 11
during the forties, 12-13
The Gay Intelligentsia, 13
Gilded, 16-18
homosexuality of, 14
influences on, 9
pagan, 15-16
postwar, 7
of urbanity, 13-14
Gay poets-of-color movement, 21-22
Generation Q poets, 23-25
Gilded Poets, 16-18
Gittings, B., 34,38-40
Gledhill, C., 178
Gonsalves, R., 21
Goyen, W., 75-86
Grahn, J., 122,123
The Great Performance (Muñoz), 162-165
Grier, B.
as editor of *The Ladder,* 41-42
gift of book and periodical collection, 2,209-210,213
kidnapping of *The Ladder,* 42-46
reprint of *The Ladder,* 28-29
use of pseudonyms, 33-34
Gundlach, R., 37-38
Gunn, T., 16,17,18

Halperin, D. M., 71
Harlem Renaissance, 6,19-20
Harris, B., 3,127,144,151
Hemphill, E., 21
Hispanic gay poetry, 21-22
Hispanic poets, 21-22
Historiography, 196-197
History
antiquarian, 183-184,186
critical mode of, 184,186
deconstruction of, 197
fiction and, 199-200
gay and lesbian, 195-196
monumental, 183,186
uses of, 183
The History of Sexuality (Foucault), 3,70-71
"Home Movie" (Rule), 105-110
Homosexuality
Black nationalist arguments and, 54
of early postwar American poets, 14
Gilded Poets and, 17
southern literary presentations, 68-70
The House of Breath (Goyen), 75-86
Hutcheon, L., 145

Inland Passage (Rule), 95-99
It Ain't Me, Babe, 118-122

Jeanmarie, R., 21
June L. Mazer Lesbian Collection, 207-209,210

Kameny, F., 37,38-39
Kitchen Table Women of Color Press, 209
KNOW, Inc., 116
The Ladder
content of, 34-35
distribution of, 35
DOB convention announcements and, 39-40
early days, 31-32
editors of, 34
final issues of, 45-47
first issue, 32-33
impact of, 29-30
importance of, 28
kidnapping of, 42-44
as networking tool, 34
1970s lesbian bookwomen and, 124

reprinting of, 28-29
research debate and, 35-39,40-41
themes of, 35

Laine, B., 9-10
Language, 105
LaPorte, R., 41-46
Latin Moon in Manhattan (Manrique), 165-175
Latino novels, 156,172
Lesbian archives, 2,207-208,216-217
challenges of, 211-213
concerns of, 214-215
regional, 209-211
scholars, 216-217
Lesbian criticism, 103-105
Lesbian/feminist bookwomen, 133
Lesbian Herstory Archives, 207, 210-212,226-235
Lesbianism, publishing and, 116
Lesbian paper materials, 206-207
Lesbian studies, 103-104
Lesbian theory, 144,145
Libraries, 207-208
Literature. *See also* Gay poetry
AIDS and, 156
creation of art and, 148-151
postmodern, 151
Puerto Rican, 159
Lorde, A., 3,63,88,209
Love Alone (Monette), 22
Lover (Harris), 3-4,144-145
creation of art in, 148-151
cross-dressing in, 145-148
Lyon, P., 30,33,34

McBride, D., 2,209-210,213
Manrique, J., 165-175
Martin, D., 30,31,34
Martin and John (Peck)
as critical history, 197-200
history and, 183-189
mourning and, 189-194
summary, 178-183
Mass media
women's liberation movement coverage, 117-118
The Mattachine Review, 29
Mattachine Society, 7,28
Monette, P., 22
Monumental history, 183-184,186
Moon, M., 194
Morirás si da una primavera (Torres), 157-162
Mourning, 189-194
critical historical approach to, 195
criticisms of Freud's account, 194
Freud's contribution to, 194-195
Muñoz, Elías Miguel, 162-165
Munt, S., 103-104
Mysticism, 15-16

Nestle, J., 29,33,211
Newsletters, 115-116
Newspapers
feminist, 118-119
gay, 8
New York City, 6
New York School, 7,9
Nietzsche, F., 178-179,183-189
Nunokawa, J., 194

off our backs, 119,121,122,132-133
O'Hara, F., 14-15
ONE (magazine), 29
Ortleb, C., 15
Otero, M. R., 159
"Other," view of, 3,6
Other Voices, Other Rooms (Capote), 72-75,86

Pagan poets, 15-16
Paper lesbianism, 116
Peck, D., 178

Performance poetry,queer poetry and, 23-24
Perkins, D., 8,9
Phelan, S., 104
Photography, homoerotic, 18
Platonism, cult of, 11
Poets of Gay Urbanity, 13-14
Poets of the Pagan, 15-16
Postmodern lesbian narrative, 151
Postmodern literature, 144-145
Poulin A., 8
Puerto Rican literature, 159

Queer poets, 23-25. *See also* Gay poets
Queer theory, 103-105,145
Queer zines, 24

Race, sexuality and, 53-57
Radical feminism, 134
Reading queerly, 88,92,97,98-99
Rich, A., 3,88,92,93,200
Roof, J., 151
Rule, J., 88-92, 103,105
Russell, S., 40

Saint, A., 21
Sale, K., 114
Sandoz, H., 40
San Francisco Public Library, 213-214
Schwartz, J., 29
Schweickart, P., 92-94
Scott, J. W., 196
Seajay, C., 122,123,126-127,129,135
Sedgwick, E. K., 67-68
Sexuality, race and, 53-57
Shelley, M., 118
Sherry, M. S., 195-196
Small press movement
  gay poetry renaissance and, 8
So Far from God (Castillo), 156-157
Southern Renaissance, 68-70
Stanford, A., 19,20-21
Stonewall Riots, 6,7
  gay identity and, 10

Talmadge, B., 31
This Not Quite Promised Land (Rule), 100-102
Tobin, K., 122-123
Torres, D., 157-162
Transvestism, 146,147

Underground press, 115

Webb, M., 132-133
Williams, W. C., 12
Wittig, M., 88
A Woman's Place (bookstore), 126-127
Women in Distribution (WIND), 128,131-132
Women in Print Conference, 1-2, 128-129
Women in Print Movement, 116,126
  decline, 135
  lack of records of, 209
  legacy, 136
Women's bookstores, 127-129,134-135
Women's liberation movement
  early chroniclers, 115-116
  media coverage, 117-118
  newsletters, 115-116
The Women's Press Collective, 123, 209
Women's presses, 134
Women's studies, historiography and, 196
Woolf, V., 199-200
World War II, social effects of, 6
Writing queerly, 88-89

Zimmerman, B., 104

COSTS: Please figure your cost to order quality copies of an article.

1. Set-up charge per article: $8.00
   ($8.00 × number of separate articles) ________
2. Photocopying charge for each article:
   - 1-10 pages: $1.00 ________
   - 11-19 pages: $3.00 ________
   - 20-29 pages: $5.00 ________
   - 30+ pages: $2.00/10 pages ________
3. Flexicover (optional): $2.00/article ________
4. Postage & Handling: US: $1.00 for the first article/
   $.50 each additional article ________
   Federal Express: $25.00 ________
   Outside US: $2.00 for first article/
   $.50 each additional article ________
5. Same-day FAX service: $.35 per page ________

GRAND TOTAL: ____________

METHOD OF PAYMENT: (please check one)

❑ Check enclosed ❑ Please ship and bill. PO # ________________
(sorry we can ship and bill to bookstores only! All others must pre-pay)

❑ Charge to my credit card: ❑ Visa; ❑ MasterCard; ❑ Discover; ❑ American Express;

Account Number: ____________________ Expiration date: __________

Signature: ✗ ______________________________

Name: ____________________ Institution: ____________________

Address: ______________________________________

____

City: ____________________ State: ________ Zip: __________

Phone Number: ________________ FAX Number: ________________

MAIL or *FAX* THIS ENTIRE ORDER FORM TO:

Haworth Document Delivery Service
The Haworth Press, Inc.
10 Alice Street
Binghamton, NY 13904-1580

or FAX: 1-800-895-0582
or CALL: 1-800-342-9678
9am-5pm EST)